Jane Yellowrock Novels

BLOOD OF THE EARTH

A Soulwood Novel

Faith Hunter

A ROC BOOK

ROC
Published by New American Library,
an imprint of Penguin Random House LLC
375 Hudson Street, New York, New York 10014

This book is an original publication of New American Library.

First Printing, August 2016

For more information about Penguin Random House, visit penguin.com.

ISBN 9780451473301

Printed in the United States of America
10 9 8 7 6 5 4 3 2 1

Penguin
Random
House

To the Hubs.
For eating lots of cold meals and putting up with
my rants and panics as I worked through this book,
tore it apart, and worked through it again.
And again. And again.

Finding my soul mate in you
was God's best gift to me, ever.

ACKNOWLEDGMENTS

Sarah Spieth and MG for all the . . . well, you know.

Cheri Whitehouse for offshore banking info.

Mud Mymudes for all the botany corrections, beta-reading for accuracy, and dog stuff.

Greg Phelps, MD, for the hospitality in Knoxville, the beta-reading, and invaluable help on the project!

The Beast Claws, best street team ever! You pushed this book without ever reading it. Your trust in me and my stories is humbling.

The Hooligans. You know how much I love you. If this book is a success, then you made it happen.

Let's Talk Promotions at ltpromos.com. You nearly killed yourselves over this book. I adore you!

Mike Pruette for website stuff, marketing stuff, and the best T-shirts ever!

Joy Robinson for the artwork on the T-shirt and on the website. LOVE the trees!

Janet Robbins Rosenberg, my fantastic copy editor who caught the terrible time line error. A week with two Thursdays . . . I am still shuddering.

Lucienne Diver, my literary agent with the Knight Agency. You believed in this book even when I had given up on it. Thank you. Just . . . thank you.

Jessica Wade, editor at Penguin Random House. There are no words. You gave me time to get this book right. You pushed me and hammered me and then sliced and diced this book and . . . I love it. This book exists because of you. Because you made me make it right.

My thanks to all the wonderful people above. If there are mistakes in this book (and there will be) they are mine alone.

ONE

Edgy and not sure why, I carried the basket of laundry off the back porch. I hung my T-shirts and overalls on the front line of my old-fashioned solar clothes dryer, two long skirts on the outer line, and what my mama called my intimate attire on the line between, where no one could see them from the driveway. I didn't want another visit by Brother Ephraim or Elder Ebenezer about my wanton ways. Or even another courting attempt from Joshua Purdy. Or worse, a visit from Ernest Jackson Jr., the preacher. So far I'd kept him out of my house, but there would come a time when he'd bring help and try to force his way in. It was getting tiresome having to chase churchmen off my land at the business end of a shotgun, and at some point God's Cloud of Glory Church would bring enough reinforcements that I couldn't stand against them. It was a battle I was preparing for, one I knew I'd likely lose, but I would go down fighting, one way or another.

The breeze freshened, sending my wet skirts rippling as if alive, on the line where they hung. Red, gold, and brown leaves skittered across the three acres of newly cut grass. Branches overhead cracked, clacked, and groaned with the wind, leaves rustling as if whispering some dread tiding. The chill fall air had been perfect for birdsong; squirrels had been racing up and down the trees, stealing nuts and hiding them for the coming winter. I'd seen a big black bear this morning, chewing on nuts and acorns, halfway up the hill.

Standing in the cool breeze, I studied my woods, listening, feeling, tasting the unease that had prickled at my flesh for the last few months, ever since Jane Yellowrock had come visiting and turned my life upside down. She was the one responsible for the repeated recent visits by the churchmen. The Cherokee vampire hunter was the one who had brought all the changes, even if it wasn't intentional. She had come hunting a missing vampire and, because she was good at her job—maybe the best ever—she had succeeded. She had also managed to save more than a hundred children from God's Cloud.

Maybe it had been worth it all—helping all the children—but I was the one paying the price, not her. She was long gone and I was alone in the fight for my life. Even the woods knew things were different.

Sunlight dappled the earth; cabbages, gourds, pumpkins, and winter squash were bursting with color in the garden. A muscadine vine running up the nearest tree, tangling in the branches, was dropping the last of the ripe fruit. I smelled my wood fire on the air, and hints of that apple-crisp chill that meant a change of seasons, the sliding toward a hard, cold autumn. I tilted my head, listening to the wind, smelling the breeze, feeling the forest through the soles of my bare feet. There was no one on my property except the wild critters, creatures who belonged on Soulwood land, nothing else that I could sense. But the hundred fifty acres of woods bordering the flatland around the house, up the steep hill and down into the gorge, had been whispering all day. Something was not right.

In the distance, I heard a crow call a warning, sharp with distress. The squirrels ducked into hiding, suddenly invisible. The feral cat I had been feeding darted under the shrubs, her black head and multicolored body fading into the shadows. The trees murmured restlessly.

I didn't know what it meant, but I listened anyway. I always listened to my woods, and the gnawing, whispering sense of *danger, injury, damage* was like sandpaper abrading my skin, making me jumpy, disturbing my sleep, even if I didn't know what it was.

I reached out to it, to the woods, reached with my mind, with my magic. Silently I asked it, *What? What is it?*

There was no answer. There never was. But as if the forest knew that it had my attention, the wind died and the whispering leaves fell still. I caught my breath at the strange hush, not daring even to blink. But nothing happened. No sound, no movement. After an uncomfortable length of time, I lifted the empty wash basket and stepped away from the clotheslines, turning and turning, my feet on the cool grass, looking up and inward, but I could sense no direct threat, despite the chill bumps rising on my skin. *What?* I asked. An eerie fear grew in me, racing up my spine like spiders with sharp, tiny claws. Something was coming. Something that reminded me of Jane, but subtly different. Something was coming that might hurt me. Again. My woods knew.

From down the hill I heard the sound of a vehicle climbing the mountain's narrow, single-lane, rutted road. It wasn't the *clang* of Ebenezer's rattletrap Ford truck, or the steady drone of Joshua's newer, Toyota long-bed. It wasn't the high-pitched motor of a hunter's all-terrain vehicle. It was a car, straining up the twisty Deer Creek mountain.

My house was the last one, just below the crest of the hill. The wind whooshed down again, icy and cutting, a downdraft that bowed the trees. They swayed in the wind, branches scrubbing. Sighing. Muttering, too low to hear.

It could be a customer making the drive to Soulwood for my teas or veggies or herbal mixes. Or it could be some kind of conflict. The woods said it was the latter. I trusted my woods.

I raced back inside my house, dropping the empty basket, placing John's old single-shot, bolt-action shotgun near the refrigerator under a pile of folded blankets. His lever-action carbine .30-30 Winchester went near the front window. I shoved the small Smith & Wesson .32 into the bib of my coveralls, hoping I didn't shoot myself if I had to draw it fast. I picked up the double-barrel break-action shotgun and checked the ammo. Both barrels held three-inch shells. The contact area of the latch was worn and needed to be replaced, but at close range I wasn't going to miss. I might dislocate my shoulder, but if I hit them, the trespassers would be a while in healing too.

I debated for a second on switching out the standard shot shells for salt or birdshot, but the woods' disharmony seemed to be growing, a particular and abrasive itch under my skin. I snapped the gun closed and pulled back my long hair into an elastic to keep it out of my way.

Peeking out the blinds, I saw a four-door sedan coming to a stop beside John's old Chevy C10 truck. Two people inside, a man and a woman. *Strangers,* I thought. Not from God's Cloud of Glory, the church I'd grown up in. Not a local vehicle. And no dogs anymore to check them out for me with noses and senses humans no longer had. Just three small graves at the edge of the woods and a month of grief buried with them.

A man stepped out of the driver's side, black-haired, dark-eyed. Maybe Cherokee or Creek if he was a mountain native, though his features didn't seem tribal. I'd never seen a French-man or a Spaniard, so maybe from one of those Mediterranean countries. He was tall, maybe six feet, but not dressed like a farmer. More citified, in black pants, starched shirt, tie, and jacket. He had a cell phone in his pocket, sticking out just a little. Western boots, old and well cared for. There was some-thing about the way he moved, feline and graceful. Not a farmer or a God's Cloud preacher. Not enough bulk for the first one, not enough righteous determination in his expression or bearing for the other. But something said he wasn't a cus-tomer here to buy my herbal teas or fresh vegetables.

He opened the passenger door for the other occupant and a woman stepped out. Petite, with black skin and wildly curly, long black hair. Her clothes billowed in the cool breeze and she put her face into the wind as if sniffing. Like the man, her movements were nimble, like a dancer's, and somehow feral, as if she had never been tamed, though I couldn't have said why I got that impression.

Around the house, my woods moaned in the sharp wind, branches clattering like old bones, anxious, but I could see nothing about the couple that would say danger. They looked like any other city folk who might come looking for Soul-wood Farm, and yet . . . not. Different. As they approached the house, they passed the tall length of flagpole in the middle of the raised beds of the front yard, and started up the seven steps to the porch. And then I realized why they moved and felt all wrong. There was a weapon bulge at the man's shoulder, beneath his jacket. In a single smooth motion, I braced the shotgun against my shoulder, rammed open the door, and pointed the business end of the gun at the trespassers.

"Whadda ya want?" I demanded, drawing on my childhood God's Cloud dialect. They came to a halt at the third step, too close for me to miss, too far away for them to disarm me safely. The man raised his hands like he was asking for peace, but the little woman hissed. She drew back her lips in a snarl and growled at me. I knew cats. This was a cat. A cat in human form—a were-cat of some kind. A devil, according to the church. I trained the barrel on her, midcenter, just like John had showed me the first time he put the gun in my hands. As I aimed, I took a single step so my back was against the doorjamb to keep me from getting bowled over or from breaking a shoulder when I fired.

"Paka, no," the man said. The words were gentle, the touch to her arm tender. I had never seen a man touch a woman like that, and my hands jiggled the shotgun in surprise before I caught myself. The woman's snarl subsided and she leaned in to the man, just like one of my cats might. His arm went around her, and he smoothed her hair back, watching me as I watched them. Alert, taking in everything about me and my home, the man lifted his nose in the air to sniff the scents of my land, the delicate nasal folds widening and contracting. Alien. So alien, these two.

"What do you want?" I asked again, this time with no church accent, and with the grammar I'd learned from the city folk customers at the vegetable stand and from reading my once-forbidden and much-loved library books.

"I'm Special Agent Rick LaFleur, with PsyLED, and this is Paka. Jane Yellowrock sent us to you, Ms. Ingram," the man said.

Of *course* this new problem was related to Jane. Nothing in my whole life had gone right since she'd darkened my door. She might as well have brought a curse on my land and a pox on my home. She had a curious job, wore clothes and guns and knives like a man, and I had known from the beginning that she would bring nothing but strife to me. But in spite of that, I had liked her. So had my woods. She moved like these two, willowy and slinky. Alert.

She had come to my house asking about God's Cloud of Glory. She had wanted a way onto the church's property, which bordered mine, to rescue a blood-sucker. Because there was documentation in the probate court, the civil court system, and the local news, that John and I had left the church, Jane had figured that I'd be willing to help her. And God help me, I had. I'd paid the price for helping her and, sometimes, I wished that I'd left well enough alone.

"Prove it," I said, resettling the gun against my shoulder. The man slowly lowered his hand and removed a wallet from his jacket pocket, displaying an identification card and badge. But I knew that badges can be bought online for pennies and IDs could be made on computers. "Not good enough," I said. "Tell me something about Jane that no one but her knows."

"Jane is not human, though she apes it better than some," Paka said, her words strangely accented, her voice scratchy and hoarse. "She was once mated to my mate." Paka placed a covetous hand on Rick's arm, an inexplicable sort of claiming. The man frowned harder, deep grooves in his face. I had a feeling that he didn't like being owned like a piece of meat. I'd seen that unhappy look on the faces of women before. Seeing the expression on the face of a man was unexpected and, for some reason, unsettling. "He is mine now," Paka said.

When Jane told me about the man she would send, she said that he would break my heart if I let him, like he'd broken Jane's. This Rick was what the few romance novels I'd read called tall, dark, and handsome, a grim, distant man with a closed face and too many secrets. A heartbreaker for sure. "That's a start," I said. In their car, a small catlike form jumped to the dash, crouched low, and peered out the windshield through the daylight glare. I ignored it, all my attention on the pair on my land, moving slowly. Rick pulled out his cell phone and thumb-punched and swiped it a few times. He paraphrased from whatever was on the screen, "Jane said you told her you'd been in trouble from God's Cloud of Glory and the man who used to lead it ever since you turned twelve and he tried to marry you. She also said Nell Nicholson Ingram makes the best chicken and dumplings she ever tasted. That about right?"

I scowled. Around me the forest rustled, expectant and uneasy, tied to my magic. Tied to me. "Yeah. That sums it up." I draped the shotgun over my arm and backed into my home, standing aside as they mounted the last of the steps. Wondering what the church spies in the deer stand on the next property would think about the standoff.

They thought I didn't know that they kept watch on me all the time from the neighbor's land, but I knew. Just like I knew that they wanted me back under their thumbs and my land back in the church, to be used for their benefit. I'd known ever since I had beaten them in court, proving that John and I were legally married and that his will had given the land to me. The church elders didn't like me having legal rights, and they didn't like me. The feeling was mutual.

My black cat Jezzie raced out of the house and Paka caught her and picked her up. The tiny woman laughed, the sound as peculiar and scratchy as her words. And the oddest thing happened. Jezzie rolled over, lay belly-up in Paka's arms, and closed her eyes. Instantly she was asleep. Jezzie didn't like people; she barely tolerated me in her house, letting me live here because I brought cat kibble. Jezzie had ignored the man, just the way she ignored humans. And me. It told me something about the woman. She wasn't just a werecat. She had magic.

I backed farther inside, and they crossed the porch. *Nonhumans. In my house.* I didn't like this at all, but I didn't know how to stop it. Around the property, the woods quieted, as if waiting for a storm that would break soon, bringing the trees rain to feed their roots. I reached out to the woods, as uneasy as they were, but there was no way to calm them.

I didn't know fully what kind of magic I had, except that I could help seeds sprout, make plants grow stronger, heal them when they got sick and tried to die off. My magics had always been part of me, and now, since I had fed the forest once, my gifts were tied to the woods and the earth of Soulwood Farm. I had been told that my magic was similar to the Cherokee *yinehi.* Similar to the fairies of European lore, the little people, or even wood nymphs. But in my recent, intense Internet research I hadn't found an exact correlation with the magics I possessed, and I had an instinct, a feeling, that there might be more I could do, if I was willing to pay the price. I had once been told that there was always a price for magic.

"Come on in," I said, backing farther inside.

I watched the two strangers enter, wondering what was about to happen to my once sheltered and isolated life. I wondered what the churchmen watching my house with binoculars would have to say about it. What they would do about it. Maybe this time they'd kill my cats too—more graves to feed the earth. Grief welled up in me, and I tamped it down where no one could see it, concentrating on what I could discern and what I already knew about the couple.

Paka seemed less human than anything I'd ever seen before, not necessarily unstable, but all claws and instinct with a taste for games and blood. Rick was with PsyLED, a branch of law enforcement, which meant he'd have a certain amount of self-control.

The constitution, the different branches of government, citizens' rights, and law enforcement were all taught from the cradle up in the church school, so all the church members would know how to debate the illegality of any incursion or line of questioning. But PsyLED was an organization that had been formed after I had left the church. Instead of learning about the quasi-secret agency at my husband's or my father's knee, I had made a trip to the local library, where I had looked up the paranormal department and discovered that PsyLED stood for Psychometry Law Enforcement Division of Homeland Security. PsyLED units, which were still being formed, investigated and solved paranormal crimes—crimes involving magic and magic-using creatures: blood-suckers, were-creatures, and such. They had unusual and broad law enforcement and investigatory powers. They worked at the request of local or state law enforcement, and took over cases that were being improperly handled or ignored by local law. Officially the head of PsyLED reported directly to two organizations, the National Security Agency/Central Security Service, and Homeland Security, and by request to the CIA, the chief of the Department of Defense, the Secret Service, and the FBI. They were a crossover branch of law enforcement, one created just for magic.

In the back of my mind flitted conspiracy reports, urban legends, government machinations, and treachery. Things left over from a life lived in the church. Even John and his first wife, Leah, had believed that the government was evil, and living in Knoxville, near Secret City (where the US government has its ultra–top secret research facilities, the ones that made the first atomic bombs and contributed to every other major military creation since) only made the stories more plausible.

Warily, keeping my body turned toward them, I backed into the main room of the house, sliding my bare feet on the wood floor into the great room that was living room, the eating area, and the kitchen at the back. I jutted my chin to the far end of the old table and mismatched chairs that had been John's maw-maw's. He'd been dead and gone for years now, but in my mind it was still his and Leah's. Leah had been sister and mother and friend. I had loved her, and watching her wither away and die had broken me in ways I still hadn't dealt with. When I walked through her house, I still missed her. "Set a spell. I got some hot tea on the Waterford."

The man waited until the woman sat to take his own seat. *Solicitous*—that's what the romance books called it. Stupid books that had nothing to do with the life of a mountain woman. City women, maybe. But never the wives and women of God's Cloud of Glory Church. I moved to the far side of the table. When I was sure we were all in positions that would require them to make two or three moves before they could reach me, I set the shotgun on the table and got out three pottery mugs. I wasn't using John's maw-maw's good china for outsiders whom I might have to shoot later. That seemed deceitful.

With a hot pad, I moved the teapot to the side of the wood-stove, where the hob was cooler, and removed the tea strainer. I could have made some coffee—the man looked like a coffee-drinking type—but I didn't want to encourage them to stay. I poured the spice tea into the mugs, smelling cloves and allspice, with a hint of cinnamon and cardamom. It was my own recipe, made with a trace of real ground vanilla bean, precious and expensive. I put the mugs on an old carved oak tray, with cloth napkins and fresh cream and sugar. I added three spoons and placed the tea tray on the table in front of the sofa. I took my mug and backed away again, behind the long table, to where I could reach the shotgun.

"Welcome to my home," I said, hearing the reluctance in my tone. "Hospitality and safety while you're here." It was an old God's Cloud saying, and though the church and I had parted ways a long time ago, some things stayed with a woman. Guests should be safe so long as they acted right.

The nonhumans took the tea, the woman adding an inch of the real cream to the top and wrapping her hands around the mug as though she felt the chill of winter coming.

With a start, I realized my cats, Jezzie and Cello, were both on the woman's lap. I tried not to let my guests see my reaction.

My cats were mousers, working cats, not lap cats. They didn't like people. Annoyed at the disloyal cats, I pulled out a chair and sat.

The man held his mug one-handed, shooting surreptitious glances at my stuff, concentrating on the twenty-eight-gauge, four-barreled, break-action Rombo shotgun hanging over the steps to the second floor. It was made by Famars in Italy and had been John's prize position. I narrowed my eyes at him. "See something you want?" I asked, an edge in my voice.

Instead of answering, Rick asked a question again, as if that was a built-in response. "You cook and heat this whole place with a woodstove?"

I nodded once, sipping my tea. The man didn't go on and for some reason I felt obliged to offer, "I can heat most of my water too, eight months of the year. Long as I don't mind picking up branches, splitting wood, and cleaning the stove."

"You are strong," Paka said, Jezzie on her lap and Cello now climbing to her shoulders to curl around her neck. "You use an ax as my people use our claws, with ease and . . . what is the English word? Ah." She smiled sat Rick. "Ef-fort-less-ness. That is a good word."

She sniffed the air, dainty and delicate, "Your magic is different from all others I have smelled. I like it." Her lips curled up, she kicked off her heels, and shifted her feet up under her body, moving like a ballerina. She drank the tea in little sips—sip-sip-sip, her lips and throat moving fast.

I wasn't sure what she might know about my magic, so I didn't respond. Instead I watched the man as he looked around, holding his tea mug, one hand free to draw his weapon. He had noted the placement of the other guns at the windows, the worn rug in front of the sofa, the few electronic devices plugged into the main outlet at the big old desk. Upstairs on the south side of the house, farthest from the road and any sniper attack, was the inverter and batteries. Rick looked that way, as if he could see through the ceiling to the system that kept me self-sufficient. Or he could hear the hum of the inverter, maybe. I was so used to it that I seldom noticed unless I was up there working.

He looked to the window unit air conditioner, which was still in place for the last of the summer heat, and up to the ceiling fans, thinking. "The rest of the year, the solar panels on the dormer roofs meet all your needs, I guess," he said. I didn't reply. Few people knew about the solar panels, which were situated on the downslope, south side of the dormers. John had paid cash for them to keep anyone from knowing our plans. I didn't like the government knowing my business and wondered if Rick had been looking at satellite maps or had a camera-mounted drone fly over. I didn't usually ascribe to the churchmen's paranoid conspiracy theories, but maybe they had a few facts right. I glared at the government cop and let my tone go gruff. "What's your point?"

He said, almost as if musing, "Solar is great except in snowfall or prolonged cloudy days. They run the fans overhead?" he gestured with his mug to the ten-foot ceiling. "The refrigerator?"

It felt as if he was goading me about my lifestyle, and I didn't know why. Maybe it was a police thing, the kind of things the churchmen said the law always did, trying to provoke an action that would allow them to make an arrest. But there were ways to combat that. I set my mug on the smooth wood table, the finish long gone and now kept in good repair with a coating of lemon oil. I spoke slowly, spacing my words. "What. Do. You. Want? Make it fast. I'm busy."

"I understand you have good intel on God's Cloud of Glory Church. We need your help."

"No."

"They killed your dogs, yes?" Paka said, her shining eyes piercing. To Rick, she said, "I smell dogs in the house; their scent"—she extended her thumb and index finger and brought them closer together, as if pinching something, making it smaller—"is doing this. And there were piles of stones at the edge of the front grass." To me she said, "Graves?"

My lips went tight and my eyes went achy and dry. I'd come home from the Knoxville main library to find my two beagles and the old bird dog dead on my porch, like presents. They had been shot in the yard and dragged by their back legs to my front door. I still hadn't gotten the blood out of the porch wood. I'd buried the dogs across the lawn and piled rocks on top of the graves. And I still grieved.

I gave Paka a stilted nod, my hair slipping from the elastic, swinging forward, across my shoulders and veiling my face, hiding my emotions.

Paka nodded absently, her eyes distant, the way some people look when thinking about math or music. "I also smelled three men. Outside. They . . ." She paused as if seeking words. ". . . urinated on your garden as if marking territory. This is strange, yes? They are only human, not were-kind." Peeing on my garden sounded like some of the men of the church, childish and mean, to kill my plants, to urinate on my dinner. "My people do not keep dogs," she said, "but I understand that humans like them as pets, like family. There was dog blood on your porch. The men should not have killed your pets."

Rick said, "That was what I smelled coming in."

Without turning her head, Paka shifted sharp eyes to me. "Do you want me to track and kill the killer of your dogs?"

"Paka," the man said, warning in his tone.

A suspicious part of me wondered why she was being so kind, while another part heard a murderous vengeance in the words, and yet a third part wanted to say, *Yes. Make them hurt.* But vengeance would only make the churchmen come back meaner, and this time they'd kill me for sure, or make me wish for my own death. The churchmen were good at keeping their women pliant and obedient, or hurting them until they submitted. I didn't plan on doing either, and I didn't plan on leaving, not until I could get my sisters and their young'uns to come with me, to freedom and safety. I shook my head and said, "No," to make sure they understood. "Leave them be."

"Is that why won't you help us with intel on the church?" Rick asked, his voice gentle. "The dogs? You're afraid of their killers coming back and hurting you?"

My mouth opened and I said words that had been bubbling in my blood since I saw them in my yard. "You were supposed to be here months ago. Jane said you'd help me stay safe. Instead, the churchmen have come on my land—*my land,*" I added fiercely, "three times and they done bad things. Threatened me. Shed blood." I lowered my voice and clenched my fists tightly on the tabletop to keep the rising energies knotted inside or maybe to keep from picking up the gun and shooting them. "And then *you* come here and want more favors instead of the help she promised."

Rick started to move. I whipped to the side, one hand grabbing the shotgun, aiming. Fast as I was, the man was faster. He had drawn a fancy handgun in a single motion, so quick I hadn't even seen him move. It was a big gun. Maybe a ten-millimeter. And it was aimed at my head.

Beside him, Paka draped an arm across the sofa back and watched him. And she purred. The sound was like a bobcat, but louder.

"Get outta my house," I said. "You might shoot me, but I'll put a hurting on you'uns too." But they just stayed there as if they were rooted to my furniture. Cello crawled around Paka's neck and nestled with Jezzie on her lap, her nose lifting close to the werecat's face. *Traitor.* Something that might have been jealousy settled firmly in my chest like a weight. I scowled. Paka blinked, the motion slow and lazy.

"Mexican standoff," Rick said, his voice soft. "Unless you have silver shot, we'll heal from anything you can do to us. You won't heal from a three tap to the chest."

I laughed, the sound not like me. It was a nasty laugh. I set the shotgun back down and placed one hand flat on the table. Paka raised her head. "I smell her magics," she said. "They are rising. Your gun might not hurt her as it would a human." She petted Cello and she smiled again, her eyes tight on me. "This woman is dangerous, my mate. I like her. Her magic smells green, like the woods that surround the house. And it smells of decay, like prey that has gone back into the earth."

"You're like Paka, aren't you?" I asked Rick, reaching through the wood table and floor, down into the ground, into the stone foundations and the dirt below the house, into the roots of the woods that gave the farm its name, roots tangled through the soil in the backyard, deep into the earth. "Werecat." I placed my other hand on the table too, flat and steady.

"We are African black were-leopards," Paka said watching me in fascination, her nostrils almost fluttering as she sniffed the air.

"Not exactly the same, though," Rick said, his weapon aimed steadily at me, even though I'd put down my shotgun. "I was infected when I was bitten. She was born this way."

"Why do you tell our secrets?" Paka asked, not as if in disagreement, but as if she was mildly curious while being bored.

"Because we need her help," Rick said. "We need to know about the Human Speakers of Truth and any possible connection to the church. Nell's the only one who might be willing to talk to me. To us," he added, including his mate.

"Who are the Human Speakers of Truth?" I asked, letting the power and safety of the woods wrap around me like crawling snakes, like vines, growing in place. All I needed was one drop of his blood and I could take his life. It was my best protection; it was my magic and the magic of my land. His blood on my land, on Soulwood, put his life into my hands. "What do you want to know? The federal and state raid on the compound told most folks all there was to know about the church."

"Do you still have family ties to God's Cloud?" Rick asked, again not answering my question. It was probably a police tactic, but it set my teeth on edge. "Someone you could go to, or talk to, safely, but not get into more trouble with the people who killed your dogs?"

"I have family there," I said, using the time to gather as much of the woods' energy as I could. "We run into one another from time to time. Farmers' market. Yard sales. Why you asking?" I said, my tone challenging, deliberately accented by years in the church.

"The FBI, state police, and PsyLED have reason to believe that a group calling themselves the Human Speakers of Truth, on the run from the authorities, stopped in Knoxville. But HST disappeared. They don't have a home base here, so they may have joined forces with a local group. We want to rule out that the HST allied with God's Cloud of Glory Church."

"Never heard of HST," I said.

"They're a homegrown terrorist, anti-anyone nonhuman, militant group," Rick said, "investigated by PsyLED for years. Our unit's been tracking their financial trail, but it went cold five days ago here in Knoxville."

"What kind of reason?" I asked. When he looked confused I said, "You said you had *reason to believe* that Human Speakers of Truth may have holed up in Knoxville. What kind of reason?"

"HST needed a place to regroup after the arrests of three high-ranking members and the freezing of the group's financial accounts. We tracked them here and then lost the trail.

"God's Cloud of Glory Church—your old cult—was in trouble with the Tennessee child services department, after the state arrested some of their leaders and placed the children in foster care. Both groups are ultra–right wing paranormal-haters, and both are in trouble with the law and financially. It makes sense for them to join up, but we can't find anything electronically that supports that possibility."

"Guesswork," I said, but I couldn't help my small smile. I'd helped damage the church. Me losing my peaceful life had meant getting one hundred thirty-eight children, some of them sexually abused, out of the clutches of God's Cloud. I had helped, even if only passively, by letting the team have access to the church's compound through my property. But I knew a fishing expedition when I heard it. There was no evidence in Rick's statements, just supposition and wishful thinking.

Rick LaFleur acknowledged my smile with a tight one of his own. "HST stopped here, we know that, so it's possible that they might have joined forces with the church, even if just temporarily. And if that's true, then HST and God's Cloud merging was a match made in, well, not heaven. Maybe in the boardroom."

"Huntin'," I said. "The menfolk would have made a deal with rifles or shotguns and dead meat for the dinner table."

Something in my tone made Rick holster his gun. I tapped off the energies from the woods, holding the gathered power under my palms, flat against the table. The wood of the table had been cut from my forest, over a hundred years ago. I could use it. "So, yes. I got family there. Some will still speak to me at market. If I choose to talk to them."

Watching my posture, Rick said, "Can you ask your family a few questions? For instance, if any new people have been admitted onto the compound?"

"That's it?" I asked. "Information?"

"That's one reason why we came up here today," Rick said.

There was a lot of wiggle room in his answer, but there was also no threat. This was a negotiation.

Realizing that, I started to let the power I had gathered trickle back through the table, into the floor, and into the ground beneath the house. I took a slow breath. "Jane Yellow-rock asked for help to save a captured vampire, and in return, she got the children out of there. My life is in danger because of her, but, if I'm honest, I think it was a fair trade. And she paid me. You ask for help with nothing in return. Why would I be so stupid?"

"Because helping us might make the church leave you alone. For good," Rick said.

"I can't see how that might even be possible." But it sounded like heaven. They had done research on me, enough to know what buttons to push to make me do what they wanted.

"You could come to work with PsyLED, on a consultant basis."

And there it was, the carrot Jane Yellowrock had suggested so long ago. A way to be safe, finally and completely, from the church, because they might walk away if I worked for law enforcement, especially one of the shadow organizations like PsyLED. I would have a different lifestyle, a different place to live . . . assuming I could leave the land, which was in doubt, but wasn't something I could say to strangers. To anyone, for that matter. I set a thoughtful expression on my face, as if their offer was okay, but not all that great. "I'll consider talking to my family." I stood straight and rubbed my palms on my thighs. "I'll think about consulting. If the money's good enough. For now, though, you gotta go."

Without replying, my guests watched as I shook open a used plastic grocery bag, filled it with late fall squash, a small plastic baggie of an herbal air-freshener mixture that contained catnip, and a bottle of local honey. I put it on the table between them. "Twenty-five bucks. Cash. And make sure the bag is visible when you go to your car. The men watching my place need to see you with it. If they stand in the road as you leave, you have two choices: run through them, which I recommend, or stop. If you run through them, be prepared to be shot at and for the local law to do next to nothing. If you stop, don't let them know you're a cop. Just act like honeymooners and tell them you bought my Blue Pill Herbal Tea and Aromatherapy."

"Blue pill?" Rick asked.

"Some men need a little help in the bedroom. They come to me for my herbal Blue Pill Blend."

He frowned. Paka smiled. I said, "Git."

"Thank you for your time." Rick placed a small stack of five-dollar bills on the side table, beside his nearly full mug.

He touched Paka's shoulder and she stood, still holding my cats. The cop moved to the door without ever quite turning his back to me. He paused at the small table beside the door, one laden with library books and DVDs. He set a business card on top. "I know you don't have a cell signal here or a landline phone, but if you need me and can get to one, call the number on that card. I'll get here as quick as I can. Tomorrow is Tuesday, and the farmers' market is going all week in honor of the Brewer's Jam fall festival." When I looked surprised that he knew that, he added, "We do our homework. In case you decide to help us, call when you get to town. We can be at Market Square early in the day. We'll find you."

They'd find me. Yeah. That was plain. No matter what I did or where I went, someone would find me. "Git," I said again, this time with a little heat, letting the power of the land writhe around my hands and into my flesh.

Paka scented the air with her lips drawn back, sucking air over her tongue, then set my cats on the floor just inside the door and followed her mate out, closing the door behind her. I grabbed up the gun and raced to the window, watching them as they entered the car, Rick carrying the bag prominently and placing it on the floor of the backseat. The small catlike creature that had run around in the car was gone from the dash. The car made a three-point turn and wheeled sedately down the drive for the road.

As I watched, Jezzie walked up to me and sat, her front feet together, posing as only a house cat can, and mewled. I bent down hesitantly and picked her up. Jezzie wasn't fond of people, but this time, she snuggled against me, purring, and scrubbed her head on my chest. Cello walked up and wound her body around my feet, and she had never done that before.

Paka had done this.

I glowered at the sight of the retreating rental car. I hadn't given them my little blue pill mixture, but on cats, the catnip mixture might work the same way. If so, Rick would probably have a fair number of scratches on him by morning and Paka would be smiling and purring. She looked like the kind of female who liked a lot of sex a lot of the time. Some women did, not that I ever understood that sentiment. It was mean of me to give them my catnip blend, and had I known that Paka was mesmerizing and taming my cats for me, I might not have. But at the time, I hadn't been able to help myself. It had seemed the least they deserved for the trouble that would follow their visit.

I stayed at the window, petting Jezzie, watching, waiting. Maybe ten minutes later, I saw a form move down the drive, keeping to the shadows. Two others followed it. The churchmen were here, and they were sneaking in along the east side of the property, not coming openly down the drive, which meant nothing good. The only good thing was that there weren't enough of them to surround the house, which meant they were likely here to threaten, not to burn me out. Looked like I'd get to use the energies I had been gathering from the forest after all. I set Jezzie on the floor and scooted the cats up the stairs, where they liked to watch birds from the dormer windows.

TWO

Moving methodically but with practiced speed, I grabbed up my guns, extra ammo, and raced to the front porch, down the steps of the house, to the ground, where my bare feet touched the earth. Power I had banked away flared up in me again, through me, out my palms, which itched and burned in reaction, my fingertips tingling. I ducked into the depression between the raised beds in the front yard, a series of narrow, twisting pathways about three feet deeper than the beds and marked with large flat stepping-stones. Places to stand and fire, paths to get away through if necessary. Paths made by the sweat of my brow and lots of broken blisters.

The walls of the beds had been made of poured concrete that came to my waist, and bloomed with medicinal plantings: spotted touch-me-not jewelweed, a dozen varieties of thyme, and some other medicinal herbs in pots that were pretty to look at, like lamb's ears, mullein, monarda, and graybeard. They were all mixed in with the ornamental impatiens and geraniums—some in clay pots—for the pretty flowers. I placed the guns on the raised beds, except the shotgun. Holding it beneath one arm, I scratched my palms one at a time until they were red from the pressure of my nails, trying to ease the pain of drawing on the forest's energies. That power still boiled inside me, hot and potent but useless at a distance and without blood. But if they bled onto my land, they were mine.

I rolled my shoulders and knelt, most of my body now protected by the concrete and the earth the beds contained, placing my back against the flagpole I'd had installed in the center of the four beds, all designed for just this purpose. The flagpole was little more than a twelve-foot-tall angle iron, and it had never flown a flag. Most people never consciously saw it.

I braced my body against the concrete and settled into a comfortable, if not relaxed, firing position, raising the loaded shotgun, and placing the back of the weapon against the flat side of the flagpole. It was an unorthodox method of firing a shotgun, but I wasn't a large woman. I had fired an unbraced one once, and the recoil had tossed me back. I'd landed flat on my backside, with a shoulder so bruised I couldn't use the arm for two weeks. I wanted to buy an automatic rifle, a weapon much better suited to a woman's physiology than a shotgun, but they were expensive, and I wasn't exactly rolling in money.

I dug my toes into the cool grass of early autumn, blew out my breath, just like John had taught me, and shouted, "Stop!" I waited a moment as the word echoed and faded away, surprised when my invaders actually came to a halt in the shadows of the woods.

"State your piece," I yelled.

"Put down your weapons, woman!" one of the men called. They were too far away for me to make out their faces yet. But they'd be coming closer.

"Don't make me hurt you!" I yelled.

No one answered. I couldn't see them well enough to identify them, but I felt them through the dirt and placed the three men in a tight grouping about a hundred fifty feet away, in the cover of the forest. At least they hadn't split up. That would make it more difficult to bring them down. They were too far away, however, for a shotgun to protect me, and plenty close enough to take me down with a rifle, providing they found a higher vantage point to fire down at me, hidden in the low paths between the beds. For the first time in my life, I wished I were a real witch, as the church had once accused, one who could bring up a protective circle or send fire shooting outta my eyes or whatever witches did to people who wanted to hurt them. Not having better options, I decided to goad them.

"You'uns come outta the woods," I shouted in church-speak. No one moved. "Cowards! Afraid to face a woman on equal terms? Whatchu gonna do, huh? Shoot me from a distance like some kinda cheat? Maybe you think you'uns is all like some kinda assassins, but you ain't! You're chicken!" I shouted. "Each and every one of the churchmen is all chickens! Come out and face me, ya chickens!" Schoolyard taunts. They worked.

No one spoke loud enough for me to hear over the distance, but I felt them start slowly toward me, widening into a triangle shape, which was unfortunate, the man in the middle hanging back, the ones on the sides coming forward faster. The man in the center stumbled, the muscadine vine catching his foot. His hand touched the ground, bare skin to the earth, and I felt a tremble through the woods. A wrongness I couldn't place, deeper and darker than the wrongness of Rick and Paka. But there was no time to dissect that feeling. He righted himself and moved faster. The trees around the clearing began to sough, branches swaying back and forth slowly, like a sensation of breathing, though I felt no wind in the lowered paths of the raised beds. The grass beneath me shifted and bent beneath my weight, scratchy between my toes.

Smoke from my woodstove swirled and twisted around the house, smelling of warmth and false reassurance. The man on my right moved out of the woods and I saw his face. It was Brother Ephraim, my personal nemesis, a small man, but one who carried a big hate. He thought all women were evil and needed to be put in their places, beneath his boot, starting at an early age. Brother Ephraim hated me for lots of reasons, all of them related to my disobedience. I hadn't done as the church decreed and married the former leader, the old pervert better known as Colonel Ernest Jackson Sr., at age twelve. I hadn't been punished for my infraction either. Instead I'd accepted a proposal from John and Leah Ingram, and gone off church land with them, away from the men who wanted to either marry me off to the highest bidder or burn me at the stake for being a witch—because even then I'd had magic enough for the churchmen to notice. My leaving had been as much a taunt as my words just now.

From that day over a decade ago, Brother Ephraim wanted me in the punishment house, my punishment left in his hands.
I'd die first.

The man on my left stepped out of the trees—Joshua Purdy. No surprise. Joshua had tried to court me starting the week John died, the moment it was discovered that he'd left me his land, instead of leaving it to the church, like any self-respecting churchman should have. The land gave me value in the church's eyes, and Joshua was determined to claim me and the property both.

I'd die—second. I almost smiled.

The man in the center walked free of the trees and the shadows starting to stretch with early evening. Ernest Jackson Jr., called "Jackie," had become the head preacher and had taken over running the church. The colonel's son and heir was the meanest human being on the face of the Earth. I'd looked up what men like him were called. Misogynists. Sociopaths. Maybe even psychopaths. Dangerous, no matter what they were called. If the others hated me, then Jackie hated me with a burning passion, like coals of hatred piled up and waiting for the smallest inflammatory incident to flame up and roar, destroying everything his path. The thoughts were too poetic for the little turd. The hatred was mutual. And Jackie had drunk vampire blood long ago, to help cure him of a childhood cancer. Drinking blood of the damned had to have contributed to changes in his brain. Likely made him crazier than he woulda been in the first place.

Maybe that was why his touch had spooked my woods. Hatred was like fire, capable of destroying everything in its path. Woods feared fire. Perhaps hate made them feel the same sort of terror.

Jackie's hatred had gotten much worse when he discovered that I had allowed Jane Yellowrock's raiding party through my property to church land, the night his daddy went missing. It made me partially responsible for the arrests and the removal of the children by the child protective services of the state of Tennessee and the loss of his daddy, both in his eyes and in my own. Jackie and I had history. I could only hope I'd live long enough to see Jackson Jr. dead and gone too.

Brother Ephraim raised his shotgun and fired, but not at me. Into the back of the house. Two shots, a few seconds to reload, and two more shots, interspersed with the sounds of breaking glass and things shattering. When the sound died away, I heard him laughing as he again reloaded.

From behind me, from along the southwest border of the property, down the mountain a goodly ways, I felt something race up the road and leap into my forest. A creature that didn't belong here. Foreign. Wrong. The forest scratched the soles of my feet in warning. The grass shifted beneath me in alarm. The leaves thrashed overhead. *Wrongwrongwrong* thrummed up through my flesh. But I had more immediate problems—the three men hiding in the shadows.

"Stop!" I shouted at my visitors. They halted, each man holding his ground and a shotgun, the weapon of choice for most hunters, for the churchmen, and for every redneck around here. "Say what you came to say," I demanded, "and get off my land."

"You're dressed as a man, Sister Nell," Brother Ephraim called over the intervening distance. He was wearing camo greens and blended into the woods just beyond. "We would counsel you in womanly ways," he said.

Nothing new there.

"We'uns jist seen you entertain a strange man in your home without the presence of a family man to protect your honor and virtue," Jackie said. "You are now sullied in the eyes of the church and must submit to punishment to bring about repentance and atonement. It's time to return to the arms of the church and the family of your God."

"You're living alone, instead of as a helpmeet to a husband," Brother Ephraim said. "Women are weak, and apt to fall into the clutches of evil men."

Again, nothing new.

The new feeling of wrongness was growing closer, much closer, from the men before me and from the gorge behind me, from where the road curved around the property. My back tensed with apprehension, but there wasn't time to look over my shoulder. There was no way I could turn from the churchmen. "There aren't many men more evil than you, you perverts! Go away," I shouted. "I don't need to hurt you."

The men laughed at my words, and Joshua Purdy stepped from the shadows. He shook his oily hair back from his narrow face and said, "I've offered for you, time and again, to make you an honest woman, Nell. Accept my offer in the manner it was intended. Don't make us do something we might regret."

"Regret this," I muttered. I fired my shotgun. The boom was enough to damage my eardrums. The butt of the gun jerked down along the length of the flagpole, the barrel rising with the recoil. The men darted into cover as I steadied the weapon, tracking Jackie, who had ducked behind the vegetable garden not far from the side of the house and was crouching his way to the house corner for better cover. I fired again, taking down a vine of second-crop string beans, in a haze of green leaf shrapnel. I was deaf from the concussion and my eyes were tearing from the blasts as I reloaded with practiced ease.

All I needed to do was wing them. Just a single scratch by a shot pellet or vine thorn or anything, and I'd have the injured one's life force in my hands. But according to what I felt through my feet, no blood had dripped onto the soil of my land, onto the soil of Soulwood.

I blinked to clear my vision, catching sight of a flashing shadow, the shadow of wrongness that had been racing toward me, up the hill. From one side, a black shape leaped thirty feet and landed on the house roof, a leopard digging in with her claws as she raced over the roof ridge. A black leopard, dark as night, dappled with spots like moon shadows on the forest floor. Shock sliced through me as if I'd slipped a knife blade along my flesh.

An instant later I heard a shotgun blast and Brother Ephraim's high-pitched wail. His blood splattered in a sharp arc across the trailing muscadine vine and the dirt at its roots. The hunger for that blood roared up like wildfire. The soil sucked at the blood, the attention of the forest awakening and turning to the fight, eager. A tremor like electricity zapped through the trees and through me. Brother Ephraim was mine. This was part of my magic, my singular powers. To take the life of anyone who bled onto my land. To feed that life to the woods.

Jackie, hiding behind the beans, swiveled his shotgun toward the commotion and Ephraim's scream. He stood, raising his gun into firing position. I took careful aim at him, my finger on the trigger. Without firing, so fast I didn't have time to blink, Jackie pivoted his body, shifted his aim to me, and fired.

But he aimed too low. I felt the shot as it peppered into the soil of the raised beds. A terra-cotta pot busted, shards flying. Two impatiens plants took balls of hot shot to the roots and died.

Which made me mad.

I steadied my gun and squeezed the trigger. The gun boomed, plant parts flew inside the garden. I reloaded. Fast. So far as I could tell, I hadn't done anything except make a salad. I tightened my finger on the trigger.

The blast shocked through my hands and arms as the gun slipped off the flagpole. The world tumbled around me, recoil sending me rolling across the yard. A fractured shiver came from the ground, one that felt heated, like fire burning the grass, ripped, like fescue torn and killed by sheep. This was fear and danger as grass understood them.

I saw Joshua Purdy as I rolled. Unbloodied. I tried to right myself. Tried to pull my shotgun into place. Tried to pull the power of the land around me and hit him with it, not even knowing if that might actually work. The last thing I saw was Joshua's fist, coming at me.

I woke choking, drowning, shivering. I coughed and spluttered, pushing up from the water. I shook my head like a dog, my hair slinging water. By the feel of the earth beneath me, I knew where I was, about two hundred feet from the house, still on my land, where a spring cascaded from the rocks high behind the house, dropping to form a crick that ran most months out of the year. The water was still, unmoving in this natural bowl of earth, a shallow pool about a foot deep atop the clay depression. I rolled, dropping my backside into the chilled water, my knees up and arms locked, holding me in a sitting position. I coughed, expelling the water from my chest, the sound ragged before it finally eased. When I could breathe, I took in myself and my surroundings.

My coveralls' straps were cut, my shirt torn away. My upper chest was exposed. Joshua was sitting above me on a rounded boulder, his shotgun resting on his knees, watching me. I couldn't tell much from his expression, but I knew that he had tried to hurt me before he threw me in the pool, while I was unconscious. Tried to hurt me and couldn't. Not in my forest.

My hands felt odd, as if I had held them too long against a heating pot, slightly burned. The power of the woods tingled on the air, up through the clay and the water, full of fury and fear, the same feeling in my hands. I had a feeling that my woods had zapped Joshua. It hadn't been enough to kill him, but enough to stop him, make him rethink, giving me a chance to pick and choose my response. But now I was drained. I had nothing left inside me, unless he was bleeding, and I felt no blood where he sat.

I worked my jaw, feeling bruises and strained jaw joints, tender eye, swollen nose. He'd beaten me and taken me to a private place to do evil things to me, if not for the eerie woods that cast long, murky shadows and burned him with their anger.

Dark was coming. The trees of the woods raised above us, massive, big enough that three men couldn't have held hands and circled the trunks with their arms, trees as big as those in an old-growth forest. My woods. Eight years ago, the trees had had less than a third their current circumference, only twenty-five to fifty years old, and showing the girth of all such trees. My magic had made them stronger, bigger, tying them to me in some way I didn't understand. My magic had made the woods something else. Something other than just trees.

Years ago, I had killed a man who attacked me, much as Joshua had and for similar reasons. In fear and terror and panic, fighting for my life, I had fed him to the forest. I hadn't even known for sure who he was. I still didn't know. But that was my secret, never shared, not with anyone.

I was still slightly deaf, ears ringing, but I saw the branches move in their artificial wind, a breeze of the trees' making. My woods were alert and eager, had been since they tasted the blood earlier. They were full of power, waiting to be used. Waiting to be fed. I hadn't fed Soulwood but the once. Eight years ago. But the forest remembered.

The woods felt . . . hungry.

I dug my hands deeper into the bottom of the small pond, the reek of decay strong. The clay held the surface water in place, and a layer of leaves, dead and decaying from last winter, coated the bottom of the hollow. I shoved my hands through the muck and the soft clay, pushing back with my weight, forcing my hands deeper. My fingers found a thin strand of a root, not much bigger than a hair, but alive and pulsing with the forest's life. I pulled on its energies and it released its life into my skin, the root instantly shriveling, dying. I'd pulled too much and I released the life force back into it quickly, rattled and surprised.

Breathing out, I was not aware until then that I'd been holding my breath. More carefully, I pulled on the energies in the soil, knowing this was dangerous, but needing what Soulwood could give me. Joshua had made a mistake leaving me here on my land, in contact with the soil and water, roots and plants, that were the surface of its soul. Now all I needed was for him to come close enough for me to scratch him. "Joshua," I said, acknowledging his presence after a too-long silence.

His face didn't change; he didn't blink; I couldn't tell if he was breathing, until eventually he said, "I'll tell 'em I had my way with you." His voice was toneless. "They'll believe me. And they'll marry us in the church to protect the reputation of a widder-woman." I didn't reply, just sat there, exposed, cold and wet with the chill of early autumn, night falling, watching him watch me. Feeling the weight of the snub-nosed .32 still in the bib's pocket, weighing it down, remembering that I had more than one way out of this—though how he had missed the gun in his destruction of my clothes, I couldn't know. I'd have pulled the gun and shot him now if I thought I could hit the side of a barn from this distance, with that gun. The .32 was for close-up work, not target shooting. I needed him closer. Much closer. Gun and magic both required me to be up close and personal with my opponent. Shifting my body weight back onto my hands, I pushed farther down into the clay and sludge.

Joshua kept talking. "They'll marry us in front of witnesses. And I'll have your land and you. The way it was supposed to be."

Joshua, John's nephew, had been my husband's heir, until I came along. Joshua had believed that everything his uncle owned was going to be his, me included, and according to church law that would have happened, eventually. But Joshua didn't want to wait. He never had.

Joshua, his brother, Jackie, and a couple of friends cornered me at the door to the ladies' restroom, alone, after church services one day. I'd been almost fourteen and, though married to John in the eyes of the church, still a virgin.

John had caught his nephew and Joshua's friends, all older than me by five years or more, pawing me, and the vengeance he had administered with his fists were images I carried with me still. My husband had changed his last will and testament soon after that. And for all intents and purposes, we left the church a year later. Everything had begun to change after that event outside the ladies' room. And now here I was, with Joshua again, my virtue and life in danger.

"You hear me, woman?" he asked, his voice rising, a thrum of anger in it.

I quoted the Bible. "'But if a man find a betrothed damsel in the field, and the man force her, and lie with her: then the man only that lay with her shall die.'"

"Take off your clothes, woman," Joshua said, his voice vibrating with threat.

In the distance I heard a sound, rhythmic, a kind of throbbing resonance that might result if a music producer combined the rumble of a powerful engine with the purr of a house cat. In, out. In, out. Purring on the inhale and the exhale both. *Paka.* The black wereleopard in her animal form was close by.

Deep in the clay, my frigid fingers touched something solid and springy, and I wrapped them around the larger root, careful this time to take only a little, not what my panic screamed I would need. Holding on to the life of the forest, I tracked the purring, chuffing sound to a point of wrongness just to my right and slightly downhill, but . . . high, high in the trees. Below the leopard's paw, hanging on the branch beside her, was a body, mostly dead. I could feel his blood on the tree bark, his breath slight and fast in the shadows, his heart fluttering. This blood felt wrong as well, but a wrongness I couldn't explain. The wrongness was Brother Ephraim, and he was dying, dragged along an enormous tree branch by the powerful jaws of the black leopard. Blood poured from him onto the tree, as if deep gouges scored his flesh. The pumping of his heart was speeding, but the circulation itself was slowing as he bled out. Paka had wounded him most grievously while saving me, and he was dying. Dying fast. Blood loss and shock would kill her victim in minutes.

Joshua shifted on his pile of boulders. "Jackie said you'd let the devil into your house. A she devil and her devil man. And we had to take you back or you'd lose your soul. So . . . you're mine. Jackie said so." When I didn't reply he said, "Put aside the Taser you used on me. I won't have my wife with a weapon."

Fear welled up in me. This . . . *this* was what I'd feared all my life. Punishment at the hands of a churchman. "No," I said, so softly it was more a vibration in my chest. "No. I won't."

Joshua heard me and his face twisted in hate. "Take off your clothes. Submit. And I won't hurt you."

There was no cell signal on my land, and as best as I could tell, Jackson Jr. hadn't gone down the road, to a place where he could call for help. He was tracking the leopard, his footfalls steady and determined. Reckless. Arrogant. But not stupid. Cunning evil on two legs. If Jackie got here first, he'd shoot Paka and help his pal Joshua rape me, while his other friend died in the trees. They'd rape me just like they'd tried to outside the ladies' room when I was a kid. I'd kneed him in the groin then and tried to run, leaving him in the dirt. The boys still standing had grabbed me, hands up my dress. Until John found me. If John hadn't come . . .

But I wasn't a kid this time. I wasn't helpless, even without a man to protect me. Even without Paka in the trees above.

"No," I said, louder. "I won't have you." I shook my head. "And I won't let you hurt me."

Joshua's fury beat through the ground, hot and cold all at once. I felt him gather himself, ready to attack.

I didn't have a choice. I pushed my hands deeper into the clay, trapping myself if I had to move fast, the suction pulling at me, the cold stealing my life's warmth, but burying me in the earth of my woods. I found a second root with my other hand, this one larger. A poplar tree root as big around as my lower arm, tiny rootlets feathering off into the soil. This one pulsed with life like a fire hose, full and potent.

With the two roots in hand, I could follow every life source in the forest, every bird, rat, snake, beaver, red deer, lynx in a distant tree, watching prey, and the wrongness that stalked my land. Jackie. Joshua. Brother Ephraim, dying overhead, all wrong. Paka, Wrong. And Rick LaFleur. He was still human-shaped, moving among the trees, silent and stealthy, more so than any human I'd ever known. He was closing on Jackie. He had the churchman's scent. With him, on his shoulder, was a large rodent or small cat, another life force not seen here before, its energies wrapped around Rick's. *Cat on the dash of the car.*

Such wasted thoughts amid everything wrong that was poised to erupt into some new thing, something so very dangerous.

Above, Paka left the body of Brother Ephraim in the limbs and began moving through the trees, leaping from huge limb to huge limb, from tree to tree, silent, except for that double purr growing closer. It reverberated through the trunks of the poplar grove and into my bones. Paka was a wrongness here in the Appalachian Mountains, the trees resisting her. I feared that my woods might hurt her like they'd hurt Joshua. Instinctively I reached out to her through the trees, accepting her, pulling her in close to me, making her part of the land. It was the same thing I did when I put seeds or a plant's roots into the soil; I claimed them for the land. In the same way I claimed Paka, giving her access to every part of the woods, making her part of them. Like the trees and plants, I could use her to help me as I desired. But I knew that by claiming her, I was also accepting responsibility for her actions. This was the good and the bad of living in Soulwood.

Joshua pulled his legs up under his body, in preparation to stand. "I said, take off your clothes, woman."

From all around came a sound that had never belonged in this forest, a sound that was powerful and terrifying. Not a roar like an African lion, but like the dark of a moonless night, half scream, half rumble, a hacking, growling roar that spoke of death and menace. Joshua cringed and looked around. Paka had moved fast through the canopy of trees.

Overhead I caught a glimpse of a soaring hawk as it dove, hurtling through the limbs, half closing his wings. He tilted his body up, his claws opening, reaching. He caught a squirrel in his talons, the prey silent, swiftly crushed to death. The hawk spread his wings and flapped past me, to settle on a branch above Joshua. It ripped into the still warm body of the rodent and tore off a strip of bloody meat, the raptor staring down at Joshua as it ate. The squirrel's blood splattered as it died. I knew it because of the roots I clutched, because they knew it, because the forest knew it all. Almost a whisper, Joshua demanded a third time, "Take. Off. Your. Clothes."

I lifted my face and smiled at him, eyes only half-open, lips closed, demure, like the womenfolk were trained. "Nooo," I said, drawing out the word.

Overhead the hawk paused, seeing the movement of a black shadow in the tall branches. *Paka*. Stealthy. Just above me. Her paws padding along a limb, about twenty feet away from Joshua. I had seen her leap onto my house. Joshua was well within Paka's range. I wasn't gonna have to kill this man, or not alone, at any rate. I laughed, the tone low and mocking. Slowly I added, "And if you touch me again, I'll make you shit your britches, *boy*."

Joshua stood, the shotgun gripped so tightly in his hands that his knuckles went white. A drop of something fell from above and hit him, square on his head. Joshua flinched and raised one hand, letting go, holding the gun by the barrel only. With the other hand, he touched the crown of his head. When he drew back his palm, it was smeared with blood. His eyes went wide; he tilted up his head, eyes darting through the branches. But Paka had already leaped. Flying through the air, silent as the shadow of death in the valley of evil.

Joshua saw. Movements jerky, he tried to raise his gun. Too late. Paka crashed into him and rode him to the earth, her claws embedded in his face, the long retractable claws holding his skull and jaw. Her back feet slammed into his middle, crushing out his breath in a strangled scream as they landed.

"Paka! No!" Rick darted into the opening between the trees and waded through the small pond, his boots sinking in the clay and splashing me with icy water.

Paka roared again, a hacking, growling scream that sent shivers through the forest and into my cold flesh. She turned greenish-gold eyes to me and hacked, asking me what I wanted to do. Rick came to a stop at the edge of the pool and looked from her to me, his eyes wide and uncertain, watching.

On his shoulder something moved, the other life force I'd noted earlier. It chittered and bounced up and down to see in the gloaming dark. When I didn't react, it leaped ahead and landed, racing from Rick, fast as a flying bird, bounding as if winged, toward Paka. More wrongness rocked through the earth, shocking the breath from me.

"Pea! No!" Rick screamed. And I knew something horrible was about to happen. The thing drew in its body to leap. Steel glinted at its feet. Wrong, so very *wrong*.

"No," I whispered. In response to my thoughts, the ground

seemed to close over its back feet. The critter whiplashed and rolled, its body stuck, as if on flypaper. It squealed, the sound catlike and mad. The small creature rippled and went still. Like the others, it looked at me. It wasn't a rodent. Not a cat. *Something else.* Something with dark steel claws the size of good butcher knives, longer than it should be able to use, small as it was. Neon green, shaped like a small cat, claws out. *Steel claws. An animal with* steel *claws longer than my hand.* It was so foreign that the forest would have rejected it and spit it out, sending the thing rolling, had I not clenched my mind around its feet. Yet, even through the ground, I couldn't get a feel for what the creature was.

Rick stared at his mate, his face and eyes fierce and angry and hurting. I had no idea what the expressions and emotions meant, but they were deep and intense, an agony of the soul. "Paka. No. Please, Pea. She was trying to save the woman, Nell."

The thing on the forest floor hissed, its claws flashing. I didn't know what it was, but I had a feeling what it intended. "Why does it want to kill Paka?" I asked.

Paka, sitting atop Joshua, growled low, the sound vibrating through the air and the earth. Her claws had pricked him, making him bleed, and I could sense that blood seeping into the ground, Joshua's blood and Ephraim's blood, strange and metallic. The earth was thirsty, so eager for sustenance that it made my mouth go desert dry and my stomach cramp with need. Eight years since I had fed it. Eight long years. Distantly I heard Joshua whimper.

"That's what its species does," Rick said, his voice empty of everything but dread. "They live with us, like pets and friends, but they're here for one reason, as a deterrent, to keep us from spreading the were-taint or killing humans. For a were-creature to kill a human or to bite and transmit the were-taint, the punishment is death. Always."

And Brother Ephraim hung on the tree limb, not far from us. Pea knew what had happened to him. Somehow. And for the weres, Pea was justice and vengeance and death. "And though Paka hurt Brother Ephraim saving me, there's no hint of mercy?"

"No. None," Rick whispered, his eyes on his mate. Tortured. But oddly I didn't see love as I understood it, or even love as the library books suggested it might be. It wasn't a happy love. It was addled. *Addicted.*

I remembered my sense of Paka as a tamer of cats. Paka had magic, and her magic was . . . I shook my head slightly, trying to figure it out in time to avoid whatever was primed to happen here, hovering over us like the sword of death.

"I smell her victim's blood," Rick said dully. "His bowels have opened. His bladder gave way." Rick took a shaking breath, the sound broken. He looked up into the trees, as if trying to locate Ephraim. "The stench of death rides the breeze." His tone made me think of poetry, as if he were quoting something.

"But if Paka hurt a human and he *didn't* die at her fangs," I said, "*and* he didn't turn into a werecat, then what?" At my words, Joshua whimpered, as if the claws at his neck and face tightened.

"The only way that could happen would be if someone else killed him before he died at Paka's fangs." And then Rick's eyes tightened and I knew his thoughts had taken a turn, hopefully to follow mine.

I closed my eyes and wrapped my fingers tighter around the roots, letting them speak to me about the body so high overhead. Brother Ephraim was near death, his heart racing, his breath so light and thin that scarcely any air moved through his lungs. So much blood drenching the tree branch, falling onto the ground in quiet splatters, the forest soaking it up, waiting for me to feed it fully. "Brother Ephraim is nearly dead," I said, "but not quite."

"Pea . . . ," Rick said, his voice clotted with emotion, his face showing conflict and pain. He didn't love Paka. But he was tied to her. *Magic,* I thought.

I shivered, my hands still buried in the clay, my fingers still gripping the roots, the power of the forest still flowing through me. "My choice," I said to them, my eyes on Pea. At the words, a foreign emotion flooded me, engulfing me. I gasped once, like a drowning victim thrown into an icy stream. The sensation flashed through me, a raging flood, steeling my breath. Something powerful, primeval, elusive. Far more than I could grasp. It washed over and through me and away, a flash flood, too much, too potent, to really comprehend. And it trickled away, leaving nothing.

They were looking at me strangely and, not sure what had happened, I finished the thought, *"My* land," I said, the words ringing strangely. *"My* enemies. *My judgment."* I knew something had happened, but it was gone, fleeting and intense.

The little green thing chittered at me, as if waiting for me to say something more, so I did, drawing on the ancient emotion that had washed through me. "He's dying. There's no way to get him to a hospital in time. But this is my land, my woods. And he's my enemy, who came to do evil to me, just like Joshua Purdy"—I inclined my head to the pile of rock—"came to do evil to me.

"Paka's fangs haven't spilled his blood, just her claws, so he's safe from weretaint, right?"

Rick nodded, the movement jerky.

"So it's just Brother Ephraim, who's dying." But the biggest problem wasn't Ephraim or Joshua. Jackie was in my woods, drawing close. I didn't have long to save Paka, who had saved me. To do so, I'd have use my strongest magic for the second time in my life. I didn't know if I could stem the flow, once I set it free.

And Joshua had bled on the land too.

THREE

Pea chittered at me, trying to say something I couldn't understand.

I tilted my head, my wet hair clinging to me with cold. My body felt numb rather than frozen, which meant I was hypothermic. "Brother Ephraim, who is near death, once controlled the punishment house," I explained to the furious green critter. "It's the place where women were sent to be reminded that they were only the helpmeet, not the man, that they were born to do and be and feel and live as their menfolk told them.

"He had my mother one time, for a whole day. She came back changed, crying in the night, flinching at the slightest move. Daddy brought her home, but he never did a single thing against old Brother Ephraim, even when she had a baby the next spring that looked more like Brother Ephraim than like Daddy." I settled my eyes on the thing that had leaped from Rick's shoulder. It sat on the ground, feet caught in roots and earth, its small body tense and rigid, prepared to attack Paka the second it got loose, steel claws glinting. "Ephraim hurt my mama. He hurt a lot of women. He came here today to hurt *me*, to take me back into the church against my will and punish me. I know that because he told me so. The judgment is mine. His life is mine. The choice is mine. *Mine.* Not yours."

I leaned forward, against the pull of the muck. My arms began to slide free, slowly. I wanted to be covered when Jackie got here.

"Joshua, now, he's just an angry, silly little boy who'll still be a silly little boy twenty years from now, if he lives. While he'll most likely continue on this road and become the same kind of evil as his friend Jackie, he hasn't actually accomplished much in the way of evil." And I wouldn't sentence him to death despite the blood he had shed on the forest floor, blood that was mine to take. The woods seemed to flow beneath my feet in reaction to my words, making me wonder what it heard, what it felt from me. The big black cat retracted her claws and stepped away, still poised over her prey in threat. With a back paw, she sent Joshua's shotgun spinning off the rocks into the darkness. It clattered down the stones.

I lifted my chin and raised my voice so it would carry up the pile of rock. "You hear me, Joshua? I'm offering leniency. I'm offering mercy." Joshua said nothing and I called out, "You hearing me, Josh? 'Cause iffen you don't answer me, I'll let that big ol' cat eat you." I almost added, *the way it ate Brother Ephraim,* but I didn't.

"You're insane," he shouted back, gasping. "You need to be locked away, chained in the attic, where crazy women go."

"That's not an answer," Rick said, his voice oddly low and without emotion. I thought it might be his cat talking. "Answer the lady."

"I hear," Joshua ground out.

I figured that was the best I was going to get. I dropped my voice again, low enough to exclude Joshua. "The leader of God's Cloud of Glory Church is nigh," I said in my strongest childhood dialect. "He'll wanna kill us all. He will not be a respecter of the law. He finds pleasure in destruction and death and the pain of his victims." I leaned harder and my left hand came free, slinging clay and pond goo across the small clearing. I swished the hand in the pond water to clean it and held my bib up over my breasts, as I swiveled and leaned away to free my right hand. The moment it was free, I swished it too, and stood, bare feet on the edge of the tiny pool. I slipped my hand into the bib and around the small .32. Joshua was incompetent, too busy feeling up breasts and not busy enough making sure his prey was defenseless. I gripped the gun with my right hand and held the bib with the left, swiveling to see the path where Jackson Jr. would appear.

"Jackie!" I shouted. "Brother Ephraim is gone and Joshua is pinned down, weaponless. You come into this clearing and you'll not make it out again!"

"Thou shalt not suffer a witch to live!" the words screamed, batting through the trees, a hollow sound, lacking in the power

Jackie always found from the pulpit and the microphone that gave him a range God hadn't.

I smiled, more a twitch of lips than anything else. "That all you got, Jackie?" I mocked. "That old line about witches? I got a gun and two helpers." I looked at Pea. "Maybe three."

"You got no help. You got no backup. You are mine; all the women are mine."

Was that the way things were now in the church compound? All the women belonging to one man? I didn't believe it. Even the rancid old pedophiles wouldn't give up all their womenfolk to the preacher. But some families might have married off the older daughters to the preacher, just as Lot, in the Bible, had offered his daughters to the crowd of rapists to keep himself and his men friends safe. That sounded like the thinking of some of the churchmen.

I said, "Wrong again. I got me a special agent of PsyLED here, Jackie."

Rick called out, "I'm Special Agent Rick LaFleur. I'd like to talk to you about a number of things, one of which is the attack up at the house. Do you know who shot up the house owned by Nell Ingram?"

There was no answer. Through the soles of my feet, I felt Jackie move away, not back toward the house, but up along the ridge, fast, weirdly fast. Running with his tail between his legs at a speed I'd need to think about later. A speed maybe given him by the vampire blood he'd drunk in years past, blood provided when his daddy kidnapped vampires for him to drink from. The forest carried his emotional overload—fury, panic, sexual frustration. Fear brought about by the unexpected presence of law enforcement.

I relaxed my shoulders and said to Rick, "He's gone." I told the leopard, "Let the little boy go. No harm, no foul. This time." I might hate Joshua Purdy, I mighta killed a man here in the heart of the woods once, but then as now, I was a judge, not a murderer, and judges should have some small speck of mercy about them, somewhere.

Paka backed away, leaving Joshua laying on the stones, bleeding and terrified. I could smell urine and knew he'd pissed his pants, not that I blamed him. I looked at Rick. "You sure he isn't gonna go catty on the full moon?"

"Yes. I'm sure," he said, his voice tight. "She didn't use her teeth. There was no exchange of body fluids." Rick moved cat fast and knelt, one hand fisted in the green fur of the thing with its feet buried in the earth. He put away his gun and petted the creature like a kitten, a swipe from ears along its back and tail. "Pea," he said, as if the animal could understand him. "Nell says the man won't die at Paka's fangs."

It didn't sound like any kind of cop talk I'd heard on the films I watched. It sounded like a paranormal conversation rather than the law of the United States, conversation with the metaphoric hand of justice rather than the hand of the written law with *I*s dotted and *T*s crossed, which was good for me. It meant that Rick was unlikely to consider my next acts as a crime. Rick added, shaking the green creature slightly, "He won't turn on the full moon. And Paka didn't kill him."

"My land. My rules," I said to Pea. "Paka goes free, so you can back off, you little green . . . *thing*."

The green thing turned to me, chittered in disgust, and sniffed the air as if perplexed. Animals picked up conversations from body language, but I was pretty sure that this one understood English. It spat, clearly repulsed, and looked up into the trees, chittering some more.

Pea went silent, its nose still working like a rabbit's, twitching and bunching.

To Rick I said, "Would you take Joshua away, outta my woods? Paka and me, we got us a little talking we need to do." The black cat looked at me, her eyes a beautiful shade of greenish gold in the early night, her black mottled coat disappearing entirely in the shadows. "We can walk back to the house together. Okay?"

Rick looked from me to his mate and shrugged. "Paka doesn't like other females. It's taken her a week to settle in with the trainees."

"She'll be fine with me," I said, hoping I was right, hoping my claiming of her for the land hadn't done something to her. I had only ever claimed plants, not a breathing animal, let alone a werecat.

Rick released Pea's green fur and climbed the stones, bent, slung Joshua's arm over his shoulder, and half carried him back down. None too gently, he helped the man back along the narrow trail to the house, shouldering Joshua's bent gun without missing a step. "I'll see him on his way and wait for you at the house," Rick said. Being part cat, Rick had no trouble negotiating the path in the fast-falling dark; Joshua stumbled a bit and Rick didn't seem to care, dragging the smaller man until Joshua caught his feet.

When they were out of earshot I reached into the woods and into the ground, feeling for Pea. I had no idea how I had buried its feet, trapping it, and I didn't want to get close enough to use my hands to free the green thing. But I thought about letting it go, and instantly Pea bowed its back, digging in with its hand-claws, freeing its back feet. Hissing, it sat and began cleaning those steel back claws on the ground, the feel of metal sharp and cutting, as if razor blades slashed me instead of the forest floor. Then it raced into the shadows, reappearing back at my feet so fast I would have missed it had I blinked. It carried a droplet of Brother Ephraim's blood on one steel claw, and held the blood up to me. Hesitantly I leaned down and extended a finger. Pea smeared the drop of blood onto my fingertip, careful to not cut with its claw. It chittered at me, its tone oddly formal sounding, as if this was a ceremony of sorts. I hoped it wasn't a death sentence aimed at me.

I wasn't sure what all this meant, and said to it, "I accept the blood, and the price, if there is one." It chittered at me, softer now, and backed away.

I searched the ground for Paka's life force, then felt for Brother Ephraim above us in the trees. Both were present in the woods, part of the earth beneath my feet and part of the woods over my head. Somehow I'd claimed them both when I claimed Paka. Maybe claiming predator and dying prey made them one? Maybe because Paka had eaten part of Brother Ephraim and his flesh was her flesh? I wasn't sure. I wasn't sure of much of anything in the land that was mine, except that it had claimed me too, long ago. With something like instinct, I had been claiming it back ever since. And now, with that same instinct, I was choosing to feed its magic, its power, again, by taking another life. That wasn't something I had ever wanted to do. Or maybe I was lying to myself and I had always wanted to use the power of the woods, always wanted to feed them. To the werecat, I said, "You feeling any different?"

Paka sat, front paws together. Watchful.

I almost said, *I did something when you were tracking Joshua an' me. The forest, it was wanting to stop you. I told it you were mine so it let you through.* I hadn't thought to claim the others, which seemed wise in retrospect. But Paka appeared no different now from before. Calmer maybe. Hunting living prey made cats calm and happy. Killing made them happier still. So I didn't tell her what I'd done, mostly because I had no idea how to undo it. I'd play a wait-and-see game instead, and maybe not ever have to confess. The coward's way, but I had often feared that I was a coward, shamed by some part of me that I never even saw, never knew. "Your prey. He's still alive, up in the trees."

Paka's big head raised up, looking into the trees, and dropped down, then back up, nodding once, her eyes aiming back at me like weapons. "His life is the forest's to take," I said.

Paka did nothing, so I turned my back and took the slow steps into the dark, to the ground beneath the tree limb where Brother Ephraim lay, as close to death as a man could get and still cling to this Earth. Blood had dripped and splattered on the leafy forest floor. I stared at it, not sure how to do this. I had only ever done this once before, in fear, fighting for my life, against a man who wanted to hurt me. So much of my woods was unknown to me; so much of my power over it was unknown as well, and I had intended it remain that way if possible. But Jackie and Joshua were never gonna let me be. Not now. And tonight indicated that the woods and I were closer, more twined, than I had previously thought.

I bent my knees, placing my palm on the blood. Blood didn't have an odor that humans could smell, not until it began to sour and rot, but this blood smelled metallic, bitter, something odd just at the edges of my ability to detect. Beneath my hand, the forest was seething with need, with hunger, the scent and patter of blood, the stench of bowels still releasing, and the reek of fear, the race between predator and prey, all had waked it. The woods thrummed through me, as if blood that pulsed and air that breathed.

I called to the blood on the earth and to the life draped high above. And I plunged my hand through the splattered blood, into the soil, fingernails breaking with the impact. I pulled on the blood, on the body hanging above me, drawing the life force to me, gathering it as if webbed between my fingers, which were buried in the dirt. I hovered my other hand over it, holding the life force like a ball of light balanced atop the ground, between my two hands a single tether of life, still secured to the body above. And I felt Ephraim begin to pass away, his spirit falling, disentangling from his body. His life force shuddering through the air. My magic caught it, pulling it to me and across my flesh like a caress, or a promise, or a threat, heated and icy both, into a glowing ball that held together, for a moment. Brother Ephraim began to slide away from me, into the ground. The process was slow and purposeful, my mind focused. The life force slid past me, clutching at me as it went, trying to slow its passage, screaming deep into the dark beneath.

The woods shivered, the soil moving in fractions of inches, fast and furious. Drinking the life away. Claiming the soul as its own. Things fell from the branch above, hitting the ground around me, bouncing, breaking, fracturing, and crumbling to powder. Bones. Hair in short strands. Fingernails. Clothes. Boots. Crumbling and sifting into piles and then into the dirt, sucked down. Along with the soul I'd stolen to feed Soulwood. Ashes to ashes, dust to dust.

And so I fed the life of Brother Ephraim into the earth.

This was resolute. Deliberate. This was judgment. Utter. Complete. And I didn't care. Even knowing that this power made me evil, far more evil than a witch, no matter what the Scriptures might say. Scriptures that had no mention of my kind anywhere in them. I'd looked.

The limbs above shook and trembled. Leaves rustled hungrily. Time passed. The earth stilled. Satisfied. Pleased. *Aware . . .*

I breathed in, smelling loam and water. Hearing the trickle of spring water. Night had fallen, dark and thick with promise, threat, and gratification. I stood and brushed my hand off on my damp clothes. My fingertips were bleeding, blood dripping onto the ground, but as I watched, the skin healed over, clean and new. I was no longer cold; I felt warm and sated and relaxed, the power still pulsing in me. I didn't know what that might mean, but it felt good. The church would call me witch and evil and murderess and burn me at the stake. But the church wasn't here. And the law enforcement officer who was here? He'd never tell what he knew or thought he knew, because if he did, Paka's secret would be out—that she had hunted a human and eaten of him. And that fact would forever alter the precarious balance of humans, paranormal creatures, and law enforcement in the United States.

I stood over the place where Brother Ephraim had vanished and quoted Shakespeare. "'If you prick us, do we not bleed? . . . If you poison us, do we not die? And if you wrong us, shall we not revenge?' You're gone now, Brother Ephraim, into a life of my choosing and my judgment." The ground beneath me went still, leaving the woods hushed and silent as the grave.

I considered Paka, a black smear on the night, and said, "You didn't eat much of Ephraim, so I reckon you're hungry. I have a venison roast in the freezer. I can thaw it and cook it for you to eat in human form, or let you eat it raw in cat form." Paka yawned, showing me her teeth, white in the night. I wasn't sure what answer that was, but I turned and led the way through the woods, back to the house. Paka followed in my path, her huge paws silent on the earth.

Rick, Paka, and I were sitting around the table, silent, me finally warm and dry, a blanket wrapped around my shoulders, drinking homemade wine bottled by Sister Erasmus. She was my maw-maw's friend, and her wine was delicious, at least to me; I'd had two and a half glasses, leaving me tipsy, twirling my goblet in my fingers, sleepy, like the forest surrounding the house. The goblets had thick stems and deep bowls, earthenware that had been hand-thrown by a local woman, cooked in a wood-fired kiln, and glazed in greens and browns with touches of blue. I'd had the goblets for two years, having traded vegetables and herbs for them, just because I liked them. I'd never used them until now, making do with water glasses or empty Mason jars. Company deserved better. The night itself deserved better.

Paka, in her human form, poured another few ounces into my goblet and I sipped, the wine dark and rich, which I liked, though Rick had called the wine too sweet. I hadn't bothered to learn much about wines, knowing I'd never have a chance to try the expensive good ones, but I had considered growing grapes for local vintners. I figured my land would grow better grapes than any place in Europe. I could plant an acre, maybe two, in the front yard, if I was of a mind, and watch over it through the front window.

Paka finished off the small venison roast, which was bloody in the center and too tough, from being still frozen when it went into the oven to thaw in heated stew juices. But she didn't seem to notice or care. Eyes dark and hooded, Rick watched her as she sliced off pieces of the roast and picked them up with her fingers, eating with dainty movement but no manners. He seemed entranced by her, but not like a normal man in the presence of a beautiful, wild woman. More as if he was pulled to her, like the moon to the Earth, held in her orbit, but always separate. I couldn't guess at the nature of their relationship, but whatever their bond was, peace wasn't part of it.

Paka looked at him, and slid one slender finger out of her mouth. It was unconsciously alluring, until she spoiled it with the words, "His blood, the blood of the man, it was . . . wrong."

"We can talk about that later," Rick murmured.

I frowned, remembering the feel of Ephraim's life as it slid along my skin. "Metallic," I said. "His blood smelled and felt, metallic and tart, like pennies soaked in vinegar." Rick didn't reply. I looked out into the dark, beyond the creature they called Pea, sitting in the windowsill, staring into the night through the glass, its tail twitching slowly. Not a cat tail—too short and too thick for that. And too neon green for any mammal on Earth. Parrot green maybe, or pea green, after which it had been named. It had hidden its huge claws, which had to be magic, because they were longer than its feet. Not an Earth creature. Something from somewhere else. If the church was right, the only other places for beings to come from were heaven and hell, but Pea looked like she—I wasn't sure about its gender and neither were the others, but they called her female—belonged to neither. Rather, she looked like something out of a fairy tale, one of the old stories, fluffy on the surface but dark and bloody underneath.

I pulled the blanket tighter around my shoulders, glad for

the warm clothes and mostly dry hair. Glad for the Waterford Stanley cookstove. Glad for a roof over my head and a house that was mine alone. Glad to have my guns back at the windows where they belong and not left outside in the raised beds, abandoned. Glad to be alive.

Not happy about the damage to the house. I'd have the insurance company out tomorrow afternoon, and I'd have to find a way to pay the deductible. I knew exactly how much cash I had on hand and it came to enough to pay for a single pane of window glass. I hadn't looked at the other mess, the damage inside. The dollar signs were adding up fast and I hadn't even gone to work for Rick yet. It could only get worse. I would be smart to kick them to the curb, but I couldn't. We were bound now, in a way, by the death of Brother Ephraim, and by my claiming Paka. I didn't know what I could do about any of it.

Having people in my house was unexpected. Except for a rare townie customer looking for an herbal remedy, I'd been alone here since John died. I'd gotten used to the feel of the floor beneath my feet, untouched by the vibrations of other people walking, used to the empty table and chairs. The silence. Used to washing only one plate. One glass. One fork or spoon.

In theory, after John died, I could have left, sold the land to a development company, moved to the city. But I stayed here, probably foolishly, waiting to see if my sisters would ever come to their senses and run away from the cult, from their lives in multiwife marriages, to freedom.

Now there were people here and the house felt full, as if it needed to stretch to contain us all. The dirty dishes on the table were . . . more. The noise was more. The more I might have had if John had given me children. But he hadn't been able to give his wives babies and the others had requested divorce, which he'd granted, and left him for other men, all except Leah. She had died here in the farmhouse, in the bed in the biggest bedroom on the south side of the house, leaving John alone except for me. Later he had died in that same bed. I hated that bed but I hadn't been able to throw it out. Instead, I slept on the sofa or in the small cot in the loft that had been mine since I came here. Or on the screened porch in the hammock. I slept with guns at every window. I slept safe, for the most part. Safe, but alone.

"Do you want to tell me about it?" Rick asked, his tone gentle.

"About what?" I asked. Tears pricked my eyes and I stood quickly, dipping my head forward so my wet hair slid over my face and shoulders and down to my hands as I cleared the table. "About what happened in the woods? What my life was like with John? Why I left the church? Why I still live here?" I glanced at him as I stood and stacked the heavy stoneware, none too gently. The *clank* of pottery and the *clink* of utensils sounded thunderous in the silent house. "What do you want to know?"

Rick tilted his head, observing me, his black eyes still kind. No man had ever been kind or gentle to me. Not even John, no matter that he'd loved me, saved me. He'd never been tender even when he finally took me to wife at age fifteen—he hadn't known how to be. But he'd given me freedom and safety and that was worth so much more than any kind of gentleness that there might have been.

I set the dishes in the sink and put the vegetable leftovers into the steel composter on the back porch, the meat scraps and juices into a separate tin, wiped off the plates. I stopped, staring out into the night, letting my senses free. Impressions came from the woods, fast and intense, much more so than only yesterday. The trees were happy, satisfied, alert, though not in any way that a human might have understood. Back at the sink, I piled up the dirty dishes, and realized that my tie to the woods was stronger. I had known for a long time that I wasn't strictly human. Hadn't been in years. Maybe forever. But this . . . this was different. This was more . . . more whatever I was.

And with the sensations coming at me from the woods, I also had to think about the fact that I had killed a man tonight. One who would have died anyway. But still.

That should have made me afraid, or shamed, or shocked, or . . . something negative. Instead, it made me happy—fiercely, ferociously happy. But that knowledge was mine alone, not something to share with strangers, no matter that we now shared the knowledge of the death of Brother Ephraim.

I turned on the spigot that let water into the farmhouse sink from the woodstove's water heater. It steamed in the air as it gathered. I added soap and watched bubbles rise.

"Nell?" Rick prodded. Gentle. His voice so tender. No wonder he was a heartbreaker.

"I was always different," I said, without looking back at them, "from the other women. I wanted to read books, to spend time in the gardens or the greenhouses, rather than in the sewing rooms or the kitchens or the nursery, chatting and gossiping. I never wanted the things the other girls did: a husband and a passel of children. I wanted a man who would treat me with respect, who would marry me according to the laws of the land instead of the laws of God's Cloud of Glory Church. A man who would wait to bed me until I was of age." I turned off the water and bowed my head, my hair sliding against me, still damp and chilled.

"When I was twelve, Colonel Ernest Jackson—Jackie's father—asked my father for my hand in marriage." I began washing the plates, my face firmly turned away from my guests. "I waited until Sunday and told the colonel no, in front of God and everybody, in front of the whole church. Made a ruckus, I did. I told him I'd rather marry a horse's backside, though I wasn't so polite about it. And then I ran out."

Rick said nothing. I didn't look his way.

"I guess Jane Yellowrock told you about the colonel kidnapping vampires and drinking their blood." Rick didn't move, not even the smallest bit, but Paka, who sat within the range of my vision, glowered at her mate. "It's common knowledge that he and his cronies did it for Jackie Jr., to save him from a cancer. They must a also figured out how it gave the old men power in the bedroom. They kept kidnapping and drinking off and on until Jane finally put a stop it. I figure the colonel was drinking undead blood about the time he wanted me. Feeling his oats.

"Anyway, I was in trouble and afraid. I hid in the barn after the scene in the church. I was still there when John Ingram and his wife, Leah, wandered in and found me. We got to talking, him and his wife and me. Leah was sick and dying. Everyone knew it. And because John hadn't given her children, she would be alone in her dying. So. She suggested John marry himself a nurse for her, someone young and strong and independent, who might not mind never having young'uns. They proposed to me; and promised that I wouldn't have to take up my wifely duties until I turned fifteen. I accepted."

In the silence of the great room, I finished washing and rinsing the plates and stacked them on the wood dish drainer that John had made in the church's woodworking shop years ago. For Leah. Everything in this house had been made for Leah or one of his other wives, not me. But I was the one who'd ended up with it all. Life was puzzling. Unpredictable. But one thing was sure. The meek didn't ever inherit the Earth. I wasn't meek. And I had the land. The others were dead and gone, and it was mine according to the law of the United States and the state of Tennessee and according to the land itself. Leah had been gone since I was nearly fifteen. John had been dead since I was nineteen. More than three years I had been alone. So maybe it was time and past time to claim the house and the things in it too, to make them mine. To maybe move from the tiny half bed to a bigger one, to make a room my own.

No one was talking and the water wasn't hot enough, so I dried my hands and opened the wood box on the side of the stove. I put a single split log inside, turning the bottom damper almost closed, the top damper shut tight. The log, sitting on the coals, would last all night, and leave me plenty of coals to start a fire in the morning. It would also heat the water. That was the first thing I'd learned when I came here, as John's affianced wife—how to maintain the stove and its attached water heater, how to do maintenance on the windmill that ran the well pump, how to check the cistern, how to pump water by hand when needed. Chores, arduous work. But worth it for the freedom they had offered me.

"I never loved John," I said, "not the way library books say is possible, all that passion and kissing and stuff, but John and me had married in the eyes of the church. I respected him and loved Leah, and nursed her through her dying, and I gifted him with my virtue and my honor when I came of age, according to the church." I'd not been happy to go to John's bed, but I had been grateful enough for his protection that I'd gone willingly at age fifteen. "Leah hadn't been in the grave a good year when John took sick and the men of the church came sniffing around, knowing he was dying, hoping to get his land." One of whom I had

killed, my first sacrifice to the earth of Soulwood, but that wasn't
to be shared, ever. And I would never know who had attacked
me. Half a dozen backsliders left the church that year. Coulda
been any one of 'em. "When I turned eighteen, we married
again, this time according to the law of the state of Tennessee.

"I nursed John as best I could, and kept him alive longer than
the doctors said was possible. And when he was gone, I inherited Soulwood." I rinsed the last of the dishes in tepid water.

"Why do you stay here?" Rick asked.

My shoulders went back stiffly. "I stay to honor John and
because my sisters are still part of the church."

And I also stayed, despite the danger from the churchmen,
because the land and I were tangled together. Tighter now than
only hours past.

I turned to my guests. "What do you want with me? Everything, this time, not just the easy stuff, asking questions. What
about that consulting you talked about? What's that really mean?"

Rick glanced at Paka, who had moved to sit at the kitchen
table with my cats, one on her lap and the other sleeping on
her shoulders, and back to me. Instead of answering my question, he asked another one himself. "What did you do with the
man Paka killed?"

Pea turned at the question and gathered herself. She leaped
all the way from the window to the back of the sofa. With
another single leap, she landed on the table, sauntered up to
Paka, and butted her in the nose. Paka hissed at her and batted
her away, in the manner of cats.

I said, "Paka didn't kill him. I never laid a hand or a
weapon on him. He died of nature. And he'll never be found."
If Rick the cop thought I meant natural causes, so be it.

"You buried him?"

"Persistent, ain't ya?"

He pointed to himself and gave a half smile. "Cop." It was
a charming expression, black eyes flashing with good humor,
showing the man he might have been once, before life, before
loving Jane Yellowrock, and maybe before being magically
tied to Paka, who seemed to be sucking him dry of life and
happiness, like some kind of spiritual vampire he couldn't get
away from.

"There was no chance of Brother Ephraim surviving. He

passed away but not at Paka's hands." I firmed my lips. "No one will ever find a single cell of his body or thread of his clothes."

Rick's smile vanished, leaving the calculating, discerning cop in his stead. He stared at me with the same intensity Jezzie used when she spotted a mouse that she wanted to eat.

"You're thinking with a different part of your brain now. Earlier you were thinking like a cat. Now you're thinking like a cop. You're thinking you might be forced to arrest me. But if you do, then you have to arrest Paka. Paka was there," I said. "She hurt him to save me. He was dying." More slowly, I said, "He was dying *at her teeth*. He was going to die on my land. So I . . . helped." I didn't have to add, *If I hadn't let him die the way he did, Pea would have killed her. Or you would have had to arrest your cat-woman.* He knew that. And he knew that I knew. "Paka was there when Brother Ephraim . . . departed. Neither of us lifted a hand or paw against him." Not as humans understood it.

Her words languid, Paka said to me, "The words you have claimed are true. I did not kill the male. The were-taint will not be spread. The male will not turn at the full moon. He will not return at all." She looked at Rick. "This woman and I did not kill. Except to protect her, no one's hand was lifted against him. He is gone."

Her word choice and syntax were odd, but she was a foreigner and maybe that was the way she spoke English, because it wasn't her first language. Maybe an African language was first for her. Or cat.

Rick glowered, the cop in him fully taking over from his other form, the cat who had been pleased to survive and eat and rest. I wondered for a moment how a cop could take off time to visit with me, but decided the answer might be in the name of his law enforcement organization, Psychometry Law Enforcement Division of Homeland Security. Living in the church with conspiracy theorists for so many years, I knew lots about the way the law worked, in principle.

Paka said, "There is no crime scene. There is no body. There is no blood. There is nothing. This is her land in the way of the ancient among many tribal peoples, and her word rules over all. Also"—she shrugged slightly—"Pea is satisfied at the woman's judgment." I didn't know what she meant about me ruling, but I'd take what I could get.

"If someone reports a crime," I said, "you can come back here and look. I give you my permission and you won't even need a warrant." The cop frowned, thinking things over, as if different scenarios were playing out at warp speed in his mind.

"Thank you," Rick said, finally.

I didn't want him to thank me. I frowned at him and went back to the last of the dishes in the tepid water. "Farmers' market is in Market Square. There's other markets, but the one in town is the best known and best attended. The churchmen drop off their women just after the traffic eases. The women set up the tables in the church booth and sell vegetables, honey, jellies, quilts—things made by the women—and handmade dough bowls, rolling pins, stools, tables, rocking chairs, and toys made by the men in the wood shop. Church pamphlets are on the booth table extolling a glorified version of the church. The market earns them money and goodwill from the townspeople and makes them look as humble and moral as the Amish. My mama and my maw-maw might be there, along with my sister Priscilla, one or the other or even all three, and if so, I can ask your questions. They might answer." I gave a small shrug and pushed my hair out of my face. "They might not."

"Why have you decided to help us?" Paka asked.

Reluctantly I said, "Because if you hadn't come back to help me, I might be dead." Or *entertaining* guests tonight in ways I didn't even want to think about. Or I mighta had to kill them all, all three, and feed them to the earth. One possibility filled me with a dread and the other with an eagerness I couldn't shake off.

I arranged the plates and glasses so that they would dry easily and turned to the couple, crossing my arms over my chest, a habit of both self-protection and succor. "You said you wanted my help. How much do I get paid if I help you? I got five hundred dollars when I let the blood-suckers cross my land to rescue a blood-sucker that the colonel kidnapped, back when Yellowrock Security wanted my help."

Rick said, "You'll be a consultant. Pay would be calculated based on what you can tell us and how much assistance you give."

I narrowed my eyes at him and walked to the desk John had used for business. "I want a contract, signed by your superiors, in my hand before I start work."

The couple exchanged glances, saying nothing, but it felt as if they reached some kind of decision. "Where is the booth so we can be in place?" Rick said.

Rick had said something similar before, before the attack on my home, when a visit to the market was just hypothetical, and not a reality. "Why do *you* need to be there?" I asked.

"We're your backup, Nell," Rick said in that gentle way of his. "You don't go in alone. Never."

And that sent a curious shaft of emotion through me, of something unknown and precious and impossibly seductive. A sense of safety. It was so elusive that I didn't know how to reply. *You don't go in alone. Never.* The words broke me in ways I hadn't known I could break.

To hide my reaction, I swiveled away and stepped slowly into the dark of the shelving behind the kitchen, where I kept preserves and seeds and dried foodstuffs, dishes and pots and serving bowls and crockery. I stood in the unlit space and dried my tears, a cold breeze on my damp face and hair. I followed the breeze and discovered the first of the damage from Brother Ephraim's shotgun. I hadn't looked for damage. Hadn't wanted to until they were gone and I was alone. My teary eyes went flinty and dry with fury as I took in the broken dishes on the floor, and the broken back window, which was spiderwebbed with cracks. If I hadn't already agreed to be a consultant, this would have decided me.

I walked through the house, noting that Brother Ephraim had shot out four of my back windows, top and bottom panes both, damaging the frames and the walls, inside and out, and some wood trim inside Leah's and John's old bedroom. But the pellets had only pierced the screening and so critters and bugs couldn't get in tonight, even without window glass.

Back in the kitchen, I pulled a magnifying glass out of the tool drawer and went over the stove and its water heater. "Nell?" Rick asked.

I held up my hand like a traffic cop telling him to stop. "I need a minute," I said, verifying that the stove system was undamaged. Repairing it would have been a time-consuming and expensive fix, but it was fine. When I was done, I stood over the stove and looked around my house, my blanket forgotten, my body heated by anger.

Women were expected to simply take whatever the church-men dished out. Take it and cry and grieve and then accept whatever they did. No more. Not for me.

The churchmen would stay away for a bit, what with a special agent involved, but eventually they would be back. I had always assumed that they would burn me out and make me wish I was dead, and there was no help for it. I could get a restraining order, a piece of paper to wave in their faces and burn in their fire. I could move, or try to. I could ask for protective custody. But that wouldn't last. Eventually the churchmen would find me.

But maybe being part of PsyLED would give me protection from the church. One of my attackers, Brother Ephraim, was dead and gone. And the cop, who was part cat, sitting in my front room, had told me I wouldn't be alone.

Not alone. That was temptation.

I went back to the great room and opened the wooden box where I kept all my records. I removed two business cards. I used a local company for roofing, the solar panels, and the windows, and they would be right out when called, but if I didn't involve my insurance company, it was going to cost me. I didn't want to contact my agent for this, but I knew that the replacement would be a lot more expensive than I could afford. I had to bite that bullet.

I said to Rick, "The men shot up my house. I could call the cops but I think it would be wiser to just call it vandalism." I handed him the first card. "This is my insurance company." For the first time ever, I blessed John's foresight in getting insurance. God's Cloud was anti-insurance, but John had worried about me living here alone and had insisted that I have top-of-the-line policies for the truck and the house. It had seemed a waste until now.

I handed Rick the second card. "This is for the people who put the windows in." I wrote a short note on a scrap of paper and put it in his hand with the cards. "If you would be so kind as to call them both, I'd be appreciative. Tell the repair people these are the damaged windows and that the siding over the logs in back was peppered with bullet holes. They'll handle it, turnkey job." Rick smiled and tucked the cards into his chest pocket. Watching him do that was oddly final feeling, as if by asking him to do this one small thing I was sealing my own fate.

Shortly after that, I saw Rick and Paka to the door, their list of questions clutched in my fingers. This time, I had to bodily drag Jezzie and Cello away from Paka, an act that left me bleeding and them mad, but once the couple drove off, the cats quieted. I doctored my cat scratches with my own poultice made of plantain, arnica, calendula, and comfrey leaves mixed with aloe, applied with soft rags tied in place. I also treated my bruised jaw and eye socket where my sweet suitor had clocked me a few. It was painful and puffy and hadn't healed like my cut fingers when I jerked them out of the earth, but the same herbs that worked on open wounds would help that, except in tincture form. I applied a bit with a heated rag, followed by a rag cold from the well water, back and forth between temperatures until the pain eased, though the bruises were an ugly purple, spreading down my neck with the pull of gravity and all around my left eye.

Once the pain was eased and the bleeding had stopped, I finished putting away the pots and dishes and brought in the dry clothes off the line, carrying up the basket to the small bed in my little room for folding later. I didn't want to do it now. I didn't want to do anything right now. I had taken a man's life tonight. He'd have lost it in moments anyway, but . . . I had hastened it on by seconds and claimed it for the woods. I should feel something about that, some guilt for killing, or happiness for vengeance satisfied. Instead, for reasons I didn't understand, I felt only overheated, itchy, and twitchy, as if my skin wanted to ripple and bubble up, like a science fiction movie I had watched one time. I stopped, bare feet on the floor, feeling the wood beneath my soles, and below that the foundation, resting in the earth that had nourished the trees used to build the house, when they had lived. Alexandre Dumas, in *The Count of Monte Cristo*, had said something like, ". . . *I have been heaven's substitute to recompense the good—now the god of vengeance yields to me his power to punish the wicked!*" I wasn't sure if God had yielded anything to me at all, or if I had stolen that right from him, and if so, he might just be taking his own good time to swat me down.

At the thought, my skin seemed to settle. This was why I had been so twitchy. Tonight I had finally found some small part of vengeance, justice, and no small measure of satisfaction when I took Brother Ephraim for my woods. But tonight, between one of Brother Ephraim's heartbeats and his last, I had also committed murder. And I felt no guilt. The dirt beneath my house seemed to throb once, the feeling it sent through me vibrant and alive. And darker than I ever remembered. I didn't know what to think about that.

Unsettled, I went through the house more carefully, cataloging damage. There were broken dishes, still sitting on the shelves up high, and I brought in John's old stepladder to take an inventory. I swept the shattered dishes into a plastic dishpan and swept up the mess of broken crockery that had hit the floor.

My fingers traced the lines of the shattered antique hand-thrown pitcher. It had been made by Leah's great-grandmother in the mid-eighteen hundreds. There had been no one to give it to when Leah passed, and I had put it on the top shelf in the kitchen pantry, thinking it would be safe, but a pellet had found it. My eyes burned and tears threatened, my throat clogged with pain. I owed her better than to let the church destroy Leah's things, her memory, or me. She had taught me better. I put the broken pitcher back on its shelf, even though I knew that there was no way I could mend it.

Later, carrying my blanket, a book, and the list of questions that Rick had placed on the stack of books where he had left his cash earlier, I wandered to the back porch. It was a lot neater than when John was alive, piled as it had been with garden tools and buckets and boots and tillers and such. I never understood how a man could accumulate so much stuff. Now everything was neat, the tools hung on nails I had hammered in the back wall, John's boots and hats and work gloves given away. The garden tools were now stored in the small enclosed space on the south side of the porch, one I'd had built with the insurance money from John's death. The church didn't believe in life insurance, but by the time Leah had died, John didn't believe in the church and so had provided a small sum for me. The life insurance money was mostly gone now, except what I'd invested in a fund at the bank. The shed took part of the view, which I hated, but it also protected the back porch from the hottest summer sun, and the small window inside kept the shed warm in winter, from radiant heat alone. The dogs had slept in there some nights, when they hadn't wanted to come inside the house, kept warm by the last rays of the sun.

Now, the floor of the much smaller porch was taken up only with the washing machine (an old model that drained into the garden), one chair, a tray on legs for use as my table, and my hammock. I'd bought the hammock from my sister Priscilla, when she was pregnant with her first child, and paid too much for it, just for the chance to make sure she was okay. Not unexpectedly, she was happy, married to Caleb Campbell, who was ten years her senior and already had one wife when they wed, Priscilla's best friend, Fredi. Priss didn't want to escape, didn't want another life. She was happy, living in a big house full of children and wives and a husband who loved them all. The very life I'd been raised to aspire to, and had run away from, was the one she wanted. Up to the moment some churchman tried to take her to the punishment house. I stayed on Soulwood for that day, to be a safe haven to run to. And I stayed because when I did leave, even just to market, I felt the land's call like a dark wound in my chest.

Priss, like my mama and my baby sisters, loved God's Cloud. They loved the life there, the people there. Mama had even forgiven Brother Ephraim for his sin against her. The churchwomen were blind to the wicked acts of the ones who did evil in the name of God. The call to forgive was a powerful weapon, used against them for too long.

I had a feeling Jackson Jr. wouldn't be forgiving me. But with Brother Ephraim missing and Joshua scared, he wouldn't make a fast decision about me this time, no matter how mad he was, not with a special agent involved, no matter how tangentially. He'd want to let time pass and things settle, and when he came again, he'd make sure he had more than three men. He'd want to come in fast, grab me, and haul me out, leaving no trace. Then he'd burn my house and garden to the ground. And he'd take me to the punishment house personally. Or at least that would be his plan, once he convinced enough of the men to help him kidnap me. And I figured he'd forget to mention to the men the presence of police or black leopards leaping from my rooftop to protect me, and maybe Joshua would hold his tongue too. So . . . I was safe for a little while. Long enough to try to derail their plans. Long enough to figure out how to use the title of PsyLED consultant to my best advantage.

I let my thoughts wander for a bit at the memory of Jackie running through the woods, his speed not quite human, too fast, too surefooted. I wasn't sure what it meant, but I knew it meant *something*, and not something good. I remembered the bitter smell of Ephraim's blood and of Paka's description of it as *wrong*. I remembered Pea offering me a drop of Ephraim's blood and her incomprehensible chitter. I wished I knew what all that meant, but whatever it was, it too wasn't good.

I wished I had a method of making the woods grow thorny vines among the trees along the borders of the property, like Sleeping Beauty's forest. Protective, passive defense. But my power wasn't magic. It didn't work that way.

Except . . . the ground had risen up and grabbed Pea's feet like a trap when I'd wanted her stopped. I didn't know what that might mean either. Not yet.

Thoughts and plans and worries swirled around in my brain, rising and dying back like fire in a brazier, hot and uncertain and potentially destructive. And possibly useful.

I crawled into the hammock, turned on the small lamp, and opened Rick's list of questions. There was a short paragraph at the top that read:

Human Speakers of Truth is an antiparanormal, anti–human rights, quasipolitical terrorist group with once-deep pockets and ties to energy. They own outright or through shell companies a small oil company in Texas; several small natural gas companies in Tennessee, North Carolina, and South Carolina; and several other less legitimate companies, possibly for money laundering. With the FBI and secret service involved, and financial assets frozen, they need a place to regroup. We know they came here, to Knoxville, Tennessee. We believe that they are still here, and we are searching for evidence to prove or disprove their location. For your contacts in the church:

1. Have there been any new men around?
2. Describe any changes in leadership and any power struggle.

3. New tensions?
4. New weapons?
5. Anything at all different?

To ask such questions of me, Rick LaFleur truly didn't understand how people lived in the compound of God's Cloud of Glory Church. The women would know nothing unless pillow talk had loosed the tongues of their men. The questions and the presence of PsyLED on an investigation told me that this was more than just an investigation into some homegrown terrorist group and church politics and finances. PsyLED was involved in the investigation because HST was a group that espoused killing all paranormal creatures. The FBI would have handled something strictly human, and the secret service would have handled any kind of financial wrongdoing. I folded the paper and tucked it into the bib of my clean overalls with the .32. I turned off the lamp. Rolled over and snuggled down in the hammock. The night was chilly and silent, even when the mouser cats unexpectedly leaped up onto the hammock and settled on me, purring. They had never done that. Never.

For a moment I missed my dogs so strong my chest ached. They had been John's dogs, working dogs, and he'd found my love of them amusing. Even before he died, they had been too old to work, but they hadn't been too old to love or to love back. But the cats never had. Until now. Until Paka tamed them for me with her magic.

The dogs had been all I'd had for years, all that loved me when I was lonely or empty or afraid. And they had stayed with me all these years, until the churchmen decided them being dead would make a good message to me. I hoped my message to Jackie was just as strong, not that he'd ever cry over Brother Ephraim's disappearance. No. He'd be after me eventually. And this time, things would be different. Because I was different.

At the thought, my hands burned and itched, as if in memory of the wood's power zapping Joshua. Or the memory of Ephraim's life slipping through my fingers. I might not have defeated Jackie today, but I'd put a hurtin' on him he would never forget.

FOUR

I woke the moment the churchmen began their trek along the boundary of my property. The feel of their footsteps yanked me from a sound sleep, and I rolled from the hammock to the porch floor, dislodging the cats, who hissed and arched their backs in displeasure. Heart pounding, I pushed through the screened porch door and stepped onto the grass. There were three churchmen, treading steadily, carrying equipment that clanked, making the animals dart away or crouch and grow still, as was their nature.

But I'd been wrong. They weren't on my property, they were a good fifty feet out, on the Peays' farm, which adjoined my property to the northeast. And they were crossing over into the Vaughn farm. I realized that these weren't men here to kill me. These were the watchers who spied on my property from the deer stand on the neighbor's land, churchmen who had been there off and on for months. And I realized that I hadn't seen them during the time when Jackie had attacked. He had sent them home, taken their place. That made sense. But, I had never before been able to feel the watchers that far out. This was new and unsettling, as if, with the gift of Brother's Ephraim's body and soul, my woods had grown, had spread their borders.

Overhead the leaves rustled uneasily.

I felt the men climb the wooden ladder nailed to an old bur oak, and settle on the deer stand that was built like a triangular treehouse, secured to the bur oak and two black walnut trees. One of them peed off the side of the deer stand. Stupid, that. Deer would avoid the place now. I didn't feel worry or anger off the men. More that friendly, chatty emotion men exuded when they were with their friends and intending to be sociable for a few hours. I had never picked up so much from people on

my land. It was more than disconcerting. Surely this awareness would dissipate over time.

I went inside and, working without light, opened up the
wood box's dampers and added two split logs to the firebox,
both summer woods—wood that burns cool. One was a hefty
piece of poplar and a smaller, dryer piece of pine. They would
make more ash than the harder, faster-burning wood, but they
were fine for keeping a fire going all day. The small pine lit right
up, and I closed the wood box door. With the hand pump I
added more well water to the hot water heater. It was something
I had to attend to carefully, because too little water in the tank
could allow the seams to melt, and replacement was expensive.
The pump to the hot water tank wasn't automatic. The well and
cistern were on high ground, so gravity kept the rest of the
entire system filled, but I had to hand-fill the hot water tank.

It was still dark when I washed up and dressed in fresh
clothes, browns and greens, muted shades. I gathered my keys,
library books, some baskets, and my purse, and walked silently
to my garden, missing the dogs in the dark of predawn, their
noses damp and cool as they poked at me, sniffing, warm bodies pressed against me, tails slowly swinging. The grass was
wet with dew that wicked up into my skirt hem. It was too dark
to get a good look at the garden, but the ground beneath my
shoes told me that a bean plant was broken and weeping from
the shooting yesterday, but was still alive; I'd lost some late
tomatoes, including a huge, dark brown purple I had been trying to save for seeds, but the garden wasn't traumatized—it
would live. I raided it for cucumbers, several brown tomatoes,
black tomatoes, and a dozen small purple tomatoes to trade
at the market, a colorful mixture of peppers, and a mess of
beans that would have gone stringy soon. All the veggies went
into the baskets I carried, while in the back of my mind I was
thinking that the plants needed pruning and the entire garden
needed mulching and nothing was getting done out here in the
soil and no foodstuffs were getting put up for winter. My garden was suffering another day with lack of care, this time
because of Rick and Paka.

I stowed the produce in the bed of the truck, along with a
few treats for Kristy, one of the librarians who was also a
gardener. We had become friends, and I didn't have many, so

the few I had were special. Whenever I went to town, I always put a thing or two in the truck for her.

I started the old Chevy, which coughed when it turned over, but ran quiet, and backed quickly around, hoping to keep the backup lights from being seen by my watchers. Without headlights, I made my way along the crushed-rock drive and on down the mountain. I was able to feel my woods all the way, which was new and a little disquieting, but it let me know that the men hadn't moved from the deer stand and probably hadn't seen me leave. They would have no idea where I'd gone, and might not know what to do about my absence, without making the long walk back to the church compound to ask for instructions. Hopefully by the time orders were relayed—on foot, thanks to the lack of cell signals—I would be back home and the repair men would be here.

It was after sunrise when I pulled into a street parking spot for the second day of a weeklong farmers' market. Normally, it ran only on Wednesdays, but the city fathers were trying new things to bring people and money into town, like an extended schedule for the farmers' market for fall produce. I parked the truck in an inconspicuous spot and made my way through the park, feeling odd, but oddly right, to be wearing one of my new skirts, sturdy shoes instead of work boots, and a button-up blouse over a T-shirt. I'd chosen a dark green skirt and match-ing T, with a white overblouse, colors and shapes close to the garb worn by the churchwomen, though theirs were all hand-sewn, and I had purchased mine at a local clothing store.

Going to market was wise in ways other than just seeing my family. I traded even or received cash for my veggies and jams and preserves. I didn't reckon I'd be getting a check from PsyLED right away. It might take weeks to be paid and enjoy the freedom of having money, a disposable income.

Fleetingly I wondered if freedom would make me danger-ous, as the churchmen claimed freedom did to a woman. And then decided that if it did, I didn't care.

Spreading a small blanket on the dew-wet grass, I tied my hair back with an elastic and sat, my small pocketbook in my lap, my back to a tree, my baskets close to my knees. I set a wide-brimmed hat on the blanket and slipped off my shoes, placing my feet in the grass and working my toes into the soil.

I leaned back against the tree bark. Contact with tree and earth shivered through me, sudden, shocking. I drew in a slow breath, feeling the power of my land even here, so far away from my woods. That had never happened before. Never had my woods found me when I was off-site. I breathed out, letting the electric tingle settle into me, into my bones and my viscera.

This was more. Too much more. Even in my resistant brain I knew my magic had changed. Grown.

Brother Ephraim's blood and death had been far more powerful than I could have known. For the first time I felt a twinge of worry about his passing into the woods, his blood smelling so odd. Maybe he had been sick. He would have died in moments anyway, I knew that, but with him gone, at my hand, only minutes before nature would have taken him . . . was that really murder? Was the blade of the merciful still murder? The garrote of the priest to the one on the stake to burn? By today's standards, yes. But it hadn't always been so. And if it was now, should I care? Was my claim and Paka's agreement about me having the right to rule on my land correct? Or had my deliberate actions changed the nature of Soulwood, and me as well, me reaping the death I had sown? I wasn't sure about the questions, and I had no certain answers. I also had no guilt or shame in what I had done, and maybe that made me as evil as the churchmen, and as dangerous as they claimed free women were.

I closed my eyes, feeling the sun rise, lifting over the horizon, the first pale rays turning golden, warming the earth. I settled into a partial lotus position, hands on my knees. The churchmen, if they passed this way, would ignore me, thinking me a modern-day hippie. Others might think me a new-age sun worshiper, or a Jesus freak out to pray, or a Hindu, or a yoga practitioner. I was none of those, but if I ever prayed anymore, it was like this, my face to the sun, in contact with the woods and the ground.

Traffic was already busy this morning, the vibrations of passing vehicles subtle under my feet. A cop on foot patrol paused by me, and I smiled without opening my eyes. "It's a beautiful morning, Officer."

I felt him start, the emotion passing through the ground and into my body. "Ma'am," he said as he moved away. I felt it the moment his attention went elsewhere. *Interesting.* I wondered again if this awareness would fade as Ephraim's energies were absorbed and commingled with the other man I'd fed to the forest. The sensation I was getting was . . . overly alert, agitated, hyper-reflexive. If I was presented with a child like this, by a concerned parent, I'd suggest he or she be given chamomile tea with lavender or lemon balm. For an adult, I'd suggest blending in valerian. But this was wasn't a human, it was the woods themselves. I couldn't see a way to feed my woods a soothing dose of herbs big enough to do it any good unless I bought out an herbal supply store and dropped the chamomile from an airplane. The image made me smile.

A voice said, "I almost didn't recognize you."

Rick. So much for being hyperalert. I hadn't known he was there. Was that because I had claimed Paka, and through her also placed a claim on Rick? That was a scary thought. I opened my eyes to find him standing on the sidewalk nearby, facing Paka, as if he was speaking to her and not me. I interlaced my fingers and stretched my arms up over my head, hiding my mouth from view as I said, "That was the idea, me in church-woman attire, or close to it." I leaned out, stretching to look at the booth. "They're here, setting up. If I'm a clock, then the church booth is at two o'clock. The women are my sisters Priscilla and Esther, and the Cohen sisters."

It was an odd grouping of churchwomen to say the least, as the Cohens had been taken from the punishment house during the law enforcement raid and into protective legal custody, last I'd heard. I was surprised to find them living back among the church folk, walking free, and out in public, unless the menfolk wanted the world to see them and assume that they were okay. Or maybe they were here so that Priscilla and Esther could watch and then tattle on them. Anything was possible in the twisted minds of the churchmen.

"Go away," I said to Rick and Paka. I felt them drift to the far right, away from the churchwomen's booth and into the market.

Hours had passed as I sat on the land. It was ten a.m. and most booth spaces were open, so I stood, put on my hat, took up my baskets and blanket, and walked across to the nearest booth. Like the others, it had a tentlike tarp overhead, a long table in front, and unopened boxes at the rear. The vendor sold unusual varieties of seeds and late-planted beans that were still in the pods for canning or eating now. Since my garden had been shot up, I traded some of my winter squash—three heirloom varieties—for some purple-podded pole bean seeds, a packet of rare Kentucky Wonder bean seeds, as my own stash was smaller than I wanted, and a packet of rattlesnake beans for spring planting. One can never have too many beans. I canned and dried mine, and sold them fresh, in season, by the peck basket at another market on the roadside. While I dickered with the vendor, offering my veggies for their seeds, I also traded for three varieties of heirloom lettuce seeds and one variety of melon—Rocky Ford, which looked good on the package.

While I dawdled over the seeds, I managed to make eye contact with Priscilla from beneath my wide-brimmed hat. I shot a glance to the outdoor latrines, and held up a hand, flashing five fingers two times, suggesting a meet in ten minutes. I got a slight nod and a tense line of lips in return, and went on to the local pickle producer. She took my largest basket full of small, firm cukes and exchanged them for five small jars of her secret recipe of bread-and-butter pickles. There were enough cukes to can more than ten large jars, but I didn't want to do the canning, so the trade was good enough for me. I didn't eat much in the way of cukes and pickles, and the face creams I made only lasted for so long in the fridge.

Out of the corner of my eye, I watched as Priscilla made an excuse and headed for the standing, portable toilet booths. Without picking up my speed, I made a line to intersect her, and caught up.

When we were out of sight of the sales booths, Priscilla rounded on me, her face pinched and drawn, made worse by the hair, bunned-up tight atop her head. "Are you trying to get me in trouble or did you'un just get stupid alla sudden?"

"Neither."

"Then talk fast. People are mighty jumpy roun' the church today."

"Jumpy how? Who's jumpy?" I pulled off my hat to see her better.

She looked back toward the booth, out of sight but not out of mind, and gripped her brown skirts in both fists. "Brother

Ephraim done went missing last night. There's those that say *you'un* are behind it, what with your witchy ways."

"I'm not a witch," I said, the words by rote. The assertion was the truth and not words I used to say to make me feel better.

I wasn't a witch. I was something else. Something worse.

"Are you in danger?" I asked her softly.

"Because a you? Prob'ly," Priscilla grumbled, but her expression softened as she took in my bruised face. "What happened? You okay?"

"I'm good enough," I said. "So Brother Ephraim's missing? What are they saying?"

"Him and Jackie and Joshua Purdy went hunting over close to your place, and Brother Ephraim walked away and never came back. And Joshua's saying as how you called up a demon to attack him."

"Mmmm," I said, trying to be encouraging, trying to decide if I should tell her more. I decided not. "That's it?"

"That's enough, ain't it?"

"I heard . . . I heard there were some outsiders around. Any new people in the compound?" Priss looked confused, and I tried to find another way to ask this, knowing how my matchmaker sister would take it, my sister who thought every woman needed a man and a dozen children in order to be happy. But I couldn't think of anything except to blurt out, "Any new *men*?"

Priss' face went from sour to happy and hopeful in an instant. "You thinking about taking a husband again? Coming home?"

"No, Priss. I'm not coming back to the church. It isn't my home. Hasn't been in a decade."

Her face fell and she crushed her skirts again, a gesture that looked nervous as her hands smoothed out the wrinkles, gripped the cloth, smoothed out the wrinkles, over and over. "You're helping outsiders again, ain't you?" When I didn't reply, she made an expression I had seen on Mama's face, a pinched, fearful look, but it slid into resolute and stayed there. "Fine. Ain't no new people. No new men. I heard that some a the younger boys was hunting and come upon a nonchurch boy and they're playing in the woods together. Jackie seemed to know his people, and approved it, so long as they don't act up or get into hooliganism and put graffiti on the houses."

That was a surprise. While it wasn't uncommon for boys or men to see or encounter nonchurchmen in the woods at hunting season, they weren't allowed to interact with them, only speak and move on. Church people didn't associate with outsiders. Even outsiders like me, who had once been insiders, hence Priss' nervousness. "Anything else new?" Gossip. I was asking for gossip, which I had never listened to when I lived there. But Rick wanted news, and I hadn't talked to Priss in a long time. I didn't know what might be important.

"Some stuff you wouldn't know 'cause a you not coming round no more," she said. "After the social services raid, Preacher Jackson took everything outta the punishment house. This month he installed a guest quarters there, with a tiny kitchen and bath and two little bedrooms. It looks nice. But then he put the winter supply cave off-limits for a bit, and we're worried about having enough foodstuffs to last the winter."

The punishment house had been a narrow structure with a bath facility and four beds, each bed equipped with straps to hold a woman down. The cave was one of three, the winter supply one used only for storage. "So where do the women go when they get punished now?"

"You're always looking for the bad stuff. The dark side." Her face went pinched again. "But this time you got a point. Jackie done built him a room on the back a his house. He's in charge of the punishing now, both the women and the men. And he's got him what Caleb's calling a *cadre of cronies* who hang out with him and take part in the punishing. It's got Caleb and Daddy and his friends all riled up. Caleb's afraid him and his own bunch might have to fight for the church leadership."

"Oh." That meant the Nicholson cadre—my family—and their hunting buddies disagreed with church policy. I had no idea how to respond to that. It was beyond any expectation or understanding of the church and how it worked. In my recollection, no one got riled up about anything. They followed along like sheep to a shearing. Except that John and Leah had backed away from the church, and then John and I had left it. So maybe I hadn't understood the politics of the church as well as I'd thought. I had only been twelve when I left it, all filled with righteous anger and—

Priss interrupted my thoughts with, "Who hit you?"

I touched my face. It wasn't hurting much, but it was a lovely shade of purple and green today. I had a black eye, which did hurt, and more bruises on my throat and shoulders. "Joshua Purdy. And then a black cat jumped him and I got away. Not a demon."

Priss' eyes tightened more, but she didn't say anything, so I had no idea what the reaction meant. I asked, "Why does Caleb think Jackson Jr. took over administering punishments? Something new going on?"

"Since the Social Services raid, Jackie's been a mite unpredictable. He blames you for the police interference. He's increased his wives to four and his concubines to ten or so. He even come sniffing around Esther and Judith, till Daddy told him none of the Nicholson girls was ever going to him, not as wife nor concubine. Caleb was there in the wood shop, and the way he tells it, Jackie was a mite riled, but he backed down. The number the preacher keeps is always changing, but he holds the power right now and not enough of the menfolk can find the guts to stop him and take back the church leadership. Yet."

Yet meant the alliances weren't strong enough to make changes. Esther and Judith were of age according to church law, and Esther was a beauty, having taken her cornflower blue eyes and blond hair from Mama's side of the family. "How do the elders feel about Jackie's wives and women?"

"Don'tchu tell I told this," she warned, her tone stern. "They been rumbling about deposing him, but my Caleb and some a his bunch got an audit in secret. All the church property and buildings belong to Jr. in the absence of the colonel. Kinda made 'em all mad and they hadda back off from kicking him out, 'cause if they do that, then they're the ones who havta leave the compound. The law would be on Jackie's side." Priss had a peculiar smile on her face, and I wondered if she had urged Caleb to call for CPA services, not that I'd ask such a loaded question.

"So who's in charge of the compound?"

"Until last night, Brother Ephraim. Now he's disappeared, and no one knows what's gonna happen."

Most of Rick's questions had been answered: no new men, lots of leadership problems and power struggles, and new tensions had occurred, all answered by inference and all partly my fault, not the fault of some new group joining the church. I bent around the portable toilet pod to make sure that Esther and the Cohen sisters were occupied. They were helping what looked like a happy couple examine dough bowls and rolling pins and hand-stitched quilts. The romantic couple were Rick and Paka, and they looked blissful together. My little custom-tailored catnip aromatherapy must be helping them, but either way, we were safe for the moment. "Any new weapons on church land? Different things from the usual?"

"More 'n the menfolk know what to do with. How many hunting rifles can one man need, I ask you, when some a the young'uns need new shoes, and the men are off buying useless stuff?" She sounded exasperated. "They brung in fifteen automatic rifles. Them things shoot thirty rounds per magazine. There wouldn't be nothing left of the deer to eat." She glared at me. "Why you asking that?"

"I'm asking because Jackie's men shot up my house," I said hotly. Priscilla's face went through a series of emotions that were too fast to follow, but she ended up looking thoughtful. "Priss, if you want to get free, I can keep you safe, you and all the sisters, as many as want to come. I promise I can."

"You always say that, but I gotta ask how, in light of the fact that you'rn sportin' some mighty spectacular bruises. 'Sides, Nell"—her expression softened with something akin to joy—"I got young'uns and another on the way." She put a hand to her belly, and something inside me clenched. I hadn't known she was pregnant. "And I got a husband I love. I don't want to leave. I'm happy, Nell." Her expression proved that, all full of tenderness and joy, the way a woman must look when she's fulfilled and satisfied. Things I didn't understand and probably never would.

"If you get in trouble," I said, hearing my own stubborn tone, "go to the Vaughns' and pay them to bring you to me. I can get you somewhere safe, to someone who can protect you."

She made a sound of disbelief in the back of her throat. "They come back last night from huntin' all cocky and talking about how you'rn a lot more *subservient* to your betters now." Her brow crinkled as she stared my jaw, her hazel eyes darkening. "Damn Joshua Purdy to the depths of perdition."

My eyebrows went up when Priss cussed. She leaned around the toilets, staring at the booth, and said, "I been gone too long. I gotta go."

"If you learn something more about the factions or troubles sometime in the next week to ten days, and you can find an excuse to get away, come through the woods to tell me."

"I can't do that," Priss said, her voice wavering. "I can't. I can't be taken to punishment. Jackie, he'd . . ." Her words stopped, her voice holding real fear now.

"Find a way to get word to me if you need me. If Jackie tries to punish you."

"*Fine*. Iffen that happens, I'll try. I'll do most anything to keep outta Jackie's hands." Priscilla paused and added, "Our brother picked hisself out a girl and is getting married in a week. Just so's you know." She took off back to the booths and I went the other way, but my stomach was sour and a knot had formed just below my breastbone. My bruises ached, and they hadn't really bothered me until now. I shoulda shot Jackie and Joshua when I had the chance. I shoulda fed their souls to the woods and good riddance. How could I protect my family against Jackie and his "cadre of cronies"? I couldn't kill them all.

"You the one they said was differ'nt."

I whirled, startled, my heart leaping into my throat. The ground hadn't told me anyone was near; I hadn't realized how quickly I had adapted to depending on the earth to warn me of things.

She was dressed in churchwoman attire—olive green skirt, brown shoes, tall socks to hide her legs, olive shirt, and brown sweater. Her hair was still down, not up in a bun, making the girl less than twelve years old, her height marking her as probably eight or ten. Her hair was the exact shade of reddish brown that Priscilla's had been when she was this age, before the red had dulled down to brown. And her eyes were the hazel gray of my own eyes. Her jaw was like mine, a bit pugnacious, her brows arched . . . like mine.

She was a Nicholson. I was sure I had seen her the last time I went to services with John, but that had been a long time ago. She was too young to be Judith.

I took in a slow breath and whispered, "Mindy?"

"Yup. But I like Mud, because I can grow things so good.

Is you her? The one that could grow most anything? The one who left?"

"Yes," I whispered.

She was my sister. I hadn't seen her since she was a toddler. I realized that my sisters knew more about me than I knew about them.

"They say you done got married in the eyes of the law. That you took land that shoulda gone to the Purdys. That you'un's independent and read books and live alone instead of in a big house with a bunch of women and young'uns."

I had no idea at all how to reply to that, so I just nodded my head and realized how much she looked like Mama, all long-limbed and skinny. And how much she looked like me.

"You like it? Living all lonesome? I think I'd like it. I like the quiet. I like planting things too, making 'em grow." Her eyes went bright and intense. "If Mama says I can, can I come visit?"

Something unknown moved deep inside me, something I had no name for. So much was new and uncertain since Rick LaFleur and his mate came to my door—so much of the strangeness within me. "Yes," I whispered again.

"You don't talk much, do you?"

A chuckle burst from my lips, quickly stifled. "No. Not much." She grabbed my hand, squeezed, and held on. Something slow but powerful passed between us, like the growth of roots in the soil, like the slow process of rock or glaciers beginning to cleave. Like nothing I had ever felt before. And then she let go and the feeling was gone. I shook my head.

"You'un'll talk if I come visit. Mama says I can make a turnip talk when I'm of a mind to. Daddy tells me I'm to be seen and not heard. I think that's stupid. I gotta go." She whirled, her skirts flying, and in an instant, she was gone.

"I think it's stupid too," I whispered to the empty place where she had stood.

My sisters had been talking about me. Remembering me. I stared at the place where Mindy had slipped between the portable toilets and disappeared. Priss, Esther, Judith, and Mindy had kept my memory alive. I wondered if my brother, Samuel, remembered me. And if my half brother, the one born from Mama, listened to the chatter about the one that left the church. Thinking about family, all the young'uns growing up, I shook my head in wonder. Sam was getting married. Amazing. The wedding would be huge, with all my full and half sibs. I had several half brothers, and I had no idea how many half sisters. I hadn't kept up with that part of the family after I left.

The thought of my sisters—of Mindy—was warm and bright in my dazed mind as I carried my seeds and pickles and empty baskets to the truck. Without looking around, I stored everything away, dropped my hat into the passenger seat, and drove off, finding my wits only after I maneuvered away from the market.

My sisters remembered me. Talked about me. A small smile played at my lips.

Like usual, I stopped at the library and left off the books I had finished, but the night without reading and watching films had put me behind, so I renewed two of the nonfiction books and both films, and visited Kristy. Today I brought her some African Blue Basil seeds, a variety that had dark bluish purple leaves and a robust flavor. I found it too strong, but she liked her basils licorice-y. Once I got past an explanation about bruises—blamed on a lie about an ax head that came lose mid swing—I leaned across the book counter, and we had a nice chat about fall plantings. I made a suggestion about an herbal tea recipe for her grandfather, who was having trouble sleeping. He was a Vietnam War vet, and his PTSD symptoms always got worse in the fall and winter, as the days got shorter and his seasonal affective disorder kicked in to exacerbate it.

Kristy was studious and dark-haired and, like most librarians I had met, she read a lot. Before I left, she handed me a new book and said, "I know how you feel about romances, but, girl, this one is a must read. It's about a woman from the Victorian era who carries a sword like a man, goes into business like a man, and still gets her man, if you know what I mean." Her eyebrows waggled.

"I know what you mean," I said, amused. "I just never thought about that being too terribly important."

"Girl, when you meet the right man, your head will spin. Happened to me when I met Harvey. We'll do coffee and I'll dish."

Which sounded fun. The visit was short, but it left me feeling more lively and positive. I took home a newspaper with a splashy story on the front page about a townie girl who had been kidnapped. The paper showed a grainy photograph of a white van with a dented back panel. Police were investigating it as a possible sex trade abduction. Sad that the police had never been called into investigate when church girls were taken that way.

Rick and Paka and the thing called Pea were parked next to the truck when I came out of the library, sitting as if enjoying the warm weather; I walked over to their car, leaned in the window, and told them not to come back to the house, that I once again had three men in the deer stand that overlooked my property. A single visit I could explain away. Two would create too many questions.

Rick's response was, "It's empty at night?" I nodded once, my hair loose now, and swinging. "Good thing. I hear we're going to have some localized straight-line winds and downbursts tonight. I hear they can do some awful damage." Beside him in the car, Paka laughed. The sound was nowhere near humorous. Or human.

I had a feeling that there was a lot more going on than the PsyLED cop and his cat-woman had told me. And that feeling suggested that I was going to get stuck in the middle of it before all was said and done. It was a mite curious that I didn't care. "Did you get the insurance handled and the repair people lined up?" I asked.

"The insurance adjuster will be there this afternoon. The Rankins will start today, and will be back at dawn to finish," Rick said. "The receptionist said she knew you rose early, so I didn't argue." I dipped my head in a small nod and Rick went on. "What did you learn?"

I told him, as succinctly as possible, but leaving out my sister Mud, what I had learned. Then, figuring we were done, I got in the cab, shut the door, and drove off in John's—no, not John's, *my*—truck.

I was home early enough to harvest some root herbs, which was hard work, requiring using a very sharp shovel, a gardening fork, a sturdy spade, and a pair of thick leather gloves to protect my hands, while keeping a shotgun close and the .32 in my overalls' bib. I thought about my day as I worked up a sweat. I needed my bare feet in the soil and the dirt in my hands and up under my nails. The feel of the soil leached the tension and worry out of me and left me feeling more peaceful, the way it always did. Before I turned to more difficult projects, I pruned back some overgrown plants and placed bricks over some rosemary limbs to root them for selling.

On the back porch, I washed and laid out the first of the burdock root, calamus, ginseng, goldenseal, yellow dock, soapwort, and snakeroot to dry, then spent the warm heart of the day working in the garden with the tiller. The engine was loud, but I had my awareness of the land to tell me if anyone was heading this way, but no one did, not even my watchers. And just like I needed to have my hands in the soil, the soil needed my attention, turned under with natural supplements. Twice a year I turned over the garden dirt, this time in the half an acre where the spring and early summer plants were dying, adding compost from the fifty-gallon drum on the south side of the house, readying the ground for winter, mulching deep, trying to make up for the time spent away from the plants. It was grueling work, but the ground liked the feel of the tiller in it, churning and aerating and adding new nutrients. It was like exercise and a good meal for the garden. Had my land been a house cat, it would have been purring by the time I finished.

The three men in the tree stand watched, but didn't come close.

The insurance lady came by and stayed for half an hour, taking pictures of the vandalism, as she called it. She assured me that the insurance would cover the damage, but got kinda pruney around the mouth when she did. I got kinda pruney when I heard the deductible.

The Rankin truck must have passed her on the road down, because the dust was still settling when it pulled in. Thad Rankin of Rankin Replacements and Repairs showed up himself to inspect the damage and give me an estimate. We had done business together ever since John and I married, and he had a set of windows in the back of his truck when he parked. I counted and the number matched the ones that needed replacement. Rick could follow orders. That was a good trait in a man. I met Mr. Thad at the front door, noting that he had another man with him, toting a ladder and other equipment. "Hear you had some problems yesterday, Miz Ingram," he said by way of greeting, his eyes on my jaw and eye, with their blossoming bruises.

"Bunch a hooligans out hunting," I said. "I reckon they thought my house was edible."

"Them hunting hooligans manage to sock you too?" he asked gently.

I touched my jaw and sighed. "Actually, in a way, yes. But forewarned is forearmed. I have a gun, and next time it won't be so easy for the vandals."

Mr. Thad chuckled, though it sounded mostly polite, not like real amusement. Over Thad's shoulder the young man with him lifted a hand, nodded, and headed to the back of the house with the batch of equipment, the ladder over one shoulder. Thad's son, Thaddeus Jr., who went by the name *Deus*, had grown a foot since I'd last seen him. He was the fifth generation to be working for the family business, which had been started back after the Civil War, by a family of freed slaves. The young man looked to be about eighteen, and was fit and trim in his company T-shirt and jeans, his dark skin shining in the sun.

"That cult you got away from," Mr. Thad said, jerking my attention back to him. "Was it involved in this 'hunting vandalism'?"

I glared at Mr. Thad and he backed away fast, down the top two steps, lifting his hands as if holding off an attack. "I didn't mean no nosiness or disrespect, ma'am. But people talk." When I didn't say anything, he went on. "We pray for the women and children at your cult all the time."

"Not my cult. Not now. Not ever," I said stiffly.

"I understand that, Miz Ingram. But if you ever need help or a new place to worship, you are welcome to come to church with us at First Tabernacle A.M.E. Zion. We accept everybody, whites and blacks, brown-skinned and Asian folk, men and women, worshiping together under one roof, like the good Lord intended. We even got a sign language speaker to interpret the sermon and prayers and such for the deaf."

I relaxed my shoulders and shook my head at Thad, not in
negation, but in embarrassment. "Sorry," I whispered. "It's
been a tough couple of days."

"I understand. I'll get your house secure for the night and
put in the windows. We'll come back tomorrow to redo the
siding over the old logs, and check again to make sure you got
no rot or termites. I'll send a crew to patch the wallboard and
paint inside, someone you can trust to let in your house. And
you remember: You need help, you call on me. I'll come. The
men from my church, we'll come. We'll help you fight the evil
of that place and them people. You understand? We'll come."

I blinked back hot tears and didn't remind him that I had no
phone and couldn't call for help. I said, "Thank you, Mr. Thad.
I'll remember. And my name is Nell. You understand?"

"I do, Sister Nell. I surely do."

The Rankins were parked in the drive for an hour and twenty
minutes, and during that time, Brother Thad and his son changed
out four windows and marked several dozen shot holes in the
siding outside and in the wallboard inside, coming and going like
family, while bread dough finished rising and I put four loaves in
to bake, picked vegetables, and thawed meat for the evening
meal. It was unexpected to discover that the Rankins thought of
me as a sister, an equal in their church, and not chattel. The entire
idea of church had left a bad taste in my mouth for years, but . . .
maybe that was just the one church, the God's Cloud of Glory
Church, or a few churches, not all churches. I had to wonder.

I accepted a tract from Brother Thad before they left, and
told him I would consider attending a service at his church. *A*
service. One. I made sure he understood that part. And he left
beaming and satisfied, telling me he'd wait until he heard from
the insurance company to send me a bill for the deductible.

I didn't really know what to make of people like Mr. Thaddeus Rankin. Good people, but foreign to my upbringing and
life experience so far.

No one bothered me that night, but I woke with a perplexing
sensation at about two a.m on Wednesday, a feeling that ants

were crawling all over me—biting, itchy, feathery, and burning. I sat up in my small bed in the dark, disturbing the cats. More than one nonhuman, and one human, had crossed into the woods on the Vaughn farm property. Their life signatures were incomprehensible, remarkable enough that I couldn't separate them into individual markers, but I knew in my blood that they were no threat to me, feeling playful rather than malicious. I felt them tramp along the property line to the deer stand, and later felt it as the stand's supports were ripped from the trees and it started to fall. I felt it in my bones when the biggest part of it hit the ground about twenty feet from where it had started, as if the air had swept up underneath and tossed it. Heard it in the nerves of my hands when the nonhumans shouted with victory.

It wasn't Paka. I'd have recognized her.

Nonhumans. On my land or near enough. Strangers.

In the ground beneath my home, I felt something stirring, something new and angry. I raced to the front windows, listening, waiting. But the flash of rage died away, gone so totally that I had to wonder if I had imagined or misinterpreted it.

In the distance, on the Vaughn farm, I felt the uninvited visitors withdraw. Relief shushed through me like water through a pipe, but it didn't last long, and worry flushed right back. I spent the rest of the night on the sofa, where I could see anyone coming down the drive, protecting my home from any direction. I slept uneasily, with John's old Colt .45 six-shooter and the Winchester .30-30 on the rug at my feet. Neither had the spread pattern of the double-barreled shotgun, but without being able to stabilize it against a flagpole or a handy wall, the shotgun was mostly a threat without teeth. Useless. I needed something that was point-and-shoot and wouldn't dislocate my shoulder. I needed a new gun.

The land quivered when humans walked onto my land just before dawn. They entered along the northwest side of the property, from the Stubbins farm. The churchmen had never come that way before, the land being steep and requiring a demanding climb, but perhaps Jackson Jr.'s anger was changing things. Or perhaps the group he'd found to help were the

Stubbins' kin. I had figured it would take time, maybe even weeks, to organize the menfolk. I'd been wrong.

I sat up, feet on the floor, and rubbed my tired eyes, concentrating. Fear spiked through me. They had sent eight men. I felt their combined life force flowing through the woods, along the ground, and up through the foundation of the house, into my bare feet, and some of the life force carried a faint taint of wrongness, similar to what I had sensed from Jackie. They carried weapons, and though I couldn't tell what kind, I knew that with eight participants, they didn't intend to use distance weapons. They intended this to be up close and personal.

I'd thought I had longer. I was a fool.

The battle I had been expecting and fearing for years—the battle to take me back to the church for punishment and rehabilitation, churchman style, or burn me at the stake—was heading my way. I'd choose my own way of dying if I had to go today.

The intruders had to come through the woods, however, and there was no path, just ridges and small creeks and rock outcroppings and trees big as redwoods. They'd be working by dead reckoning, in the dark of predawn, giving me time to get prepared. The trees were so tall on the steep hill that the leafy canopies cut the line of sight to nothing. I wished again I could do magic like a witch in one of the silly movies I watched, making roots rise up and trap them, thorns rise up and form an impenetrable wall. I remembered Pea and the earth that had stopped her in her tracks. In some form of trepidation, I reached out to the woods and thought, *Stop them.* Thinking that maybe the roots and the soil would indeed reach up and trap their feet as they had trapped Pea. But nothing happened.

So . . . I was gonna have to deal with this. With the men.

Real life was always a lot more bloody and had a lot fewer happy endings than movies.

Working in the dark, I double-checked the loads in all the weapons and laid out ammunition at each window. I washed up with the last of the night's warm water, bathing the sleepless exhaustion from my eyes, before slathering on my homemade emollient cream. A cold wind was blowing, tossing multicolored leaves, and even stripping green leaves from their stems, flinging them through the air, so I braided my hair back out of the way, dressed in long-john underwear, layered on T-shirts, overalls, and work boots. For an extra bit of safety, I strapped John's old hunting knife around my waist while extra rounds went into my pockets—preparations that settled me. I was gonna die. But I'd take a few of them with me. I took a moment to wonder what life would be like if I were able to pick up a phone and call the police for help. But the woods made that impossible. Cell signals just didn't reach in here. Even satellite signals were iffy once one entered the edge of the property.

Soulwood ate the energy.

Though my heart was stuffed up high in my throat and my guts did little pirouettes, I ate leftovers from the fridge and stoked the stove before putting the drip percolator on the hottest section of the stovetop for coffee, making a full pot in case I got to be hospitable instead of a good shot. Or in case someone made it inside and I needed an unexpected weapon. Scalding coffee was a good one.

I shooed the cats out of the house. It was safer outside this morning than inside, despite the owls and coyotes and foxes that thought house cats were tasty. And the churchmen would likely kill the cats like they'd killed the dogs.

My heart rose up in my throat at the thought of the dogs, and I suddenly could feel the cold, hair-covered flesh of their ankles as I dragged them across the lawn to bury them. Tears threatened and I blinked, closing my lids over hot, painful eyes. I would not mourn. Not now. Grief was paralyzing. Grief slowed reflexes. Grief was an emotion I didn't have time for.

I sat on the back porch with John's hunting rifle, the sun rising at my back on the front of the house, the screening hiding me in shadows, and I felt one of the churchmen trip and fall, barking his arm on the root he landed on. His skin ripped and his blood dropped, two tiny splatters. But it was enough. His life was mine the moment I needed it. Another tripped and bit his tongue when he landed, jaw-first, in the loam. He spit bloody spittle. Two were mine now. Six to go.

The churchmen walked closer, tramping over my land.

Maybe I could convince them to go away.

My laugh was humorless. Maybe pigs would fly and I'd find gold nuggets in the water that my windmill pumped up from the ground. Best bet was I'd die fighting and take a few with me.

The sky was bright in the east, climbing above the mountain ridge, the sun's rays shining through clouds like a deceitful promise of survival, when dark forms appeared at the edge of the woods, stopping just outside the cleared area of grassy land. I lifted John's binoculars to my face and tracked down until I focused on one of the men.

Only it wasn't a man. It was a kid. A boy. Maybe ten or twelve years old. He was wearing a plaid shirt like the older churchmen wore on weekdays. Jeans. Boots. He had dark red hair and freckles. He carried a hunting rifle almost as big as he was. And he wore an expression too callous and too determined for his years. And yet . . . *he was afraid.*

Oh . . . No . . .

I moved my binoculars right, slowly, then left, until I had seen all eight of them. Not one was older than fifteen. None of them even needed to shave yet. And they all wore faces that said they had come to do something they already regretted. Ernest Jackson Jr. had sent children to murder me. And I owned the lives of two if I set my hands into the soil and dragged them under.

"No," I whispered. "No."

They are not going to make me kill children.

FIVE

I stood and set the rifle against my shoulder, opened the back door, aimed out into the dark, over their heads, and fired a warning shot. The biggest child, maybe the eldest, raised his weapon on the house, but with me standing inside the door, lights off, and with the sun rising on the front of the house, throwing the back into darker shadow, he was blinded. "What you'uns want?" I demanded in my best church accent.

"We're looking for Brother Ephraim," one of them shouted. "My daddy thinks you got him here. We'uns aim to set him free and then take you back to the church, where you're supposed to be."

"The Brother isn't in my house," I said. "And I'm not of a mind to go back to the church." My comments seem to flummox them, because no one answered. I figured that they hadn't thought much beyond telling me what they wanted and then expecting me to obey, like a good churchwoman did. But they forgot. I wasn't part of the cult anymore. I didn't obey anyone. At that thought, a fierce delight welled up in me and pulsed through my body, through the floor, and into the ground.

In the rising sunlight, the boys looked back and forth between each other in consternation. I studied their faces, thinking I spotted some family resemblances. There was a Cohen, two of the Purdy boys—Joshua's cousins or half brothers—a Campbell, a boy I didn't know but maybe a Stubbins, maybe a Lambert, and a McCormick. But the biggest kid was dressed differently from the others, wearing city-boy jeans and a T-shirt with something written on it in yellow and orange, the design shaped almost like a target over his heart. He wasn't Aden family, though he had slanted, narrow eyes like the family patriarch, maybe a similar shade of blue. His

rifle was different from the other boys' guns too. It was one of
the modern ones that fired off three-burst rounds and could be
set to fully automatic with the right gear and know-how. Like
an AR-15 or -17, something or other, a gun like I'd been lusting
for and could never afford. Like the automatic rifles Priss had
mentioned. This boy was clearly in charge, urging the others
forward with his gun barrel, his face full of anger and hatred
and devoid of fear, the kind of emotions learned at Daddy's
and Mama's knees, family hatred shared along with prayers at
the dinner table. That hatred and the AR-whatever would
chew up this house in a heartbeat, and me along with it.

"Witch!" the unfamiliar kid shouted, stepping forward,
into the light of dawn. "I call thee out, in the name of Jesus
Christ, to face your punishment and the justice of the church."

I thought a minute, not seeing any other way except to
shoot him. My guts curdled. "I'm not a witch," I shouted back,
trying to buy some time, trying to figure out what to do, how
to save these children and still keep me alive. "I'm a baptized
Christian just like you, only I don't try 'n kill people who are
different from me."

"You're a woman. You gotta do what you're told," he said.

I took a breath to reply when I felt the change up through
the floor. I might have felt it sooner if I'd still been barefoot,
or had my boots in the dirt, but two factors were detrimental
to my knowing what was happening until it was close: wearing
boots in the house, and my attention on a more obvious threat.

A truck had pulled up the hill and turned into my drive, the
headlights illuminating the boys with their guns. The boys
froze like deer in the headlights and the sun peeked over the
horizon, tinting them in the bright red and gold of morning. I
heard a voice, a bull horn or loudspeaker from the truck. "You
children get back to your own homes!"

I closed my eyes in relief so strong it sent acid up my throat.
It was Thad Rankin, and he sounded mad as a hornet. *"Git!"*
he shouted.

The boys turned as one and raced back into the trees, the
outsider boy in the lead. He might have shouted to the others. I
couldn't hear, but I felt the remaining boys race toward him,
back the way they came. I sprinted to the front, staring through
the windows. I felt more than saw Thaddeus get out of his

truck and slam the door, muttering under his breath about hooligans. And I laughed, the sound a panicked wheeze.

I dropped to the sofa, following the stranger boy and his comrades back to the Stubbins farmland. I felt the land rise up, as if aware, as if tracking them as a threat, as if it *knew* who they were and where they went. As if the woods had . . . learned something about the threat they posed to me. Something dark and wild raced through the ground, following the boys. It was more cohesive now than it had been. More complete, less divided, and that was unexpected. I wrenched my thoughts away from the land and the sick feeling that the dark thing brought me.

I went to the door, and opened it to my rescuer.

Thad Rankin asked, "Are you hurt?"

I shook my head and realized I was trembling. A sob burst out, as unfamiliar as the dark thing in my woods. I was *crying.* Again. I wrapped my arms around myself and shuddered, backing away to let Mr. Thad and Deus into my living room. "I didn't know what to do," I said. "I didn't know what . . ." I trembled so violently my teeth rattled. "They were children. Just babies." I sobbed again, the sound harsh. I hadn't cried in front of people since Leah died. My knees hit the sofa, and I stopped moving. "Copying their daddies and the hateful men at the church. I couldn't even defend myself. *They were just children,*" I said fiercely.

Mr. Rankin pointed at the sofa and I fell onto it, wiping my face.

"I heard a shot. Did they shoot at you?" he asked.

"No. I fired a warning shot over their heads."

"What did they want?" he asked. His eyes were tight and dark with worry.

"They came looking for a churchman who went missing while hunting. They accused me of having him prisoner in my house." Rankin's eyebrows went up in surprise. I shrugged, feeling tired. "They said they were here to set him free and take me back, by force."

Rankin said, "We'll check the house. Do you want me to call the sheriff when I get into cell range?"

"No. I won't send a bunch of children to juvenile detention for nothing. I put on coffee," I said. "Help yourself."

I went to the bath and splashed water on my face, which was white and bloodless, my eyes too big. I freshened up and felt a sight better when I came back out, and better still when I realized that Thaddeus and his son were checking the house and the woods out back.

When they came back in, I had a loaf of homemade sliced bread, plates, spoons, three cups of coffee, real cream and sugar, and a jar of peach-hot open on the table. My peach-hot (peach preserves made with hot peppers) was the best in the county. After exchanging a glance I couldn't interpret, the two sat at my kitchen table and made up their coffee to suit them, Deus taking his with sugar and his daddy taking his black. We sat there, silent, and I realized that it was the first time they had ever sat at my table. Which was a shame.

"Thank you for being here," I said, the coffee sitting uneasily on my stomach. I tore a slice of bread and chewed, hoping to settle it, which led to Deus taking a slice and smearing preserves on it. He was a young man, and young men were always hungry.

"Why did you leave the cult?" Thaddeus asked.

I understood his curiosity on all the levels—curiosity about the cult, curiosity about why someone would shoot up my house. I chewed, and drank my coffee, and said, "I stopped attending God's Cloud for several reasons," I said. "One, when I inherited this property I fell into 'sin and disfavor.'" I made the words a quote with my fingers, and both men showed surprise. "This property, by church law, should have gone to the church upon John's death, since he had no sons. But after Leah died, John and I were married by a judge, legally, under the laws of the state of Tennessee, instead of according to church law. And his will had been filed properly. I was his widow, and I inherited.

"The church objected, but they lost in court. They had to pay the legal and court expenses too." I knew that the men heard my satisfaction. I'd been practically blissful when the judge had ruled that the church had to pay my lawyer and all costs.

"Reason two," I said, "a proper churchwoman would have taken her deed to the land and gone right to the church and married according to her next male relative's wishes or according to the will of the leader of the church."

"What?" Deus said. "That's not right."

I smiled behind my cup at the statement, but it faded when his father said, "There's lot a things wrong in this world, son. It's important to remember that others have troubles we don't always see." He was right. My problems were small potatoes compared to the problems of others.

Deus slurped nosily. "Mama'd a killed them boys."

Thaddeus laughed. "Your mama is a pistol, boy, but she wouldn't have killed some foolish children."

"Okay. She'd a made 'em wish they was dead."

Thad laughed softly. "You got that right." The men bumped fists. The coffee was strong and bitter, but they drank it anyway. "You were saying," Mr. Thad said.

"After John died, I declined to do anything they thought I should. Mostly I declined to marry one of them," I said, at last, with a distinct lack of enthusiasm.

"John and I attended services at the church on the occasional Sunday morning, in order to keep the peace, but when he got sick, and then passed, I stopped going altogether, even though that meant I had to sneak around to see my own sisters and Mama."

"And that's why schoolchildren came to shoot up your house?"

"Land and property, patriarchy and hierarchy, are all important to them. Women aren't. I'm never going back to the God's Cloud and their punishment."

Deus looked puzzled. "Punishment?"

"I'll explain later," his father said, his tone grudging and sad. It seemed that Mr. Rankin knew something about the church and how things worked after all, likely from the time the compound was raided by the sheriff, social services, and the child welfare people. The media had released all sorts of information to the public then, including the existence of the punishment house. Which, now that I thought of it, was a good reason for Jackie to have turned it into a guest cottage.

"Thank you for the coffee, ma'am," Mr. Thad said, standing. "Come on, son. We got work to do." He left through the front door for the driveway, his son trailing.

I could hear them chatting as they unloaded equipment from the truck, voices low. I figured that Thaddeus was explaining church things to his son. I closed my eyes and thought about my land. They were the only two people on it. The boys were back on Stubbins' property, nearing the farmhouse. Some things I shouldn't be able to know this far away, this far from my property's boundary.

On the Vaughn farm, the new nonhumans were back, but deep in the woods, tramping on the far side of the hillock. I was curious what they were doing, but not inquisitive enough to go ask. I was tired and sleepy and sad, but with all the workers here, I was safe.

My forest was changing fast, yet it hadn't killed the boys, not even the boys who had bled all over it. I had the feeling that the woods could have stolen the life force even without my intervention, but . . . I hadn't wanted to kill children, so the woods hadn't killed.

I needed to find out the limitations and boundaries of my woods' power, but I had no idea how to go about that, short of some deadly experimentation.

While keeping a close mental eye on the woods, I put a meal together and cleaned house and started some oregano tinctures and weeded the garden again and generally stayed out of the way as a variety of men and one woman came and went, repairing my house. Most of the work was done before supper, and when the trucks drove off and the dust had settled, I stepped out onto the front porch and made a megaphone of my hands. "I know you're out there!" I shouted. "Come on in."

I turned my back and went inside, watching through the front window as the snoops I had been feeling on the Vaughn farm slowly worked through the trees, onto the property, across the lawn, and up to my house. I had determined that there were three nonhumans and one human. The three nonhumans moved differently from the churchmen. They moved differently from the Rankins, differently from people at the market or at the produce stand, differently from the people I saw on the television shows I checked out of the library. They glided, slid, slinked their way to the house, all but the human, who tramped as if tired. The small group came slowly, out in the open, across the grassy lawn that would soon need to be cut, whether it wanted to or not. They looked watchful, scanning the house for attack, the woods for attack, and everywhere for danger. They gathered at my front steps in a thin semicircle, and there they waited. One of them had my mouser cats on his shoulders, much like Paka had carried them, and he was taller than the others, with long blondish hair and a whip-lean form.

Once I was satisfied that they had all come, I walked out of my front door, without a shotgun, the way I'd met Mr. Thad— in peace. "You're Rick LaFleur's people," I said. "You'uns broke the deer stand into pieces and sent it flying."

"Yes, ma'am, we are," the blond male said in an accent. Texan, maybe, but then I knew next to nothing about accents. "Newly graduated from Spook School, on temporary assignment here in Knoxville for some advanced training, a little liaison work with the FBI, and a little light night work here in your hills." His eyes roamed my bruises and his expression darkened. "I'm just sorry we weren't here when the coward hit you, ma'am."

I tilted my head uncertainly, not sure where this conversation was supposed to go or what they wanted. "Thank you," I said, relying on manners.

"You knew when we broke it?" he asked, his head jerking in the general direction of the destroyed deer stand. His tone implied that he already knew the answer, but I nodded anyway.

The man glanced around the group and back to me. "I'm Occam, ma'am. Wereleopard," he said, moving a hand down along his body like a carnie magician displaying himself, "from Texas, originally." He pushed his pale hair from his long jaw, and I saw the hint of dimple in one cheek, low down.

"I'm T. Laine." The woman smiled, showing straight and even pearly whites, the kind that came with a high price tag and a youth living with a metal mouth, or very good genes. "I'm a moon witch with strong earth element affinities and enough unfinished university degrees to satisfy the most OCD person on the planet. But that's what made me attractive to PsyLED."

"I'm JoJo. I'm the token human in the group." JoJo was African-American, maybe mixed with something else, like Korean, and she was pretty, with tip-tilted eyes and a small bow of a mouth, but she also had piercings everywhere: nose, eyebrows, lips, all over her ears. She had tattoos too, the small tips of some picture peeking out of her shirt collar that must have gone down her chest. One side of her neck displayed the only tattoo that was completely visible—a small full moon with a spotted leopard stretched out on a limb, and below the leopard, a pool of water in which the leopard was reflected. It was delicate, fine work in oranges and reds and blues, with midnight outlining. I had never known anyone with tattoos, and all I could think was that they had to make it impossible to go undercover and not be recognized. Which was a very surprising thought for me.

"Tandy," the other male said. He hadn't taken his eyes from me the whole time they stood there, and both hands held on to the edge of the porch as if to keep him from falling or running off. "I'm an empath. I pick up on emotions and feelings and . . . I love your woods." He smiled with his whole face and the skin at the corners of his glistening brownish-red eyes crinkled. His accent was different, and I didn't know how to place it. American, but from somewhere else. "They whisper," he said.

"They do," I acknowledged, oddly pleased that someone besides me could tell that.

"Do they talk to you?" he asked, his peculiar eyes widening with delight and what might have been exhilaration, his hands clenching on the porch. "Is that how you know about the deer stand?"

"In a way. I guess," I said.

Tandy had puzzling reddish tracings all over his exposed skin, as if a child had drawn on him with a red pen. There was no meaning to the erratic lines, which appeared at his hairline, as if they started on the top of his head, beneath his red-brown hair, and jerked their way down and across his body and limbs. They looked like lightning in scarlet miniature, traced across the very whitest flesh.

"Why were you watching my house?" I asked them.

"Rick said to keep an eye on you," JoJo said. "Protection duty. We thought we were done until we heard a gunshot."

I tilted my head, hearing the question in the words. "Vermin needing to be scared off."

T. Laine said, "But we're really still here because once we came close to your land to break the deer stand, we couldn't keep Tandy away."

"Your woods. They call to me," Tandy said.

I gestured for them to come in. "I'm Nell. You'uns been out there all day. You thirsty? Hungry?"

They answered all at once with opposing responses. "No." "Yes." "I'm a vegetarian." And the strangest response, from Occam, "I'd gladly pay you on Tuesday for a hamburger today."

The other three laughed at the obscure statement. I frowned, not knowing why it was funny. "I don't have hamburger. I have cubed venison steak thawing, bread in the oven, and a garden full of vegetables. Welcome to my home. Hospitality and safety while you're here. As long as you act right," I amended. "You act wrong and I'll kick your butts to the curb."

Subdued by my threat, but curiosity leaking off them like heat from a stove, they came in. Beneath my feet, the woods were aware and alert, but not upset or angry. From the trees came a low hum of what felt like contentment. I pulled my cardigan closer, uncertain at the changes taking place around me, the people—beings—with me. I closed the door on the dying day, and wished I had gotten more sleep.

They ate a mountain of food, much like John had when he was working the land, before he fell ill and had to be nursed like a baby. And they talked. And talked. And made jokes I didn't understand. And referenced movies I hadn't seen and books I hadn't read. I might have felt as if I was being shunned in my own home, if they hadn't worked so hard to include me, especially Tandy, whose reddish eyes followed me as I cooked and served and ate. It was a little unnerving having him around, knowing he was reading my emotions, but it wasn't like I could kick him out. One did not kick out a guest after one had offered hospitality.

And the cats loved Occam as much as they had Paka. Seems they had a thing for werecats.

As soon as I politely could, I stood, began removing plates from the table, and started dishwater in the copper kitchen sink. As it scudded into the bottom, suds rising, I began washing and felt a jolt of shock when Occam joined me there. He picked up a dry rag and dried a plate. "What're you doing?" I asked.

"Drying the dishes, ma'am," he said simply.

"Why?" I demanded. "That's women's—" My words cut off abruptly.

"Women's work, Miz Nell?" he asked mildly, his words Texan slow, his dark blond hair swinging forward to his jaw as he worked.

I looked down at my hands in the dishwater, suds up to my wrists. *Women's work*. The foolishness the church taught.

As he dried another plate, Occam said, "I spent a lot of my life in unpleasant conditions, but back when I did have a mama, she taught me to clean our house, wash my own clothes, and cook, though I admit I'm a sad excuse for a chef. I can mop, sweep without stirring dust, and iron, if I don't mind the risk of scorched britches. And I make a mean pot of chili, hot enough to burn out your gullet."

"Totally," JoJo said from the table. "If *gullet* means esophagus, stomach, all your small and large intestines, and the plumbing you empty that chili into. He served it to us at Spook School when we signed up for temporary duty with him. I thought we were going to have to call out the fire marshal."

"I warned her," Occam said, sliding me a crooked grin as he dried two forks, and a green glass so old the glass had bubbles in it, hand-blown early in the previous century. "She didn't listen."

He tilted the big stockpot I'd used to make enough pasta for them all and dried the inside, then the outside. "I even know how to work that mysterious device known as a vacuum cleaner." He sent me that small, uneven grin again.

"I've seen men on films wash dishes," I said reluctantly. But even when Leah was dying and I was so busy caring for her, John hadn't washed dishes or cooked or done any of a hundred chores that needed doing with a sick woman in the house. He'd never done a lick of women's work in his life.

"Culture shock," Tandy said from behind me.

Occam said, "I had it when I got here from Texas. I'd spent twenty years in a cage there, a spectacle in a traveling carnival."

"Twenty years?" I asked as shock spiked through me. I shot a look at Occam's face to see if that was some kind of horrible joke, but he nodded in that slow, easy way of his.

"From the time I was ten until I was thirty," Occam said,

though he didn't look a day over twenty. Maybe that seeming youth was part of being a werecat.

"You were kept in a *cage*?" I asked. "Like you were some kind of *animal*?" My next thought that the women in God's Cloud were kept like animals too.

"I *am* an animal," he said softly, "by most of humanity's definition."

"I've never been too impressed with humanity's ability to use its noggin, when it's so much easier to hate for no good reason. You are *not* an animal," I said. But Occam just sent me that uneven grin and dried the next plate I handed him. I wasn't sure what to do with a man who thought less of himself instead of more, and one who didn't argue with me, to boot. And who washed dishes.

I let my eyes slide to Tandy's face and the reddish lines that marked him, trailing down his cheeks and jaw and chin, dividing and redividing like the veins in a leaf, feathering along his neck into his collar. The empath looked distinctly uncomfortable, and I figured he was picking up my agitation. He had to be a walking, talking lie detector. I'd have to be careful what I thought and felt around him, which I didn't like at all. I wasn't good at playing games.

Occam, on the other hand, radiated calm, despite the direction of our conversation, placid as a cat sitting in the window staring out at the day.

"What's your story?" I asked Tandy. "If you don't mind me asking."

His face lit with delight at my question, as if most people stared without asking, and being asked was a sort of a compliment. "Permanent Lichtenberg figures—broken capillaries after being struck by lightning. Three times in one summer."

"Three times."

"I'm serious. Three times. No one could explain it." When I didn't reply he said, "Statistically the chance of being struck by lightning is one in three thousand, but realistically, it's much more like one in thirty or fifty thousand people are ever struck by lightning. That's my number, not a statistician's number, but it seems to fit." He pointed to the plate I was rinsing. "You missed some spinach there. But there are people who get struck more than once," he said as I rewashed the plate. "There's a YouTube video of a guy getting struck three times in a row, but I think it's fake. It takes a long time to get over being struck. You don't just get up and walk away. But there is the case of a man in Colombia who was struck four times, and a man in North Carolina who was struck three times, like me. Roy Sullivan was struck seven times over the course of his life. None of them became empaths. Being struck by lightning." Tandy looked at me out of the corner of his eyes. "Worst superpower ever."

I giggled. It came out as a squeak, air bubbling through my lips, making them flap. My eyes went wide and Occam laughed with me, his eyes lighting up. Tandy stopped moving. He didn't lift his eyes back to me. He just stood there, staring down. "You don't laugh," he said after a too-long moment. "Ever. You can actually remember the last time you laughed. It was months ago. And before that when you watched a movie."

"Stop that," I said, my tone sharp. "Get outta my head."

"I'm not in your head," Tandy said softly. "I'm an empath, not a mind reader. Normally."

"What's that mean? *Normally.*"

"I can feel your reactions, just as I can feel other people's, but with you, after having spent the better part of the day hiking along your land, in your woods, I can . . . I can feel much more with you." Tandy lifted his eyes from the floor to my face and he smiled, his reddish eyes bright. "I like you. But you think you're too dangerous to be anyone's friend. You think you'll do damage to them, put them in danger from . . . your cult? No. That's not it. But something. You also think that having friends will call attention to you in ways that will bring trouble down on you and them."

"Stop that," I whispered. "I got no friends. Women aren't allowed to . . ." I stopped, horrified at what I had been about to say.

"Have men friends?" Tandy asked. "Only women friends, and then only women that their male authority figures approve of?" He held my gaze with his own. "Only friends that their husbands or fathers say they can have? Their own sister-wives or cousins or half sisters? Only people in the church?" I backed slowly away, until I felt the heat of the stove at my back.

"In your own way," Occam said, drying the last clean dish, "you were just as caged as I was when you were a child. Still are, I'm thinking."

"That's not religion," Tandy said. "That's cult talk. Real religion is about love and redemption and healing, not putting people down, segregating them into smaller and smaller groups so they can be controlled. Controlling people is evil, real evil. Even God doesn't control people. He gave us free will."

I blinked at the words. At the truth in them. For years I'd been reading and studying about cults and how they affected people. How they squeezed them down into a small constricted place and kept them there. *Controlled.* That was it exactly. Converts had no free will, the cult taking away that one right given by God. To choose.

T. Laine brought over the last of the dirty dishes and set them in the sink. "You got a deck of cards?" she asked me. I shook my head. *Cards?*

Tandy plucked my washing cloth from my hands and wrung it out before he elbowed me aside and continued washing the dishes. Occam nudged me away from the kitchen, with a soft, "'Scuse me, ma'am. We got work to finish here."

I stood at my kitchen table watching two men—*men*—washing my dishes. There was something practically obscene in the vision. Obscene and wonderful.

"Well," I said. "How about that."

Tandy turned around and winked at me and then went back to washing. Tandy's clothes hung on him as if he was wearing a big brother's hand-me-downs. Occam's jeans and tee fitted to his form as if he'd been poured into them. Both men were barefooted, like me, and the sight was strange. John had never gone without shoes or slippers. Neither had Daddy.

Feeling odder than I had since I was twelve and first came to live here, I walked into the living room and curled up in John's old recliner, watching as the witch and the human woman found a deck of cards in one of their backpacks and started a fast-paced game of cards. And I noted that the devil himself didn't rise up out of the cards and set the place on fire.

SIX

Things got more bizarre when I felt a vehicle on the road, driving up the hills, and I knew, without a doubt, that Paka and Rick were inside. My awareness of the cat was far stronger than it should have been, as far away as they were.

My heart raced; my breath came too fast. I shouldn't know this, except that I had claimed her.

"Nell?" Tandy called, his voice filled with the same alarm I was experiencing. Barefoot, I left the room for the front porch, the chill in the air biting through my bare soles. Orion hung in the Southern sky, revealed above the tree line as the lawn slid down the arch of the hill. I pulled my cardigan closer and waited.

Behind me, in the house, Tandy watched me through the window, outlined by lantern light. The empath looked twitchy the few times I looked back, feeling the emotions I was feeling, but not knowing why. It had to be confusing for him. But with people in my house and others on the way, I was out of my element. I waited, seeing the vehicle's lights flicker through the trees, hearing the strain on the engine, climbing the rutted road.

I was still alone on the porch when a van turned in, its headlights picking me out where I stood in the cold, my feet on the smooth boards of the porch as the engine was turned off and as Rick and Paka got out, the doors closing quietly. I wrapped my arms around me as they approached in the total dark, sensing Paka's sexual satisfaction in her body language, and Rick's dissatisfaction in the stony look on his face. He was most unhappy and swatted Paka's hand away when she clung to him. They stopped at the bottom of the stairs.

"You think giving us catnip is funny?" he asked, his tone far too mild for the roiling emotions I was picking up from them.

"I had me a fine giggle at the time," I said. "Now, not so much." I had a feeling that a were-creature who was born in her animal form treated mating a mite differently from the way a human did, making my actions more dangerous than I had expected. "You all scratched up?"

Rick blew out a breath and rubbed a hand over his face, which was bristly with whiskers. Something peeked over his shoulder at me, furry face inquisitive. Pea. She ducked her head back down, and I realized she was playing hide-and-seek, clinging to his shirt back. "If I said I was still bleeding," he said, "would you be happy?"

"Not really. Not anymore," I said. "I see the attraction of Paka—believe me, I do. Her magic makes my cats tame, and my land practically dances in anticipation every time she's near." I didn't add, *but you don't want to be tied to her,* though it must have been in my tone, because Paka slanted her cat eyes at me. Rick sighed a curse, a plain old American curse.

I said, "You know, that word always seems to lack in imagination, as if you ain't got the learning to communicate what you really mean." Rick nearly laughed, surprise bubbling up in him before dying away. "You can come in," I said. "Hospitality to you both." I went in and sat in John's recliner, pulling my feet up under my body to warm my toes.

Once inside, Paka raced to T. Laine and JoJo, gathering them up in a group hug, as if she had missed them for days. Carefully bypassing Tandy, she also hugged Occam, who patted the seat next to him, the way a human would tell a child where to settle. The neon green creature leaped from Rick's shoulder, where it had been play-hiding, across the furniture, to join her on the sofa. My two house cats—no, three, as the one from outside raced in through the open door—were a big ol' pile of cat, on top of the humans. The human forms. I wasn't sure how to refer to them all. The cats were growling, spitting, and purring, and finding laps and nooks and crannies between bodies to curl up in. I'd been trying to catch the feral cat for weeks so I could get her shots and neutering. But it looked like she had decided that werecats on the premises was a good reason to make an appearance.

I figured I'd have to name the new mouser; she was making herself at home and becoming domesticated fast, rolling her

scent all over Occam, batting at him, scratching him to show
affection. He batted back, gently, murmuring in his Texan
accent, "Hey there, sugar. Ain't you a purdy lil' thang." With
her black head and aggressive personality, I decided she would
be Torquil, Thor's helmet, not *Sugar.*

Rick, on the other hand, who was supposed to be a werecat
too, was standing at John's desk—no, at my desk—ignoring us
all, his back to the room as he paged through papers he had
brought in. He was the lone cat, maybe? Like a lone wolf, but
a leopard version? Rick ignored the chatter as if he didn't
really care what the others did, arranging printed papers and
a laptop on the desk.

Several long, narrow, parallel trails of blood dotted his
starched shirt as he moved, reopening the wounds in his back,
wounds scratched there by Paka, in what had to have been wild
and bloody sex. I shook my head. I had been mean to give
them catnip. I should be ashamed. But I wasn't.

I turned my attention back to Occam, who was now watching the card game. These people were bewildering and fascinating. While I was thinking, Rick placed two six-packs of
beer on the center table, passing bottles around. I'd been so
focused on other things that I hadn't even noticed he'd brought
them in. Beer. In my house. My eyes went wide, and I covered
my mouth.

John would come back and haunt me. He'd had a fit when
Leah traded for the muscadine wine the first time, saying, "We
will not consort with the devil in my house, woman." But he'd
settled when Leah had starting quoting Scripture about the
health benefits of wine, and ended up muttering about drunk-
ards, eternal judgment, and uppity women. He had even
learned to enjoy a glass from time to time. He'd have done
anything for Leah. And later for me.

John had been honest and kind, and that was a far better
compliment than I could offer about most humans. And he had
been hospitable in his way. I could almost hear his voice saying, "Hospitality means more than opening the door. It means
accepting the person you welcomed, warts and all." If Leah
Ingram had offered hospitality to strangers, then she would
have let them drink beer in her house. And she wouldn't give
them catnip. At that thought, shame gushed back.

The three others, Tandy, JoJo, and T. Laine, were playing a loud and energetic game of cards, which included lots of cursing, insults, name-calling, and flipping each other off when a point was scored. It looked like fun, but I didn't know how to play or how to ask if I could learn. They clinked bottles and drank, sticking the rest in my refrigerator. The beer made them more unruly and noisy. I frowned mightily at them, but they ignored me, and I didn't know how to take that.

I was studying the people and the cats so intently that I missed what Rick said until he repeated it. "Your work at the market was helpful. Here's the contract you asked for, signed by the head of HR, for the position of consultant." He tossed a sheaf of papers into my lap, sealed with a fancy clip. "You said you wanted to know what we're investigating. Sign everywhere it's highlighted in yellow, and I'll read you in. You can skip the drug testing for the moment."

I neatened the sheets of paper and scanned the first page. The paperwork was for hiring me to be a temporary consultant with the Psychometry Law Enforcement Division of Homeland Security. Beer and cards and now this. John was probably rolling over in his grave with horror.

But *I* wasn't rolling over in horror. Excitement leaped up in me like a flame through gasoline, a hot, bright *poof* of exhilaration and anticipation that washed away the momentary guilt. I wasn't sure what was happening in my life, but I wanted it, whatever it was.

Feeling flighty and capricious, more things no good woman should ever be, I scanned and signed everything and folded a copy of the three he had tossed at me. I'd read my copy more thoroughly later. Not reading something the government had thrown at me meant John would be double rolling. I smiled at the thought and tossed the two copies back at Rick. "I signed. Read me in." When he looked at me, inquisitive and surprised, I said, "That's what you said. You'd read me in. So do it."

Rick cleared his throat and the rowdy room fell silent as he addressed his crew. Team. Whatever they were. "You were all assigned to Knoxville for temporary duty when you graduated last week, assigned to take on the investigation into the Human Speakers of Truth for the purpose of tracking them online and researching their financial activities. This was a job in line with your lack of experience, an on-the-job training exercise, predominately paperwork, social media, and Internet, Deepnet, and Darknet searches, to be overseen by the local FBI agent and me, to prepare you each for inclusion into existing PsyLED units elsewhere. As of this afternoon all that changed. Look around, people. This is the first official meeting of the newest PsyLED Paranormal Investigative Unit."

Occam whooped, sounding like something from a rodeo.

T. Laine said, "Us four? All probies?"

Over her questions, Tandy said, "We're Unit Eighteen. Or is it nineteen?"

"Eighteen. But we can discuss unit designations later," Rick said, relaxing and letting that rare, charming smile out. "For now, we have official orders." He read from a short paper he pulled from a file. "'A team of recently graduated special agents will be assigned to the new Knoxville/Asheville/Chattanooga region, under newly promoted senior special agent, Rick LaFleur.'" There were catcalls—literally—and hoots of delight.

"Why here?" Occam asked, his words laconic but his tone laced with something darker, suspicious. "Why us? Because we're mostly paranormals, so they stick us together in a backwater?"

"No," Rick said. "Secret City is my best guess. They want us here to protect it, and they think a human/para unit is the best way to do that."

A line appeared between Occam's brows as he processed what that might mean. He didn't argue. Secret City was the name of the underground testing and R&D part of the US government.

"Unfortunately," Rick said, "our first investigation just went from looking around and asking questions about the homegrown terrorist group, the Human Speakers of Truth, getting our feet wet, and writing reports, to a higher priority." A sensation like electricity flashed through the people in the room and through me. Outside, the woods rustled in anticipation. To me, Rick said, "We were initially only intended to see if the Human Speakers of Truth had moved into the region, an easy, strictly information-gathering and investigative assignment as part of the FBI's investigation into the organization.

As of this morning, there was a confirmed kidnapping of a human teenaged girl in Knoxville."

I stood and went to John's desk, pulled the small news sheet, and handed it to Rick. He made a face. "Yes. Fortunately, for the girl's sake, it's being downplayed by the mainstream media, and it hasn't hit social media yet. In fact, the latest info is that this photo and the security camera it came from were part of an early Halloween prank." He handed it back to me and booted up his laptop.

"HST raised funds through kidnapping in the past," Occam said, sitting forward.

"Correct. But we're not jumping to conclusions. We don't yet have independent confirmation that HST is in the area. No confirmation of HST involvement. And the methodology of the kidnappings didn't precisely fit the previous pattern," Rick said.

"But PsyLED and FBI took down three of the top people in HST," JoJo said, "so maybe someone else is in charge, putting their own ideas into play."

Occam said, "I get all that. But why are we involved? We work crimes and cold cases with paranormal connections."

"Correct again," Rick said. He whirled the laptop and we watched as fuzzy black-and-white footage moved across the screen. Four girls were standing in a clump, all wearing identical short skirts and showing a lot of bare leg. A grayish van pulled up. Three men jumped out. They grabbed one girl, threw a sheet over her, and pulled her into the van. The van roared off, leaving behind a puff of dark exhaust and a group of screaming teenagers. There must have been three more people standing nearby, as the group increased in number. Cell phone cameras went to work. A moment later, a police car pulled up.

Rick played the sequence again, and the others detailed physical characteristics of the kidnappers. One large and clumsy. One small and jumpy. One halfway between the two. All wearing toboggans, the kind that cover the whole face.

Rick said, "Two hours ago, the FBI received a ransom demand on the girl. One million dollars for her safe return, with an offshore account for the transfer of funds. They let her talk to her mother. She was alive, terrified, but unhurt at the time. The call was on a cell phone, but by the time the agents triangulated it and got a team there, the only thing left was a cheap burner crushed in pieces on the roadway. No cameras in the area. No prints but the girl's on the cell. We'll know more when they get more.

"There is one paranormal connection. It's tenuous, but was enough to read us in. When the ransom call came for the girl, it was for one million, to be deposited into an account in the Turks. The family said they could get the money, and then called a blood-servant of Ming Glass, the Master of the City."

There was a soft sound of interest from JoJo.

Rick nodded. "It took the feds by surprise. Apparently the family thought a century-old relationship couldn't be part of their current crisis, so it wasn't initially disclosed to the feds, but they have a link and a prior attachment to Ming Glass or one of her scions, back a few generations."

"You're right, though," T. Laine said, pointing at the laptop. "That is definitely not the MO of HST."

"MO?" I asked.

"*Modus operandi*," Rick said. "Latin for 'method of operation.' The kidnapping took place on school grounds in front of witnesses in a nonfamily, stereotypical kidnapping."

Modus operandi, I repeated to myself. I was gonna have to learn Latin? I needed to watch more crime shows and fewer comedies. And was there such a thing as stereotypical kidnapping? As if reading my mind, Tandy opened a saved file on his laptop with information from a .gov site on kidnappings. And *stereotypical kidnapping* was a proper term claimed by the National Incidence Studies of Missing, Abducted, Runaway, and Thrownaway Children.

I had so much to learn.

"Until we know more," Rick said, shutting down the replay, "we've been assigned to assist as needed, with the FBI, local law enforcement, and the Tennessee state police. We'll be going back over their reports and the actual crime scene looking for anything paranormal that might have been missed. What we have so far is sketchy. A sixteen-year-old, taken after cheerleading practice at Farrington High, Caucasian, from a well-to-do, politically connected family.

"The definition of the security footage is too low to make much out, except that it matches the white panel van with a dented back bumper and no license plate described by the witnesses."

"No info on who set up the account used for the ransom demand?" T. Laine asked. "Nothing that ties to HST?"

"Not yet." Rick went on. "All we have is current information on the church from our civilian operative, which indicates no outsiders on the compound. We have no new intel on where HST has gone to ground, and we've not been assigned the case, but because of the tenuous paranormal connection, we have been asked to assist in a joint task force, primarily as backup and as a training exercise for us. Our participation will be mostly observational. For now."

I counted up the people he might be referring to as a civilian operative and came up with me. My mouth turned down harder, and I caught Tandy looking at me, reading my emotions. I wasn't sure how to handle having someone around who could read me so well, but so far I didn't like it much. I felt a childish impulse to stick my tongue out at him, and when he laughed unexpectedly, I figured he had gotten the message. He looked away, his expression lightened.

"The victim is considered to be in peril of injury or death, though thanks to the ransom demand, the element of abduction for sex trafficking has now been taken off the table. Because of our lack of experience, the FBI will consider us warm bodies, but we have databases and paranormal experience they don't have. As we are integrated into the team, I expect you all to take orders and follow their leads unless you find something concrete—and I mean rock solid—to offer. Otherwise, come to me first. Pick up coffee and donuts, be agreeable, listen, and learn."

Rick's black eyes settled on me. "We aren't leaving anything to chance. While it isn't likely that God's Cloud is harboring HST, if it's determined that the girl is inside, we may need help getting onto the compound to find her."

Such an action would bring down the wrath of the church onto me. I took a slow, unsteady breath, and placed my feet on the wood floor, reaching out to the woods for steadiness and calm.

"It isn't likely, Nell," Rick said, "but kidnapping is an HST moneymaker. *If* all of this is connected, and *if* they are at the compound—lots of *if*s—we'll need you."

Tandy said, "No one will use you, Nell, not any more than we use each other. It's what a team does: borrows on one another's strengths, holds one another up through our weaknesses."

The empath had been reading me again. "What are you? My confessor? My psychologist?" I stood up, transferring my weight to my bare feet on the floor, feeling the restless forest outside and the massed emotions inside, agitated and tense, the sensations mixed up and tangled through the old wood of the floor and up inside me. I leaned toward Tandy. "I told you to get outta my head."

"You belong with PsyLED," he said, "with this team on our first gig." He smiled uncertainly, showing slightly yellowed teeth, the enamel cracked in fine lines, like the Lichtenberg lines on his skin, but paler. "You will bloom working with us."

Bloom. I couldn't help but love that word and, despite myself, some small, tight place inside me warmed and stretched, like a bud trying to open. "I'm not a plant," I said, stubborn.

Rick said, "You said you wanted to be a consultant."

"You should a told me things had changed, before I signed the papers."

"You might not have signed them, then." It had been intended to be humor, but when I sent him a look, Rick added, "Fine. I'll tear them up right now—no harm, no foul. And you can walk away from a girl in peril, simply because there is a remote—very remote—chance that she is on the church grounds."

Silently I turned and walked out onto the front porch again, feeling like I was running away, and maybe I was—maybe that was what I did, *run away.* The swing hung on chains, on the south side of the porch, facing north, into the drive and the hills and also angled toward the front door, which meant I couldn't turn my back on the house and show with my body language that I wanted to be left alone, but I sat on it anyway, pushing off with a toe. When I took a breath, the air chilled my throat all the way down, and my lungs ached with the cold. Come morning, the trees would have started to turn. In a week, if the weather held, we'd have fall colors. If it turned out that the church was involved, and if I went against them, in a week, I might be in the new punishment house. I might never see my trees again. I might be dead.

Any excitement I had felt at having a real job, working with a team to a good end, like crime fighters did on a few shows I had watched, shriveled up and died at the thought. But then I thought about a young girl, kidnapped and possibly treated like God's Cloud did. *Culture shock*—the words Tandy had used. What a girl would go through if she refused to do whatever her kidnappers wanted would be so much worse than just culture shock.

The door opened and Paka walked out, closing it behind her. She curled into the swing beside me and put her head on my shoulder in a gesture that felt all wrong. No one had put her head on my shoulder since my sisters and half sisters had when I was a child. I didn't want Paka here, but I also didn't want her to go away. I wanted to hit her. And I wanted to put an arm around her shoulders. I didn't know what was wrong with me, but it felt awful. I frowned into the night and crossed my arms tight across my chest.

"He's worried," she said, her odd, catty voice raspy and deeper than I expected each time she spoke, her African accent liquid and melting.

"He could put me in danger. Put my people—my sisters and brother, my mama and my maw-maw—in danger." If she noticed that I didn't mention my daddy, she didn't say.

"He will keep you safe. He will keep them safe. He is no longer the police officer he once was. Now he is different. He stands in both worlds—in the cat world, with me, and in the human world. As a PsyLED special agent, he has much freedom in interpreting laws that affect us nonhumans, the laws that he must enforce. If you became in danger from the church again, if they took you, he would take a gun and go into the compound to save you, no matter what those in authority over him decried."

I had been surrounded by men with agendas my whole life, and Rick having an agenda that was more important to him than the rule of law sounded a lot like the churchmen. Even John had had an agenda, and had used me to accomplish it: the honest and good and faithful goal of helping his wife to die with some kind of dignity. After she'd passed and we'd both mourned, he'd married me, and even then there had been an agenda, partially to protect me, partially to have a woman in his bed, but mostly to flip off the church, though he'd never made the obscene gesture used so easily by the PsyLED team.

John had loved me there, near the end, I knew, but it was difficult to love an old man who was dying, awkward to do my wifely duties, even though I wanted to show him how much I appreciated his keeping me free and safe from the church, how much I appreciated his plans to leave me his family land once he was gone. It was hard. Loving a man was nothing like the shows and films and books that talked about romantic love. Fiction. That's all love was.

But the other thing I'd always thought was fiction was that women could have equal power in the world, working alongside men without being abused or punished. That supposed fiction had been proven reality tonight, proved by the way the team acted together, men and women on equal footing, with equal power. I wanted more of it. Foolish, foolish me. I wanted more of it. And it might be my undoing.

I said, "If I had to go in . . . or if I was taken into the compound against my will, other people, innocent people in my family, would get hurt. And more people would get hurt if Rick went into the compound to save me. And the consequences for after, after he's long gone and can't protect or save the people left behind, those consequences could be disastrous."

"And the consequences for a girl taken by evil men?"

I dropped my head down, my hair covering my face and sliding against Paka's in a silken shimmer. "That's not fair."

"No. I am a cat. I was born a cat and found a human form long after I was weaned. Cats are not fair."

"No. They're sneaky."

"Be sneaky with us. Help us find the girl."

"And if I have to go inside to do that? If my sisters are placed in even *more* danger because of something I do?"

"He will go to the cult grounds only if there is no other way. As to your family, if they decide to leave the cult, Rick will provide them a safe house until they can settle permanently elsewhere."

Hope, flagging through the conversation, leaped like flame to dry wood. I sighed and felt the trees move in a cold wind, leaves stirring, sliding together, and slipping apart. Whispering in a language even I couldn't understand. The tight bud of *something* inside me, something I had no name for, shivered with the leaves, straining toward . . . something else I didn't know. From unknown to unknown. But there was one certainty. My sisters wouldn't leave God's Cloud until there was no other choice. And by then it might be too late. At that time, I could be their only hope.

"I have . . ." I stopped and started again. "There's another woman I can ask about the Human Speakers of Truth, the wife of Elder TJ Aden, the elder who acts as judge in disputes. His second wife helps run the vegetable stand where I sell my farm produce and herbal mixtures. If anyone has heard or seen anything, she and her sister-wife would know." I thought about what I was saying and what I was offering, and went ahead anyway. "Some of the local women will be there, not just churchwomen. I'll . . . I'll see what I can do. What answers I can find."

Paka batted my side with her hand, and I felt the prick of claws—cat claws, not human claws. It was cat talk for approval. I looked down at her hand in the dark, expecting to see . . . I didn't know what I was expecting, but the cat claws extending from the tips of her fingers were shockers. So was the black cat fur on the back of her hands. Paka could become part cat, which was surreal and so out of my understanding that my skin pebbled into chills. I forced myself to be still and think it through. Her catty approval meant that working with a law enforcement agency was a good thing. According to the churchmen, that meant I was going to hell. My lips moved into a smile in the dark, and I patted her hand, feeling the soft cat hair and the sharp prick of claws. Cat claws, explaining why Rick was scratched up, but not why Paka wasn't. Very strange, these nonhumans.

I stood from the swing, Paka at my side, moving with cat-fast reflexes, the swing corkscrewing. Paka behind me, I walked back inside, the warmth of the Waterford Stanley stove hitting me in the face. I glared at Rick. "You got an odd combination of honesty and deceit in you, like what the churchmen warned me about from the time I was able to understand English." Rick lifted his eyebrows in amusement and what might have been condescension. I scowled at him, feeling heat rise to my face. "I'm accustomed to men *taking* what they want, and you *charm* people into doing what you want. I'm not sure if that's any better, but I reckon it's easier to live with." I looked from him to the others in the room, hearing the depth of the silence after I spoke. "And you others got your hearts in the right place. So I'll help." I took a breath and said the words that needed to be said. "Even if it means going onto the church grounds."

Tandy started, "It's not like—"

I held up a hand to stop the words. "I know it's not likely. But it had to be said." I explained what I would be doing at the vegetable stand at dawn. To Rick I said, "So, turn in those papers. And leave me anything I need to read so I can ask the right questions. And now that you got what you wanted, you'uns *get out of here.* I'm tired of company, especially company that came to make me *like* them and manipulate me into doing what they wanted." Tandy had the grace to shift his eyes to the floor. The rest of them were just staring. "Git! I need to sleep, and I'm sure you got a lot of Internet stuff and texts and e-mails to deal with."

My guests looked from one to the other and slowly stood, dropping house cats and gathering up books and useless phones and tablets and laptops. They all headed to the door. Silent and subdued. I knew I'd been rude, but the noise was too much. The people were too much. It was too much like the life I'd lived as a child, noisy and . . . and happy. Happiness grated across my skin like a rasp, abrading and painful.

Yes. I *had* been happy as a child in the compound, happy until the day the colonel told my father he wanted me, the day all my illusions about the possibility of a good grown-up life came crashing down. "Please," I said in a softer tone, my eyes on the floor, not meeting theirs. "I need some time alone. I'm not used to"—*being happy*—"so many people around me. Anymore."

When my house was empty and the dark blue van was long out of sight, I stoked the stove and turned off the lights. I carried a blanket outside to the edge of the trees, my bare feet picking up the chilled dew from the grass. This was where I used to sit when Leah was napping, and I needed to get away from the smell of sickness. It had been far enough from the house to feel free, yet still close enough to hear Leah if she called. It also offered the best view, down the hill toward the lights of Oliver Springs, Oak Ridge, and Knoxville. In my loneliness as a teenaged girl, I used to put my hands into the soil and touch the tree roots, taking solace from them.

I still took solace from the trees. Unfolding the blanket just enough to keep my backside dry, I sat and put my hands and feet in the dew-wet grass and on the bare earth, my fingers finding a root and resting over it. It was a large root from a huge poplar tree. The same one I used to cling to when I was tired or distraught. A sycamore's roots ran along beside it, intertwining, and I pushed my fingers into the meeting place of the two roots, the marriage between one kind of tree and another.

Instantly I felt a sense of peace and contentment flow into me; I felt the hum of the earth, the soughing of its breath, the slow movement of its tides, and the pull of the moon that was rising over the skyline. It was a waxing gibbous moon, big and bright, the color of a yellow gourd, hanging on the horizon. The feelings were more than merely peaceful and wonderful. Taken all together, they were life and goodness; they were all that was noble and beneficial and fecund and lovely about this Earth. This moon. These two roots. This grass beneath my feet. I caught a glimpse of an owl flying past, most silent of predators. Saw bats' wings flickering in the moonlight. Heard a night bird call, a whippoorwill. My woods had a lot of whippoorwills, though the birds preferred open fields, planted with grasses.

"Did I do the right thing?" I asked the night. "Have I made the right choice?"

Nothing answered. The earth never did. Neither did God, so far as I'd ever heard. But I felt good about it, about the choice I had just made. And maybe that was enough.

A splotched shadow moved across the ground, four legs in dappled shades of moonlight, looking like a headless cat. "Torquil, You coming to give me an answer to my question?"

The cat, her black head invisible in the dark, walked up to me, and leaped across the blanket into my lap, where she curled and relaxed, her breath a soft purr. And that was an answer. Torquil had been wild, a loner, a people hater who'd hung around just for the rats and voles that came to my garden and for access under the front porch when it rained. And then

Paka and Occam and the others came, and suddenly she was
curious and accepting. She bumped my hand with her head,
asking for attention.

Torquil was tamed.

Was that what the people who visited tonight wanted to do
to me? Tame me?

Maybe my life as a loner and a hermit and an independent
woman was over. Maybe it had been about to be over for a long
time and I just hadn't noticed.

In the distance, gunshots rang out, staccato and overlap-
ping, echoing through the night. Creatures moved uneasily,
not liking the sound of gunfire resounding over the ridge separating the church grounds from mine. This was night target
practice, not hunting, and far more firepower than usual.

Through my hands and both soles, I felt someone walking
along, outside the boundary of my land and my full awareness,
even as extended as those boundaries had become following
the death of Brother Ephraim. It was as if the watcher knew
where they were and stepped just beyond where I could sense
him. He walked to the broken deer stand and stopped, unmoving, for a long time. Then he slipped away, off my land, and
was gone.

Belowground, something dark raced around and around the
boundaries of Soulwood, as if learning the limits of its prison
or searching for weaknesses in the wood's walls. It felt frantic,
and to my knowledge, this hadn't happened the only other time
I'd fed the woods. But it would settle. Surely it would.

I went inside to sleep, in the tiny bed I had claimed so long
ago, upstairs in the nook that was mine, had always been
mine, even when living with John. Even when I'd had wifely
duties to accept. When we were done with marital relations,
I'd always left and come upstairs under the eaves, uneasy in
Leah's bed and unable to rest with John's snoring.

I brought a stack of books to bed, fearing I wouldn't fall
asleep tonight, with all my questions, with the house somehow
continuing to ring with the noise of people. And with three cats
on my bed. That was foreign, especially with Torquil being so
demanding. She chose to curl up under my chin, purring. I just
hoped she didn't have fleas. I perused the books by a single
lantern (the solar batteries having been mostly drained by the

guests and all the lights we'd used), trying to clear my mind, but it raced, uneasy, excited, fearful.

Sleeping alone in my house had never been challenging, not with my early warning system in place. Soulwood Advance Security System. I made an acronym of the name and thought that SASS worked well. It was funny, and I wished I had someone to share it with. I rolled to my side and closed my eyes, but they popped back open. I picked up a novel to read when sleep fled from me. Long after I usually was asleep, I finished the romance book and threw it across the room. It made me feel weird and uncomfortable and not myself. And more lonely than ever. People in the real world *and* the fictional world were baffling. Purely mystifying. Moments later the lantern flame sputtered and died, taking the last of the light and leaving me in the dark, alone but for the cats.

Thursday morning came with the cold, though not quite cold enough to coat the grass with ice, not yet cold enough to sparkle frosty white in the dark of early morning. In the predawn, still in my nightgown with thick socks on my feet, I lit a lantern and stumbled around the house, washing up, stoking the stove, putting on the percolator. I prepared a breakfast of the last of my eggs, the last of a loaf from yesterday's bread, and honey, fully waking up only when the coffee hit my system. I ate and studied the material Rick had left me, paying close attention to the photographs of the girl. I memorized the new list of questions Rick wanted me to answer.

When I was satisfied that I knew what he knew and also what he didn't, I dressed for the day. Missing my dogs. I still so missed my dogs, and never more than in the morning, when I'd usually turn them outside to guard the premises and sleep in the sun. But I wasn't going to risk getting another dog, not while I could be still be in danger from the church. The cats were sneaky. They'd survive anything except a sharpshooter's long-range, carefully placed hit. Cats wouldn't come when called. They were half-wild, still, or had been until Paka showed up. They wouldn't wag their tails hoping for treats while someone targeted them from inches away.

I let the cats out into the garden with the admonition, "Watch out for hawks." Cello and Jezzie raced to the patch of catnip and rolled in it, vocalizing loudly. Torquil started digging instantly, chasing a vole. "Get it and eat it, Torq." A second later she had the vole in her teeth and another second later it was dead. She looked to me and I said, "That's a good girl. I'll bring you some fresh cream for dinner." She sat and started eating her raw breakfast.

Satisfied that they would be okay for the day, I loaded my truck up with late-season veggies, a variety of dried herbal teas and spicy meat rubs in plastic baggies, some natural flea collars I'd sewn, each containing my herbal flea repellent, and some jars of honey I had traded for. I folded the last bit of cash money into a pocket. It wasn't my day at the stand, but it would be handy to sell some stuff today to buy groceries. Feeding six extra mouths was pricey. Next time they'd have to bring the food and feed me.

In the yard, I extended my senses to discover that the land's boundaries were empty of churchmen. For the moment, the destruction of the deer stand had been successful. But that wouldn't last.

Remembering my hat, which I'd left in the truck, I went across the damp grass and opened the passenger door. It squealed, old metal on old metal. I lifted my hat. Beneath it was a folded piece of paper. Like something torn out of a notebook, spiraled side ragged. My heart did something strange, a painful beat, as if it knew what was there. I reached in, my hand pale in the cab light. Took the note. Opened it.

In a blocky print, the note read,

I HAVE SMELLED YOUR SISTERS.
COME HOME OR THEY ARE MINE.

It wasn't signed. But it was Jackie. It had to be.

SEVEN

The vegetable stand was at the base of the hills, in a crossroads where cars backed up to drop off kids at a school, where commuters slowed on the drive into Knoxville, and where the through traffic was heavy in mornings and evenings. The building was nothing more than a kid's playhouse that had outlived that job and been repurposed to more profitable ends. I was the first to arrive, and I keyed open the dead bolt and turned off the alarm, one that went straight up to Old Lady Stevens' house, alerting her that someone was here who was supposed to be here.

I swept out the night's spiders and a blacksnake that had chosen to winter here. I didn't mind the snake—it kept out the rats—but some customers got a bit riled at the thought of snakes. I rearranged the canned goods, placed my offerings on the shelves (with prices clearly visible on the tops), and the veggies in baskets on the porch railing. My vegetables were large, sweet, unblemished, and firm, the best veggies anywhere in the Knoxville area. I never took any home.

In the rafters, strapped to the collar ties, stirrups hanging, there was a Western saddle, an Australian saddle, and a jumping saddle, along with half a dozen sets of reins, a set of well-used saddlebags, a hackamore, and other horsey stuff. Quilts weren't kept in the little house, but brought each day by the women who made them, along with handmade baby clothes, and leather-worked pocketbooks and belts. Some of the pottery from the potter in Oliver Springs stayed here overnight; so did the canned goods. Most everything was priced with a business card so lookers could contact the people later via e-mail, go to Web sites, and see more offerings. I didn't have a Web page, but I was thinking about making one. If I could figure out how it was done, I could do it all through the library. And maybe even open a PayPal account, dealing with the establishment and the government.

The shop was small, but it held a lot, and had three small handmade rocking chairs on the front porch—for sale, of course. There was also a bulletin board with business cards advertising such things as hay, split wood, well diggers, septic system installers, antiques stores, farms, horseback-riding lessons, gunsmiths, and much more, with little spaces on the shelf below where visitors could find extra cards to take with them. My cards were there too, with my e-mail address on them, even though I could only access it through the library system. I neatened up the business cards and threw away some that had become sun-bleached or moisture-wrinkled.

When I was done, I unchained the rocking chairs and sat down in one to wait on Sister Erasmus, my mother's friend and the church's winemaker. Not that there would be any wine sold here, not with the laws on alcohol and the taxation problems. It was just too much trouble for the small bottler to deal with, but lots of horse trading and bottle swapping went on under the table. The rest of us pretended not to see.

Sister Erasmus drove up at six thirty, gave me a stern nod, and started unloading her truck. She brought many of the same kind of items the church sold at the market, but at lower prices, since none of us had to pay for booth rent. I helped her carry hand-stitched quilts and dough bowls and set them up along the railing and banisters of the low porch. When most of the toting was done, she looked me over with severe eyes and pinched lips. "I heard tell you was caught by the church-men wearing them overalls. It's good to see you in a skirt; proper clothing for a woman. I like your hair bunned up. You look like your maw-maw when she was a young'un." She took her accustomed place in a rocking chair, and I sat in another one, tipped back with my toes, and rocked, the runners thumping on the uneven porch boards.

"How's Mama and Maw-maw?" I asked after a polite spell.

"They're fine. Or as fine as they can be with you gone. Living aside from the church, in sin."

"I'm not sinning," I said, my tone impassive.

"Your daddy would like to see you settled and safe. Back in the arms of the church, as a good and proper woman should be."

My daddy. Who had colluded with the colonel to marry me off to the old pervert. And who would collude with someone else to marry me off. Except that Priss had said he had refused to allow my sisters to go with Jackie as concubines. Maybe Daddy had learned something new. But Priss was right. I wasn't strong enough to protect my family, not alone. I touched the note through the cloth of my pocket.

I have smelled your sisters.

Come home or they are mine.

Jackie hadn't signed the note. He hadn't needed to. He hadn't been on my land, so he had put the note in my truck in town somewhere. The library, most likely.

I had joined PsyLED to make some spending money, to help with the investigation, an investigation that had gone sideways to include a kidnapping. But there might be a way to use PsyLED, and my position with them, to help protect my sisters, if I got the chance.

If they were willing to leave, I'd need help. Lots of help. People with special abilities like T. Laine with her magic, and stealth abilities like werecats, and a badge, like Rick, to save my sisters. And a safe house, like PsyLED might provide. My fingers traced the note through my pocket. But I'd need to lay the foundation for that. Come up with a strategy. A plan.

I opened my mouth and said the words I'd never thought I would. "Iffen I thought I could get on and back off the compound, I might come visit. Might even bring a few friends who need to see how the Lord's people live." The words tasted like char on my tongue. I'd never bring a *friend* into the compound. And my worst enemies were there already. But that was what I might have to do someday—bring people into the compound to get my sisters out.

Sister Erasmus shot me a calculating look. "You'd come back onto the church grounds?"

"Maybe. For a visit. If my right to leave was assured."

"Your right to leave is always . . ." She stopped, the sentence unfinished.

"In danger. My right to leave is always in danger," I said, still without emotion, "and you know that's the good Lord's honest truth." The rocking chairs thumped softly, the day brightened, and traffic picked up. We both glowered into the day, not liking our thoughts or the worst memories of the compound of God's Cloud of Glory Church.

"I'll allow, there's some truth in your statement," the sister said, grudgingly. "'Specially now."

I blinked in shock. Not one member of the church had ever agreed with me on anything, and certainly not about my danger from the church leadership. Cautiously I nodded, a single bob of my head, church-style. "Why 'specially now?" I asked, easing into the questions Rick wanted answered.

"Jackson and his cronies driving around at night, vehicles coming and going through the compound at all hours, some of the men meeting up in small groups to talk. *Secrets*." I managed to keep my mouth from hanging open, and Sister Erasmus clasped her hands in her lap, staring out into the day, her mouth tight with disapproval. "We had three whole families up and move away in the last year. In the dead of night. That ain't never happened, or not in such numbers.

"Some of our own menfolk reading secret papers, talking about doing wrong in the name of right. Speaking against one another in secret. Saying things like 'The end justifies the means.' Niccolò Machiavelli espoused that and he got it wrong. The end only matters *because* of the means."

My head dropped and my eyes went wide. I couldn't have been any more surprised if Sister Erasmus had stripped naked and danced across the front porch. Her pinched mouth didn't smile, but the corners of her eyes wrinkled up in amusement. "You think you the only one a us churchwomen to get an education? I got books that would a caused Preacher Jackson—the old one, not the new upstart whippersnapper—to bust a blood vessel in his brain box. You come on the church grounds. I'll give you a basket of bread or some such to take home, and you can hide some of my books in the bottom."

"Thank you," I whispered.

"Things might be getting better. I seen two backsliders with my own eyes, wearing city clothes, talking to Jackson Jr. They thinking about coming back to the Lord, so that's good."

"Oh."

"Them backsliders, that family was shunned, ostracized a generation or so ago, and they up and moved, the whole kit and caboodle of 'em. They been in and out of the church half a dozen times. Word is they been looking around, thinking about coming back again, repenting and being baptized. Though that's just talk. Ain't no new house going up, no new stores being used. But I'm ever hopeful."

I thought about her statements. Backsliders on church grounds wasn't an anomaly. It also wasn't the multiple men who would be required to stage a kidnapping. Three men and a white van had been involved. Some of the churchmen are bad enough. New people, especially backsliders, people who were driven out for who knows what sin, might be worse. But then, I was a backslider. Glass houses and all that. I gave a mighty sigh.

But Sister Erasmus wasn't finished. "Now, I'm not saying everything is fine as frog's fur. And I am not one to gossip," she said.

I hid a reflexive smile at the barefaced lie.

"But iffen you wanna talk about trouble"—her rocking sped before evening out again—"we can talk about the new boy. He ain't nothing but trouble with a capital *T*."

"Oh?" I asked, encouraging her in the sin of gossip.

"Him and his newfangled gun, shooting at everything in the holler. Gunshots rattling the windows. Chasing off deer we need for winter stores. Wasting ammo that we need against the coming evil times." Erasmus was a firm believer in the end of the world, a postmillennialist, believing that the end was nigh and the downfall of humanity imminent. Believing that resources needed to be kept for such times as the sun went scarlet and the seas boiled.

I remembered the sound of gunfire at night, echoing up and down the hills, target practice at a much greater volume than ever before. Yes. Wasteful. And expensive.

I wasn't sure what I believed about the end-times, but I nodded earnestly, remembering the boy with the assault rifle, standing in my backyard. Not a church boy.

"Menfolk acting like fools. Keeping good churchwomen from getting in to take care of our *own stores*. Winter's coming on, we need access to the hay and the feed stored in the winter cave to do an inventory and change out the rat traps or we'll have a starve-off of livestock like back after the flood of 1937." She made a sound that was part grump and part snort, and that I couldn't have duplicated if I'd tried all day. But then I didn't have the nose Sister Erasmus had, not by half. And I'd learned something interesting, without asking.

"Who's got the caves blocked off?" I asked, trying to sound incredulous, as if I'd heard wrong. "All of them or just the winter stores cave?"

"Jackson Jr. and his playmates. They got the smallest cave all to themselves, keeping the womenfolk from our fall inventory. That's where them menfolk are studying some secret papers like they're the King James Bible."

I said, "Keeping secrets to themselves? That does sound divisive and contentious." I should have felt guilty for encouraging the sister to gossip, and I should have felt guilty for not feeling guilty. But I didn't. I felt stronger. Like a real PsyLED investigator.

"Exactly," Sister Erasmus said. "I see all them years away from the church didn't ruin your understanding of Scripture. What's worse, though, is none of us women got a lick of an idea what kinda books and papers they're studying on, and none of the men with access are sharing, even in pillow talk. It's vexing, it is."

"Oh. I can see how that would be frustrating." But I wasn't interested in some new conspiracy theory. Those went on all the time. "Sister Erasmus, can I tell you something and ask you a question? Private-like? Not to tell no one, not even your husband?"

"Only if it don't involve sin, child. I won't keep no secrets that put your soul at risk."

"No sin, Sister," I said. She nodded and I went on, my voice quiet, the way a secret and a semiconfession should be. "I was in town for market day. And I overheard some people talking. I won't say who. They said a group called the Human Speakers of Truth were on church property. That they brought in a young girl kidnapped from town." I lowered my voice even more. "According to what I heard, the sheriff seems to think the churchmen might be involved."

"Gossip. Pure gossip. No girls or mysterious people on the property, excepting the backsliders, and I know them. One of them hellion Dawson boys and his father. And besides, the church wouldn't condone kidnapping girls. Who ever said that was misinformed or lying outright."

I looked down at my hands for a moment, not meeting her eyes. Softly I said, "You know as well as me, that some a them churchmen is evil incarnate. They'd get away with anything they could, everything they could. They'd hurt women. You *know* it's so. Just like you know some a them would burn me at the stake if they could, for me being a witch."

"You ain't no witch," the sister said smartly. "Never was one. Just good with the soil and the gardens and independent like some other Nicholsons I can name." Instantly I thought of Mindy, my full sib. *I have smelled your sisters. Come home or they are mine.* "Perhaps a mite ornery and wild. But *not a witch.*" She looked at me from the corner of her eye and then back at the road, the way church folk always held private conversations. Not looking, preserving privacy. "Your maw-maw had you tested when you come of age and whispers reached us that the colonel might want you. You was not and are not a witch."

My throat closed up in disbelief and confusion.

"You don't think Maude and Cora would let the girl children go to him so easily or so early, did you? Not without a fight. Maude wanted you proven a witch so we could expel you and send you to live with her people down the mountain."

Maude was my maw-maw; Cora was her daughter, and my mother. *She had me tested? Before the colonel had declared for me?* "Her people?" The words were a whisper of bewilderment.

"The Hamiltons. They was downhill, city people, townies, the Hamiltons was. I reckon you got cousins and second cousins in town. Not that they ever tried to speak to Maude once she married into the church. Disowned her right fast-like. Anyways your maw-maw was wanting to get you declared a witch so she could get you away, but the townie witch said you wasn't. Then you made a mess a things, calling the colonel a horse's ass in front of the whole church. Maude had to act fast-like to get you safe. Her and your mama hatched that plan with John and Leah, and the rest is history."

I felt something slow and glacial flow through me and settle in my belly and limbs, heavy and poignant. Sister Erasmus sounded so normal. So ordinary. As if she were speaking commonly known information. As if she hadn't just turned my world upside down. The women in my family had been working to keep me free of the colonel? The women had set up my proposal from John and Leah?

Disbelief raced through me and tightened my flesh. My breath expelled in a rush and then came too fast. I blinked my eyes as hot tears gathered and dissipated, dried out by shock. The women of the church had always seemed so weak. But maybe there was more to them than I had seen. "You know, well, you *should* know, that I never heard that tale till now."

Seen from the corner of my eye, Sister Erasmus scowled. "John told you. Him and Leah."

I felt light, as if a cavern had just opened up beneath me and I was falling into the dark. "No. No, I never heard this. Never."

Sister Erasmus slanted another look my way, surprise in her quick glance, the expression scarcely caught from the corner of my eye. "That ain't right. He said he *told you*." The last two words were inflexible, laced with underlying anger and disbelief.

I shook my head, the motions jerky. My eyes hot and dry. My world falling away from beneath me. My hands and feet tingling, my breath too fast.

Erasmus stared out at the traffic, her lips working as if her front teeth hurt. A chewing motion. "Your maw-maw . . . She would a told you when you married John in the church, proper-like, with your family all around and your daddy to give you away. But you and the Ingrams did it so fast-like, standing up in church and stating your intentions and then just leaving.

"You kept to yourselves, kept private-like, even after you come of age and he took you to wife according to church law. John said you didn't want your family around, 'cause you was still scared of the colonel." The flow of words stopped abruptly. Out on the road, the traffic increased. The light of morning began to reveal the day.

I blinked, and my eyes felt hot. I'd been staring straight ahead, focused on nothing for too long. When I tried to speak, my throat felt hot and dry, and it ached as I forced words out. "I never spoke to my family after John and I married, except at market. He said you'uns wanted me back, to sell to the colonel. He kept me safe from my family. That what he said. *Safe*."

"And John never said nothing about your family and your womenfolk suggesting you marry him?" There was heat in Sister Erasmus' voice. Anger.

"No," I whispered.

"*Men*. Sometimes they got nothing between their ears and too much between their legs."

The sound I made was more sob than laughter, but it eased the terrible pressure that had been building inside me. I curled both lips into my mouth and bit down on them with my front teeth to keep from making the sound again.

"You need to talk to Maude and Cora," Sister Erasmus said. "We can make that happen at market next week. But iffen you want to come on church grounds and bring some a your friends to hear a sermon, you let me know. I'll tell your people, and my husband will arrange it."

I caught my breath. "Thank you, Sister Erasmus." A sense of relief spread through me. "You are warrior for God, Sister, equally proficient with Bible quotes and a shotgun, and full of wisdom and grace."

The sister made a sound like "Pashaw," but I could tell she was pleased.

I held out the note. Sister Erasmus took it and opened it. Read it. I said, "I think Jackie left it for me. To threaten my sisters."

She nodded stiffly and said, "I done heard he was after Esther in particular. I'll see your daddy knows. He'll handle that little whippersnapper. I can keep this?" I nodded. She stuffed it in her skirt pocket, and changed the subject. "Mrs. Stevens has twenty-seven dollars for you from sales last week. She'll be bringing it today."

"That's right fine," I said. "I need some gas for the truck and a few groceries."

My heart felt inexplicably lighter when the next car pulled up, and two other women, including Old Lady Stevens, climbed out with loads of stuff to display. I helped set up extra tables, and it was only when I drove away in my truck, much later in the day, that it all came back to me. My family hadn't abandoned me. And—John had known, had *always* known.

And he hadn't told me. He had lied to me directly and for years. Suddenly I realized that my safety from the colonel had come at a much higher price than I had ever realized. And that John had spent our entire lives hiding the truth from me. Using lies to control me.

After the morning in the vegetable stand, I drove into town and went to the library. It wasn't my regular day, but everything was different and off schedule this week, and I had books to turn in, even the nonfiction books that I wouldn't have time to read, not now that I had a temporary job. Kristy was off and so I made it quick, answering e-mails from some repeat customers, including a spa in town that purchased my cucumber cream for facials, took some new orders for herbs, vinegars, and infused oils, and had the payment money sent to the group PayPal account owned by Old Lady Stevens, who used to be in the church but had broken away some years before John and I did. She handled all the churchwomen's (and my) noncash Internet financial transactions. She gave us cash when we sold something online, and when we needed to buy something, we gave her cash and she did the paying. It was handy for us "off the griders." I did some more research on PsyLED, but didn't learn much more than I had already.

I sent Rick LaFleur an e-mail, telling him that I had information, possibly pertaining to the case. He sent one right back, asking for a meeting out on I-75 outside of Knoxville. In a hotel. A business meeting. In a hotel! I'd never been in a hotel.

Excitement fluttered under my breastbone, displacing the disquiet that had settled there from the conversation with Sister Erasmus. I checked out and drove sedately to the hotel. It was called the Hampton Inn and Suites, Knoxville North. And it was amazing. There was shiny stone on the floor and carpet all over—and not handmade rag rugs, but big carpets made on commercial looms. It wound through the lobby and down the halls, perfectly woven. When I finished goggling, I asked for directions to the room and gave my name. I was given a little plastic card, like a credit card. I had no idea what to do with it, but I accepted it and the directions that came with it. I had ridden in elevators before, at the hospital where Priss went when she had trouble birthing her baby. I went to see her baby boy, looking through the windows into the nursery. After hours. When no one from the church might catch me there. So I knew how to get to the fourth floor, and followed directions to the suite at the end, where I knocked to be let in.

Tandy opened the door, his reddish eyes perplexed, until he looked down, to see the plastic card in my hand. Smiling, he left the room, closing the door behind him. "The room key works like this," he said softly, taking the card in his red-lined hand and demonstrating the way it fit into the slot and the little green light that said go.

"Oh," I said, embarrassed. They must think I was a little country bumpkin. Which I was, I realized. Face burning, I said, "My thanks for demonstrating the proper methodology."

He pulled the door back closed. "'How then shall they call on him in whom they have not believed?'" he quoted. "'And how shall they believe in him of whom they have not heard? And how shall they hear without a preacher?' Or a teacher."

"You quoting Acts to me, Tandy?" I said with a small smile, feeling better, which had to be what the empath had intended. "You don't look much like any preacher I ever saw."

"The church where you grew up would burn me at the stake should I presume to preach to them," he said, showing a disturbing knowledge of God's Cloud's politics and reaction to outsiders. Especially outsiders who looked so different.

I nodded slowly. "Maybe so." I inserted the key card and pulled it back out, the little green light showing. I entered the suite, Tandy behind me, and heard the door close. The others were engaged in heated discussion, which I ignored as I surveyed the suite. It was wonderful, like a tiny little house but all modern and electronically up-to-date. Beyond the entrance door was a seating area with a sofa, too many chairs for the small space, a coffee table, desk, a huge TV, a small refrigerator, and microwave. A curtained window opened out onto the hallway beside the door.

Occam was seated on the sofa, his ankles crossed, feet on the coffee table, encased in thick socks. Paka was curled on the sofa's other end, one hand holding the toe of Rick's boot possessively. Rick sat in a cloth-upholstered chair with one ankle folded on the other knee, where Paka gripped his boot. T. Laine, the witch, was curled up in a chair beneath a blanket. JoJo, with her multiple piercings and tattooed dark skin shining in the lamplight, sat on the floor with her legs crossed like a guru, barefooted and slouched, wearing multiple T-shirts and a patterned skirt. There were two vacant chairs, one for Tandy and one, I guessed, for me.

A hallway opened into a bathroom, with a stone cabinet top and tub big enough to lie down in. Through the opening I saw a bed that could only be a California king; I'd never seen one that big, but I'd read about them in my novels. Doors hung open to other rooms, and I wanted to wander through and look in, but such nosiness was rude in the homes of the church, where a man and his several wives and children all lived under one roof. I guessed it might be rude here too.

"We have a laptop for you," Tandy said. When I didn't turn around, he said, "Nell?" And I realized he was speaking to me.

I shook my head and clasped my hands behind my back. I didn't have the money for a laptop.

"We each get one. From PsyLED," he added, still picking up on my emotions, which should have been unnerving, but I seemed to be getting used to it. "It's part of everyone's gear," he added. "They provided one for your use for the duration of the case."

"Oh," I said, and I couldn't help the delight that suffused through me.

Tandy opened a laptop and punched a button, making it come on. I eased between all the knees around the table and took my place on the end of the sofa, beside him, watching.

"This is your log-in and password," Tandy said, passing me a small folded piece of paper. "Change your password and memorize it." The small paper contained a user ID and a list of numbers and symbols, nothing easily memorable. "It will get you into the case files, the HST files, the Internet, FBI.gov, and PsyLED intranet, but not much else. Consultants don't have full access."

I nodded, following his directions, typing quickly, not caring that I was on the outside. I'd been there all my life. "I'm in," I said, surprise mixing with the delight.

"Good," Rick said, all business, in distinct opposition to Tandy's gentleness. "You said you had an update."

"An update on the church and on my safety," I said, "and two men Sister Erasmus saw in the compound." I started with what Sister Erasmus had said about the backsliders and the stranger boy with the automatic assault rifle, likely the one who had threatened me. I told them about the secret meetings and conspiracy papers not being shared among the entire congregation. I mentioned the overly wasteful target practice last evening. Told them that I had laid the groundwork to get back inside, if needed, and concluded my report with, "Nothing she noticed is unusual. Backsliders repent and go back to live on the compound all the time. Boys shoot and target practice and hunt all the time, on church lands, even off season and against the law," I concluded.

"Sugar," Occam said, "what are the chances that they would make you stay if you went back inside?"

I had never been called *sugar*, and the endearment sounded wrong on my ears, but he had also called my cat *sugar*, so maybe the word was just a Texan thing. I pressed my lips together and dropped my eyes to the laptop screen, thinking about his question. That was actually fairly likely. I didn't want to go in, no matter what the benefit. Not ever again. Except . . . If I could get my sisters off the compound, I'd go in. I'd risk it.

"They'd make her stay," JoJo muttered, the rings that pierced her lips moving. "I'd like to kick 'em in the nuts."

So would I, but I'd never have said so aloud. An unwilling smile tugged at my lips.

Watching me, JoJo said, "Tell you what. We get the chance and no one's looking, I'll hold the new preacher down and you can kick him in the nuts." I laughed, shook my head, and covered my mouth. The others laughed too, mostly at me, not at JoJo, who clearly said such things all the time.

But if I got the chance alone with Jackie Jr., in the proper circumstances, I'd prick his skin until he bled, and give him to the woods. Which would be far more satisfying, and far more permanent, and that thought made my insides quiver with a sense of dismay at my own cruelty. So I didn't answer, keeping my eyes on the computer screen, where they couldn't read my intent in my expression, and not meeting Tandy's gaze, which might indicate a deeper understanding than I wanted. I shook my head and wished I'd left my hair down to cover my face when I tilted my head forward. "Sister Erasmus says the winter storage cave has been set off-limits to the churchwomen. It isn't anything to do with the HST or a kidnapping, but it is different. I can show you if you have a map of the compound."

And boy howdy, did they have maps! Amazing satellite maps, so clear that I could identify every building and pathway, and even people who were walking. There were maps from summer, with a leafy tree canopy, and maps from winter with bare branches revealing the ground. The maps turned the focus of the meeting from me to the compound of the church. I showed the team where the three cave entrances were, all hidden beneath canopies of tall hemlock trees that were still growing when most of the Appalachian Mountains' hemlocks were dying from the hemlock woolly adelgid. It was an aphid-like insect that fed on hemlock sap. The trees were alive, possibly because of me, though I didn't tell the team that. It wasn't any of their business that I'd tended the trees when I was little and willed them to live and be strong, long before I had known I had magic.

"This is the entrance to the smallest cave," I tapped the map. "When the FBI and the state police raided the compound, they didn't find it, so it never got inspected or investigated. This is where the seeds and the winter supplies are kept. The canned goods, the stored grain, the stuff the women need. The others are here, and here." I pointed to the bigger caves, closer to the main part of the compound, closer to the chapel and the home of the preacher. "They have weapons and farm equipment and generators and ammunition and suchlike in them. Survival stuff. The one in the middle has a water source and is the place where we'll—where they'll—hole up when the government comes to attack." I thought for a moment before adding, "Not that it helped when the government actually did come to attack. Anyway, all three caves have reinforced poured concrete walls set just inside the entrances and steel core doors built into the walls. The plan was to bring down the cave walls outside of the fortified entrances with planted charges and then open passageways to the caves to either side. The tunnels are mostly finished, and it won't take long to chip a ways into the other caves.

"Some say that there's an entrance to deeper caverns from the center cave, but I wouldn't know. My best thinking is that only the inner circle of churchmen would know that, and I have no way of finding that out."

"Planted charges? And if the roof comes down when the charges go off?" Rick asked.

I shrugged. "The menfolk debated that possibility, but they figured that wouldn't happen because God wants them to survive. So far as I've seen, they might be right, because God hasn't stopped the evil done by so many of the church's menfolk. Not that they think of it as evil, but . . . I do." Quietly in the back of my mind, I had always thought it, despite the Scripture that said, "Thou shalt not judge."

The others were discussing the backsliding men Sister Erasmus had seen—the Dawson men—and how they might, or might not, fit in with the kidnappings. And how to find out more about them without having photos or fingerprints or anything else. I let them talk, learning about options that included cameras outside church property, trained on the road, drunk-driving checkpoints, again with cameras but this time on the officers' vests, and half a dozen other ways. The churchmen would have been appalled at the legal ways to surveil the road leading into the compound. I thought it was amazing.

We were nearly finished when Rick received a call on his cell phone. Another girl had gone missing.

EIGHT

He said, "No witnesses, and she may have wandered off, or taken off with a boyfriend, but no one has heard from her. And her cell phone was found a block from where she was last seen.

"The FBI hit the twenty-four-hour window without the return of the first girl. The ransom was paid, and there hasn't been any activity, which violates traditional HST procedure, which provides for return of the abducted within one hour of receipt. As you know from Spook School, when this window of time elapses, there is, statistically, a drastically reduced chance of warm-body rescue. After that, it usually means a recovery attempt, not a rescue."

"Warm body?" I asked.

"Rick's shorthand for living and still human," T. Laine said. "He has personal experience in that department."

"Not relevant to today's briefing." Rick stepped into the back room. When he returned, he pulled behind him a whiteboard on a wheeled stand. It had been divided in two with a marker, and a photograph hung on each side, with pertinent information beneath, like height and weight. I knew without being told that they were the missing girls. Rick passed JoJo a sheet of paper with two names written on it and an address for an FBI Web site. "JoJo, you type faster than the rest of us. Will you merge and update our files?"

JoJo grunted and said, "Sure. Make the black girl play secretary," but there wasn't any heat in the words.

Tandy smiled as if he was feeling pleasure from her. He said, "Not secretary. Computer geek and all-around IT specialist."

JoJo said, "I can live with that, if I can have the superhero name of SuperGeek or SuperHacker. Or maybe Diamond Drill." The last one made no sense to me, but I didn't ask, continuing my practice of sitting still and silent and learning by listening.

Amused, Rick said, "You gave up that lifestyle, Diamond Drill." JoJo's full lips spread into a wicked smile, and I didn't understand the humor. Rick said, "Because of the expired window, we've been asked to meet in person with the FBI."

He tapped the left side of the whiteboard and the photo that hung there. "Let's recap everything for Nell and update our board. Girl One was taken from school grounds following cheerleading practice," Rick said. "Witnesses and security cameras indicate that three males jumped out of a white panel van, no plates. Slight dent in the rear passenger-side panel. All three wore hoods and gloves. They grabbed the girl and threw her into the van. The van has since been confirmed to be a 1994 Dodge Ram panel van." He looked at me, "This is the stereotypical kidnapping I was talking about. It fits the textbook, nonfamily, political, ransom-style kidnapping. It required planning and an intimate knowledge of the girl, her whereabouts, and her schedule, all of which was posted to social media."

JoJo whispered a curse under her breath, her fingers tapping on her laptop keyboard so fast it sounded like rain, a steady drumming.

"Girl Two disappeared after ballet class. Her mother had engine trouble and was late to pick her up. No witnesses. Cell phone left behind. Private security cameras two blocks away caught sight of a panel van matching the description in the first kidnapping, no plates. There was no confirmation of the small dent, due to camera angle and low def, but it's assumed at this point that the girl was taken by the same people. That will be confirmed when and if they get a ransom demand."

I remembered what I had read on the government study about stereotypical kidnappings. "So some kidnappings are crimes of opportunity," I said, "but these kidnappers have treated this like a hunt." Rick looked at me curiously. I lifted one shoulder and said, "The church is pretty good about planning things. They're hunters. Hunters plan, stalk, build duck hides and deer stands to wait, watch, attack, and kill. Hunters are patient. These people are hunting humans, so they track their prey, but instead of tracks in the ground or spoor or territory marking, they track social media. Right?"

Rick gave me a small nod, and a flush of pleasure sped through me. "The FBI is also looking into whether the discarded cell was synced to a stranger's."

"Why do you call them Girl One and Girl Two. They got names," I said, frowning at Rick. "Names and histories and pictures." I pointed at the boards. "Rachel Ames and Shanna Schendel."

"He does that for me," Tandy said softly. "It's . . . difficult for me to work cases. Any cases. Everything is so personalized, everyone on the team feels the pressure. It can hit me hard."

"In training, we learned how to work together," T. Laine said. "It's all business, no emotions allowed. At least not in front of Tandy."

"Oh." That made some kind of sense. Strange sense, but sense. "Did the girls know each other?" I asked.

"They both attend Farrington High School and had French class together last year, but there isn't anything else to connect them, not that we've been able to discover, beyond that casual acquaintance."

I studied the pictures of the two girls, both pretty, looking vivacious and happy and fulfilled. And . . . soft, somehow. Not exactly innocent. Just untried, unpunished, as if they had lived easy lives. By the time I was their age, I had buried one sister-wife and been married according to church law for years. My sister Priss had married and had a baby on the way by the time she was fifteen. Looking at the faces of the missing girls, I felt odd and old and worn, as if I were fifty years old, not twenty-three, feelings I stuffed deep inside as all good women are taught to do from an early age, and plastered a smile on my face, hoping Tandy hadn't noticed my change in emotions. This was going to be problematic, working with what had to be a human lie detector.

Rick's cell made a tinny burbling sound and he picked up. "Special Agent LaFleur." He made a face and walked into the bedroom, shutting the door. The others talked and Tandy made a pot of coffee while I experimented with the laptop, opening the new file JoJo had sent, with all the information updated on the abductions. Once I got the file opened, I could see everything the FBI had on the girls, and I could also watch JoJo work in real time, updating and editing as she went. As the others said, this was "so freaking cool." When Rick returned he said shortly, "The feds say we have permission to take a look at the kidnap crime scenes. Gear up. We'll eat on the way."

I said, "I'll need to go home and eat lunch, since according to the contract I signed, I don't get paid for three weeks. Which is really not a good way to do business. When I make a deal with someone I get half up front. That way if they stiff me, I'll at least have something."

"You're getting paid by the federal government," Rick said, closing up his laptop, his smile making him look younger and less harried. "They don't stiff people."

"The federal government has been bankrupt since nineteen thirty-three, when they devalued the dollar and got rid of the gold certificate. Look it up. I wouldn't trust them to pay for a bag of flour." Which I still needed to pick up at the store. "I prefer to barter when I can. Plants for eggs and meat and chicken. Whatever I have for whatever someone else has. That's value. And right now, I'm hungry and nearly broke, so I have to go home."

T. Laine made a *pfft* noise.

JoJo said, "No way are we letting you drive all that way back out there, girl. Good God, it's like fifty miles. I'll feed you."

"I don't need to take charity," I said tartly. "I have food at the house."

"When we're doing fieldwork, expenses are covered," Rick said. "And that includes meals. You can submit an expense report. But for now, don't worry. I'll take care of it. You're part of this team."

"But—"

"What was that you said to us?" Tandy interrupted. "'Welcome to my home. Hospitality and safety while you're here'? You're in our home now." Which left me totally nonplussed. To the others he said, "Mexican?"

"We did Mexican already this week," JoJo said, closing her own laptop. "Burgers." Still bumfuzzled, I followed them out the door.

Following a fast-food meal that was mostly beef and potatoes, we drove by the school where Girl One was taken, and we all

got out to suss around a bit. There was crime scene tape blocking off a large area, all of it concrete or asphalt and no place
for me to take off my shoes and feel the ground. The werecats
didn't smell blood or semen or urine, just a lot of humans.
Rick used a little device called a psy-meter. It was about the
size of JoJo's playing cards, and it measured what he called
psy-energies, the energy left behind by all living things, even
more so by magic-using nonhumans and by magical spells or
workings. But there had been too many people around for anyone to get a good reading.

At the ballet studio it was pretty much the same, except for
a strip of land in the parking area where one tree, a dogwood,
had taken root and another had tried to and died. The ground
was covered in pine needles, and when I pushed a hand
through to the soil, it was to discover that the lone tree was
afraid, *fearfearfear* leaking through every rootlet and stem
and reddening leaf. It had been afraid since its partner tree
had died, thinking it the last tree on the face of the Earth. I
willed it to listen to me, while the others sniffed around and
muttered to themselves. I willed it to live and promised it I'd
bring another dogwood back to plant in the place of death,
and I'd bring fertilizer and water and help them both to survive. When I pulled my hand away, it was . . . not happy. But
maybe looking forward to winter rather than fearing death.

We had done all we could at the old crime scenes, and headed
back to the hotel. I hadn't gotten enough sleep and was nodding by the time we were ensconced in the suite of rooms
again. I fixed coffee while Rick and the others checked e-mail
and made calls. From the few comments they made, I deduced
that Girl One was still among the missing, meaning that the
Human Speakers of Truth were looking less likely to be culprits, and the girl was more likely to already be dead. The
team's emotions were both excited and fearful, and Tandy
looked drawn and worn from trying to ward them off. I made
sure he had coffee with plenty of sugar and cream, and I stood
over him waiting for him to drink, trying to project happy
emotions toward him.

I had just taken my own first sip when Rick stepped in from

the back room, ended a call, and said, "Listen up." His face was empty and cold. "The news media finally caught up with social media about the abductions. An hour after it hit the airwaves, a third girl went missing, a human girl with a strong paranormal association to one of Ming's scions. Her mother is Claretta Clayton, and so her daughter falls completely under PsyLED jurisdiction."

The tension in the room ratcheted up so high it took my breath away. T. Laine sat up straight. JoJo grabbed her laptop and started a search for something on the Internet. Tandy's skin went a bit pale, his Lichtenberg lines going brighter.

"Who's Claretta Clayton?" I asked.

"A VIV—Very Important Vampire," T. Laine said, her eyes focused far off.

Occam paraphrased from his tablet, "The Clayton family helped settle Knoxville in the late seventeen hundreds, and Claretta married into the family in the eighteen hundreds. Her husband died in the Civil War, and she was turned by a marauder. She broke with the family. According to our files, Ms. Clayton has a human daughter, age eighteen."

"How much was released to the public?" T. Laine asked. "The paranormal family, compounded with the time . . . Could this abduction be a copycat?"

Rick made a noncommittal sound, his face grim. "We can't rule anything out at this point. But with the FBI already entrenched and because the cases are currently linked, the director decided that the feds will remain in charge. This unit will be offering our expertise and our data on HST. But this has nothing to do with the readiness of this team to take on an assignment, nothing to do with division of responsibilities, and everything to do with needing a bigger team than PsyLED can offer at this time. So we're working with the feds, and everyone in this unit will accept that. Understood?" There were impassive nods around the room, but Tandy looked distressed, and I knew that not everyone agreed with the decision to work under the FBI. Or maybe some thought that the FBI wouldn't work with them.

Someone turned on the huge TV, and I saw a gorgeous blond woman talking about three missing girls in Knoxville, believed to all be abductions, but it was quickly clear she knew that and nothing more, because she immediately went to a specialist on nonfamily kidnappings. I downed my coffee, thinking about what I knew and what I didn't.

"There are other significant differences with the third girl," Rick said. "She didn't attend Farrington High. No white panel van was seen. However, she did disappear from school, after being dropped off by a limo driver. He's at FBI headquarters being questioned now."

"Which school?" JoJo asked, typing again.

"Private school. Senior at Wyatt," Rick said. His cell chimed again and he turned back into the bedroom, saying, "LaFleur."

I didn't know much about nonchurch schools, but even I had heard of the private Wyatt School of Knoxville, and I pulled a map of it up on my laptop. Wyatt had a soccer field, a baseball field, a lacrosse field, whatever that was, a tennis center, plus two arts buildings and a theater, a sciences building, and a swimming pool. I'd never been in a swimming pool, hadn't even seen one except on films. There was one teacher or staff member for every ten kids, which, according to the Wyatt Web site, was much lower than in public schools. Wyatt was a day school for rich kids, though financial aid was available. Tuition and food went for nearly twenty thousand dollars per year. Per child. I'd never made that much altogether in a single year. And I'd been homeschooled all my life, until I had taken over my own education at age twelve. Photos of the student body suggested they all were from a financial upper class, all with perfect teeth, athletic bodies, and artistic, scientific, or political leanings. The future artists, doctors, lawyers, and politicians of the state went to school at Wyatt.

"Theodore Roosevelt said," I quoted, "'A man who has never gone to school may steal from a freight car, but if he has a university education he may steal the whole railroad.'" Trying not to be sour but not succeeding, I added, "Looks like these kids might be on the way to greatness stealing railroads."

"Meow," Occam said. The others laughed, and I realized I was being gently teased, as if they were testing the waters to see if I had a sense of humor or if I was going to be difficult to work with.

Even *I* knew I'd sounded catty, and fought off a responding blush. I wasn't accustomed to being sarcastic or snide and it left me feeling itchy and odd in the face of their careful laughter.

Rick walked back in, his face holding an expression I couldn't identify. JoJo said, "What part of the campus did Girl Three disappear from?"

"We don't know," Rick said, studying me for reasons I didn't understand, that odd look still on his face. "The chauffeur dropped her off at the Upper School Building this morning, but she never showed up for class."

"Are there security cameras on campus?" JoJo asked, fingers tapping like a snare drummer.

T. Laine whirled her computer so we could see the screen and said, "Two facing the entrance. The chauffeur had to pass them when he dropped her off. Neither one was working that day."

"Neither camera was working?" I asked, clarifying. "I don't particularly like happenstance or coincidence," I said.

"You got a quote for that?" Rick asked.

Tapping the keys of my laptop, studying the map of the grounds before starting a virtual tour, I said, "A paraphrase. Once means happenstance, twice means coincidence, three times means enemy action. Ian Fleming said something like that, I think in one of the James Bond books." I spotted the cameras on my computer. Both were facing front, both big enough to see at a glance. "If I was planning a kidnapping and I had a way inside, I'd dismantle both of them the night before and then take out my target. A bigger question is how the kidnapper knew she would be let off at that entrance and not one of the others."

Silence settled around the table, and I looked up. They were all staring at me with looks that ranged from surprise to outright suspicion. I sat back in my chair and folded my arms over my chest, feeling protective and proud, the latter of which was a sin, but not one I could honestly repent of this time, even if I was of the mind to. "What?"

"Trained investigators would know that sort of thing. Not a . . ." Rick bit off his words.

"Not a backcountry *hillbilly*?" I said stiffly, my church accent creeping back in. "I keep telling you'uns. I was raised by hunters. I snuck around a lot when I was a little'un, listening to the menfolk talk and brag. I also had a husband who intended me to be able to take care of myself when he was gone. I know how to bait a trap, set a snare, shoot a varmint, and skin and dress a deer if I need to. I never have, not since the lessons, but I know how. I also learned how to observe and draw conclusions—that was called deductive reasoning, which linked premises with conclusions or potential conclusions. Or brought up more questions and observation leading to more conclusions.

"And back to that quote? This looks like enemy action," I finished hotly.

"She was right," Rick murmured. Paka snarled and, from her reaction, I realized that the "she" Rick was talking about had to be Jane Yellowrock, the vamp hunter who had brought me to the attention of this group. Jane must a said something to him about me, something good, to get him interested in my consulting with his team. Maybe I owed Jane an apology for all the bad things I'd thought and said about her.

"Yes, she was," Tandy said, his Lichtenberg lines glowing a bright, unvarying red.

T. Laine was watching me with delight; Occam and Paka with something like the way cats look at a new toy, as if they wanted to sink their claws into me and see if I'd bleed. A small smile crept over my face. Here I was in a hotel room with a bunch of people I'd not met until recently, men and women both, in a *hotel room*, not a one of the people related by marriage or blood—and no one had molested me, not once. The churchmen had been wrong about the constant danger to the womenfolk. And I was having fun. How 'bout that? I hadn't had fun since before I became a woman growed, but I was having fun.

"So, if we were in charge, what do you think should be our next move?" Rick asked, "Assuming we won't interview the family until tonight."

I *felt* the test in the question. He was checking out my vaunted deductive reasoning. I tapped my pursed lips with a finger. "The police are probably all over the crime scene, messing up the scent patterns for the cats among you. But just in case we can pick up something that a human can't, I say we should go to the school as soon as possible." Rick didn't indicate an answer, just waited patiently, like a cat staring at a mouse that was acting distinctly un-mouse-like. "And it'd be nice to get the chauffeur driver to the school to show us exactly where he dropped her off. Exactly. Not in general. It would be even nicer if the local cops were told to stay away from the site so you could all smell it, but I'm guessing that won't happen." While there, I'd also be able to take off my shoes and put my toes into the soil where Girl Three stepped out of the car, to see if I could pick up anything, but I wasn't gonna tell them that.

I said, "If the FBI hasn't already done it, somebody should talk to all the girls' friends about whether any of them were seeing someone on the side. Boyfriend, someone their parents were against them seeing. Something secret that they might not put on social media." They were all looking at me even more weirdly, as if I were some new critter they'd caught in one of my own snares and they weren't sure what to do with me.

Crossly, I said, "I've read a few mystery books. It's called looking for clues. Like, were there fingerprints where the cameras were disabled?"

"The FBI is on-site, checking everything you mentioned and a good deal more besides," Rick said.

"But you got cats, and they can smell around to see if anyone new was in the school. The cats can also smell for Girl Three's scent patterns and blood or body fluids where the driver let her off. If she was scared, she mighta peed a little, and some cats can see body fluids in ultraviolet, in the dark. Can you'uns, when you change into cats?"

Rick laughed softly. "She *was* right. And yes, Watson, the FBI crime scene techs are doing most of those things, and we will redo anything that looks pertinent. The ones that haven't been done are on the list for the day."

Near sundown Rick got word that the FBI crime scene techs were finished with the private school, and we headed for Wyatt, where Girl Three, the vampire's daughter, had been taken. The team chattered and entered things into their synced laptops as we rode toward Wyatt School. Here, there were trees, enough to actually make a wood.

I studied the roads and the surrounding area the way a hunter might, taking in details like high ground for observation spots—not many—roads in and out, nearby streets and buildings, bodies of water, the thick woods, subdivisions, and a trailer park. Dutchtown Road took us to Wyatt School Lane, and that road took us to the school itself, which occupied a lot

of acreage, bigger than most family farms in the state. The
school had multiple entrances off Wyatt School Lane, making
any observation about the cameras less than helpful. A black
limousine was waiting for us at the entrance to the Upper
School, parked in a small, paved, circular turn-around area. I
got out, looking around like the others were doing. The cameras on this entrance were the ones that had been disabled. On
the other side of the road from the school were trees and what
most people called natural areas, in this day and age, though
the trees were only a few decades old and a grounds crew kept
the undergrowth clear. The rest of the team went to talk to the
chauffeur and sniff around the spot where Girl Three had been
let off by her chauffeur. I went to the woods.

They were oak varieties, maple varieties, poplars, longleaf
pine, and sweet gum. This time of year the leaves had started
to form a carpet on the ground, but there were enough still on
the limbs and twigs to hide a good climber. I walked deeper
into the trees, studying, letting the woods recognize me. Trees
in general—despite the scared dogwood—are deep thinkers,
slow to become aware, slow to recognize new beings in their
midst. But if someone spent any time in a wood, they might
have been noticed, especially if he, or she, hurt one of them.

According to the maps, there were residences nearby, a
mobile home park, a few businesses. Nearer the school, there
were running paths through the woods for the school athletes,
the tracks and the grounds near the campus all neat and weed-
free. Farther off, the grounds crew had been less interested in
landscaping, just keeping the paths clear. Beside the sculpted
paths, there were lower trails used by rabbit and opossum and
raccoon, where the shorter vegetation had been reshaped by
their passage, higher paths used by deer, the ground cover thin-
ner where the deer hooves had damaged the low plants and
higher where their bodies had pushed aside and broken the
branches and stems on the way to the water of Kilby Lake, not
far from the school. And there were the littered paths employed
by nonstudent humans. Random beer cans, plastic water bottles, and used condoms on the trails leading to the mobile home
park. I walked toward it along one especially trashed path, and
wondered if an upscale teenager had a thing for a trailer park
teenager. Or maybe, unbeknownst to her family, this missing

girl was on drugs and walked here to buy them, or alcohol. Or any kind of secret a teenager might keep. I studied the metal homes for a while before I turned and went back through the woods. The trees were awake now, and recognizing me, recognizing Paka and the other big-cats, the life force of the woods a low, deep, vibrant pulsation I could feel along my skin. Overhead the leaves rustled as a breeze stirred through them, the trees stretching limbs against the pressure of movement.

The air was brisk, leaves falling steadily now as I walked back toward the school. When I could see glimpses of the limousine again, I stopped and sat on the ground, took off my shoes and socks, bent my knees up under my chin, and, my skirt demurely tucked around me, put my bare feet on the ground, flat, soles evenly distributed, toes pressing in. I put my hands flat beside me. I closed my eyes and sought out the spirit of the trees as I could do so easily at home. Back at the single dogwood, all I had needed to do was touch the ground, because the space was so small and the tree so alone. Here it was harder, the trees not accustomed to communing with anything not plant-based. But they were aware of me now, and they were curious. At which point I realized I had no way to find out what I needed to know.

Even in my own woods, the trees can't see. They experience the world around them through touch, temperature, pressure, and vibrations of sound. My woods don't *see* anything, only the vibrations and awareness telling me what was going on. Here, all I could tell was that people passed through these woods with regularity, from the school and from the residences nearby, some at speed, pounding along, some meandering, some with stealth. Athletes ran. Bored people meandered. The stealth part was disturbing, however, and I was able to narrow it down to two humans who had moved like foxes, one from the trailer park, and one who came back and forth across Dutchtown and into the trees there.

According to the maps, that part of the area was heavily residential, with the woods broken up by roads and tract house neighborhoods. Little by little the trees of the woods had been slaughtered and hauled away. There wasn't a significant woods until Hardin Valley Road, and that was earmarked for destruction. There wasn't enough connection for the woods where I sat to speak to the woods across the way, so I had no idea if the stalker routinely came through there too. The woods weren't strong enough to show me much more.

If the missing girl had spilled her blood here, I might be able track her. I had followed an injured deer once, across Soulwood, its blood dripping onto the earth. Blood was easy to follow. Tracking a human had to be similar. But I was not going to get her blood.

I blew out my breath, opening my eyes, stretching out my legs, flat on the ground. And saw the bulbous moon hanging in the trees. Night had fallen.

"Whadju find, sugar?"

My head jerked toward the sound. It was Occam, high in a tree to my left. I frowned up at him. He shouldn't have been watching me. "What do you mean?"

Slower, he said, "What did you discover when you"—he made a rolling motion with one hand—"communed?"

Tandy leaned out from behind a tree and softly said, "That was incredible. I never felt anything like it before."

A spike of fear shocked up through me, like being stabbed and electrocuted all at once. The fear multiplied in intensity. *They had been watching. Watching me.* Around me, the breeze picked up, colder than only an hour earlier. Chill bumps rose on my skin, prickling, and my fingers started to shake. Hiding my reaction, I pulled on my shoes and stood up, brushing down my skirt and smoothing strands of my hair toward the tight bun. The wind had pulled some loose while I was unaware. The two men still watched.

Watching me. Watching me use my power. I shivered hard.

Occam said, "I never saw anyone commune with a forest before." There was something like awe on his face. "That was amazing."

They had *watched*. They all *knew*.

"Nell?" Tandy asked. I didn't look at him. "Oh," he said. "Oh! I'm so sorry. I didn't understand. Occam, please give us a moment. We'll meet you back at the van."

"I said something wrong, didn't I?" Occam said, leaping from the tree limb with cat grace. The jump was marred when his index finger caught on the sharp bark and drew blood. He landed between Tandy and me on the balls of his feet and his fingertips, microdroplets of his blood hitting the earth. Droplets that I felt through the ground, sharp and heated and . . . Something tugged at me through the ground, needing, wanting, *hungering*.

Occam rose fluidly to his full height. "Whatever I said, sugar, I didn't mean to hurt you."

Blood. Hunger wrapped itself through me and wrenched, demanding. I turned and ran.

My breath came fast, my heart speeding. I raced through the trees, a zigzag course as if to unsettle a hunter who had me in his sights. Birds startled and called out, the alarm tones shrill. The trees caught my fear, throwing out warnings that felt like, *Fire! Fire!* Their greatest fear except for man. I could feel them through my thudding feet, their deep rootlets spreading like fingers, siphoning up water from far below ground as my fear spread and they prepared for danger. They shared the warning root-to-root, tree-to-tree, species-to-species—the old fear, *Fire! Fire!* I ran faster, my breath burning. Leaves fell like rain, hiding my passage.

I realized I was on a path and I spun away from it, into the underbrush. I must be far from the school, because here, there was heavier growth. Blackberries that scratched my skin and pulled at my clothes and hair. I dropped to hands and feet and crawled into a patch of bracken, pushing aside the large fern-leaves and ducking beneath low limbs of trees. Hiding. Heart pounding. Around me, field mice, lizards, and snakes dashed and undulated away in fear.

Lungs burning, I crawled deeper into the bracken until I was surrounded by ferns and my bare hands were buried beneath last year's leaves, into the mosses and the damp soil. Things crawled over my wrists and arms, many-legged and fast, as my hands disrupted their lives.

People were watching me. Always watching me.

And . . . Occam had bled. Were-blood, hot and potent, all across the earth beneath him. The wood had wanted that blood. I had wanted that blood. Had thought, just for an instant, about what it would feel like to feed him to the earth. I was . . . I was evil.

I was evil, just like the churchmen had said.

And . . . the moon. Were-creatures and the full moon. That meant something, explained something, but I didn't remember what. I only remembered that I had been terrified, and when I was terrified I wanted blood. Always, even if just for a moment, I wanted blood for the earth, to give the trees strength and power and to claim it for my own as I had Soulwood. *Oh God. What am I? What kind of devil am I?* My leg muscles twitched, my heart and lungs pumped, my skin burned. With each breath, my lungs made a retching, tearing sound.

My unbunned hair was tangled in a snarl and draped around me like a lank veil, sweaty and full of twigs. I realized I was crying when tears dripped forward and off the tip of my nose and from my chin, falling to the ground like a salty offering. I didn't know why I was crying. No one had hurt me. No one had even chased me. They had let me go. But . . . but I had seen something inside me. Something I didn't know was there. Something I couldn't quite identify, didn't recognize. Something that I feared.

Occam had bled. Beautiful, strong blood.

I heaved breaths until my trembling eased. Until the tears stopped and dried on my cheeks. Until I heard-felt through ears and palms the sound vibration of someone slowly approaching. I rolled to my butt, sitting up, hidden in the ferns, and wrapped my skirt and my arms tight around my legs, holding myself like a child, my back to a pin oak, the bark rough and soothing against my spine. Night had fallen, the darkness harsh and deep and encompassing. Shadows were long and lean across open ground and hovered, like raven wings spread into darkness, over the bracken.

And then I remembered why the moon was important. I had read once, long ago, about were-creatures. They were moon-called, their blood infected with something called prions that initiated changes in their genetic structure. They changed shape into another creature most easily on the full moon, when the lunar cycle made their blood potent, the prions multiplying during the full moon and forcing the change upon them. Which . . . which might be why his blood had affected me so strongly. His blood was powerful and vital, and, right now, the earth knew that. Liked that.

Twigs snapped, in what had to be a deliberate sound, since the creature tracking me was probably werecat.

"Nell?"

It was Occam. If he had cat eyes in his human form, then my trail was likely lit up, bright in every misplaced leaf, every broken stem, every disarranged fern, my fear sweat in droplets everywhere. My scent was probably hot on the air from running, from anger and fear pheromones, smelling like prey when I was a bigger predator than anyone, even I, had guessed. I hugged myself tighter.

"I see you in the dark," he said softly. "May I come in?"

I laughed silently, and wondered if I was a mite insane. An invitation into a wood that wasn't even mine? *Fine.* "Yes. You may. But the moon's gonna be full in few days, and I don't know how much control you have at this point. So please refrain from eating me."

I could hear the smile in his words when he said, solemnly, "I promise." A long-fingered hand, the skin tanned in the daylight, was nothing more than a pale glow in the night as he pushed aside the tall ferns and crawled beneath the trees on his hands and knees. He settled himself near me, leaning his back against a tree across from me. I stared at my arms, hugging my legs.

"Can you tell me why you ran?"

I shrugged in uncertainty. How did I tell him, anyone, about . . . everything? The breeze grew more chilled and the shadows abruptly darker as clouds covered the waxing moon. Occam waited patiently, and the silence pushed against me, demanding an answer even if Occam himself wasn't pushing. I frowned. "I was running away from myself more than anything," I admitted unwillingly. "But I don't like being watched. Wasn't right."

I said nothing about the blood on his fingers, but as I sat in the bracken, I realized that the wood no longer hungered, or if it did, then I had somehow cut my awareness of it. Run away from it. I didn't say, *And this wood wanted you.*

Occam nodded, his face serious. "You're a very private person. I get that. Rick said you might be a *yinehi.* Or a couple of other Cherokee names. I know I'm not pronouncing it right in the Cherokee tongue. But he was talking about fairies, maybe wood nymphs, though in your case, mostly human. He said you were intensely private. And I forgot that. I promise that it will never happen again. I'll never watch you, not without your permission."

I thought about that, from the perspective of the church and the menfolk and the way they did things. Nothing was ever free.

"If you're thinking about quitting," he said, "I'd like you to stay. All of us would. We'd like you to try again. Find a way to merge with this team. Learn how to get along with all of us."

I looked into the dark orbits where his eyes hid in the shadows. In the daylight, they were amber-brown eyes, but in the dark they were just holes in his skull. "Don't watch me unless I ask you to. I been watched and spied on my whole life, hiding who I am, what I am, whatever that is. Been watched by the men in the church as I approached womanhood. Been watched from the deer stand for years. Nothing I can do about none of it. But you. I can stop you."

"Understood. No one watches you without your permission. Anything else?"

"Never lie to me."

Occam thought about that one for a moment. "I will never lie to you unless I have to."

"Why would you have to?"

"Secrets that aren't mine to share," he said instantly. "Need-to-know info on cases unrelated to you. PsyLED has certain levels of security clearances. Yours is much lower than mine."

Occam stuck out a hand and I studied it a moment. Menfolk sealed deals with handshakes, man-to-man. Deals with a woman were usually different. Sealed with other words or in other ways. I had signed a contract, but I had a feeling that this handshake would be much more final, much more permanent. This handshake was about trust, and expectation, and protection, and commitment. Hesitantly I placed my hand into his. His palm and fingers were heated, like a furnace, and in an instant, something wild and fiery flowed through his flesh, skin-to-skin, something that made his eyes glow golden in the night. My hand felt small and cold inside his grip, but just as strong. I gripped his hand back. We shook on it. His eyes faded to human amber. When he let go, he rolled to his knees, all feline grace, and crawled out of the bracken. Silent, wondering if I had made the right decision, I followed him through the deepening dark, toward the lights of the school.

NINE

When I emerged from the woods, walking silently behind Occam, Tandy raced toward me, some unfamiliar emotion on his face—part fear, part sorrow, part something else—his strange hands reaching as if to grab me, pale in the night. I jerked back several steps and Occam stepped in front of Tandy's hands. "Not without her permission," Occam said. "Not to watch or to touch. Never again without her permission." He looked at the rest of the group. "She's not a cat in a pride or a den. She's private. We abused her sense of privacy, Tandy and me. No one watches her unless she is in danger or she asks. Understood?"

"Yes, yes, yes," Tandy said, the words running into each other, his hands gripping Occam's arm, his face nearly frenzied, his words running together. "I'm so sorry, so sorry, so sorry. I didn't understand." I recognized the expression on his face then. Pain. He was feeling some inexplicable kind of ache, like a throbbing in his red-lined flesh. "I beg your forgiveness for overstepping my bounds. But I find you . . ." He shook his head as if searching for a word he couldn't find. He settled on, ". . . *fascinating.*"

I took another step back at that, surprise slipping through me like a cold rain down my collar, knowing my posture was still defensive.

"We all do," Occam said, "the ones of us who aren't human. You smell like . . . like home, sugar. Like safety, perched in the trees with fresh kill before us."

"You smell of jungle and tall trees," Paka said. "Of deep water and rich earth. And death. Much death, the earth wet with the blood of prey, an offering, a gift, that I might eat and live."

T. Laine had been leaning against the van; she pushed off

with her hands and came to stand near Rick, many feet of space between us when she stopped. "I don't have Tandy's sense of empathy or the cats' sense of smell, but my magic likes you. I think I could bounce a spell through you, like a routing, like the way a comet picks up speed when it circles a planet and boomerangs off into space. But I'd ask first. I'd always ask. Men? And worse, cats?" Her tone was incredulous. "You have no idea. They have no sense of privacy when they turn catty."

I nodded, the agreement jerky. I'd seen house cats do things that would sear my eyeballs if a werecat did them. I turned my attention to JoJo, the token human of the group, wondering what she would say. "I don't get the whole privacy thing," she said, pulling on all the earrings in her right earlobe, sliding them through her fingers, which pulled her lobe out of shape, to rebound, earrings swinging. "I'm a party girl. Gimme a beer and bucket of wings or some of Mama's cooking and a bunch of half-drunk pals all piled on the couch watching a game, and I'm down with that. But I also don't get hunting down prey and eating it raw or shifting on the full moon—or not shifting and going nutso over it."

That part made no sense, but I let it go.

"But I don't have to get it. I just have to live and let live," JoJo said. "And if that means not following you on a hike into the woods, I'm down with that too. And, hey, you don't smell like anything to me. Sorry."

I let a half smile curl my mouth. "Down with that," I repeated, shaking my head. "I guess I'm down with that too."

"Good," Rick said. But there was something in his tone that said my taking off like a cat with her tail on fire was a problem I needed to work on. "Now, if you can stand it, we need to know what just happened. Not the little chat you had with Occam. We get what happened and how we overstepped and what we need to do to keep it from happening again. We all saw you sitting near the trees. Your scent changed, just like it did in the market, when you sat under the trees. Something was happening. Tandy calls it communing. To the cats' noses you released something almost like a mating pheromone."

T. Laine said, "I felt magic. And not a magic I ever felt before."

"What was happening?" Rick asked.

"I . . ." I shrugged uncertainly. "I ain't never—I have never explained it. Or talked about it. But I guess *communing* is as good a word as any. I learn things from a wood, if it's old enough. I learn things from individual trees sometimes too."

"Okay," Rick said, his voice even and controlled. "Tell us what you discovered in the woods. Please."

I gave a small shrug. "Runners on the trails, people having sex in the woods—two people, probably male, who were . . . not good people," I said, trying to find English words for the trees' emotions. "Dangerous people who come here often. One came from the trailer park and one from somewhere across the road."

Rick nodded. "No more games, people. T. Laine, you and Occam check out the trailer park, a quick magic and scent search. See if you see or smell anything wrong, out of place." He handed Occam a plastic baggie with a T-shirt in it. "Get a good baseline. If you pick up Girl Three's scent, I want you back here to recheck."

Occam took the baggie and opened it, sticking his nose into the bag and sniffing, fast and hard, several times, through his mouth and nose both before handing the baggie back to Rick. The two disappeared into the shadows, moving fast, and I realized Occam had been taking a scent, like a tracking dog. I figured werecats must have a better-than-human nose, and decided that they had gotten the T-shirt from the chauffeur.

To the rest of us, Rick said, "We have one more stop to make tonight. Girl Three's home. Then I have reports to write up." He opened the side door of the van. "Let's go. We'll pick up Occam and T. Laine on Dutchtown Road." I remembered that this girl's mother was a vampire, one of the scions of the Blood Master of Knoxville, Ming of Glass. Even the church knew about Ming of Glass, the vampire used sometimes as a threat against unruly children. *You be good or Ming of Glass will snatch you outta your bed.*

Because I was only a consultant, the team didn't always think to explain to me what was going on. Worse, I didn't pay enough attention to the team's chatter while we drove, letting the events of the last few hours ring and thrill and settle through me. Trying to decide if I'd made a bad mistake signing the contract to help out these people, trying to decide if shaking Occam's hand had meant less than I thought it had. Trying to decide if I really cared that I had done any of those things. Because though they had to learn to understand me, and I them, I liked the idea of being part of a team. And maybe, just maybe, having friends. Except for Kristy at the library, I'd . . . been alone . . . for a long time.

Sequoia Hills was a fancy place, gracious-like, the roads weaving up and down in long curving lanes; the center area between lanes was planted with trees and shrubs and exotic grasses I didn't recognize in the dark, but I guessed that they had been imported. Nothing like these was native to the hills or the Tennessee Valley. The lawns were also bordered by and filled with gardens full of plants I didn't recognize; they looked healthy and pretty and froufrou, placed for effect, but not a one of them was grown for eating or medicinal purposes.

Unlike the tract housing I had glimpsed on the drive this afternoon, where every home was a cookie-cutter version of the others, none of these houses had . . . *homogeneity* might be the right term. They were each and every one a different style and built of different materials. Most had smaller houses in the back or an extra wing that had been added on to it, though likely not for the reasons the churchmen added on to theirs—more wives. I guessed that each house held only one family, which the churchmen would say was a waste of real estate. I smiled slightly, seeing my reflection in the van's middle window.

We pulled up into a driveway and stopped, the van on an incline, so that Rick set the parking brake. He looked to me, sitting in the passenger seat and asked, "What impressions did you get as we drove through?"

I looked back at the others, but they appeared to be buried in their laptops, which meant the question was probably directed only to me, maybe some sort of test. I said, "Money. Good breeding." I thought a bit and added, "Exclusivity. They import their plants and pay someone else to do the designing and the work. They probably never put their hands in the soil or ever get dirty. When they do good deeds, they do it by writing a check. They spend money on cars for luxury instead of practicality or the environment. I could tell more if I could put my feet on the ground."

"Knock yourself out."

I hesitated a moment and then remembered that phrase from a film. It was a peculiar way of telling me I could do anything I wanted. I nodded and slipped off my shoes, opened the door, and stepped out onto the concrete drive, which sent spears of cold into my soles. The night was more than chilly; we had frost on the way, and the air bit and nipped my exposed skin with icy teeth. My hair, which was still down from my run, swirled and twisted like mare's tail clouds in the wind until I coiled it around my hand. I should have brought my coat.

I walked across the two feet of drive to the lawn and stepped slowly onto the grass. It wasn't a wild grass, of course, but it was happy grass. Some variety of centipede, the mat stretching across the open spaces, the leaves and roots and runners heavily steeped in time and good water and care and nitrates. It felt . . . *satisfied*, maybe, and very oddly, it also felt . . . snobbish, if grass can feel snobbish. My own mixed grasses at home felt useful, functional, and beneficial. *"You* are supposed to be eaten," I told the snobbish grass softly, "by sheep and cattle and goats and geese. You are foodstuff."

"Nell?" Rick asked.

"Nothing," I said, walking away, the grass tickling my arches and pressing up between my toes. "Just talking to the grass."

I walked around the front yard, which was rolling and landscaped with flowering fall plants. Purple pearls, brandy-wine plants, late-blooming varietal hydrangeas, and black lace. The plants were deeply layered, the ones that had been in place for years feeling superior and the newest ones feeling uncertain, but settling roots deeply into the well-mixed soil. I had a feeling that the owner of the house was going to be snooty. And maybe even the gardener.

The lawn surrounded Girl Three's home, a house of . . . *stately proportions* might be a good term—nothing forbidding like the Batman family home, Wayne Manor, or glamorous like the Biltmore house. I'd seen pictures of that house, and it was ultrafancy. This wasn't a small house, nor a large one either, though I had only the multifamily, multiwife, many multichildren homes of the church to go by in measuring size. This house had what they called a brick façade with rock faces, stark white window trim and mullions, a black door, and several peaks in the roofline. The roof was made of slate, the tiles curved on the lower sides, making it look like a gingerbread house, and the slate had been there long enough to grow moss. There were skylights in the roof and a big screened porch near a pool on one side. A full basement sat in the earth underneath it all. In back was a garage with three doors and a small second house, totally separate from the front house, the windows dark. The pathways in the back were poured concrete in curving arcs, plants with big leaves curling at the path edges. Yes. Gracious. And elegant. Except where the dog had peed. There was dog urine on many of the plants, the backyard marked by a large and stinky dog. I was reminded of the men who had marked my yard, and made a mental note to look for a dog in the house and to have the werecats in the group double-check my assessment.

I walked back to the van and said, "The people who take care of the yard have good taste in plants and know how to keep them happy. But whoever keeps it up is snobby, and most gardeners and lawn care people aren't snobby —they're too busy and dog tired to be snobby—so it's confusing."

"No one new came through here?" Rick asked.

"Plants don't understand *new* things. They understand things that they can note over time. But if someone new just walked across the lawn, they wouldn't notice unless he set the grass on fire, or pulled plants and weeds out of the soil, or killed something on it so the blood drenched the ground, or cut down some of the trees.

"One thing. A dog marked the backyard recently, but the urine hasn't killed any of the plants like it would have if the dog belonged to the house and regularly did his business out here. Just to be safe, you might send a cat nose to double-check."

Rick nodded, his gaze beyond me into the night as Paka, in her human form, slid out and through the shadows around the house. Moments later she returned and said, "Dog. Big dog." Her nose curled; she sneezed a tiny cat sneeze and shook her head as if at something foul. JoJo chuckled in sympathy. "It does not belong to this house. It wandered through. It stinks like wet, sick dog."

Rick said, "Okay. A stray. Let's check out the house. T. Laine, you're on point with evidence gathering, close attention to magical signatures and trace magic."

I looked up at that, wondering why he'd said *magic*. But before I could ask, he went on.

"JoJo, you'll be with the feds." He led the way to the front door and up the brick steps to the porch. I followed at the back of the team, shivering and carrying my shoes, my toes frozen, chill bumps all over my arms and legs, looking for a place out of the way to sit and put on my shoes, and watching what the team did, how they moved, and what things they said to each other. Curious. Captivated.

The door opened before Rick knocked and a woman stood there. She was dressed in dark slacks that had been tailored to her; it was fine, delicate work, the kind the best church seamstresses did on the side, to supplement their incomes. White shirt, gray sweater, her hands fisted in her pockets, dragging down the sweater in front. Her hair was brown with blond streaks, and pulled back into a short ponytail. She looked jittery and shaky, and I could see the effects of tears on her skin, long hours of tears, and stress, and worry. Her skin was the pale white of undeath. This was a vampire.

Vampires had crossed my land before, and I remembered the feeling that had crawled over my flesh of *death, death everywhere*, but that was on my land, my wood, where every sensation was intense, dazzling to my senses, and I hadn't been prepared for that. Here, I had been prepared, but the vampire didn't spend time in the yard. The house would be a different matter, but—I took a stabilizing breath—I was ready.

Rick flashed his badge and ID and said, "Mrs. Clayton, I'm Senior Special Agent Rick LaFleur. These are my team members. I called earlier about your daughter's disappearance. Do you mind if we come in?" It was all official-like, until he added, "I'm a wereleopard, as are two others of my team. Will our scent be a problem for you, ma'am?"

I didn't hear what the woman said, but saw her step back and gesture us in. I was still carrying my shoes when I stepped into the foyer. Onto the wood flooring.

The moment my soles touched the wood, the feeling of death hit me, stronger than at home, that last time. Maggots and slime and rot beneath my feet, remembered by the wood of the floors. Absorbed by the floor. And given back to me tenfold. Rot, decay, putrefaction, corruption. The stench and texture of the air and of the floor were as real to me as if I had fallen into a pool of rotted flesh and the things that fed on it.

I sucked in a breath, and it froze my lungs. Before the door closed, I whipped around and back outside. Into the night. Running. Running for the largest copse of trees at the boundary of this lawn and the neighbors, running from the dead that crawled all over me like maggots and worms and filth. *Vampires.*

I thought I was prepared. I wasn't. The wood of the floor had given a best-forgotten memory back to me.

Retching, I crawled under the protection of the trees on the neighbor's side of the boundary, and I scrubbed my feet into the bark mulch. It was commercial stuff, dyed black, horrible for the plants both from the chemicals and the heat the black retained. But better on my feet than nasty vampires. I twisted my feet until I worked them through the mulch and into the soil, rubbing them into the dirt, cleaning off the death that clung to them. Only then did my gagging cease. Then I sat and pulled on my socks. Shivering so much my teeth chattered.

I should have been wearing my shoes. This was nobody's fault but mine.

I had the left shoe on when I heard my name called. It was T. Laine, the earth witch, and she could see me in the landscaping lights. I had her pegged as a no-nonsense woman, and her words didn't surprise. "Honey, you gotta quit running away when you're scared."

"I don't have my shotgun. I couldn't shoot her."

She came to an abrupt stop in the night. "Come again?"

"I've never been in a vampire house. The wood floor." I gagged again and thought I'd lose my supper, but I kept it down. "The floor absorbed the undeath. And I was barefoot. I felt them through my feet on the wood floors. It's . . ." I picked a word I had heard them use. "It's gross."

T. Laine breathed out a soft "Ohhh. Really?" She crossed the mulch to me and asked, "What do they feel like?"

"Like I'm walking on maggots and worms and rotten 'possum. I stepped in one once when I was a little 'un. Barefoot. It was horrible. I gagged for a week." I pressed a hand to my stomach. "Until I could get that rotten feeling off my feet."

"Ick. Sounds gross. So that was what you felt when . . . ?"

"When I put my foot on the wood floor. Maggots. Dead things. *Vampires.*"

"But you didn't feel any of that when you walked in the yard?"

"No. She's an inside vampire." I pulled on my right shoe, still thinking. "But maybe I can go inside if I keep my shoes on." *And with a nice thin layer of dirt on the soles of my feet,* I thought, standing.

T. Laine said, "I could . . . well, I mean." She stopped, perplexed.

"You could what?" I asked.

"I could put a temporary ward around your feet so you don't feel the floor as much." Before I could ask she said, "A ward is like a fence or a wall, but made of magic. I know your church believes that all magic is Satan worship or something, but it's not. Really." When I didn't reply, she added, her tone growing acerbic, "I don't need to sacrifice a goat or a chicken or call on the Lord of Darkness. You don't have to drink warm blood right out of a dying animal. Magic isn't evil, it just *is.* It's everywhere around us, in everything, everyone, every rock and blade of grass. It's mathematics and atoms and electrons and protons. It's dark matter and light matter, time and space. *Not evil.*"

I couldn't hide my amusement when I said, "I agree."

"You do?"

"Yes. I should be fine with shoes on." *I hope.*

T. Laine backed away as I scrambled to my feet. T. Laine was medium height, nearly black hair, eyes the same color, a round face but with an aggressive jaw. Pretty. Stubborn. Honest to a fault. Despite Occam's admonishment to not touch me, she grabbed my hand and headed to the house at speed. I'd have had to hit her to get free, which I had no desire to do, so instead, I ran to keep up as she towed me up the drive, up the steps, and into the front of the house.

When my feet touched down it wasn't nearly as bad as before. I made a face to show her it was still *ick* but not unbearable, and she pulled me into the front room and through it, closer to where I could hear Rick talking. I didn't get a good look at the house except for the orchids. Orchids everywhere, all kinds of varieties. And all in bloom. That wasn't right. I yanked my arm free, breaking T. Laine's hold on me long enough to stick my fingers into the coarse wood chips of the orchids nearest.

T. Laine got her fingers back around my arm again and dragged me into what had to be the great room. It was huge, with vaulted space and skylights and a fireplace big enough to roast a whole hog in. The room was decorated in greens. All kinds of greens. And here too were orchids, hundreds of them, lining the shelves of every wall. All blooming. All. *Not possible*. It simply wasn't possible to get every variety of orchid to bloom at once. *Not* possible. Not even for me, and I was *real* good with plants. I rubbed my fingers and thumb together, evaluating what I had felt when I touched the orchid bark mix.

The vampire woman, Mrs. Clayton, looked up when I entered the living room and now stopped talking. Her head tilted weirdly, and she seemed to be sniffing the air, her nostrils fluttering like a horse's did when it sniffed new people, when it was deciding if it was gonna let them close or kick them. Or, in this case, bite them.

"And what is she?" Mrs. Clayton asked, tilting her head to me. "She isn't human."

My head shot up. "At least I'm not rude enough to ask," I said, stung by the question. "Kinda like I wasn't rude enough to say that your floors feel like dead 'possum."

"Nell!" Rick said.

He sounded shocked, but I didn't look his way, keeping my eyes on the dead thing, who seemed, oddly enough, to be holding in a small smile now, buried beneath heaps of worry and fear, but there. "What do *you* think I am?" I asked the vampire.

"I have no idea." Her head tilted again, this time too far, the not-human too far I'd heard vampires could do, which was creepy. "I haven't smelled a creature like you before. I'd be honored to taste your blood someday"—she smiled at last—"despite your appalling lack of manners."

I let my scowl deepen, let her read on my face that drinking my blood was not gonna happen. "Who tends your garden?"

"Nell!" Rick said, a hint of anger in his tone this time.

Again I ignored him. Mrs. Clayton said, "My daughter does." Her smile disappeared, replaced by the weight of her fear. "My daughter is wonderful with plants. She can grow anything, anywhere, anytime. She is in great demand even now, still in high school, with her university degree not yet acquired, to design and work with landscaping."

"And the orchids? She tend them too?"

"Yes. She is—"

"Not a human. You're hiding whatever she is. Maybe to protect her. Maybe for some other reason. And I'm betting she isn't even your daughter, at least not biologically."

Mrs. Clayton's shoulders hunched up and her pupils went black and wide in scarlet sclera. "Hoooow do you know thisss?" she hissed. A real hiss, like a snake. And she leaned forward in the wood chair she was sitting in, her neck stretched out like a lizard's. Her fangs slowly snapped down on their little hinges, and fell into place with a soft *schnick*.

I felt the weight of Mrs. Clayton's whole attention on me, and I nearly flinched, but something told me that if I did, I'd be perceived as breakfast. The chill bumps that been left from the cold tightened again, this time from fear. "The orchids told me. *You* told me when you said she's the gardener. Because no gardener *ever* can make this many orchids bloom at once."

The vampire blinked. Blinked again. And went back to aping human, just that fast. She looked to her left, from orchid to orchid, and her brow crinkled. "I . . ." She twisted her head the other way, taking in the dozens and dozens of plants. "I never thought . . ."

Rick nodded to T. Laine, who put her fingers into the orchid pot nearest. The earth witch jerked her hands away and stumbled back, almost as if she had been shocked by electricity. She flung her hands back and forth, as if shaking water from her fingers, and nodded to Rick, then shrugged, her gestures saying that it was magic, but not something she recognized.

"Mrs. Clayton," Rick said, speaking gently. "If your daughter isn't Mithran or human, we need to know what she is. That might be important to the investigation and to locating her. To getting her back to you." He didn't add the word *alive* at the end of the sentence, but it hung in the air, unspoken but powerful.

From the hallway a woman entered. No. Not a woman. Another vampire. Blond and limber looking, as if she did yoga every day, but with the broad shoulders of a plowman or a boxer. She was pretty in a deadly-looking way. She looked vaguely familiar, which meant I had probably seen her back when Jane Yellowrock had come through my land, but I didn't remember her name, and no one introduced her. Or the vampire behind her, a slender male with long red hair. It was no wonder the floors felt maggoty.

The head vampire's lips pressed together, and she shook her head, but it wasn't in refusal, more as though she was conflicted. "She is gone. In danger." Mrs. Clayton shook her head again, and seemed to decide what she wanted to say. "Mira was a foundling." Her gaze met Rick's, and she added, "Most literally. Clan Blood Master Ming found her on her doorstep sixteen years past. I . . ." The vampire was wringing her hands, and I was certain I had never seen anyone do that. She seemed to notice, and she placed both hands on the arms of her chair, over the knobs, which were carved like African lion heads.

"When no one came forth to claim her, she was placed in the foster care system for a short time before one of my human servants arranged that I might adopt her. She is the only child I've ever had, and I thought her part elven, though mostly human, until last year, close to eighteen months past, I suppose, when her scent began to change. It was only slightly at first. She still smells human, but human and something else, perhaps. Her gift with plants manifested then too."

"Did she start having her menses then?" T. Laine asked. "When the gift with plants started?"

"My daughter has not yet begun her menses."

T. Laine eased into the great room, massaging her fingertips as if they still tingled. "Perhaps her species doesn't have them?"

"We don't know what she is," Mrs. Clayton said uncertainly. "We had considered asking the Europeans when they come to visit the Master of the City of New Orleans, but there is some fear that the oldest Mithrans might claim her as their own under the Vampira Carta. Her lack of humanity may make her fair game to them."

Not much in that sentence made sense, so I made a mental note to look it all up—on my new laptop. When I got time.

Rick said, "Your daughter is an American citizen, no matter what species she is. They can't take her. You'll have the help of PsyLED, the US Department of Homeland Security, Immigration and Customs Enforcement, and the State Department on that. But first we need to find her. What else can you tell us?"

Mrs. Clayton clasped her hands, the fingers of which wore sparkling diamond rings and one single huge black pearl. As if again sensing that she was broadcasting her emotional state, she looked down and spread her fingers wide for a moment, stretching them. Her attention settled on the black pearl ring, and she rotated it with the fingers of the other hand, around and around the digit. "Her . . ." She stopped and started again. "My daughter has . . . pointed ears." No one in the room said anything, and the silence went on a beat too long, making me aware of where every member of the team was. Tandy stood against a wall, his eyes flicking from person to person, as if he was picking up emotional tags from each of us as well as from Mrs. Clayton. Occam was kneeling, his fingers spread on the floor, his weight on the balls of his feet, and something made the posture look very catlike and dangerous, as if he was about to pounce on prey. Paka stood behind Rick, watching, her eyes slit, gaze piercing. Other humans stood in the opening to the great room—law enforcement, wearing suits and ugly shoes. The FBI, I decided, the team that had set up the electronic equipment, waiting to hear about a ransom call. JoJo was standing with them.

The vampire went on, still twirling her pearl ring around her finger, her attention on only it. "They were noticeable on her baby photographs. For some years she wore her hair over them, until they kept growing and her hair no longer hid them. Now the points are quite pronounced. I purchased a charm for her with a glamour in it to keep the tips hidden. The glamour must have sunlight to recharge it. It looks like this." She extended her hand to display the black pearl. "She wears it on her left hand.

"And Mira also . . ." The vampire's brows came together. "She has no body hair at all, though her brows are quite unruly and difficult to keep shaped. She also has acute seasonal affective disorder." Mrs. Clayton looked up for a moment, her eyes sweeping the room before returning to her hands. "She needs far more sunlight than most people. If left too long in the dark, she becomes ill, physically so. In winter, when the days are shorter, Mira is badly affected by the early nights, and so we have installed artificial lighting in her room, to give her bright lights, what they call *full spectrum*, and she uses them several hours each day. If the people who took her don't allow her enough sunlight, her glamour will fail. Her ears will show." She frowned and shook her head, the heavy worry sloping her shoulders again. "She will become angry, sometimes violent. Enough darkness and Mira's hair will begin to fall out, she will fall into a deep depression, and she will sleep away the day. Day after day."

The vampire smiled, a bittersweet expression that made her look totally human. "My daughter is gentle and full of life and can make anything grow. And she hates the dark. She is so very, very unlike me. We are total opposites in everything. And yet, in the hours of dusk and dawn, we have built a life here. I would give up all that I am and all that I have to see her safe and free." She looked at the FBI team, two men and a woman, still standing in the doorway. Her voice dropped an octave, almost to a growl when she added, "No matter what they ask, I will give them. Make certain that they know that when they call."

The phrase hung on the air between us all, unspoken: *If they call*. So much said in so few words, when I was accustomed to lots of words, and total clarity of intent from everyone, in the way of God's Cloud of Glory. The cultural differences were making my new job challenging.

"Agent LaFleur," the FBI woman said. "We'd like a word with you, please."

Rock nodded and left the room. The others drifted back into the other parts of the house, leaving me alone with the vampire. Mrs. Clayton didn't seem to notice they were gone for long seconds before she looked up from her hands to see the room, empty but for me. "I had wondered if you were the same species as my daughter. There is something of the same scent about you, but"—she shrugged—"different as well. Are your ears . . . ?"

"Not pointed," I said, and pushed back my hair to show the rounded curves. "No glamour. No surgery to make them round." I didn't add that if I'd been born with pointed ears, I might have been smothered in my cradle.

An uneasy silence settled between us, and I felt like I should go closer and sit near her. It was what the churchwomen did when there was distress. Hugs and kind words. But I couldn't get any closer to the death feeling I got from Mrs. Clayton. So I said, "I'm sorry I got all riled. I don't know what kind a species I am either, so I took offense when none was intended." I mimicked her shrug. "You're not my first vampire, ma'am, but this is my first vampire house."

She smiled slightly. "Do I still feel like dead opossum?"

"No offense intended, ma'am. Honestly."

She stared up at me suddenly, her eyes black again, and scary looking. I grew instantly still, like a rabbit under the eyes of a hawk, and tried to draw a breath that seemed stuck in my throat. "My daughter's life is in your hands," the vampire said. "Yours and the others'. Please. Get her back for me."

"We will do everything possible, Mrs. Clayton," Rick said coming back through the door. "PsyLED will be taking over the investigation of your daughter's disappearance, with FBI assistance. The Bureau has done a spectacular job, and will still be working the case, but we'll be dedicating *all* of the efforts of our entire team on Mira. Mira alone."

I realized that with Mira not being human, responsibility for her case fell directly into PsyLED's lap. Anxiety I hadn't expected wrapped itself around me and tightened like a boa constrictor.

The vampire looked to me. "You. You will get her back for me," she commanded. Before I could reply, Mrs. Clayton got up and left the room. Fast. Way faster than a human. Scary fast. With a little snap of air that made my ears pop. But at least the maggoty feeling dissipated some with her gone.

To us, Rick said, "Their systems are already in place and FBI will continue to monitor the house and phones. We'll be handling the investigation on the streets and electronically. JoJo, you'll liaise with the FBI, remaining here. You being human will make them happier than any of the rest of us. I want to know everything they learn the moment they find it out.

And I'm rather certain that they haven't told us everything, so be nosy. If Mrs. Clayton or one of her Mithrans come back out to visit, be nosy with her too. See if she left out anything, any detail. Even if it doesn't seem important."

JoJo smiled and flicked a ring in her nostril, leaving it swinging. "I'm real good at being nosy, boss."

Rick smiled and nodded the rest of us to the door. "Let's go."

The special agents talked while Rick drove, and this time I took a place in back, on the bench-style seat, beside Paka, who curled up like a cat and fell instantly asleep. Again, I had nothing to offer and sat silent, listening to the woman's purring breath.

We were nearly back at the hotel when Rick said, "It's almost midnight. Tandy, you and T. Laine are the night owls. You take the first shift and go over all the FBI information on all the cases. Compare and contrast everything with the other cases and with Girl . . ." He stopped. "With Mira Clayton." I realized that using pseudonyms for the girls wasn't going to work anymore. We had been to her house. Touched her magic and her personal belongings. Met her mother. We had our own girl. That had made it personal, even if it wasn't supposed to become so. Rick said, "The rest of us will get some shut-eye."

T. Laine said, "I need caffeine and sustenance for an all-nighter. Coffee and lots of it, and pizza. And it comes off the company plastic."

"Done," Rick said, tossing his cell phone to the witch. "There's Community dark roast coffee in my bag that I'll contribute to the cause. Order a couple of large. One supreme and one veggie lovers."

"Boss, I love you."

Rick chuckled, and I didn't understand what had happened until Tandy said, "Community Coffee is from Louisiana, and it's hard to get here. Rick has it shipped in monthly for his personal use. It's *really* good coffee. And the pizza just went on the unit's credit card, so we don't have to figure out how to list things on our expense reports. Makes things easier."

I nodded, suddenly exhausted. The weight of the day landed on me, the prickly feeling of being around all the people and creatures and their multitiered and interlaced emotions, the need to be alone, on my property, with the woods at my back, all heavy. "I need to go home," I said, stretching. "How soon do you need me back in the morning?"

Rick looked at me in the rearview mirror and said, "How does six a.m. sound?"

I'd have to be up long before five o'clock to make that. "Horrible," I said. "But I'll be at the hotel by six."

"Good," he said. "Because if Mira Clayton is being held somewhere in the dark, we may need to move fast. This abduction wasn't exactly like the others, so the first thing I want to do is rule out any copycat involvement."

I considered that statement in light of the girl's need for the sun. Would she really die if she was kept in the dark too long? I felt my ears, rounded and human. I sometimes wondered if I'd die if I left Soulwood for too long a time, as if I was tied to the land. Maybe it was like that for Mira, with the sun. Out of nowhere, Pea leaped across the room and landed in my lap, chittering loudly, distracting. Pushing her away, I repeated softly to myself, "Six a.m. I can do that."

TEN

The cats were on the front porch, yowling, when I got home. I let them in, fed them enough cat kibble to keep them around without keeping them from working, and while they ate, I stirred up the last of the coals in the stove, added some kindling and winter wood that would burn fast and hot, to warm the cold house. The chill of fall had left the place miserable, and I'd need a shower to wake up in the morning. For tonight, I was simply too tired to wait on hot water. I dumped some beans into a pot, checked them for rocks or grit, rinsed them, and added more water, leaving them to soften on the warming shelf above the stove. Then I used the tepid water in the stove's water heater and a washrag, standing in the tiny bathroom behind the kitchen to give myself, my face, and my feet what Mama called a sink bath. I brushed and braided my wind-snarled hair, pulled on my winter flannels for the first time this season, and climbed the stairs to my cot. At least it was warmer upstairs. After a few spoonfuls of cold stew, I fell into bed with the cats for what would surely be far too little sleep.

As the chilly sheets warmed and sleep enfolded me, I thought about my woods. I had never been away for so long at a time before. And never so late into the night. It was strange to contemplate, but I felt as if they were sighing with relief at my return. As if they had missed me.

I lifted a hand out from the covers and touched the wood floor, feeling, somehow, the chill of the wind outside, stirring the trees with the thought of winter's sleep. Feeling their leaves closing off with the season as they changed color and fell. It felt as if the woods had been searching for me for hours and were finally at rest. At the fringe of the property was the darkness I had felt, restless and fragmented and afraid, if broken shadows could be any of those things. But it seemed calmer than before. That had to be good. In the distance, gunfire again echoed through the night, new and worrisome.

I rolled over in the warming bedding, pushed a cat's body off me, closed my eyes, and let sleep take me.

I was awake at five a.m. on Friday, gripey, gritty eyed, cold, and wanting coffee. I hadn't used any of the battery power the night before and so had lights to help wake me, and soon had coffee percolating on the woodstove and fresh wood heating the house. To make it easier to heat the main part of the house, I kept the extra bedrooms closed off in the winter—the bedroom once used by Leah and John, and the bedrooms upstairs that had been used by his second and third wives, Brenda Bell and Leota, the wives who had left him when he couldn't give them babies, long before he married me.

I'd met them a time or two after I married John and before we left the church. They were happy women, full of satisfaction, with a passel of young'uns between them. After they each had divorced from John, they had married brothers, twins, and lived in a huge house of merged families. They seemed nice enough and happy enough, and if I was honest, I was glad they hadn't stayed with John. He'd not have needed me if they had stayed, and I might have been given to the down-the-hill Hamiltons, Maw-maw's folk, or given as a junior wife or concubine to the colonel. Or maybe not, if Sister Erasmus was right about Maw-maw and Mama conniving to keep me out of the colonel's hands. If John and Leah hadn't been around, maybe my family would have found another way to keep me safe. I wanted to talk to them soon and . . . and see if I could determine the truth from the untruth of John's tales to me about my family. Just thinking that he had misled me left a hurting place in my heart.

I showered while the coffee perked, and washed my hair. There was enough leftover power to dry my hair with the handheld hair dryer that I seldom used. And I had one clean gray skirt I could wear, with leggings underneath for warmth. Over two T-shirts and a buttoned blouse, I added a thick, hand-crocheted cardigan. On my feet I pulled two pairs of socks and my best pair of heavy, lace-up ankle boots. The boots were scuffed and needed to be polished, but they were comfortable and warm enough for all day. The outfit's colors didn't match, but the soft grays and greens didn't clash either. I could shuck layers as the day warmed, if it warmed. I braided my waist-length hair into a crown around my head and slipped a thick hairband around my neck, one I could pull up around my ears and over my head to hide the crown, which might be considered too proud for a childless widder-woman to wear in public.

Dressed, I stopped and looked at myself in the mirrors. And frowned. I was wearing clothes the church would approve of. Until just this moment, I hadn't even noticed that . . . that I didn't own anything that the church would scowl over except my gardening overalls. I didn't wear jeans like T. Laine, or the wildly patterned, filmy skirts like JoJo wore. Or the flesh-hugging tank tops and slacks that Paka wore. I was . . . I was still a *churchwoman*.

I studied myself, my face pale in the mirror. My skin was good thanks to the creams and oils I made for myself, but I could use some makeup, some blush to pinken my cheeks. Maybe some lipstick. And mascara, though I feared I'd poke out an eye with the wand. *Makeup.* And lessons to use it. Maybe some colorful shirts. Pink. *Red.* And maybe I'd get my ears pierced and buy some earrings. Tingles flew through me at the improper and unholy thoughts. And I smiled. Next time I had money, I'd stop by the CVS and peruse the aisles.

I ate an apple, drank two cups of coffee, and rinsed the beans and added fresh water, salt, and a packet of hot peppers and herbs I kept premixed for beans. I dumped in a cup of apple cider vinegar and some dried onion. Putting the stew pot on the hottest part of the stove, I set the dampers to last the day, then surveyed the house. The sheets needed to be changed, the stove's wood ash cleaned out, and sachets in Leah's old closet needed to be replaced. Out in the garden, the trellis was listing, needing to be staked up. My tools were going to rust if they didn't get cleaned. The dead plants needed to be pulled, diseased leaves removed. But none of that was urgent; it all was going to have to wait.

I picked up my keys and small bag and let the cats out. I

stood on the back porch and *knew* that no one was on my land. No one was watching. I walked through the dark and started up the Chevy, pulling out of the drive and down the mountain.

I beat the rush-hour traffic and stopped at the store to pick up a big bag of flour, some flax meal, and black quinoa, wishing I had money to buy one of the insulated coffee cups that the special agents used so often. This was what the churchmen taught—that association with nonchurch members would change a body and soul, sending a believer into covetousness, idolatry, and sin. I was already heading down that road to damnation, but I discovered that I didn't care. I wove through the near-empty streets with a dark resolve, hands clinging to the steering wheel with a death grip, as if making this drive was sealing me into something I had never imagined and would never be able to return from.

I was at the hotel early. There was no light under the door at the room, and so I went back to the lobby and got the desk clerk to remind me how to log on to the hotel Wi-Fi. Once in, I e-mailed them on the laptop that I was downstairs. I also discovered several orders for herbal treatments and oils, and the good news that I had received nearly fifty dollars through Old Lady Stevens' PayPal account, which meant I could stop by her place, pick up the money, and buy more groceries. I could also put some cash aside for the stove wood I'd need in order to get through the winter. I firmly turned away the temptation to buy lipstick and fripperies. When I got paid—if I got paid—by Rick's agency, I'd see about giving in to that particular delicious sin.

The smell of coffee met me at the suite's common room when I opened the door with my card key, that and stale pizza, and multiple creatures under stress. Unwashed humans and cats, sweat, sleeplessness, and frustration gave the air a strong, unpleasant tang. It made me wary, and I stopped just inside the door, surveying the small space.

Tandy and T. Laine looked the most strained, which made sense as they had pulled the all-nighter. They were curled on the sofa, heads at either end and feet in the middle of the sofa as if they'd been playing footsie. T. Laine was dressed in wrinkled black sweats and a flamingo pink turtleneck T-shirt, and was wrapped in a blanket. Tandy was dressed in what looked like flannel pajama bottoms and a sweatshirt. It was an intimate scene, too personal and cozy for my comfort level.

Tandy stopped my reaction with, "We haven't been fooling around, Nell, despite the comfy impression."

"Good God, no," T. Laine said, swearing. "I adore Tandy, but having sex with a guy who can tell what I'm feeling would be miserable. I couldn't fake anything."

Tandy offered a small tired smile, as if they'd had this conversation often. "True. There's no cheating with an empath, but then again, we always know what our partners want and need. Empaths make the best lovers."

"I'll make you a coffee mug with that on it for Christmas, but since you're the only empath any of us know, I'll have to take your word for it. I need my bed." She called louder, "Rick! Nell's here and we can pass the baton. I'm beat."

Pass the baton?

The door to the room with the super-king-sized bed opened, revealing the foot of the bed and the rumpled covers with Paka still curled in the twisted blankets. Rick was dressed, like T. Laine, in sweats with socks on his feet. He turned and crossed the room to tap on one door into an adjoining room. Occam stepped out instantly and glided past the king bed without looking at the occupant.

Unlike the others, Occam was dressed for the day, in black jeans and a black T-shirt, though without shoes. The tops of his bare feet were thinly dusted with a lace of light brown hair and his toenails were rounded and smooth. Something about the smooth toenails struck me as so very odd. John had never smoothed his nails. He had kept them clipped, but the ends had been jagged and the nails themselves had been thick and rough. They had always been rough on the sheets, ripping them more than once. And they had been grating on my calves and thighs. I'd hated his toenails. But Occam's were . . . nice. Even his fingernails were rounded and smooth.

A flare of something unknown sped through me, and I dropped my laptop on the low table, went to the coffeemaker, and busied myself at the machine. When I had a fresh pot gurgling I turned around and caught Tandy watching me. His face was solemn and intent. I realized that he'd felt my spike of . . . whatever that had been. And my reaction after. He gave a small nod that I couldn't interpret.

I glanced at Occam. He was eating a slice of cold pizza, his blondish head bent to capture the cold pie in strong white teeth, his hair swinging forward and curling on the ends. Such long hair wasn't all that rare to see on a man, but such beautiful hair was. His hair gleamed in the lamplight. It had to be the cat genes.

When all but Paka were assembled, and coffee had been passed around, and a second pot started, Tandy said, "To rule out God's Cloud of Glory Church and to search for signs of HST, the FBI is making RVAC flyovers of the compound at dawn. We have prelim footage and some still shots of panel vans that could match the description of the snatch-and-grab kidnapvan used by the kidnapmaniacs, except they had plates and the camera angle wasn't sufficient to determine if any vehicles had a dent to match the kidnapvan."

Kidnapmaniacs. I had the feeling that Tandy was using the jargon to help me relax. The terminology sounded like made-up words or street slang, not cop lingo, unlike *RVAC*, which sounded all law enforcement with the initials instead of words. "RVAC. Is that like a drone?" I asked.

Rick lifted his hand and dropped it fast, hesitating, as if he wished those words hadn't been spoken. Almost unwillingly, he said, "RVACS are remote-viewing aircraft. Smaller, quieter, easier to control than a drone."

I let a tiny smile soften my face at the hesitant and complicated body language in the small room. Rick was against letting me know things about their practices and technology, but Tandy's complacent expression said that it was too late now, and had been done deliberately.

Tandy placed photos on the tabletop, saying, "Each one shows the cult compound from different vantage points. Note the vans parked here"—he pointed with his strangely marked hand, one finger tapping pictures that had been printed out on plain paper—"and here, all pale-colored, gray, blue, or white."

I said, "If I remember, that's where the church's passenger vans have always been kept. God's Cloud buys old vans and paints them white."

Rick raised his eyebrows at me. "And you didn't think to tell us that until now?"

I realized that with the church and the kidnapmaniacs using white panel vans, I probably should have mentioned that. "Sorry," I said softly. "Not used to thinking about everyone and everything being some kinda clue."

"Where do visitors park?" Rick asked.

"Beside the chapel building," I said, pointing.

"No vehicles there at the time this was taken," Tandy said.

"We also have good visual intel on the building that Nell said was the old punishment house and is now the guest quarters. There is no sign of anyone using it. Our contact on the FBI will do an infrared and low-light cam flyover tonight to verify." He tapped again. Four pictures, this time each one from a different side of the building, but all from above. RVAC height. The churchmen had been right about the government invading privacy and keeping watch. Their conspiracy theories had been confirmed.

Part of me wanted to make a scene about privacy. Another part was in fear for the missing girls and my own sisters. And yet another part was wondering why the outsiders were so important, why missing nonchurch girls were worth a hunt, but the evils taking place against children within the church had deserved a blind eye for so many decades. Social services had returned so many children after their raid that it seemed the atrocities committed by some of the churchmen had been swept under the rug and the children there again forgotten.

T. Laine took up the narrative, saying, "County and state canine units have spent the last twenty-four hours on the first two scenes, in the order the girls were taken. They got a hit on the ballet school site, though the feds can't tell us what it means. Or won't. What I was told was that the dogs went, and I quote, 'Squirrelly.'" She made finger quotes in the air. "Frankly, we were there, so we might be to blame. They now want to keep the dogs separated, not mixing up dogs and scents on the nonhuman case, so we have a new team coming in from Nashville. This team has worked paranormal cases before and will be here by one p.m."

"Specifics on the K-nines?" Rick asked.

"One tracking dog, one air dog. We haven't had rain, so we might get a scent," Tandy said.

I knew a lot about hunting dogs. A tracking/trailing dog followed a scent on the ground. An air-scenting dog followed it through the air. Some dogs did both tracking and air scenting. If there was little wind and no rain, air dogs with really good noses had been known to follow scents for miles. The official record was twenty-four miles to rescue a kidnapped girl. But I remembered the wind yesterday and had serious concerns about that possibility.

Rick said, "When JoJo gets here, we'll get a quick debrief, and then I want her and you two"—he pointed to T. Laine and Tandy—"to have five hours of downtime before joining the canine unit, to keep the dogs from wigging out at our cat smell. The dogs will start at Wyatt School and move into the woods nearby," Rick said. "And before you say anything, yes, we should have stayed out of the woods until the dogs had a chance on-site, but we have better noses than humans, even in human form, and I had hoped we might find something. I've requested a dedicated dog team. We might get one, making it easier to track with dogs accustomed to our scents, but I'm not holding my breath. And even if we got a team, we'd have to share them with all PsyLED units nationally."

"Brute?" Tandy asked and then yawned hugely.

Rick looked at me. "Brute is a werewolf stuck in his beast form. He's usually part of this team, but he's . . ." Rick paused as if trying to figure out how to say the unexplainable. ". . . not someone we can compel. He's in New Orleans, spying on, or maybe working for, the Master of the City there. Unless he asks to join us, that's a no.

"The rest of us smell like nonhumans, and that's why I'm pulling JoJo off the FBI and back to us for the day. We might confuse the dogs' noses, so she can take point. The all-nighter means we'll have three team members out for the morning. While JoJo, T. Laine, and Tandy are getting shut-eye, we'll divvy up the teams differently today. Occam will still handle the trailer park door-to-door, but, Nell, can you go with Occam today, once the canine units are done? See if you feel anything about our girl?"

I nodded slowly. I could work with Occam. That funny feeling I'd felt when I saw the smooth toenails and fingernails on the werecat was gone.

"I want T. Laine in after the canine unit completes its search, to see what she can pick up magic-wise once we have a trail. *If* we have a trail."

Tandy said, "While we've been talking, I got a text. JoJo has news, and she should be here in—" JoJo shoved open the door and flung herself into the room, dropped two boxes of Krispy Kreme donuts on the table, and raced through the room saying, "I gotta pee like a racehorse!"

I thought about that peculiar statement while Rick opened the top box, took one and passed around the box. Through a mouth full of donut, Tandy murmured, "Dear God in heaven, they are Hot Nows. Thank you, Jesus, for the Krispy Kreme company, and may you bless them and JoJo forever."

I had a feeling he wasn't really praying, so it might have been blasphemy. Or I thought that until I bit tentatively into a glazed ring of fried dough. It melted in my mouth. Sugary sweetness flared through me. I wanted to pray thanks too. It was, by far, the best thing I had ever eaten. It beat Leah's apple uglies by a mile and a half, and her uglies had been declared the best pastries the churchwomen had ever made. It seemed the others in the room agreed, as there was no sound but moans of pleasure, the soft sounds of chewing, licking and the slurping of coffee. I drank my coffee from the Styrofoam cup and ate some more and thought that this donut might really *be* holy.

I finished my donut and licked my fingers. Into the silence I asked, "How sure are we that all the girls were taken by the same people? I mean, we only have timing and age. What if someone heard about the first kidnappings and used the opportunity to take Mira? If someone had figured out that she had some kind of magic, she might be useful. Or maybe someone wanted control over the vampires."

Every eye came to me. It was unnerving.

"What did I say?" I asked, taking a second donut.

"Part of the briefing this morning," Rick said, his face too rigid to be expressionless, "that we have yet to get to. Part of what we discussed last night after you left. In this room."

"I did a sweep," T. Laine said, starting on her own second donut. "No electronics."

"Except we didn't sweep the electronics themselves," Occam said.

"And there's no way to sweep her gift," JoJo said, coming back into the room, "since we don't know what it is."

"And I didn't set a circle at either meeting," T. Laine said.

None of which made any sense at all.

They were all staring at me. Evaluating. Calculating. *Accusing.* I had been looked at this way by the church for years, so it didn't surprise me. Too much. But, oddly, it hurt. I bit into the second donut and thought about what we had all been saying, trying to figure out what was going on and how to get beyond it. Whatever *it* was.

"She doesn't know what we're talking about," Tandy said, "except the accusation part. She understands *that*, as if she expected to be accused of something. Or, rather"—he tilted his head, his eyes half-lidded—"as if she has always been accused, all her life, and why should we be any different?"

And then I did understand. They were accusing me of planting listening devices in their room or listening in some magical way. I stopped chewing and sat there, in the uphol-stered chair, thinking about the accusation, gooey dough in my mouth. Thinking about the conspiracy theorists in the compound of God's Cloud of Glory Church.

I felt something strange bubble in my chest, push its way up and out through me. It was that strange sound again. *I was laughing.* It was a peculiar noise, sort of giggly and high-pitched, muffled by the donut in my mouth. I chewed and giggled some more, investigating this new feeling inside me. Giddy. Silly. The others looked baffled. I shook my head and managed to get the bite of donut swallowed, without choking, and drank some coffee to make the half-chewed bite go on down.

"She had no idea what we were talking about," Tandy said, "until she started laughing. And now she's . . . I don't know what to call it. Drunk on amusement?"

"Nell?" Rick said.

I sipped more coffee, still giggling. When I could speak, I

said, "Conspiracy theorists." Tandy started laughing too, one hand over his mouth as he chewed. Much more slowly, as they pieced together what I might have meant, the rest of them started laughing.

Rick shook his head. "We are . . . conspiracy theorists? Like your cult is?"

"Not *my* cult. I told you that." I licked delicious sugar off my mouth. "And I told you that I'm capable of deductive reasoning. And you told me that you wanted me because I thought on both sides of a box, inside and outside. So either you trust me or you don't." My amusement died in an instant, and I glared at him to make my point, my church vernacular hitting its strongest twang in years. "But iffen you accuse me of cheating again, I'm outta here, slicker 'n goose grease. We clear on that?"

Rick's humor fled as well, and he studied me with steady eyes. "We're clear. I'm sorry, Nell."

"Forgiven. Besides, you mentioned that word, *copycat*, yesterday, and I looked it up. And, logically, I understand why you have to watch me. Now what's in the other box? 'Cause I want more."

Tandy smiled happily. "Nell has never tasted a Krispy Kreme before."

"Never?" JoJo said, incredulous, opening the second box as I finished off my second glazed. "Try this one. It's blueberry filled." She took another and bit down, something gooey and red poking out a hole in the side of the donut. "Thish 'uns raz'ber'. You go' try one deese too," she said, with her mouth full. She swallowed. "That cult is evil through and through to keep the women from eating one of God's finest creations. 'Cause I'm betting the men eat them all the time."

She had a point. And it made me mad. Something to think about later.

Rick said, "JoJo? Report."

JoJo said, "Two things. One, Mrs. Clayton told me that over the course of the last ten years, six of Knoxville's fangheads have gone missing. Disappeared, like poof"—she snapped her fingers—"and never returned. I got to thinking about the men at God's Cloud and wondered if the one suckhead they took— the one that Jane Yellowrock got back—might not have been the first or only. Something to look into."

She stopped talking and drank down a bottle of water in one continuous glug. When the bottle was crinkled up empty, she tossed it into a plastic garbage can and said, "You should see me chug beer. I'm only two seconds off the world beer mile champion."

I had no idea what that meant and jotted it down for future research.

"The FBI has received a ransom demand on Girl Two, one million dollars for her safe return, same account numbers in the Turks for the transfer of funds. Again, they let her talk to her family. She was alive and unhurt. Call came in on a cell, but by the time the agents got a team there, they were gone. No cameras, no prints but the girl's. They have this down to a science, just like the HST always did things, with multiple abductions and multiple ransom demands so that law enforcement is overwhelmed.

"FBI has run all the taped calls through various kinds of software and determined that every conversation took place in a vehicle, diesel engine—unlike the kidnap van, which was gas-powered—and the engine was an older model with some kind of knock," JoJo said. "That is the total of what they have. Our unsubs are low-tech, fast, and smart. No mistakes. Rach—sorry, Girl One's family deposited the money they got through Clan Master Ming, but she has still not been returned to her family. The family of Girl Two has taken similar steps. The Clayton family has not been contacted for a ransom. The feds did prelim evals on the bank account number given by the kidnapper. Because it's a foreign, private financial institution, it's hands-off as far as getting depositor info, but they're applying political pressure and financial leverage. The feds might be able to buy the information on the offshore account."

I didn't know what the Turks were, except people from Turkey, maybe, so I tapped laptop keys to check on that.

JoJo pulled on the earrings of one ear as she talked, something she had done before. The motion looked like something she did to calm herself or to focus. Or maybe, this time, to stay awake. "Oh. I'll update our files as soon as I get some shut-eye. I'm too tired to type right now. Where was I?" She yawned hugely. "Oh yeah. They're using sat maps and ALDS," she said, "to narrow down where the next call might come from, and trying to figure out what make and model might sound like that diesel. Nothing's been determined yet. There isn't enough manpower in the state to cover all the possible locations."

"ALDS? I asked.

"Algorithm for Location Differentiation Software," T. Laine said. "It's an acronym for the algorithm software used by law enforcement and the military to determine comparison of locations. For instance, if a military or civilian enemy typically uses one type of location to commit a crime, or drop off money, or make an exchange, that locale could be assigned a number to each set of parameters. Like, no cameras might get the locale a ten. Easy access to four outbound streets would get an eight. Three streets would get a five. Traffic might be accessed and numbered by time of day. But they assign a number for each facet of each similar location. It sounds fancy and high-tech, but so far, the math has shown little use in real-life sitches."

Sitches, I thought. *Situations. Got it.* Info popped up on my screen. Not Turkey the country, but the islands. The Turks and Caicos Islands were a British Overseas Territory consisting of tropical islands. The larger Caicos Islands and smaller Turks Islands were in the Lucayan Archipelago, which were located between Cuba and Haiti. I had never heard of them, but they were big business in the financial world, with seven licensed banking institutions and several private financial organizations.

I said, "Can we go back to *offshore accounts*? I don't understand."

"The HST uses them all the time," Rick said. "Using offshore accounts and rerouting the money through other banking institutions and countries is the best way to get through an abduction without being caught. Of course, they would need to go to the island country to open the account. So far as I know, opening an initial account isn't something that can be done from home. Everything about the ransom MO, if not the kidnappings themselves, points to HST, which means that the Human Speakers have ties to this. They have to be in Knoxville."

JoJo said, "So someone in the HST—and yes, the FBI is assuming HST is behind at least some of the abductions—had to go out of the country. They'd need passports and money in hand; cash is preferred to open most offshore accounts. Dozens of HST members have passports, and the feds have to know how many have traveled out of country recently, but they didn't share that info with me or the local LEOs. So I ran my own search, through our own databases, of known HST members who've traveled outside of the country. We have four."

All I got from that was more questions, but the only thing I could think to say was, "Leos?"

"Law Enforcement Officers," Tandy said gently. "Ease up, you guys. She's . . . rattled."

"I want a travel mug like you have," I said. The words came out of nowhere as I kicked off my shoes and pulled my legs into the chair, smoothing my skirt, wrapping my arms around my knees, hugging myself. "I have to use a Styrofoam cup, and you have cool metal travel mugs. I want one." They all stared at me for too long, silent. I said, "That was a non sequitur. I needed time to think."

Occam's mouth stretched slowly into a grin, his lips wide and his eyes unblinking, much like a cat—maybe *his* cat, his werecat. He stood and took a mug from beside the sink near the microwave. His back to the room, he said, "Non sequiturs are also very catlike." Which made me blink. As the others watched, he rinsed the steel mug, poured coffee into it, and turned to me. "Sugar? Creamer?"

"Both," I said, my voice hesitant. "Thank you."

"Anytime, sugar. Anytime," Occam said, his voice a deep burr of sound as he prepared my coffee. It all felt oddly intimate. John had never fixed my coffee. In my experience, men didn't fix coffee, not even their own. He pushed down the travel mug top and held it out to me.

I unwrapped my arms, accepted the mug from him, and drank. The coffee was perfectly heated and sweet. I smiled up at him, knowing there was relief in my eyes and, from the way his nostrils fluttered, probably in my scent. He smiled back, and I felt less stressed about being in the hotel room, with people who had been strangers only a few days ago.

Rick passed around several lists of HST members for all of us to study, all hard copies in a purple folder. One was a universal list, of every family and family member in the organization. There were files for each, listing crimes they were purported to have committed or been an accessory to, before or after the fact. There were lots of photos, some clearly selfies from social media, most taken with long-distance cameras, which again proved the church's claim that the government was spying on its citizens. Sometimes conspiracy theories were real, but sometimes they were for a good cause.

There were even some children, which means they were being brought up in an environment where hate was not only acceptable, but looked upon as good and righteous and proper. Which was the way the church did things. Raise up a man in the way he ought to go and he will return to it when he is old—a Bible paraphrase I had grown up with. I thought about the boy with the assault rifle, and the gunshots at night, and paid close attention to all the photos of young men, but none looked like him, which relieved me more than I had expected.

Rick's phone rang, that odd little tinkle sound of his cell. He answered it, "Senior Special Agent Rick LaFleur," which meant he didn't recognize the number. I was learning things, and that small bit of awareness made me feel good about myself in ways I didn't understand too clearly. This time, Rick didn't leave the room for the call, just listened and grunted a few times. He said, "Copy. Thank you."

Moments later Rick's cell rang and again he took the call. Tandy's minute cringe told me it was bad news. Rick hung up and said, "We now have a Girl Four. She's a little older than the others, age nineteen, a college student, working off campus. We think she was picked up when she got off work about half an hour ago, from Sweet P's Bar-B-Que and Soul House on Maryville Pike. A group of fishermen saw her go outside to wait on her ride. Approximately four minutes later, they saw a white van pull off. Two minutes after that time, they left. When the girl's ride got there, approximately two minutes after that, she was gone. Eight minutes, give or take. That's a very small window of time to plan for, but someone pulled it off. When the Amber Alert hit the airwaves, the fishermen realized they had probably been paying their bills during the abduction, but by the time they called it in, too much time had passed. A team already ruled out complicity by the fishermen."

By the time he finished speaking, all the unit were buried in their tablets and laptops, keys tapping softly. Girl Four was named Anne Rindfliesch, and her parents were land rich, owning acres of the Tennessee countryside. No known connections to vampires.

"We need to see the crime scene," T. Laine muttered.

"We will," Rick said. "As soon as the feds are done. The family of Girl Four has no known current association to Ming, but they also have liquid funds available and won't need to contact vamps. The feds are at the house of Girl Four, on high alert, waiting for a call."

"HST has never taken more than two abductees at one time," T. Laine said.

"Yeah. This isn't a characteristic HST MO," JoJo said, fingers tapping on her keyboard.

"No. It isn't," Rick said, his tone grim. "The feds think they need money, and that's why the exceptionally large number of abductions. And the family of Girl Two just paid the ransom demand to the account in the Turks."

ELEVEN

With a quick look my way, Rick said, "The account for the bank in the Turks is under the name Johnson Campbell, DOB eleven twenty-five, nineteen eighty. That name is not on the list of HST members, but the bank is resisting turning over any more information than the name and date of birth. Nell? Is he a God's Cloud member?"

I leaned forward a fraction of an inch and then sat back against the cushions and nursed my coffee. After a bit I said, "I don't know a Johnson Campbell of any age in the church, or any other Campbell in that age range, but Campbell is a common enough name, not solely a church name. And the churchmen don't do offshore banking. They don't get passports. They don't travel."

JoJo stood, looking wobbly on her feet. "Looks like things will get interesting today, but I'm for a shower and bed. Clearer heads than mine can come up with our next move. Night, all."

"Me too," T. Laine said, following JoJo back through Rick and Paka's room. To her roommate, she said, "I showered at four to wake me up, so we don't have to flip for who gets to shower first. I'm setting a silence circle around my bed. Don't touch it."

JoJo mumbled something vaguely obscene under her breath and they closed the room door. Tandy studied me a moment and then smiled. "I'm going to turn in too. Have fun, you guys."

That left only Occam, Rick, and me in the small sitting area, Occam staring at his laptop, eyes scanning left and right as he read, his blondish hair hanging loose around his jaw. Rick was tapping keys on his. I didn't have an assignment, so I spent the time reading online about all the kinds of paranormal crimes and creatures that fell under PsyLED's purview, and looking over case reports from previous PsyLED investigations. And then studying about PsyLED itself. PsyLED was a semisecret government organization under the leadership of Director Clarence Lester Woods, and he was a former special forces guy, a Green Beret who had seen active duty. He had lost an arm to an IED—an improvised explosive device—and when he left the military, he'd taken a job with DoD. He'd put PsyLED together and still ran it, directly under the authority of the Department of Defense.

Each PsyLED agent (no matter how well trained in other law enforcement agencies or departments) received more training at a PsyLED instruction facility. The person who ran the school that trained all PsyLED special agents was the CA—chief administrator, Dr. Smythe. A *woman*. I smiled at that. A woman in charge of an entire school. The Training Facility for the Psychometry Law Enforcement Division of Homeland Security—called Spook School by the trainees—was located near Langley, Virginia, on the grounds of an old private school.

I closed the search into PsyLED and started one into the accumulated case files on the church raid. I was still studying them when Rick called for lunch break to KFC. My head was filled with all sorts of thoughts and questions, none of them leading to good outcomes under the current situation. Or *sitch*.

Before we could get out of the room, Rick's cell phone rang. He answered with, "LeFleur." Then he said, "We'll be there in twenty." He pressed a button on his cell and said to us, "Grab your gear. The body of Girl One was just found."

Body? The room went silent, and Occam and I turned to the photo of the girl. Her name was Rachel Ames. And she was dead.

Into the silence, his voice gentle, Rick said, "I said to grab your gear. The FBI has requested an update on the abductions. In person."

"HST does not kill its abductees. They *always* come through. It's their rep," Occam explained. "Even law enforcement knows it. It's less likely that people will pay if they know their loved ones turn up dead."

"This changes the focus of the investigation," Rick said, "from HST members as primary suspects to multiple potential groups."

"Okay." I was sitting in the backseat, listening and eating fried chicken livers as Rick drove and talked.

"We knew that two of the kidnap victims were related, several generations back, to Ming, the Mithran Master of the City, and of course Mira Clayton's mother is one of Ming's scions. Things were starting to point back to vamps on every level, which was also unusual for HST. During the night, JoJo was building lists of possible suspects from an HST Mithran perspective, trying to narrow down to any HST leader who might know all the families. She came up with several names, and the FBI found something that interested them in the lists she sent. Then we got this." He handed his cell phone to Occam with one hand and said, "Open the note file at the top."

We rode in silence as Occam opened the file. He sent all the information to his own cell and passed me Rick's. It was a statement from PsyLED Unit Twelve from an informant. It claimed that HST had a list of paranormals from all over the United States and was planning to bring their version of ethnic cleansing to the vampires, via staking and beheading. Rick took a turn too fast, making the wheels squeal. I rocked into the seat belt and back upright. My cherry soda sloshed. Rick said, "Too much hinky on this case. With the vampire connection, the murder of Girl One, and the lists, this just became more of a joint effort. Everything we previously ruled out and everything we never looked at because it didn't fit HST MO will have to be reconsidered."

The FBI office on Darrell Springs Boulevard was built to impress, a fortress of a building, four stories with cameras everywhere, few trees to obscure anything or anyone who might want to approach, four massive columns at the front entrance, lots of good lighting so that enemies and criminals couldn't hide in the shadows and the night couldn't lessen the cameras' effectiveness, and a five-foot-tall black iron fence surrounding the property, the fence topped by sharp points. The building was constructed atop an artificially bermed hill, which meant that there were likely more stories underground. We pulled up in front of a guardhouse staffed with an armed guard and a dog, and Rick talked to the guard through a speaker and bulletproof glass. Once Rick held up ID for all of us, the gate rolled back, more quiet than the clanking I had expected.

Rick parked, and he and Occam got out of the van. More slowly, silently, I followed, my laptop tucked inside a tote bag under my arm. I didn't really expect to get into FBI headquarters, but they surprised me. Even with so little background to be checked through, living off the grid, not having banking records, which could have made me out to be a terrorist in hiding, they let me inside. But that was as far as I made it—the front lobby. Without any attempt at politeness, I was told to take a seat and wait. So I did, ignoring the sign that said no food, no drinks, and finished off my KFC livers, mashed potatoes, slaw, and biscuits, and then slurped down my jumbo cherry drink.

By the time a uniformed guard came up to tell me about the no-eating rules, I was finished and politely stuffed the greasy papers into the bag and handed it to him, while wearing my best churchwoman, I'm-too-dumb-to-know-better smile. I might no longer be among the church conspiracy theorists, but I still didn't like big brother. Not one bit. The uniformed guard stood there holding my garbage for a few moments while I cleaned my hands on a moist-wipe and opened my computer, ignoring him. I had research to do on who might want to anger the Knoxville vamps.

I spent two hours on the laptop searching through the avenues open to me—the government and nongovernment sites that the laptop allowed me into. And I found nothing.

So I took the easiest route and contacted one of Jane Yellowrock's business partners, Alex Younger, on e-mail and simply asked if he knew anyone who might want the vampires in the Knoxville area harmed. He sent me back a short note with links to all the online sites I had found and a dozen more, and he added a single terse paragraph at the bottom of the list.

For what it's worth—after Jane Yellowrock rescued and delivered the abducted fanghead to the Master of the City, Ming did a massive bleed and read of her humans and

determined that a white male knew quite a lot more about
the kidnapping of her blood-servant by the church leaders
than he first expressed. He was sanctioned and punished
by removal from the food chain, went through vamp-blood
withdrawal in rehab. It's possible that he blames the Knoxville MOC Ming Zhane of Clan Glass for his situation. He
doesn't happen to be very bright, but he might want to
draw out the suckheads, hoping for a chance to hurt them.
Or he might want to get back at the church people who
contributed to his loss of liquid dinner. His last name is
Dawson. Hang on. Looking for more.

The name *Dawson* wriggled in the back of my mind like a
worm on a hook, luring me in. There was something I'd read
or heard about the name, maybe something in church history,
from the establishment of God's Cloud? But it wouldn't come.
Moments later, Alex sent another e-mail that said, *Simon A.
Dawson Jr., age thirty-three, has three prior convictions, two
for assault and one for stalking. See attached rap sheet.* And
then it clicked. *Dawson* was the surname of the men Sister
Erasmus had referred to as backsliders.

I sent a polite thank-you to Alex Younger and downloaded
the information. Fingers tapping on the arms of my chair, I
studied the rap sheet—which stood for "record of arrest and
prosecution." Dawson was born in Knoxville. He attended
Farrington High School, the school attended by two of the
victims. That made my insides clench in agitation. I came up
with questions but no definitive answers. I had what the cops
might consider circumstantial information on a guy who
might hate vampires, and nothing pointed to an HST connection or to involvement with another organization that might
target vampires and their human servants. But the coincidence
bothered me. Once means happenstance, twice means coincidence, three times means problems.

How likely was it for this particular Dawson to be the
church backslider? Or tied into HST? Would the FBI ask Ming
about Dawson if I gave them the name? Would they call Yellowrock Securities for information? I almost smiled at the
thought that I might have a source they didn't have or wouldn't
use. When I gave them the name and the source, would they

follow through? Would Rick LaFleur call Jane? I had the feeling that he might want to, very badly. Want to and not do it because of the whole man-woman thing.

So. Unless I gave them the name, or the cops went to Ming Zhane herself, or to Jane, and asked, they might never learn the connection of Simon Dawson to the local vampires. And he wasn't on Rick's lists of suspects with ties to the vampires.

I compiled all the data I had, leading with the paragraph about my confidential source suggesting that Dawson had been a blood-servant, punished with withdrawal, and sent an e-mail to Rick with an attached high school photograph I found online.

Ten minutes later I heard a faint *ding*, and Rick strode from the elevator across the carpet to me, an unreadable expression on his face. He stopped a foot short of me, bent over me, and dropped his hands to the arms of my chair, using his height to intimidate me, making his body and my chair into a cage. Quietly, too quietly, his voice a cat's low burr, he said, "How the hell did you find out something *we* haven't? Have you been shielding God's Cloud from this investigation?"

My first reaction was shock. Then fear raced across the shock and through me like quicksilver, the fear of a child who had been beaten, the fear of a young woman who had been threatened and . . . My breath stopped; my heart raced as memories spun through me. And then fury slammed into me so fast that my skin felt like it had been set on fire. So softly even Rick, with his cat ears, had to lean in to hear, I said, "My foot is perfectly positioned to kick you. If you don't get off me, *now*, I will."

He didn't move.

So I kicked him.

And had the satisfaction of seeing him fall, his hands holding his crotch. JoJo had been right. It felt really good. Well, for me.

The uniformed security guard was back so fast I hardly saw him arrive. I was in handcuffs faster than that. And then I was hauled upstairs, my arms lifted painfully high behind me, and thrust into a room filled with men and women in suits, each wearing the same expression—cold anger. The security guards, three of them by this time, shoved me into a chair and looped a second pair of handcuffs through the first set and wrapped them around a chair arm before latching them shut with a ratcheting *click* that sounded sharp and final in the quiet room. I was seated at the center of the table, my back to the door, the tabletop littered with papers and electronic devices, screens up all over the room, lit with photos of crime scenes, including one of a dead girl. She lay in weeds, fully clothed except for one shiny blue shoe, which was missing. Heart racing, I dragged my gaze away from the photograph of the body.

On the tabletop there were dozens of laptops and tablets and papers strewn in loose pages or stacked neatly. The people sitting around the table looked tired, angry, forbidding, and a little mean.

The man at the head of the table was older, colder, and by his expression seemed perfectly willing to have someone beat me for information. I gave him my best churchwoman smile, sweet as honey. He frowned back.

From behind me I heard something. Or maybe felt something. Twisting around, I saw one of the guards holding a black thing about the size of a pack of cigarettes, lifting it directly over me and then along the contours of my body. I didn't know what it was, but I didn't like it. Not one bit. Finally, he backed away, and I could see him communicating something nonverbally with the man at the head of the table.

Rick, walking slowly and slightly bent over, took a chair across from me and placed my laptop and other things on the table between us. I didn't look his way, not once, but when he finally got seated, he demanded, his voice slightly more breathy than usual, "Explain yourself."

I kept my gaze on the man at the head of the table and pulled on all my childhood accent when I answered. "'Bout what? There's a lot I could explain, from why I ain't adopted a new dog, to the reasons I prefer organic vegetables over ones grown with poison, to why I kicked you in the nuts. Be more specific."

Someone in the room started to laugh and turned it into a cough. The man who was clearly in charge steepled his fingers in front of his mouth. "Why did you kick Senior Special Agent Rick LaFleur?" he asked from behind his hands.

Everything about the man declared him to be the boss, from his steepled fingers to his fancy suit to the brass nameplate in from of him. They rest of the people had folded paper cards with their names written or printed in marker. I figured he was either right proud of his name or he came from unimaginative stock, seeing as how they'd used the name for five generations.

"Mr. Thomas Benton the *fourth*," I said, hearing the sarcasm in my tone and trying to tamp it down a mite, "I done told him to get off a me and he didn't. I been used and abused by men all my life. Men who believed that they had a right to tell me where to go and what to do, when to get bedded, when to get married, when to pretend to be happy, and when to suffer. Men who used threat of rape to get their way." I leaned toward the man at the head of the table, my cuffs clinking. "No man is ever, *ever*, goin' to tell me what to do like I'm stupid or ten years old and too dumb to know better. Not ever again. Or threaten me again. Or hurt me again." I looked at Rick. "You got that?"

Neither man answered for a long-drawn-out moment. The man at the head of table spoke from behind the protection of his fingers and asked, "Senior Special Agent LaFleur, did you by word or deed threaten or injure this young woman?"

Rick had gone tense as the man spoke. "I suppose, by the standards under which Nell lived for most of her life, that I did appear to be about to . . ." He stopped and started again, more stiffly. "I may have appeared as if I was threatening. My apologies, Nell."

"Accepted," I said, not looking his way. "Now iffen you want to know how I found out what I did, Mr. Thomas Benton the fourth"—I dropped the accent and went on—"it's called *analogical reasoning*. There are two steps to analogical reasoning: recognizing that two or more things have one characteristic in common, and assuming that if they have *one* characteristic in common, they may have *others* in common. Fact one: a thirty-three-year-old man named Simon A. Dawson, a man who, so far as I can tell, has never had the brains to plan anything more complex than how to serve himself up as dinner and sex partner to vampires, has reason, in his own deluded mind, to be angry at the vampires. Fact two: two

Dawson men were seen on property belonging to God's Cloud. Fact three: someone has carried out some very complex kidnappings—possibly, but not definitively, an organization called Human Speakers of Truth. If, however, the kidnapper was Mr. Dawson, then by use of *deductive reasoning*, we can deduce that he didn't act alone. You need a dictionary explanation of deductive reasoning?" I asked.

Surprisingly the man nodded, a single incline of his head. From a girl with a church background, it was an alien gesture for a man who had been mildly insulted, one without heat, calculating and probing and totally without emotion. I realized he was curious about me and what I might know and how I might think. I said, "Deductive reasoning, also called deductive logic, or logical deduction, or, if you want to be informal, top-down logic, is the process of using one or more statements or premises to reach a logically certain conclusion. The thought process links premises with conclusions, which is somewhat different from analogical reasoning. None of the reasoning processes work perfectly alone, but using them together, they offer a chance of reaching a cogent and correct conclusion or a satisfactory correlation.

"Back to Mr. Dawson. My use of analogical and deductive reasoning suggests that the man named Dawson, if he was the kidnapper, almost certainly had help, because he ain't real bright and we know that three males and an unknown driver carried out the kidnappings. Now I'm moving from reasoning to instinct. Instinct is based on past experience, current information, and a lifetime of deductive, inductive, and analogical reasoning. It's always personal and might not be based on anything one can put a finger on. Instinct says if he is a kidnapper, then he might be part of the Human Speakers of Truth."

The man at the head of the table said from behind his hands, "That doesn't explain how you found the name when we have not."

I grinned then and looked at Rick. My tone might have been full of satisfaction. Or maybe even malice. "Actually, Sister Erasmus found it. I just researched it. I called Yellowrock Securities."

If it was possible for Rick LaFleur to look any worse than when I kicked him, he did. Paler. More pained. Stunned. From down the table a voice purred, "I *told* you to call her." It was Occam, and his voice was gloating and growling in the way of cats. "I also told you Nell would if you didn't."

I stretched against my handcuffs and looked down the table at Occam, whose eyes were on Rick. Occam's expression shifted quickly from delighted and insulting, the way house cats look when they've done something they shouldn't, to something else when he caught my eyes. He rose from his chair, moving along the table, his body slinky and graceful. He bent over me, but from the side, not making me feel trapped. I felt his breath against the side of my neck and realized he had paused in bending down to sniff my scent. The warm feel of his breath made the little hairs raise along my nape in a prickling wave, like grass moving before a summer wind. He whispered, "It's okay, Nell, sugar. Everything is all right." And I knew, somehow, that I'd be, forever more, *Nell, sugar* to him. An endearment that was totally improper for a widder-woman and a strange man. My daddy would bust a blood vessel in his brain. Embarrassment and hint of fear flushed through me, and I knew Occam could hear my heart rate speed.

With his bare hands, Occam took the two cuff bracelets holding my wrists together and pressed them apart. The two chain links that attached one bracelet to the other separated with a soft sound of metal bending and tearing. My hands were free of the chair, and I placed them on the tabletop, still wearing the bracelets. A woman two places down from me stood and used a key to open each. Mildly, she said, "Impressive display of nonhuman strength. But keys are less destructive."

"I'm totally unconcerned about destruction, little lady," Occam said, a challenge in his tone. I had a feeling that the woman had never been called a *little lady* before and she didn't like it. I did, however. To Rick, Occam said, "You and me will talk about this later," and his voice was deeper this this time, an unquestioned challenge. Occam dropped beside me to the floor, one knee down, one foot down, one elbow on his knee, and one hand on the arm of my chair, but not touching me. To me he said, "Fill us in, Nell, sugar. And don't leave nothing out."

* * *

The feds were rude and snooty and too busy to observe even the most casual, minimal form of manners; they made sure I knew I was the outsider and useless, despite my unexpected and, as they put it, *accidental* addition to the list of suspects. What they meant was that I had provided them with the only real, viable suspect, with ties to vamps *and* the church, which they had been looking for, but they didn't have the breeding to say so. I informed them that they needed a lesson in manners and maybe a spanking with Mama's hairbrush. They didn't take my comments well, though the man at the head of table seemed amused. But once I finished my monologue and answered questions, they banished me from the room again. I didn't care.

Rick slid the keys to PsyLED's van across the table to me. I nodded, picked up my things, and left without telling him where I'd be or asking how he and Occam would leave when they were ready. Mostly I was wondering if he was still in pain or if his were-taint abilities healed his nuts faster than a human male's would.

I didn't feel guilty about kicking him. In fact, every time I thought about it I felt a welling sense of satisfaction. As if by kicking him, I'd kicked every other man who had tried to hurt me. But I also thought that maybe I shouldn't have kicked him quite so hard. Maybe he hadn't deserved the fear overreaction or the amount of muscle, momentum, and force I'd applied. But instead of guilt, I was carrying a sinful amount of selfish delight at having taken a stand against a man *before* he managed to hurt me.

What's good for the goose is good for the gander, I thought, though that particular saying had been looked down upon most strongly in the church, as it implied that women had the same position as men and might be allowed to take multiple husbands, a fundamental sin for sure. In my case, it meant that if a man could hurt me, could threaten me, then I could threaten or hurt him back. Maybe hurt him first. I was still trying to decide how I felt about that unexpected violent side of me when I unlocked the van and tossed my laptop into the passenger seat.

It was warm inside, and I hadn't noted the cold of the air

until it was gone. I closed the van door and took in the sky and the clouds that were gathered there, and decided that we might have early snow in the hills by nightfall, a dusting, too light to stick. And something about the sight of the clouds made me want to buy some laying hens. There was nothing better than fresh eggs for breakfast and chicken and dumplings from a fresh hen for supper. And chicken poop became excellent fertilizer when it was properly handled. But chickens would be good targets for the churchmen. Maybe later. If I survived all this.

I figured out how the van's controls worked and started the engine, making my way through the steel gate and out of the FBI's compound. I drove back to the main Knoxville library, questions about the name Dawson tangling in my mind like roots circling around a pot—getting nowhere but more tangled. I parked in back under the gnarled limbs of an oak tree, and the sight of the oak called to me, making me want to rest my face against its bark and my feet against its roots. It was a need that thrummed through me like a bass drum, low and deep. I locked the van and stepped to the trunk of the oak. No one was around, and so I placed the laptop on the ground at my feet and leaned in, laying my cheek against the rough bark, my arms around the trunk. Leaning harder, I rested my body against the trunk and took a deep cleansing breath. And relaxed. I'd no idea how exhausted I was until the tension flowed out of me and through the tree into the ground. I took another breath and let clean, healing energy flow up through the tree into me. I could feel my woods through the oak, pulling on me, calling me home, sending me energy and calm.

I stayed hugging the oak for what felt like a short time, but later I discovered that I had lost half an hour as I communed with the tree. Tandy's words. Occam's words. Communing. Feeling calm and focused, I went inside the library to the computer access room and logged my new laptop on to the Internet through the library's Wi-Fi.

Using the laptop was much faster than using the old computers in the computer room. I could get spoiled with this. After an hour of tracking down different search words under three different search engines, I discovered a oodles of information about the church's recent legal troubles, but there was nothing

useful on the Internet about the history and establishment of
God's Cloud of Glory Church, except one hint from a World
War II newspaper. The article suggested that the church was
allowed to keep their land when the government stole all the
other farms at pennies on the dollar, because a certain powerful senator interceded. Maybe he attended services there. That
senator wasn't named, not that it mattered. Back then newspapers didn't mention some things because the nation was at
war. What mattered was that some few hundred acres on the
long hills that bordered the Tennessee Valley was left in private hands.

Other than that, there was only the information that the
church itself had on their Web page, which, according to the
photographs and the listing of church elders, hadn't been
updated in five years or more. However, there were other avenues open to a persistent researcher.

I drummed my fingers on the keyboard before signing off
and went looking for a librarian. Fortunately, Kristy had just
come on shift, and she knew that I had used microfiche before.
"Come on, girl," she said, flipping her hair back and leading
the way. "I'll let you into the historical records room. You help
yourself to any old newspapers, police reports, land deeds,
marriage licenses, death certificates, and business transactions you want. Everything from every old newspaper and all
the old deeds are on microfiche. Eventually we'll get the rest
of Knoxville's history scanned into the Library's Internet, but
at least the microfiche is complete." She opened the records
room with an old-fashioned key, and turned on the lights.
"You remember how to change from one source to another?"

"I do. Thanks, Kristy," I said. "Coffee on me someday?"

"That'd be fun," she said. "But not for this. This is my job.
Call on the in-house phone if you need something," she said,
pointing to the wall phone.

She closed the door behind her, and I heard the lock click
shut. I could get out, but no one could get in without being let
in, which gave me a feeling of security I wouldn't have had
otherwise, so far down in the bowels of the building. I started
with my most obvious option—newspapers. The information
storage system was set up by newspaper and by date and was
not complicated to search, though it was time-consuming.

The *Knoxville Gazette* and the *Knoxville Register* were early pre–Civil War newspapers, the *Gazette* with pro-slavery leanings, the *Register* more pro-emancipation. The *Western Monitor and Religious Observer* was a newsletter. I wasn't sure what the difference was between a newspaper and a newsletter, but the newsletter was violently pro-emancipation. And it had taken a stance against the newly founded God's Cloud of Glory Church late in 1823.

Every child in the church was taught the tale of the church's establishment and early history, all about how the founder, the first Jackson, had come from Wales and bought land, nearly a thousand acres outside of Knoxville. About how he had gathered like-minded Christians around him and started a church, and how the townspeople had hated them, despite the heroic and gallant actions of the God-fearing churchmen. The history I had been taught was full of Scripture verses and photographs of the founding fathers, mustached and bearded, holding weapons that they had used to defend their way of life. The accounts in the newspapers were different. In October 1823, the *Western Monitor and Religious Observer* newsletter described the churchmen as particularly immoral, forcing their vile acts upon the weaker sex.

The churchmen had fought back in a series of letters, and the rhetoric from both sides had been described by the *Gazette* and the *Register* as rancorous, malicious, venomous diatribes. Not something that should have been allowed in print where the more delicate-minded might be forced to read. The language was old-fashioned and eye-opening.

In one attack, the newsletter had called upon the God-fearing populace to "cease to provide goods and services" to the churchmen, and to "shun the churchwomen as equal to those who live in sin, as surely as any strumpet or harlot!" There were lots of exclamation marks and weird spellings. But at the bottom of a special edition, the newsletter had listed the names of the early churchmen and their strumpet womenfolk. The publisher hadn't alphabetized the names, but I scanned them, from the founder, Quincy S. Jackson, and his four wives, to Ralph A. Emery and his three wives. There were a lot of surnames in between, some that were spelled differently back then, like the Stubbenses, the Edens, and the Mcormiks, who were surely the Stubbinses, the Adens, and the McCormicks. There were also some that I didn't recognize, including a Pullim family, a Gramour family, and a MacMackins family. It seemed as if the church membership had decreased over the years. Midway down, between Roxbury T. Bantin and his two wives and Jormungand M. Sanders and his four wives, was the name Elias S. Dawson and his three wives. And his many, many children.

It took only a little more work to track the family tree of Simon A. Dawson Jr. back to his illustrious—or not—ancestor. I didn't have much money on hand, but by dint of raiding the change from the bottoms of the cup holders and the floor of the PsyLED van, I managed to scrape up enough to print out the most important pages for the team. Assuming Senior Special Agent Rick LaFleur allowed me back into the unit after the kick I'd given him.

Before I left the library, I did an Internet search for Simon Dawson from his birth to five years ago, when he seemed to drop out of sight, presumably into a vampire's embrace.

TWELVE

Still feeling much better, I touched the oak tree in thanks as I left the library. Pages in hand, I drove to the hotel. With some trepidation, I parked the van in the hotel parking lot and headed to the entrance. Night had fallen and a chill wind blew straight through my clothes, giving me the shivers. Tomorrow, if the weather hadn't changed back to summer, as it did with great regularity this time of year, I'd get out my winter coat. I smelled Italian herbs as I traipsed up the hall, and though I had overeaten on the fried chicken liver dinner, my mouth watered at the aroma. I knocked and used my card key at the same time. The door opened.

Tandy leaped at me and hugged me. With both arms. I froze. But it wasn't sexual. It was . . . nice. Rick had told them not to touch me, but Tandy was an empath and he had emotional needs that were different from most humans'. Uncertainly, I patted his back. Tandy was skinny to the point of emaciation, his shoulder blades sharp beneath my palm, his spine a line of acorns. I wondered how he ate, being so attuned to the emotions of others. When others were hungry, was he? When they were overfull, was he? I had some herbal mixtures that might help him eat more. Relax more. Surely there was a legal herb somewhere that helped empaths tune out the rest of the world. Marijuana would probably work perfectly, but Rick had said something about a drug test and I figured that particular illegal herb would be tested for. I needed to do some research.

Tandy stepped back without releasing me, his hands holding my upper arms. He studied my face, but I had a feeling that he was really studying my emotions, feeling his way through them the same way I felt my way through the soil when I needed to plant something new into an existing bed, trying to see if the plants nearby were willing to accept a newcomer, trying to see if the nutrients were the right ones to succor the new rootlet or seed. Leaning in, he softly said, "No one worries about me."

"Oh. No, Tandy. I do worry about you. We all do."

I didn't know how to categorize his expression; calling it a smile was to trivialize it, to make it less significant. The light of it brightened his face and made the Lichtenberg figures more pronounced, the flesh between more pale. And his eyes seemed to glow with happiness. It was an overreaction to my words.

"Really," he said, his voice holding some emotion that might have fallen under the category of wonder. "No one."

I patted his forearm and backed out of his embrace. It was just too bizarre. And unfamiliar. And awkward. Though in some odd way, the embrace reminded me of the way I had hugged the tree earlier. He stepped back and I entered the suite. Occam's eyes found me instantly, his expression hooded.

JoJo stepped between Tandy and me and closed the door, offering a flat box centered with three-fourths of an oozing, cheesy, vegetable-laden, sausage-covered pie. Tentatively, I took a slice, the crust crispy and doughy all at the same time. Tandy murmured softly under his breath. "She's never eaten pizza before," he said. That stopped the chatter in the room as every eye turned to me. Not meeting anyone's gaze, I bit into the pizza. And I nearly swooned at the taste as it practically exploded in my mouth. It was fabulous. Spicy. Greasy. Fantastic. *Wonderful.*

Pizza was . . . delicious. Almost as good—in a totally different way—as the Krispy Kreme donuts.

I instantly began thinking of how to make bread that would rise like the pizza dough and which herbs to add to my homemade canned tomato paste to make it taste like this. Then whose cheese might make it even better. Maybe goat cheese and dried tomatoes. Basil, which I could easily coax to sprout. I took another slice and chewed, differentiating the flavors into the base herbs and spices. There was a lot of oregano on it, and I grew the best oregano in the county. My pizza would be even better than this one.

I was halfway through the second slice when Rick cleared

his throat and the half-heard babble of the team ceased. I opened my eyes, took a quick glance around the room, and sat in the empty seat—the same one as before.

"First," Rick said, "I'm sorry."

I realized he was looking at me, talking to me, and I didn't know what to do. So far as I could remember at the moment, no man had ever apologized to me. I held up a finger, asking for a minute, using the excuse of chewing to find some equilibrium, swallowed, and said, "Ummm. Okay. I accept your apology." I thought a moment more and added, "But, I have to warn you, you ever bend over me and trap me again, I'm probably gonna kick you again."

"It's a push-button reflex," T. Laine said. "He pushed your buttons, you kicked. You both need to think before you act."

That sounded like sensible advice, something Leah would have said, and I nodded. One of the others poured Coke into a cup and passed it to me. I drank cola and continued eating pizza. It was a small slice of heaven.

Rick said, "We have nonfamily abductions of four females. The family of Girl One was contacted with ransom demands and proof of life of the abductee. Then the family of Girl Two was contacted via an MO that falls within acceptable parameters used by HST in the past, with exactly the same ransom demands and delivery account numbers. Yet we have the body of Girl One, in a ditch near Dead Horse Lake Golf Course."

The room went silent. Tandy went pale and gripped the arms of his chair.

The photo of a girl lying on the ground, on the crime board I'd seen in the conference room at FBI headquarters, leaped into my mind. She had been dead. Thrown away. Like garbage.

"That's near Wyatt School," T. Laine said, putting a hand on Tandy's knee. I couldn't tell that she did anything, but he drew a breath and relaxed, and T. Laine patted his knee before removing her hand. It was the sort of gesture a mother did for a child, but it felt like more. I wondered if she had used a spell to help him stay calm when the emotions of everyone in the room were spiking.

Rick had continued, using acronyms I didn't understand. "Prelim PM indicates several things pertinent to the case. Liver temp suggests TOD was around the time of ransom delivery. External physical assessment also indicates that except for the COD, she was not abused or mistreated. COD is a blow to the back of the head, showing significant bruising, indicating it *might* have occurred at the time of the kidnap, and *might* have resulted in her later death. The word *might* was emphasized by the forensic pathologist. She'll know more about the blow in a few hours, after they open her up."

I had a short list of acronyms to look up. PM, TOD, COD, and *open her up*, though I sorta understood them from the context.

"HST does not kill or abuse kidnap victims, which is why they have been so successful," Rick said. "However, the forensic pathologist suggests that the girl fought her attackers and was injured early on, perhaps with a wound that didn't look immediately life-threatening. Bruising on the brain, called"— he looked at his tablet—"a secondary hematoma or secondary hemorrhage, can happen much later.

"Assuming the ransom demands were made according to a sequence, the Clayton family should have received a call hours ago. It didn't come. However, the death of the victim may have complicated the situation for the unsubs."

"Oh!" I said, jumping up and handing Rick the papers I had somehow ended up sitting on. "Dawson, the man who used to be addicted to vampire blood, had a connection to the church way back when. If someone in the church wanted to do harm to vampires, they might have called him. I need to talk to Sister Erasmus to verify that he's one of the backsliders she mentioned.

"I couldn't find any connection between Dawson and the HST, but I don't have access to all the databases you do, and I don't know how to dig deep electronically. He would have known the ins and out of vampire households because of being their dinner."

I ate more pizza as Rick went through the poor-quality copies. "Huh," he muttered. "I tend to forget about microfiche. I bet there's not a lot about vampires in the old papers."

"If you know their names at the time and what to look for," JoJo said. "The way they changed names to protect their lifestyles—"

"Lives of the rich and fangy," T. Laine interrupted. "Or maybe, not lives. Undead. So, undeaths of the rich and fangy."

"Okay. Back to what we were doing before Nell arrived. JoJo, see what you can find that might link Simon Dawson with HST. Nell, we might need you to ask your Sister Erasmus if the men have been back on church grounds and if they have any current church contacts." He tapped the photocopies and changed the subject. "Debrief on the trailer park canvass," Rick said. "T. Laine's pair first." Which reminded me about that part of the day's planned activities, events that had taken place without me.

T. Laine was chewing and waved at Tandy, saying what might have been, "Him first."

I started to tell Tandy to keep eating and let the others talk, but stopped myself. It really wasn't my place. But his wrists were more scrawny than mine, and I was far too skinny.

"Three who didn't want to discuss anything," Tandy said. "Emanations of guilt, anger, and fear. Probably hiding weed or other small-time crimes. Honest confusion about the missing girls. Two occupants who didn't come to the door, though I could feel people inside. And one very chatty type."

"She asked Tandy to take off his clothes so she could see more of his 'tattoos,'" T. Laine supplied, making little quotation marks in the air with one hand. "Said if she liked what she saw he could come inside for beer and fun and games."

Tandy blushed. The others laughed. Scowling, I shoved a piece of pizza at Tandy and said, "Eat." Tandy looked at me in surprise. "You haven't eaten anything since I got here." Tandy took the piece and nibbled on the point. "Eat!" I said, putting a faint command into my voice. Tandy took a big bite and chewed. Swallowed. He ate two more bites.

And I had my first taste of understanding the life of an empath. Because Tandy picked up the emotions of the people around him, it was easy to make him do most anything. This was not good. Very, *very* not good. But I kept my opinions and my thoughts to myself until he finished the pizza slice. "Okay," I said then. "That's good. You can stop unless you're still hungry."

He looked at me and smiled uncertainly. "I'm . . . hungry." He took another piece and ate it too, with most of a beer as chaser.

Occam smiled at me with an expression I couldn't read.

T. Laine watched the exchange with a dawning comprehen-
sion and glanced at me, her expression appraising and calculating and seeming surprised. As Tandy ate, T. Laine took up
the narrative, and I listened for anything that sounded promis-
ing about the missing girls and the trailer park, but didn't hear
anything interesting, except that when T. Laine cast what she
called a "searching working," she picked up traces of magic,
old and worn. They were probably spells from a water witch
who had moved out long ago. And she remembered hearing
sirens from off in the distance as they worked the trailer park.

The second pair of canvassers agreed that, on the surface,
there was nothing about Mira at the trailers. Or there wasn't
until Occam had shifted and sniffed around. He had some
pithy Texan slang for a leopard having to wear a collar and
leash, but he'd picked up the scent of wet dog. The scent pattern was similar to the dog they had smelled at Mira's, but he
admitted that, "All dogs smell the same to me. Rank and
doggy." Coincidence. But we weren't ignoring coincidence
now. We were reporting everything, even seemingly unimportant things, in case they became important later.

Unfortunately, the mobile home where Occam had
acquired the scent had been vacated recently, and the tenants
had left no forwarding address. They had paid in cash and had
been asked to provide neither identification nor references,
had lived there for two months, and had disappeared three
nights past. They rented week to week under the names Perry
Mason and Paul Drake. Occam found that highly amusing and
told us that the names were characters from an old detective
TV show. Apparently Occam lived and breathed old black-
and-white shows—cartoons and films, with a preference for
Popeye, who I had never heard of.

I decided that most of an investigator's job was boring. I'd
rather be working in the garden, getting caught up with my
fall-weather work, not that I'd tell them that. Tandy stood up
like someone had stabbed him, his eyes wide. He said, *"Run!"*
sounding panicked and strangled all at once.

The others all dove for weapons. Rick shoved Tandy and
me to the floor behind the sofa and rolled to one side.

Bullets rained into the room at waist height. I covered my
head with my arms and curled into a tight ball. Splinters,

debris shrapnel, and glass from the curtained window went everywhere, cutting into my skin. The noise was horrific. No one in the room returned fire.

Tandy's mouth was open; I thought he might be screaming. I reached out with both hands and pulled him into my arms, wrapping myself around him. I shoved emotion into him the same way I might shove purpose into a seed—*grow, be content, all is well.* Tandy shuddered and I felt him take a breath. I tightened my arms around him and wrapped my legs around him too, keeping him safe. Claiming him.

Over the roaring deafness in my ears, I heard Rick shouting orders. He and two others raced from the room. I didn't look up. I didn't move until Tandy tapped my forearm and wriggled free. He gestured me and Paka—who I hadn't even noticed—into the next room, which he locked behind us. This room had two beds, no seating area, no kitchen. The bed linens were made, though the room was lived-in and smelled musky with male sweat. Tandy and Occam's room. This one had no bullet holes, and Tandy pushed Paka and me to the floor between the two beds. He pulled pillows and a blanket off one bed and over us. Then he pulled a mattress over us too, like a fort the young'uns might make on rainy days. I didn't think it would be much protection but I didn't object. It was better than the nothing we'd had. Pea chittered and inspected the mattress fort with the playful energy of kitten.

Paka repositioned the pillows, patting them like a cat might, until the shape pleased her, then pulled me against her body and curled around me, sliding the blanket over us. It was dark in the cavern of pillows and blankets. It felt safe though we clearly weren't. Tandy spooned into me from my other side, pulling Paka's arms and mine around him. His skin was cold and his flesh beneath flaccid. Belatedly terrified, feeling all our fear.

Something dampened my clothes at my waist. Carefully I said, "Paka, you'uns bleeding."

"It is nothing. I will shift and heal."

"The others?"

"I smell blood. But not death."

"Okay. That's good, I reckon. Tandy?" I asked. He made a mewling sound of terror, his breath panting, heart racing, pounding against his rib cage. I forced myself to think. To figure out what needed to be done. "I'm okay. Paka says the others are going to be fine." I crossed my fingers at the interpretive lie. "I want you to become calm." I pushed a feeling of tranquility into him. The mewling sound stopped. After a few breaths, Tandy's skin grew marginally warmer.

He said, "Thank you."

I nodded, knowing he could feel my movement in the dark. "I thank you for getting us in here and safe. You done goo— *did well*." My ears were coming back on because over the ringing in them, I heard sirens in the distance. Later, I heard Rick and police officers. Tandy eased us out of the little mattress fort he had made and pushed the mattress back into place. He gave us each a bottle of water, and I realized that Tandy might have some type of compulsion ability himself, because I was suddenly thirsty. I drank the whole bottle and followed him back into the main room, while Paka shifted and healed herself.

It was a mess, covered in Paka's blood and debris from the shooting. I stood in the doorway with Tandy observing as Rick talked to the local police and to the hotel manager while being bandaged by a paramedic. I understood that the rooms were a crime scene and the unit would have to vacate the premises. PsyLED was no longer welcome in the hotel. The police said that we might not be safe anywhere in the city and should consider moving to a safe house, which they could arrange by tomorrow night. That was going to mean twenty-four hours living and sleeping in the van.

I heard myself say, "You can sleep at my place. You can't use your cells or the Internet, but I'll know if anyone comes onto the property." Instantly I wished I hadn't spoken, but it was too late. Just that fast, I had houseguests.

I stopped on the way home to pick up money from Old Lady Stevens, trading most of it for a slab of bacon, two dozen eggs, a chicken ready for the pot, and a small beef roast. I would have hours alone at the house before they came. The three mouser cats met me on the porch, mewling and unhappy at having been left outside all day. I opened the door and they raced inside, one of them leaving behind a dead vole on the threshold. I made a face, said, "Thank you," and kicked it off the porch into the yard. Reaching inside, I turned on a light and closed the door behind me.

In the kitchen, I put two small pieces of dry firewood into the stove, winter wood to heat the oven fast, but not enough to make it too hot for baking and cooking, and started a double batch of bread. The stove would warm the main rooms well—the distant rooms, not so much, but I had lots of quilts and blankets. I took a quick shower with the leftover tepid water, pulled out a couple dozen splinters I hadn't noticed until now from my upper arm and applied a salve and thin bandages, filled the water tank, pulled on winter thermal underwear and a pair of overalls for modesty, and put out washcloths and towels. I started coffee, tea, and then put a load of bloody and damaged clothes into the washing machine on the back porch and refilled the water tank again.

I was still moving fast, as if some part of me didn't want to slow down, because the PsyLED unit was coming, once they finished with the crime scene experts, filed reports with local police, the FBI, maybe ATF, and the director at PsyLED central. They also had packing to do and showers to take before coming here. It would take them hours.

I was still in shock at the gunfire attack. And at having invited the team to stay here. And even more shocked that Rick had said yes to a place with no Internet or cell service. But he'd said that no one would expect them to be here, and they could get caught up on paperwork and such. And, though he hadn't mentioned it, Occam and Paka could race over the mountain ridge in cat form and spy on the church compound. I wasn't stupid. The location of my property was valuable to them. And they had to wonder if I'd missed something about the church's involvement.

Rather than think about my former church affiliation being the main—only?—reason that they had asked me to join the team, I sliced the bacon and placed a dozen slices in a cast-iron frying pan to sizzle slowly, along with peppers and my bean-herb mix. While it cooked, I put clean sheets on all the mattresses, wondering if they'd mind sharing beds. They were all queen-sized beds, so there was plenty of room, but to people who likely grew up with their own rooms and beds, it might smack of an invasion of privacy. To be on the safe side, I rolled up blankets and lay one up the middle of each of the two upstairs beds. Rick and Paka would be downstairs in John's and Leah's old room, and I left their bed undivided. I brought my cot downstairs and set it up in the storage nook behind the kitchen, where I could add wood through the night to keep the house warm.

I filled lanterns and set them in every room, and cleaned and lit the lantern hanging at the landing in the bend in the stairs, to brighten their way. The lanterns were attached to the walls with screws and bolts so they couldn't be accidentally kicked over in the night. Modern people—nonchurch people— weren't used to doing without electric lights and if they needed to get up in the night, in an unfamiliar place, the access to more primitive lights would help.

I had no illusions about how long the stored power would last with so many people here; it wouldn't be long. A few hours at most. Bigger solar arrays and a battery system hadn't been something John bothered with, not once he knew that he'd never have children running up and down the stairs and his other wives had left. And I didn't have the money for an upgrade I would seldom use.

When the bacon was done I poured the spicy drippings into the beans that had slow-cooked all day, tasted them, chopped the bacon, adding that to the beans too, and placed the pot to the side to keep warm. I liked my beans spicy.

The church compound had electricity, but most households didn't use it often, as it tied them to the grid, made them dependent on systems that they believed would eventually disappear. Not the zombie apocalypse, as all the zombie films suggested, but the "illegal and immoral government closing down the electrical grid to punish and control its own citizens." Stupid thinking, because the best way to control humans has always been to give them the things that they want, not deprive them.

I cleaned my tiny bathroom and moved my few toiletries into the storage nook off the kitchen. I took a look at the cistern up the hill. It was fine, as was the windmill at the back of the property, the sound a soft, accustomed creak in the night wind. I dust mopped the floors and took the rugs outside to shake before deciding that the rooms looked nice enough for company.

Back inside, I worked the dough again and put it in trays, leaving it to second rise. With the bread from earlier in the week, I'd have six loaves. Beans, rice, bread, and a salad was a full meal for a large number of people. I started the rice cooking and realized that my hands were shaking and I was jittery and uneasy.

Guns shooting in a hotel.

People in my house. Overnight.

Men and women. *Guests.*

People. *In my house.*

I had made a dreadful mistake.

And in the middle of what might, just maybe, be a full-blown panic attack, I wondered who had been shooting in the hotel. Shooting at the suite. Had they followed me there? "Ohhh . . . ," I breathed, "nooo . . ." What if someone—Jackie?—had been watching the library, a place I was known to frequent, and had followed me from the library to the hotel? I hadn't noticed anyone behind me, but I wasn't used to the van and had been less observant than usual. Was it possible that *I* was the target? But then, it didn't seem like something even Jackie would do. He would much more likely have lain in wait in the hotel parking lot and killed me there, or here at the house. The hotel had security cameras inside and out, and the PsyLED team had been studying them before I left.

Rick had said he would bring photos of anyone suspicious for me to look at. Did *he* think I was the target? Or did he think I had led the shooters to the hotel to kill them? If I was the target, then it had to be churchmen who fired the shots, churchmen who chose to kill me and take out the PsyLED police at the same time. Jackie and Joshua might think they had such a reason. Vengeance.

Even more rattled, I turned off the electric lights, pulled off my shoes, grabbed a quilt, and raced out back and into the shadows beneath the trees. I sat with my back against the big sycamore tree, my bare feet on the roots that entangled with the poplar tree nearby, and pulled the quilt over me. The tree bark was mostly smooth, the tree itself humming with power and life. I started shaking, quaking like a leaf in the wind. I turned and laid my cheek on the sycamore, my left palm on the trunk. Tears gathered in my eyes. This was all wrong.

People were coming to stay in my house.

Overhead the leaves stirred in the night wind, dry, desiccated, shifting together, a murmuring, whispering sound, vaguely soothing. A rain of leaves fell around me, shushing, landing on my head and shoulders and the blanket over me like a blessing, a benediction. In the distance, a barred owl called, the who-cooks-who-cooks-for-you notes carrying on the cold wind. I shivered and pressed almost violently into the tree. Far away, a second owl answered the six-note cry. Territory marking, maybe. Or family talking, taking note of who was where in the dark.

People. Coming to my house. Onto my land. My *territory. To stay here.*

But . . . it wasn't the church people. These people weren't going to hurt me, shoot me, burn my home. These people were going to simply sleep here. Paka. Occam. Tandy. T. Laine. JoJo. Rick.

When I managed a breath, it shuddered in my throat and I wiped my nose on the back of my hand, dried my tears on my long john shirt. It wasn't church people. These people wouldn't hurt me. "Okay," I breathed to the tree. "I can do this."

I gulped breaths, calming my heart, and shifted position until I could place both hands on the dirt, both soles on the roots, my spine and the back of my head against the tree, looking up into the limbs. It was miserable cold, but I could feel the ground beneath me, solid and sandy, rock and stone and fill dirt, clay and layers of long-rotten leaves, water rising through the ground, under pressure, surface water falling down the hills, under gravity. Water spreading out, feeding rootlets and moistening seeds and dancing through the air as it splashed over rocks. My breath came easier, and the panic began to slide away. With the sun gone, the earth was at rest and yet never resting. Always alive and breathing and moving and pumping nutrients. Animals slept in the nooks of trees and rocks, in nests, in dens, and curled in tall grasses. Others hunted. I reached out with my senses, into the ground, and felt of the earth, the contentment that was life, and the health of the trees.

But . . . something was different. I repositioned my palms and my feet, pressing down on the ground into full contact, fingers and toes reaching and pushing.

There was still something wrong. Something dark that had been there ever since Brother Ephraim's life was taken by the land. I had expected that the disturbance would settle, would integrate with the land quickly. But the new life force was still a darkness that raced away from me, to cower at the far boundaries of the property, like shadows deep in the ground, like death in the deeps. It was strongest at the edge of my property and the Stubbins' property, right at the place where the church boys had crossed over to get onto my land, and . . . something was different there too, above- and belowground. New roots and new growth. Thick and far too mature to have not been there only days ago, yet clearly it was new growth. I couldn't tell what the plants were at first. They weren't trees. Not shrubs. Not grasses. More like . . . vines, several species and varieties all growing together, tangling as they rose.

One was catbrier, a local weed that had hooked claws on it, like a cat's. One was silver leaf nightshade, a deadly plant if eaten. And the third was poison oak. A wild rose threaded itself through the thorny mess. All of them were growing out of season. They hadn't been there before. And now they were. They were creating a wall.

When the boys ran back over the crest of the hill, I remembered wishing that I was a witch. That I could snap my fingers and create a magical ward there to stop people from crossing over to my land. Like a protective wall.

The wood was building one for me.

Surprise, and something darker, like primitive joy, flashed through me. And a breath of fear about what such an act on the part of the woods might mean. I curled my fingers into the dirt beside the sycamore roots, digging in with my fingernails. Trying to see what else was different.

On the far side of the wall of thorns, a creature paced, back and forth, back and forth. It wasn't human. It walked on four legs and through its feet came curious vibrations, deep and menacing, like the sound of growls carried through the creature's body and into the ground, to me. The darkling shadow that I felt on and in my land, the shadow that raced through the deeps, wanted the creature, was reaching toward it. But the being that inspected the thicket of thorns wasn't aware of the darkness, separated from it by the new wall and by the power that marked the boundaries of Soulwood. I felt frustration from the one beneath the ground and fury from the one pacing aboveground. Three new things on and in my wood, a wall, a creature, and a . . . a *thing* that shouldn't be there, that should have been soothed and absorbed, but was still independent, dark, and frantic-seeming. The darkness of shadows was agitated, spinning and rootling through the earth, reaching out, trying to get free. But the borders of my woods stopped it, a boundary in the soil. It was trapped. Inside Soulwood. With me.

That was disquieting. I reached out, trying to soothe the shadow as I might soothe a rootlet or encourage a seed. Rather than lean in, as plants did to receive the soothing, or race away to avoid my touch, it broke apart and fled in streamers deep into the ground. In an instant, it was gone. On the other side of the spreading wall of thorns, the four-legged creature was moving away as well.

I pulled my thoughts out of the ground and back into myself; I opened my eyes. The night had grown darker and deeper, and the moon hung as if trapped in the grasping limbs of distant trees. Despite the darkness of shadows in the ground, and the wall of thorny vines that hadn't been there before, and the four-legged creature on the Stubbins side of the property boundary, I felt much better: calmer, settled, if far colder. I breathed the icy air, tasting snow on it, feeling the sting of fog freezing. The house windows glimmered with lantern light. The smell of burning wood danced on the night breeze. I hugged myself, thinking.

Despite the edicts of the church, I had never had to be hospitable to guests. I had few social skills to draw upon. I would likely be considered taciturn and remote and uncommunicative. A prickly stick-in-the-mud. I also wasn't human. But tonight I'd try to act against my nature and be gracious, courteous, and genial. I didn't expect to be successful at any of it.

I went inside, standing near the stove so I might warm up. I turned up a lantern, added a bit more wood to the fire, and tested the dough, which wasn't quite ready to go into the oven.

My toes were frigid but felt good pressed into the wood flooring, connected to the forest outside.

I wasn't afraid—not exactly—of anything I had sensed in the land, but it was . . . disturbing. I splattered water droplets on the stovetop in various places to test the temperature. Moved the rice off the hottest part of the hob.

People in my house.

I wondered if I would be able to sleep in a houseful of people. I hadn't done that since I was twelve. The panicky feeling welling up in me again, I pulled on boots and went to the garden. In the dark, by touch and feel, I harvested the last of the salad greens, hoping there would be no frost and the plants might yield some more, and raked the mulch up higher over the plants as protection. I pulled up a mess of turnips. I gathered the clean clothes out of the washer and into a plastic basket. Back inside, I hung the clothes up to dry on wood racks placed behind the cookstove to humidify the house as they dried, and turned on the overhead fans for a bit to move the warm air around. I cut up a fresh salad, put the greens to cook, and the turnips themselves to the side for later. I got out jars of preserves in case someone had a sweet tooth. Busy. I needed to stay busy.

I began pulling dried herbs off the shelf to make a tea to stimulate Tandy's appetite. The boy needed to eat.

The beans and rice were done and the bread was just coming out of the oven when I felt Paka racing across the land. Another cat ran beside her, through the dark and up the hill, toward the church's compound. I felt them startle a deer and, in the way of cats, they changed direction midstride, leaping to the side, almost choreographed. Together they took down the deer and started eating even as the buck struggled and kicked.

City folk would have been horrified—the ones who didn't hunt or fish. For me, it was simply part of the wood. Part of the land. Part of the cycle of life and death and rebirth.

The van's lights cut through the trees in strips of light and shadow as it pulled up the hill and into the drive. The PsyLED team—the ones still in human shape—piled out of the van. I had company. And just in time. Tandy's first appetite tea was freshly brewed.

Rick had brought groceries. As if he'd lived here all his life, he put things into the refrigerator and freezer, while my mouser cats trailed around behind him, mewling as if he carried raw fish. I sat in my chair at the table and watched as he lifted the top off the bean pot and tasted the beans with a spoon. He pronounced them perfect. "As good as my mama's. And you made rice. Even more perfect. Red beans and rice. It must be Monday." Which made me blink because I didn't make beans and rice only on Mondays, and it wasn't Monday anyway. Maybe it was a New Orleans thing. Without a change in expression, he asked, "Where are Occam and Paka?"

It was a trap. I knew that even as I answered. "Eating a deer. They'll be a while before they get to the compound. And then they'll stop to eat again on the way home."

"How do you know what's happening with them?"

I shrugged. I knew. I wasn't sure how I knew, as this knowing was different and unexpected. It had started when Brother Ephraim fed my woods. How it worked was something I was still figuring out.

T. Laine and JoJo started setting the table, asking me which stoneware to use, and hunting through the drawers for flatware, in the cabinets for glasses and paper napkins. They were stunned that I didn't have paper anything in the kitchen, washing cloth ones as needed instead. "Paper's wasteful," I said, pointing to where the cloth napkins were stored.

Sounding horrified, JoJo asked, "*Toilet* paper?"

I let a tiny smile claim my mouth. "I do use toilet paper," I said primly, knowing my mama would be horrified if she heard me talking about such personal subjects with a guest at the kitchen table. "But I don't have much on hand. Be sparing."

"Good God in heaven," T. Laine muttered. "How do people live like this?"

"Efficiently," I said sharply. "Cheaply. Off the grid as much as possible."

T. Laine's face tightened, an expression like a mask, covering up whatever she was really feeling, holding the world at bay. "Don't get your panties in a wad. I get the theory. I just don't get the practice. Is that why you only have lights lit in the rooms where we are?"

"Mostly," I said. "With this many people, we'll run out of stored power and be forced to use lanterns early, so the lanterns are in place, some already lit."

"So the night we visited . . . ?"

"I ran out of power shortly after you left."

"No cable? No network news? No TV at all?"

"Movies on DVD," I said. "If you go into withdrawal, there's a battery-powered radio with a good antenna."

T. Laine said, "Son of a witch on a switch," which was cussing for witches, or so I'd heard.

There was a lot more grumbling, mostly under their breath, but with so many people working, dinner was served within half an hour after they arrived, Rick ladling up beans and rice, T. Laine cutting a loaf of bread, JoJo passing out beer and pouring well water into glasses, and Tandy sipping his tea while trying to hide a look of distaste. I watched and let people serve me in my own house, knowing that these activities—things they could control—were helping to calm and settle them.

Three of the team had new wounds and bandages. Rick's was the worst, with blood seeping through his dress shirt. When he came near, I said, "Paka said she would shift into her cat and heal. She and Occam shifted and they're feeling fine." Rick's face went stony hard. "You're still wounded from the catnip sex. You can't shift into your cat, can you?" He didn't reply, and I said, "You mentioned a werewolf called Brute who's stuck in wolf form. You're stuck in human form, aren't you?"

JoJo said, "It isn't something he talks about." I turned to the pierced and tattooed woman. Her hair had been fluffed out in tiny ringlets, her skin oiled and shining. She had slashing cuts on her cheeks, the result of flying glass from the shooting, but in the shadows of the lanterns she was all angles and sharp planes, shadow and light, like an African priestess. "It hurts, not being able to shift. Hurts like hell. He's learned to live with pain for most of the lunar cycle, but it nearly drives him crazy during the full moon. He has a music spell he plays those three days."

T. Laine said, "I'm working on a backup spell to help him

deal, but he needs the services of a full moon witch coven, and those are harder to find."

"I wasn't supposed to know?" I asked.

"It was Rick's place to tell," Tandy said.

"I was going to tell you before the full moon," he said, grudging and resentful.

"Okay," I said. He had a timetable. I understood that. It was a way of maintaining control in a life that had little. "I got a healing salve that will help your cuts." I brought out a jar of salve and set it on the table. "Arnica, gotu kola, calendula, yarrow, and aloe. I got one without aloe, if anyone is allergic."

As if it was an invitation, they gathered and sat around my large kitchen table and JoJo applied some of the gel to her facial wounds. "My gramma would like this," she said, which sounded like high praise. And the mood seemed to lighten, which was a good thing. It had gotten tense in the house.

My guests served dinner, and we ate. No one talked business or the cases at dinner, focusing on downtime, as they called it, telling jokes and picking at each other just like families did. Pea jumped onto the table, and Rick fed her small chunks of bacon from the beans, which she seemed to love. The mousers took up places on the couch and on the open shelves, bored. I sat quietly, taking it all in, and it was . . . nice. Pleasant.

I feared it might take a long time to find pleasure in the silence of my empty home once they were gone again. Perhaps a very long time. Perhaps never. So I savored the moments, paying attention to every small detail, watching Tandy eat every morsel and complain about being too full, as if that was uncommon, letting my emotions take a respite in the presence of so much activity and chatter. It was like my childhood all over again—the good parts of it, the parts I hadn't realized that I missed. It left me with an impression of melancholy and nostalgia and a peculiar sense of regret that I couldn't put my finger on and tried to banish, to no avail.

After dinner, T. Laine and JoJo washed dishes, saying it was their turn, and Tandy sat on the sofa with his tablet, tapping keys, occasionally rubbing his stomach and hiding tiny burps.

Rick and I went over the hotel security camera footage of the shooting, which required the constant moving of the mouser cats from the desk and his laptop to the floor and to Rick's lap. The cats were drawn to him like a magnet, and I pretended not to feel jealousy at their affection for him. They never chased me like that, but then I wasn't a werecat, I just fed and provided for them, which should have earned me some loyalty but didn't.

In the first footage taken from an outside camera, an older-model, dark-colored SUV, with a big, roomy cab, raced into the hotel parking lot. Two figures in the front seats stayed in the SUV, barely visible through the tinted windows. Two others leaped from the passenger side and raced through the outer doors into the hotel. All I could tell about the fuzzy images was that the men wore toboggans, the kind that covers the face except for eyeholes. And they carried what might be fancy assault rifles.

A second camera picked up the men as they raced in from the parking lot and through the lobby, a big man in front, a smaller just behind, as if being protected. There were three seconds of visual as the hotel clerk dropped behind the front desk.

A third camera showed the men racing through the hallway and up the fire stairs. This video camera was crisp, and I could make out more details. The man in front was heavy but fast. The man in back was lithe and wiry, probably average height. Both men wore jeans, flannel shirts, and work boots. There wasn't audio, but I could tell that the heavier man was stomping with each step. Both were in good shape, running without stopping to the fourth floor, and when they paused at the fourth-floor landing to confer, neither appeared winded. Some kind of discussion took place at the landing. Maybe directions, orders, last-minute reminders of a plan.

The big man tore open the fire door, and they raced into the hallway and directly to the suite. They positioned themselves to either side of the door, the bigger man nodded, and they began to fire. The wood of the door and the glass of the window exploded outward and inward, shrapnel flying. The men fired, changed magazines, and continued firing until the second magazines were empty. Then they turned and raced back the way they had come, down the stairs, through the lobby, and back into the SUV, still idling at the front door. The vehicle gunned away, leaving a cloud of black smoke. The license plate was missing. I thought the SUV was dark green. Or maybe dark gray.

Rick said, "The others have seen this. What do you think?"

I shook my head, uncertain. "The little guy moves like one of the kidnappers, jerky, quick-like. There was a big man there too. Their toboggans match, both with a stripe and diamonds on the forehead. Their clothes could come from anywhere. Play it again, please?" I watched, shaking my head, trying to force it all to make sense as the shootings took place again, and then a third time.

Rick asked, "Could they be churchmen?" When I didn't reply, he said, "Nell?" His voice was nudging, pushing me to make a claim one way or the other.

"They're dressing to look like churchmen. Flannel shirts. Work boots. But the jeans aren't hand-stitched. I can see a leather tag on the little one's belt when they talk at the top of the stairs. The toboggans are store-bought headwear, and no churchman would wear a store-bought toboggan. They don't work as well or keep people as warm. It almost feels like they're *half* churchmen. Play it again, please?"

Silent, Rick pushed buttons on his tablet and repositioned a cat whose brushing tail was in the way. "We're starting over, looking at everything, beginning with the FBI's info, which we received before we left town. Some of their analysts are still proposing that the church might have taken them in, might be providing them a safe haven."

"Why?" When he looked at me blankly, I asked, "Why do the feds think that?"

"Probably because neither the FBI's nor PsyLED's analysts can find where they moved on. HST is here in Knoxville. We're pretty sure of that. So where else would a cult hole up but with another cult?"

That sounded like wishful thinking to me, but I wasn't experienced enough to feel comfortable voicing that opinion. I didn't know what to make of it. Not exactly. But one thing was pretty clear. "I had been thinking, but"—I stopped—"they didn't follow me from the library. They came in fast, and they knew which room we were in. They were after the team, not just me. If the shooters are churchmen, then they've been watching long enough to follow someone in and get the room number. Or they got the information from a hotel clerk earlier."

I sipped my tea, thinking. "Something else about it doesn't look like churchmen. God's Cloud of Glory trains hunters, not shoot-'em-up assassins or Old West gunslingers." Slowly I said, "But the one in front moved like a farmer, not a soldier, not a police officer. He ran with heavy feet, not light feet, but stomping. The smaller man is more light-footed." I frowned, talking my way through it. "He flowed. He moved like a dancer."

"Or a predator," Rick said.

"And there's an odd back-and-forth movement with their shoulders hunched. It's strange." I cocked my head, considering. "Play it again? All the way through?" I watched the entire sequence again from arrival to departure. "The little man," I said, "he's in charge. He's giving orders, except at the end, when it was time to fire. But the bigger man has the experience with the location and maybe the experience with the automatic weapons. There." I pointed at one short section of the action on the screen. "The way they turn their heads and raise their shoulders. That's a strange movement. Their heads swivel back and forth the same way, a ducking motion like lowering their heads between their shoulder blades."

Rick grunted in what sounded like surprise. "I didn't see that. You're right. It's not the same motion a vamp makes, but it's not . . ." He paused and something like pain crossed his face. "Not normal."

"I'm guessing you brought all the security footage from the time you checked in, and someone's been looking through it for the men."

"Yeah. My copious IT department with their dozens of video-search programs."

Even I heard the amused sarcasm in the comment.

"Thanks, boss," JoJo said.

"But it wasn't as hard to find as expected," Rick said. "JoJo?"

She typed something on her tablet and new footage appeared on Rick's laptop. I saw JoJo and Tandy troop into the hotel, carrying gear and a stack of pizza boxes. They were wearing the clothes they had been in before the shooting, and were followed a moment later by a big guy who looked like he knew where he was going. His head was down, so I couldn't see his face, but his hair was short, dark, and worn in a stubbly brush cut. The cameras followed him as he passed the team, seeming to ignore them as they got on the elevator. When the doors closed, he reversed his course and pressed the UP button, watching the lights as they took the team straight up. He followed and stepped out of the elevator. He went left, then turned around and went to the right. He followed slowly, pausing, then moving on, his head down, but with that odd twisting, ducking motion to the left and the right as he moved. Moments later, he passed the suite, stopped, and went back. He stood in front of the team's door for a moment before moving at speed back through the hotel to the parking lot. He got into the same SUV with no plates and left, the tailpipe blowing black smoke.

"How did he follow us to the room when we were already inside?" Rick asked.

"Pizza," I said, giving him a grin. "He followed the pizza smell. Then he stood in the hallway until he heard a voice he recognized."

Rick asked, "Do you know him?" He punched a button. A photograph of the man appeared on the screen.

I breathed in, a quick intake of air that whistled as my throat tried to close up. This photo might have been pulled off the security video feed, but it had been cleaned up and enhanced. It wasn't crystal clear, but it was good enough. And it changed everything. I pulled my feet off the floor onto the chair and wrapped my arms around my legs. "Yes. I think so."

When I didn't go on, Rick looked at Tandy and back to me, fast, as if he was waiting for cues from the empath. Rick asked, "You want to tell me who?"

"I'm pretty sure his name is Boaz Jenkins," I said, my words toneless.

"What can you tell us about him?" Rick asked.

"Last I heard, back when I was a girl, he was a churchman with aspirations of becoming an Elder. He's a paranormal hater from way back. Says all paranormal beings are the devil's work."

"Which would make him the perfect person to be brought into the Human Speakers of Truth," Rick said.

"Satan's spawn, he called me. He's been wanting to burn me at the stake for a decade." The room was dead quiet, except for the purring of a cat, stretched out on Rick's feet. "He has two wives, Elizabeth and Mary." Mary was my friend when I was growing up, but I didn't say it aloud. It hurt too much.

"Outside of wanting to kill all witches, he's steady and patient, can sit in a deer stand or a duck blind all day without moving, and he's a good shot. Brings a lot of game to the compound and gives a portion to the widows and the people too old to hunt or farm. He's . . ." The words stuck in my throat, and I swallowed to make room for talking. "He's said to be heavy-fisted with his women and children. Strong. Works hard. Not real bright sometimes. A follower, not a leader. He'd never make it as an elder."

"You're upset," Tandy said.

I scowled at the empath, who was staring at me. "You reading my mind again?"

Tandy shook his head. "You're sad. Grieving. You loved him?"

"Me?" I squeaked on the word. "Love *Boaz*? No! But . . . his wife was my best friend when I was little. Her, I like a lot. Liked." Mary had been rebellious, like me, and we had spent one entire summer skipping sewing class, running into the woods after morning devotional, damming up creeks and chewing gum stolen from my brother, Sam. Talking about dolls and toys and books and God. She hadn't laughed when I told her that God was everywhere, in every rock and tree and bush and blade of grass.

Marriage to Boaz had changed her. The last time I'd seen her, she was pinch-faced and hadn't made eye contact with me.

"Who do you think the other man was?" Rick asked. "When they came to shoot," he clarified.

"I don't know. Joshua Purdy moves fast," I said. "He's mean as a snake and he'd do something like this. So, Joshua. Maybe. My second choice would be Jackie Jr., but I think Jackie's too smart to pull a stunt like that on his own. He'd send his friends."

I remember that Sister Erasmus had hinted at divisiveness among the men. Divisiveness sometimes created factions. This could be the work of one. "This looks bad for the church."

Rick said gently, "Yes. It does. Though perhaps not for the reasons we think. They may or may not be working with the

Human Speakers of Truth. If they are a paranormal-hating church faction, then they could have discovered independently that a paranormal unit of law enforcement—PsyLED—was in town and decided to make a statement."

All that was true, but it still came back to a fight too long avoided. To me hiding in the safety of my house in a defensive position instead of taking the fight—*my fight*—to the churchmen. I was a mouse hiding in the shadows. If I kept on hiding, someone other than me was going to get hurt. Hurt bad. Killed. Or . . . "Wait," I said. "What about the two in the front of the SUV? Did you get photographs of them in traffic cameras?"

Rick's eyes crinkled in a smile that didn't reach his mouth, and tapped a key and touched a spot on the computer screen. A close-up of the men in the front seats appeared. The driver had changed some since the high school yearbook photo I had of him. But I was fairly certain that he was Simon Dawson Jr. "The backslider," I said. "And I bet you bunches that the older man in the passenger seat is his daddy, Dawson Sr., both seen on church grounds by Sister Erasmus. This faction of men— the Dawsons and Boaz and the little guy—might have gone over to the HST."

Rick punched a button on the laptop and said, "Meet Oliver Smithy, the fourth man in the SUV and an HST organizer. This puts HST and a church faction in the same place at the same time, attacking federal agents."

"Ohhh." A feeling like static electricity stung its way through me, leaving me overheated and breathless. The church I had run from for so long was even more evil than I had expected or believed.

Through the floor, something moved on the land to the southeast, at the Vaughn farm, something motorized, traveling in the dark, toward my land. I leaped to the front window and picked up a shotgun, checked the load. "Company coming," I said. Rick followed me, a weapon in each hand, and I was reminded of how fast he was the first time I saw him. Behind me, the lanterns went out one by one.

"An all-terrain vehicle," I said, pointing, "is moving through the night in our general direction. I think it's on an old farm road."

Silently Rick slipped outside. T. Laine followed, a gun in

her right hand and something in her left. Probably a magical trinket. JoJo took up a place near me. Tandy stood between the open front door and the window, protected by a wall. "Two people," he said, loud enough for us all to hear. "One is furious. Her energies and emotions boil like water on a hot stove," he said. "The other is quiet, uncertain, but determined. Male." Tandy's face wore something like awe, the expression crinkling over his pale white skin. "I've never experienced emotions over so far a distance before. I love your woods."

The lights of the ATV cut through the trees, creating long lines of shadows and illuminating strips of land in washed-out tones of gray and green. I walked onto the porch, the night air icy as the roar grew in volume and the lights bumped from the old farm road down to the road in front of my house, and across it onto my land. It swerved to miss the dogs' graves and then swerved to miss the raised beds. The lights brightened the porch for a moment, where we stood with guns, waiting. The vehicle stopped. The motor went silent, leaving the smell of exhaust, the lights still on but directed at the stairs, not up at us.

"Miz Ingram?" a voice called. "It's Clarence Vaughn. I got your sister Mindy here. She's mighty upset and desirous of talking to you. Said you'd give me twenty dollars to bring her here and take her home."

"Mud?" I had expected Jackie, here to cause trouble. Or at best, Priss, coming to me for safety. And I didn't have twenty dollars.

Rick holstered one of his guns and pulled a twenty from his wallet, holding it in the glaring headlights. "Mindy, come get the money, and take it to the man."

My little sister appeared in the dark, long gangly limbs and scrawny body beneath the churchgirls' clothes. She was wearing a dress with no apron and boots with no stockings, no coat or sweater though it was cold out tonight. Mud took the bill and sprinted back to the ATV, then raced to the porch again.

"Daddy said I wasn't to come," she said. "But somebody done took Esther. She was standing with her intended, Jedidiah Whisnut, after evening devotionals, and somebody done run up and hit Jed. When he woke up, Esther was gone. Somebody took her. Priss said you would know what to do."

Shock stole any response from me, and all I could think of

was the note. I had known. He had told me what he intended
to do. And I hadn't done anything to stop this from happening.
"Jackie," I whispered.

"We'll take care of it," Rick said.

"Promise?" Mud demanded.

Rick smiled slightly, making me think he had sisters.
"Cross my heart and hope to die. Stick a needle in my eye."

"That's yucky," my full sib said. "But it'll do." She raced to
the ATV again and climbed aboard. "Hurry. Afore Daddy
knows I'm gone," she demanded. Vaughn started the engine
and made a small circle, the tires grinding into my grass. The
ATV roared and quickly disappeared back up onto the disused
farm road. Rick took my arm and led me back inside, closing
the door on the night. The heat was smothering. I could hardly
breathe. But someone placed a cup of tea in my hand and
forced me to take a sip. Someone else put a blanket around me,
though it was too hot. I sat there. Thinking. All I needed was
some of Jackie's blood. A single drop would do.

I pushed the blanket away and set down the tea, which was
cold now. Time must have passed.

Surprising even myself with the words, I said, "I'm going
to the church tomorrow for dawn devotional. I'm taking bread
and some canned goods. And I'm gonna make a ruckus and
get back my sister."

Rick said, "No. That is not going to happen."

THIRTEEN

"You're no longer a civilian asset. You're part of this unit, and you don't have the training or the experience."

"I'm the *only* one with the training and experience," I said softly, feeling the tremor of shock as my words ricocheted through me. "I'm going in to show the photo of Boaz and the Dawson men to an elder and his wives. People I trust. And tell them what happened. If Boaz is hiding on church land or if they've heard where he might be, they'll tell me. Boaz is a weak link. He's a bully and a coward. You get him, and you can make him talk about the people he's involved with and where they are. Boaz is the way to stop the kidnappings." I paused for a moment before I finished with, "And then I'm gonna raid Jackie's house and take Esther back."

"She's quite serious," Tandy said.

"They believe that women are weak," I said, "and stupid and easily led by men. They think a woman will do anything, be anything, a man tells her to. In their experience, they're right. Being hurt will make most people agreeable to anything, to stop pain, men and women both. So I'm going in and hope I can get back out."

"Tomorrow doesn't give us time enough to put anything together," T. Laine said. "Make it the day after." There was something in her tone that set my teeth on edge, but I ignored it. "It has to be Saturday morning," I said, hearing the quiet burr of my anger, "not Sunday, because Sunday means services all day. They won't stop services to deal with *feminine accusations*," I said, using the term the churchmen would use. "If I don't get to Elder Aden and the Nicholson clan on Saturday, the problems will be shelved until Monday." My voice rose. "The church doesn't *deal* with *problems* on Sunday.

That's a day of worship and rest. Nothing else, and I mean nothing, is dealt with on Sunday. The elders will demand that I be locked up and left until Monday. And if it's true that a church faction is involved with the kidnappings, it won't be the peaceable menfolk who have them, it'll be the crazies, the women haters. It's likely none of the girls will last very long."

JoJo said, "This is stupid, first, because none of us is letting you go in—"

T. Laine interrupted, "No, she's right. It needs to be fast, when they least expect it. But we could wire you."

"No wires," I insisted. "Now. Not later."

"If we give her a laptop or cell phone, we can track her with it," JoJo said.

Rick's face was a stone.

I said, "They'll just destroy any electronics. They're not all uneducated. Churchmen have been to college and then come home. They designed the security systems, the communications systems; they even set up a Web site for the church, though it hasn't been updated in years." Which suddenly struck me as curious. Had the college-educated men left the church? I hadn't heard rumors, but I wasn't exactly in the middle of things anymore. Rick was watching me, and I had no idea what he saw on my face, but he didn't like it.

"I thought God's Cloud of Glory didn't believe in education," JoJo said.

"Mostly you're right. Education isn't valued much; that's part of the whole prideful thing. But Jackie Jr. went to college. So did some of his friends."

I tried to remember the names of the two men who had set up the security systems. To Rick I said, "See what you have on Nadab and Nahum Stubbins." I stopped. The boys who'd come to shoot up my house had come across Stubbins property. The odd hedge of vines was growing up at the Stubbins boundary. But I couldn't see how those things would coincide with the shooting at the hotel. None of the men in the SUV had been a Stubbins. I shook the thoughts away. "Their family land adjoins mine." I pointed vaguely off to the wall of vines and thorns.

"The Stubbinses used to be part of the church in the nineteen fifties or something. Then they got into a disagreement with Colonel Ernest Jackson Sr. on some key point of spiritual interpretation and left." Or were ostracized? Had the Stubbinses been kicked out of God's Cloud? Had they been friends with the backslider Dawsons? I pulled on old memories, trying to recall things I'd never had an interest in. "About twelve, fifteen years ago, some of them reconciled and came back. The elder Stubbins had grandsons by then, who had been raised out of the church. They didn't fit in and were sent off to school. I don't know where they studied, but they left and then came back. I remember them on the compound when I was a young'un."

All the unmarried girls—and a number of the married ones—had cast their eyes at the older boys. They had been in their early twenties or so, and clean-shaven with soft-looking hair that fell across their brows, touchable and forbidden. There had been a lot of sinful gossip about the men, couched in ways to get them to stay.

I shook my head at the memories. "Last I heard, to keep the brothers near, the Elders offered them their pick of wives. I remember that one or the other took two girls, married according to the church, and settled down." I squinted, pulling at old, seemingly unimportant, relationships. "I remember seeing the brothers in services when I went with Leah and John, before she died. Must a been nearly eight years ago, but things change. I remember a list of current churchmen in the PsyLED files," I said to Rick. "Pull them up?"

Without demur, he opened a file on his laptop, and I studied it. Neither Stubbins was listed, but maybe they lived on the farm still, not on church grounds. I had remembered thinking that one of the boys who had come to my house had been a Stubbins. It would make sense what with them coming up the steep hill from Stubbins land. A gully on the Stubbins farm had been used for decades as a shooting range, and the late-night target practice still echoed up the hills from there.

And Priss had sent Mud for help. Priss had married into the Campbell clan, the Campbells were kissing cousins to the Vaughns, and the Vaughns lived off the compound. And a Vaughn had brought Mud to me with the warning. The Vaughns would know things. It was all tied together the way church-women tied things, with a quiet word here or there, a nudge, a prod, a whispered word of pillow talk. The way mice—and people who had been abused—did things. Undercover, with secrets and whispers. Churchwomen, mice, *Priss*, sending information to me to give to PsyLED. Yes. That was it, surely as the sun set in the west.

But all this understanding was useless unless I could get to the church and save Esther. If I didn't, I had a feeling that nobody would. I was changing from a mouse into something bigger. Something stronger. And I was gonna do this—save Esther—no matter what.

To T. Laine, I said, "I'll have my clothes, my Bible, my breadbasket, my pocketbook with ID and driver's license. Anything I take in has to fit in those." *With my gun.*

"You're not going in tomorrow," Rick said, his voice cold and closed, the way a man sounded when he brooked no argument. "There was a shooting directed against federal officials. One of the gunmen, Boaz Jenkins, was positively identified— by you—as being a member of God's Cloud. The feds are trying to put together enough evidence to convince a judge of the need for a subpoena to raid the compound. I won't let you disrupt that possibility." This was information that he hadn't been going to tell me, I could tell by the look on his face, his and T. Laine's— that they all knew about a potential FBI raid. All but me.

Rick added, "And you need to know something. When we were researching who had passports among the HST and the church, we found something about your family. Two weeks ago, there were passports issued in the names of Priscilla Nicholson, Fredericka Vaughn, Caleb Campbell, and six children with the last name Campbell. A Johnson Campbell is involved in this in some way. I thought you said that church people never leave the US?"

The cold that had settled in me froze my veins again. He was trying to suggest that Priss' husband and she were working with HST. "No." The word came out a whisper. I started to cross my arms over my chest and stopped. I realized that I must spend a bit of time in the presence of people with my shoulders hunched. Like a churchwoman with a mean-fisted husband. But I wasn't hiding or protecting myself anymore. I knuckled my hands and put my shoulders back. The posture was odd to me, but somehow empowering.

Rick studied my bearing and a half smile settled on his

mouth. I didn't know what it meant, but he seemed pleased. "Nell. You can't go in to the compound." He added, almost gently, "I won't let you."

Anger flashed through me like a crick in a flood. I almost shouted, "The only way to find out anything and save Esther is for me to go inside!" Instead, I bit my mouth closed on the words. I was a woman grown. My decisions were mine. My rebellion was mine. My sins were mine. Someone—Jackie?— had attacked my sister. *And me,* a new small voice whispered in my head. *I'm important too. I should have taken the battle to them long ago.* Alien thoughts. Rebellion pushed down deep, where, hopefully, Rick couldn't see it and Tandy couldn't feel it.

But I was going to have to do this the way churchwomen did things: by subterfuge, not by direct confrontation. I hated it. *I hated it.* But I let my shoulders droop in defeat. I let tears fill my eyes, easy to do because of fear for Esther. Lying. All of it a lie. But the only way. And because Tandy was watching, I let the fear fill me.

I knew that the end didn't justify the means, and that I was lying to them all. Evil was evil and a lie was a lie, no matter how well intentioned, but I couldn't think of another way to do what needed to be done in time. By Sunday, Esther would be broken. "Fine," I whispered, and let my tears fall.

I stood up and walked away, shoulders hunched. I put away clean dishes, swept the floors, dusted—even the four-barreled shotgun hanging on the stairwell wall—and replenished some herbal remedies, packaging others. I made up some herbal aromatherapy lotions and body scrubs.

Hiding other actions beneath the women's work, I also packed a breadbasket to be ready for the morning. Loaded John's old six-shooter. Packed my laptop in the basket under a cloth and the gun beneath that. I seldom stayed up this late, but I couldn't go to bed. So I worked, keeping my mind occupied with chores and fear as I schemed and planned.

Long after midnight, there was very little power left, the house windows dim, the motion-detecting security light in the yard off due to lack of activity. Inside the house, the special agents were sitting in the light of oil lanterns, working on their computers, draining the precious final power by charging their batteries.

There was nothing I could add to the investigation at this point, so I was curled on the swing on the front porch, sitting in the dark, a fuzzy afghan and a blanket wrapped around me, watching the first snowfall of the year as it dropped in lazy spirals and melted upon contact with the ground. In Knoxville, in the Tennessee Valley, the snow would melt in the air and be pure rain by the time it landed. Here, I had the first hint of real winter.

I was halfway dozing when I heard/felt the werecats leap across the border into my wood. They moved in long loping strides, Paka in front, the vibrations of their travel drumming through the ground. They weren't running at full speed, more a stretched-out jog that covered ground fast. They stopped at the deer carcass, chasing off a family of foxes that had taken temporary possession. I heard the squeals and growls, but the foxes gave ground to the bigger predators, who ripped into the meat. When they had eaten their fill, the cats rose and groomed each other with coarse tongues that pulled the blood and viscera off their coats. The grooming was strangely intimate, but it wasn't sexual, not as cats would consider it, though humans would have thought it all about mating. The cats were just cleaning each other of the scent of death, a familial endeavor, something littermates might do together.

Then they batted one another and rolled in the brush, play-fighting, biting, scratching, and growling. Paka and Occam were having fun in the falling snow, but I was tired, and I knew there would be no sleep until they were back at the house, so I tried something I had never done before. I put a bare foot on the icy porch floor and thought about Paka being back here. Thought about her curled up on the sofa with Rick, a warm cup of milk in her hand.

I felt Paka's head snap up, ears pricking. And then she was racing down the hill, along the old logging road that wound under an arch of stone, around the hill's crest, and down toward my house. I pulled my foot into the warmth of the blankets and waited, wondering what I had just done. I had . . . summoned her, like a witch might summon a demon. Or a familiar. That's what the churchmen would say of me, and of her. Witch and demon, devil and familiar. Both deserving to be burned at the stake.

I was able to follow Paka and Occam as they sped down the hills, and at the same time could feel the foxes, a mother and three grown kits, as they descended on the deer's remains once again. When the two big-cats hit the road in front of the house, I stood and gathered up the blanket and afghan. The cats had to change, and seeing them shift back to human, naked, was too personal an act for me to witness. Or perhaps I was a prude. Despite being raised in polygamous families, most of the churchwomen were. I got a glimpse of the cats, though, one spotted black and orange gold, the other melanistic, the spots nearly hidden beneath the black, as they raced through the falling snow. The vision was beautiful and deadly, and my woods liked them far too much.

The heat of the house once again hit me like a dry fist, and I dropped the blankets on the sofa, walking through the lantern light to the stove where I put on a kettle to humidify the space. Poured milk into a mug to heat for Paka. "Paka and Occam are in the yard," I said over my shoulder. "They have clothes out there somewhere, right?"

Rick, sitting at the desk again, sounded distracted, said, "Yes. Gobag in the van. Have you seen this man before?" He whirled his laptop, which cast a sickly bluish light across John's old desk. The photo wasn't very good quality, but it wouldn't have mattered. The man was old with a grizzled face and slack, bluish lips. Dead. I shook my head, uncertain. I asked, "Is he the older man from the SUV? Could it be Simon Dawson Sr.?"

Rick said, "We have no independent verification. According to his fingerprints, he's a leader in HST, but there's no name or ID to go with the prints. He was found, deceased, by Knoxville PD. The alert went out and downloaded to my system the last minutes before we climbed your mountain, and I just now opened it. His body was full of mixed metal silver shot."

"Why silver shot?" I asked. "That's expensive." And then I felt horrible, thinking of cost when a man had been killed. Was that what I had to look forward to if I continued working with PsyLED? Thoughts less about human compassion and more about forensics and evidence?

"Yes it is," Rick muttered, sounding worried. "And it's for weres and vamps, not humans, though it'll kill them just as dead."

I wondered suddenly if silver shot would kill me and decided I could live without knowing the answer to that one.

"If he's Dawson Sr., then that gives us a second link between a faction of God's Cloud and of the Human Speakers," Rick said. "Your friend, Sister Something. What's her name?"

"Sister Erasmus?"

"Yeah. At some point, can you show her the photos of the men in the SUV and our dead guy? She might remember if Boaz and the Dawsons were involved in some way."

"Yes," I said, keeping my tone soft and beaten, all the while mentally berating him for not wanting me to go onto the church grounds first thing in the morning. I didn't like being a cheat.

He handed me a tiny thumb drive. "Pics on here."

"So did Simon Dawson Jr. and Sr. help the churchmen in the kidnappings or just in trying to kill us all?" JoJo asked.

"All we *know* is that they helped shoot up our hotel room," Rick said, looking around the room the same way he had the first time he came here. "If we catch the driver, a charge of conspiracy to murder federal officials will get him to roll over on his gun-happy pals. And I hope that will lead us to the people in charge of the abductions."

"If you can get the driver to talk before the rest of the girls die," JoJo said.

"I checked in with Benton before we lost contact with the outside world. No one has called in a ransom demand on Mira Clayton," Rick said, rubbing his eyes. "Mira could still be a copycat. The first two girls were taken and the media got hold of the story before the next two were taken. There's no video footage of the last two disappearances, no witnesses, and the white van the fishermen saw when Girl Four was taken might not be the same white van we're looking for. One thing the FBI found out, courtesy of a helpful judge who allowed them access to his medical records, is that Dawson had some contact while in rehab with a member of the HST. It's our second connection. Or third, if you count Oliver Smithy." Rick scrubbed his face with both hands as if trying to rub the exhaustion away. "Dawson seems to be the single link that brings the two organizations together, the abductions and the shooting of our hotel together, and HST and the church together. So far, everything else is circumstantial.

"No one picked up a scent of Mira in the woods and neither did the canine units." Rick shook his head, as if shaking away things that didn't add up.

I remembered that the police dogs' search had been planned in the patch of woods near Mira's private school. It was difficult to keep up with all the things that went into an investigation, everything fluid and shifting from moment to moment, different members doing different things at the same time, and then debriefing as needed.

I had never thought seriously about leaving my woods, but I wondered what it might be like to be an investigator for real, to go to PsyLED school and train in all the things the team had. The very thought of leaving my woods made my heart race and my breathing come fast.

But . . . what I had planned for morning would ruin any possibility of that. I'd be surprised if they'd pay me for my work until now.

The thoughts fled as the two werecats came in through the front door, wearing baggy clothes, barefooted, their eyes glowing the pale gold of their cats, Occam's faintly browner, Paka's slightly greener. Occam went straight to the kitchen and opened the refrigerator, pulling out the container of left-over beans, and poured some into two bowls. He brought them across the room, cold, a serving spoon in each. Paka slinked through the room and settled on the sofa. Occam put one of the bowls of beans at Paka's knees and they both dug in.

Occam closed his eyes as he swallowed. "This is fantastic, Nell, sugar." His face warmed into an expression close to ecstasy as he took a second bite. "Holy hell. Best thing I've tasted since I left Texas." He looked at Rick. "Even better than your chili, boss man."

"Even better than a deer, fresh killed?" I asked.

Occam slanted his cat eyes at me and smiled as he chewed. He swallowed and said, "Nothing is better than fresh-caught venison. But this is a close second. I might have to marry you."

I knew he was teasing back and some of my awful fear for my sister eased. "I'm not the marrying kind anymore. But I'll happily fix you hamburgers on Tuesday."

Occam chortled and nearly choked on beans at the Popeye reference. I had done a little research on the phrase and the cartoon character while in the library. "Well, blow me down," he said, quoting another Popeye line. "Nell, sugar, is all up on popular culture."

"I don't think Popeye counts as popular," I said. "More like post–World War Two."

"What you say? 'I'll take you all on, one at a time!'" Which was another famous line. "Seriously, good beans," he added. "I ain't had nothing better since I joined PsyLED."

A remembered warmth filled an empty place under my ribs as I watched him eat. I had forgotten how satisfying it could be to see someone eat food I had prepared. John had been a delight to cook for, eating second and third helpings all the way up until he started to lose weight and died. The dinner table had been the only joyful part of our married life. Suddenly I recalled his laughter, booming in the tall ceilings as he told a joke. I ducked my head, thinking, remembering. Perhaps there were good times in among the bad, the difficult, and the compromises I had made to stay alive and safe.

Rick shuffled papers and clicked on his laptop with the intensity of a cat on hunt. Not paying the rest of us attention. Giving the cats time to fuel up. The others were working on laptops, keys tapping softly.

I brought the mug of tepid milk to Paka, not sure what else I could do except be a hostess. "Why did you join?" I asked Occam. "PsyLED, I mean?"

"I spent twenty years in a cage," he said between bite, chew, chew, swallow. Bite, chew, chew, swallow. "I'm making sure paranormals get some protection. And no other law enforcement agency would have a were."

He said it without anger or bitterness, the same way he would have said that his car needed washing or he needed a new pair of Western boots. As if he was used to the prejudice, hatred, and fear all were-creatures lived with every day of their lives.

"Please, sir. Can I have some more?" he asked, affecting a hungry and pitiful mien, holding out his empty bowl.

That was a cultural reference even I knew, and I dipped up more beans for him. When I came back from the kitchen, Rick pushed his laptop away and looked around the room. "Well?" he asked the cats.

They continued to shovel in beans as if they were starving, as if the dead buck had meant nothing to their caloric needs. Four spoonfuls later, Occam said, "The vantage is excellent, with a cliff from Nell's property that looks directly over the compound." Bite, chew, chew, swallow. Repeat. "But the church has cameras pointing up, probably motion sensing. Don't think we triggered them. We found places in the limbs of trees and sat awhile, watching. The placement of, and number of, guards has been changed since Jane Yellowrock's team raided it back in the summer." Bite, chew, chew, swallow. "They're carrying automatic rifles with extended mags, similar to the weapons used to shoot up the hotel. All mature men, all with training that seems much better than what Jane's team reported. About half the teams have attack dogs. We think we located all the cameras." Bite, chew, chew, swallow. "This is wonderful. Nell, sugar, you are a goddess in the kitchen."

I knew he meant it as a compliment and not a comment about idolatry, and I ducked my head, letting my hair slide forward to hide my pleasure. He shoveled in the last of the beans, moving to the sofa, stretching out his legs, bare feet beneath the coffee table, his toes pawing the braided rag rug like a cat.

Paka took up the narrative in her hoarse, scratchy voice. "Cat eyes are better than human eyes," she said. "We saw three white vans, but they were turned so that we could not see if dents were present."

At some point, Rick had printed satellite views and RVAC flyover photographs of the compound and taped them together, forming one huge aerial-view map, with the use of each building noted in red ink. He spread the large map on the coffee table, each detail crisp and clear. Paka, holding her cooling milk one-handed, traced her finger beyond an open area where perhaps a dozen cars were parked in the daylight shot, to a smaller space behind a building. "Here. The white vans are parked behind this building, where they cannot be seen from the entrance or by driving casually through."

"That's where the vans are always parked," I said.

Occam said, "There are more men here." He pointed to a spot along the cliff wall that bordered my property. It was near the entrances to the caves. "And we saw some lights moving along from here"—his finger traced a line—"to here, before disappearing."

"There's no road there," I said. "Look at your maps. There was no road there when I was a young— when I was a child, and there's no road in your satellite maps. Not even in your flyover drone thing, the RVAC."

Rick shuffled papers and found a printed view of the camp. "Remote-viewing aircraft. And you're right. No road. So what's over there?"

A peculiar tingling swept through me, a knowing, a coming together of possibilities that smacked of all kinds of reasoning and settled into a hunch. "The Stubbins farm. The drone—the RVAC," I corrected, "that took photos of God's Cloud's property didn't go past the property to other farms, did it? You believe that HST took sanctuary in Knoxville, maybe with some nonaligned or disaffected or former church family. The Stubbinses, they sound like good candidates to have offered their property as sanctuary. And the place you saw lights moving?" I said to the cats. "That's near the boundary of the Stubbins farm." When I stopped talking, the house was quiet for a long stretch of time, marked by the faint creak of the windmill out back. Rick lifted his eyes from the satellite map and met mine. His were glowing greenish gold, a supernatural glow that spoke of the werecat he couldn't shift into.

"Could be something. The feds will be happy to hear it, when we get back to someplace with a signal. Okay, people," Rick said, folding up the map and turning off his laptop. "Nell's out of power, and dawn comes fast. Tomorrow, we need to gather as much intel on the Stubbinses as we can. In the morning, Paka and Occam, you'll shift again and we'll rig you with radios. You'll go back as close to the Stubbins farm as possible and get intel. If Nell's right about a faction of the church being involved with the Human Speakers of Truth, then maybe the Stubbins farm is a possible location for HST and our three missing abductees."

I noticed that he didn't include my sister as a missing girl. Something inside grew tight and hard at that omission. With one major exception, the local law enforcement had always felt that God's Cloud's girls brought whatever happened on themselves. Protection wasn't offered to us. "I thought radios didn't work on Nell's property," T. Laine said.

Rick answered, his tone without emotion, "Jane's crew found a way to rig a system, short-term and short distance. I've got similar equipment in the van, so I'll park here"—he pointed to a road on the map—"and set it up. But we have plenty of time to work it out in the morning. Let's get some shut-eye."

Though I was intensely aware of all the noises in the house, I did manage to get some sleep in the four hours before I had to get up. It felt abnormal to not have cats on my narrow bed, but they had deserted my blankets for the beds of the big-cats. It felt even more odd to feel the purrs of cats reverberate through the floors; were-big-cats often purred in their sleep, it seemed. Everything felt unfamiliar in every way, and my dreams were chaotic, visions of running across my garden and through the woods, chased by vans that purred like cats. And more horrible dreams where I raced into a room to save Esther. And was too late.

It was difficult getting dressed for the day in silence that allowed my guests to sleep on. In my small nook, keeping my thoughts clear and calm so as not to wake Tandy, especially, I dressed in the clothes that had dried overnight in front of the woodstove, clothing appropriate for a repenting churchwoman—gray skirt to my calves, heavy leggings, black boots to my knees, covering all the skin between hem and boot. Chemise, two layered pull-over shirts, a sweater, and a coat. I was hoping that I could force my daddy to go with me after Esther this morning, or I'd go after her myself if necessary. I also needed to show Sister Erasmus the men in the photos, the ones in the SUV and Boaz from the shooting. I needed to get in and out easily even if it meant lying blatantly about everything. I wasn't good at lying. I wasn't good at any of this. But I had one chance to get in, get Esther, learn something, and get out. And I was taking it.

I pulled my hair up into a tight bun, the kind that made my face looked pinched, the kind the women wore after they had been to the punishment house, to show they had learned whatever lesson they had been taught. I had a peculiar thought as I was dressing. What if men had a punishment house, and women administered justice there? Impossible. But intriguing. And it made me smile in ways that were surely vengeful and sinful.

There was no way to get a real breakfast, so I made do with two slices of bread and some of last year's blackberry jam and last night's coffee, hot and thick as mud. And then I was in John's old truck, driving down the dirt road, a cell phone I had stolen on the way outside in my breadbasket, along with the laptop and John's old six-shooter. The phone was turned on and had a GPS tracker in it so the unit could find me if worse came to worst. It would go into my pocket, and the laptop would stay in the basket beneath the bread. The phone was surely programmed with Rick's number and all the numbers of the team. When I got ready to go into the compound, I'd call Rick, leave a message, tell him what I was doing, hide the cell, and drive in. And hope the electronics weren't discovered and destroyed.

As I took the dark roads, my brain started picking at me, poking holes in what was a holey proposition in the first place. On the surface going back to the compound was a stupid move, but in reality, it was a now-or-never move to try to save Esther. And if I managed it right, find Dawson, find Boaz, and . . . maybe even bleed Jackie dead.

I had been waiting for years, just sitting there on Soulwood, mouse-like, suffering increasingly more dangerous attacks from the churchmen, waiting to be burned out, waiting to be raped and dragged back to God's Cloud, punished, and killed. Burned at the stake. *Waiting.* For *years* I had been *waiting.* Sitting on my land like a duck on a pond in front of a duck blind, in the faint hope my sisters would come to me for protection—a protection I could scarcely provide for my own self. Priss was right. I was just plain stupid.

For the first time ever, I had what PsyLED called backup, assuming they *would* back me up when I was going against direct orders. While I was there, I needed to see about the white vans, to check if, just perchance, one had a dented bumper. I needed to see with my own eyes if there were strangers in the compound, which I could do only at devotionals, when the whole church was gathered together. I needed to get in safely, which was easiest in the predawn hours. I needed to do this. For everyone. For me. Rick would be . . . probably madder than when I kicked him in the testicles.

Getting there so early, before dawn devotions, meant there would be much less attention paid to arrivals. I was bunned-up and dressed like a churchwoman. A cursory search would be made by guards, who would glance inside the vehicle, probably nothing more, as church members who lived off church grounds traditionally drove in to join the daily morning and evening devotions and Sunday services. The guards were always men, and churchmen were naturally predisposed to think of women as no threat, so there was less of a chance that I'd be thoroughly searched than if I were a man.

Nervous thoughts buzzing my head like bees, I drove down the mountain through the dark of predawn. Excitement began to build in my bloodstream. I was fighting back. Finally. I was fighting back.

The guards at the gate didn't know me, and after a perfunctory look inside with a high-powered flashlight, they waved me through. I had turned off the cell phone and hidden it under the seat, but I broke out in a hot sweat, worrying that it would ring anyway and give me away. That was guilt thinking, accusing me for acting against the church and against PsyLED. My childhood training still held sway over logic and sense, and I had to wonder how much of my other thinking was tainted by a childhood where my mind had been molded by the strict confines of the . . . *the cult . . . the cult, not the church.*

I was breathless when I was finally cleared to enter, and I motored slowly along the tree-lined drive to the compound, my headlights picking out tree trunks and brush and a new chain-link fence, twelve feet high and topped with barbed wire. *Escape-proof,* I thought. I drove into the compound with no impediments, directly up to Sister Erasmus' house.

The sister was married to Elder Aden, who acted as an arbiter and referee during church disputes. They would be either my best allies or my worst enemies in what I had come to do. There were lights on inside, indicating that the family was up, doing morning chores. *Now or never.*

I turned the phone back on and dialed Rick's number, which was programmed in, expecting to get voice mail, because the cell signal wouldn't reach through my land. Instead, he answered, yelling, "Nell?" He sounded furious, the roar of a vehicle in the background. I figured my escape had been discovered and they were already on the way, after me. I said, "Ummm. I'm in the compound. I'm going to see Sister Erasmus. And find what Erasmus knows about Esther's whereabouts. And if they know about the men PsyLED is after." *Against orders.*

Rick cursed. I wasn't that familiar with cussing of any kind, but his sounded mighty inventive. Followed by a growling, "Do you want to tell me why?"

"I'm a civilian informant. I got information that a girl was being . . ." I stopped, finding it hard to take a breath. ". . . was being brutalized. I'm going in to ask questions about her and about a faction of the church that might be working with HST. I can't sit around no more, waiting for orders. And iffen you wanta back me up, I'd appreciate it."

"Keep the cell on and in your pocket," he snarled. And he sounded just like a cat when he did.

"I will," I said. "And thank you."

Without listening to his reply, I placed the cell phone in my skirt pocket and stepped from the truck. Trepidation snaking through me, I walked to the Adens' house and knocked on the door.

Sister Erasmus' sister-wife opened the door, still dressed in her nightgown, her back hunched and her shoulders rounded with age, blinking blearily into the dark. "Who is it?" Erasmus asked, appearing behind Elder Aden's first wife, Mary. Erasmus was dressed, her hair braided and bunned-up. Early as it was, I had to wonder if she'd slept that way. "Forgive me the early visit, Sisters," I said, "but I need to talk to you."

"Nell?" Erasmus said, sounding curious but not surprised. "It's fine, Mama Mary. I'll take care of her. You go back and get dressed for devotionals." To me she said, "I just put coffee on. Come in outta the cold. Hospitality and safety while you're here."

I entered and took the chair she indicated at the kitchen table. Over my head I heard the stamping of little feet and the sounds of children's voices. I didn't have to ask. Sister Erasmus said, "This old house was too big for TJ, Sister Mary, and me. My boy Douglas lives on the second floor with his wives, Mharvy and Lisa, and two little'uns. Mary's newly married son, Larry, and his wife, Colleen, live on the third floor, and four of our unmarried girls stay on the top floor, helping with us elders and all the young'uns at the same time, Laurie, Joelle, Barbara, and Carol—good girls, but not of a mind to marry young. Independent. Like you," she finished, and placed a mug of coffee in front of me. I sipped and put the mug on the table to cool as Erasmus settled across from me.

"Thank you, Sister, for seeing me. I'm guessing you know I'm not here for me." She inclined her head in acknowledgment. A visit to the church wouldn't be for my own self. I lifted my laptop from my basket and opened the traffic camera photograph of Simon Dawson and the older man. I slid it across to her. "Are these two men the Dawsons? Father and son?"

Sister Erasmus didn't look at the laptop photos, blowing on her hot coffee. "Who's asking?"

"PsyLED and the FBI. Trying to find some kidnapped girls."

"I done told you they ain't on church grounds."

"I know." I indicated the laptop. "Please?"

The sister leaned over and studied the photographs. "That's them. Simon and his boy, the pervert and fornicator and blood drinker. That boy lay with vampires and fed them his blood. His father . . ." Her voice trailed off, and she didn't finish her thought. "Both of them are backsliders. If they done wrong, it weren't with the church." Her dark eyes stabbed me. "You gonna cause this church trouble and pain?"

"No, Sister. I'm trying to keep the church safe and turn the police attention to the backslider factions breaking the law."

"See that you do."

I punched a key and brought up the photograph of Boaz Jenkins in the hotel. "The only knot in my plans is this. I don't know if Boaz is still in good standing with the church. Because if he is, the church needs to turn him over for shooting up a hotel and attempting to kill federal agents."

"Dear God in heaven," she murmured, closing her eyes after a single glance at the screen.

"I reckon that's a yes. Is he still living on the compound?"

"No. Him and his moved down the hill to Oliver Springs last winter. But he attends services time to time. Hunts with the men."

"Did you know that Jackie took Esther last night?"

"I heard that *someone* did. I gave TJ the note Jackie left for you. He's got men out, trying to find her, working with the deacons and the elders."

"Jackie took her. You *know* that. She needs to be rescued. *Now.* If she isn't free by the end of devotionals, I'm going after her. After Jackie. Myself."

Sister Erasmus closed her eyes and finished her coffee in a single steaming gulp. "I'll tell TJ. Now you git. I gotta dress and be ready for devotions. Do I need to bring a gun?"

"I don't know, Sister Erasmus," I said, startled. "I purely don't know."

Back in my truck I asked Rick, "Did you get all that?"

"Every word." He sounded less angry, which was a relief.

I heard the ambient sounds of the van driving, and knew he was still on the move. "Are you coming to help me or to stop me?"

"I don't know yet," he growled.

"Good enough. My next stop is the Nicholson house." He didn't reply, and I drove through the dark gray of early dawn to the Nicholson house, the place where I had lived for the first twelve years of my life. Lights began appearing in homes in the compound as lanterns were lit and electric lights were turned on. I heard chickens clucking and roosters crowing from all over the compound as the world of God's Cloud woke to greet the day. Everything looked just as I remembered it from my childhood, except for a single glimpse of a dog and a man armed with a gun meant to kill people instead of deer.

Yet, even with the newfangled gun as evidence of change, there was no way all of this would be so easy if the church proper was involved in the kidnappings. I'd have been stopped at the gate. The small, alert, PsyLED part of me began to relax. The larger, cult girl part me got more nervous because factions inside the church made all I thought I knew into different things entirely.

I pulled into a parking spot beside a red truck. My father

had always driven a red truck. My palms were sweaty, my skin was damp, and my breathing was too fast. I was going to knock on the door. I was going to see my . . . my family. My mother and maw-maw. My father. A man I never, ever thought about. The one person I had never forgiven because John had insinuated that Daddy had tried to sell me to the colonel as a minor wife when I was twelve. Which I now understood might have been a lie. I turned off the engine and pocketed the key. But Daddy was still the man who'd let Mama go to the punishment house. Unless I had that all wrong too. Was it possible? But no. I had a half brother from Mama and Brother Ephraim. That part was right. Had to be.

Lantern light poured from the lower windows, flickering on the pathway, illumination so unlike electric lights. The house looked the same—four large front windows, four stories, one for each wife, one for the older kids, each floor with a bathroom, three or four bedrooms, and a tiny sitting area. Mama hadn't been the first wife, and we had been forced to climb stairs constantly, our feet loud on the wood steps. The layout came to me clearly, the rag rugs and hand-finished wood furniture. The white walls hung with handmade quilts and shelves full of knickknacks made by children. The huge kitchen and wide living room with its big fireplace. Mama Carmel and Mama Grace bantering with my own Mama Cora. Maw-maw in the kitchen kneading dough. Micaiah Nicholson, my father, sitting at the head of the table, coffee cup in one hand at his side.

"Okay," I whispered to myself in the silence of the truck, absently using a word Rick so often employed. "I can do this."

I lifted the cell phone that Rick was taping from and pressed the OFF button. A moment later I heard the soft *ding* that told me he could no longer listen. I put that cell in my pocket, opened the truck door, and set my face.

I took the basket in hand, made sure the gun was tucked beneath the laptop, and slid from the seat to the ground, closing the truck door. Silent, I climbed the short steps to the house, and crossed the porch, every step making me feel more vulnerable. I knocked on the door. It opened immediately and a small child looked out at me. He shouted, "Mama Grace! We'ns got company!"

FOURTEEN

The children raced in from everywhere, most of them young teenagers, but some much younger. Seemed Daddy had kept his wives busy. I had not put a foot in this house in over ten years, and I didn't recognize anyone until Mama Grace came toward me with both arms out in welcome, her face lined with happiness and creased with sheet marks. Mama Grace's hug was like being enveloped in a soft down pillow and cradled in love. "Welcome to our home. Hospitality and safety while you're here." When I didn't respond, she pulled me tighter and said into my ear, her voice soft, "Baby girl. We missed you. Have you eaten? There's oatmeal on the stove and biscuits in the oven." She turned to the hovering, wide-eyed children, "This is your sister and half sister, Nell Nicholson."

"The one who ran away!" a small voice piped.

"That's not what happened," another voice answered. "The womenfolk made an arrangement for her!"

"My mama says—"

"Who hit you? Did you get punished?"

"Hush, all you'uns!" Mama Grace said. "Such awful manners shame this family. I'll whop every one of you'uns, you don't hush!"

"Get outta my way!" Mindy—Mud—spun a little boy away, elbowed her way through the other kids, and grabbed my hand, pulling me into the house. With her free hand she slammed the door. "You came! I knew you'd come."

Judith was here in this mess of young'uns. And Mud, of course. And my half brother who wasn't daddy's. Zebulun, an innocent child, over twelve years old by now. Would I recognize him? Then the half sibs. So many of them, children everywhere.

"Hush, all a you'uns," Mama Grace said. "Martha, go tell Mama Cora, Nellie is here.

"Lemme take your coat, child," she said as Mud let go and took my basket. I shrugged out of the outer layer and took the basket back, not wanting Mud to have access to my gun. Mama Grace gripped my jaw as I turned. I hissed. I hadn't thought much about my healing bruises until now.

Mama Grace's keen eyes scanned me as I handed her the coat, moving stiffly. "You need a doctor?" I shook my head no. "We thought Joshua was lying 'bout him hurting you. Priss said she seen you at market and you had a bruise on your face, but she didn't say how bad it is. You got more injuries?" Mama Grace asked.

"No. It just . . . hurts iffen I touch it." I pulled the childhood vernacular around me and ducked my head like a penitent. And hated myself. I raised my head and put back my shoulders and met Mama Grace's eyes like something other than a mouse. "I'm honored to accept your hospitality. I have things to say."

Mud pulled a rocking chair in front of the fireplace and fluffed an afghan across it. I took the seat and placed the breadbasket on the table beside me. I indicated the loaves. "For your hospitality, Mama Grace."

"Never mind your manners," she said, taking the bread from the basket and pointing to another child, who raced up, grabbed the two loaves, and dodged between his sibs to the kitchen. The laptop shifted in the bottom of the basket, beneath the dish towel I had placed there, and clinked on the gun beneath. "Tell me what happened," she demanded. "We know there was menfolk, heathen police officers, at your house. The *new preacher* told us."

Her voice was hard when she said *the new preacher*. I took a slow breath. "I'd rather just tell it once," I said in city talk, "to you, my mama, and Mama Carmel, all together. And I need to know about Esther."

Mama Grace's eyes went steely. "We'uns all got things to share, then. Your daddy needs to hear too, girl," she said.

I didn't respond to that one. My daddy had let my mama go to the punishment house. He had let Esther go with Jackie.

I *hated* Daddy.

"Nell?" I swiveled in the chair and into my mama's arms. She enfolded me, her body muscled and strong, even after ten years. "Oh, baby girl. Your poor face."

"We need to talk, Mama, but first we need to rescue Esther."

"The boys are looking for her. Sister Erasmus showed us the threatening note," Mama said. "You think it was Jackie who wrote it? You think he took Esther?"

"Nell?" It was Daddy's voice, and I pulled away from Mama, turning his way. Daddy was coming out of his private bathroom, a minuscule closet of a room that he had carved out of the space behind the kitchen wall. He was older. His face lined, tanned, showing age spots. He was smaller than I remembered, but his hands, rolling up the sleeves of his plaid shirt, were still large and rough. Daddy liked working with wood and tools, making things. He made a good cash-money living out of it. His face hardened as he took in my bruises, and he frowned. "Tell me everything."

I thought about that carefully before saying, "I got some questions first. What's being done to save Esther? Is something strange going on at the Stubbins farm? And did you know about the churchmen keeping watch on my house from a deer stand on the Vaughn farm?"

Daddy held up a hand in a gesture I recognized as one I used all the time. I stopped talking. "You little'uns get on upstairs and get dressed for morning devotional. You older girls go help. This is for adults only."

"Us too, Daddy?" a deep voice asked.

I followed the sound and saw three older boys—young men, rather, in their midtwenties, by the door. They hadn't been there when I entered and must have come in behind me. The one who had spoken was my brother, the one getting married. Amos and Rufus, half sibs, flanked him. Sam wasn't the eldest, but there was something about my elder full brother that said he was the leader of the group. He was no longer a child, no longer the braggart and tease I had known. This was a man grown.

"Did you find anything?"

"No, sir. We'uns saw the truck and came to check it out. Whisnut's still looking."

Whisnut was the family name of Esther's intended, Jedidiah. *Still looking* meant—

"Sam, you can stay. You others get to chores. Your mamas will be busy this morning and the chickens still need to be fed and eggs gathered. Wood needs to be cut. I don't care how you split the tasks, but *you* do 'em. *You*. Not your sisters. They're busy taking care of the little'uns. And there'll be no discussion. Git."

Two of the boys left. Sam stared at me. I shifted my gaze away and firmed my mouth, feeling Mama's expression form on my own face. So many of my gestures were Nicholson traits, and I didn't know how I felt about that. Mama watched the exchange and her mouth hardened too.

Daddy said, "Nell. You'un look like you might pass on out." Daddy looked into the kitchen, which was suddenly empty and quiet. "Carmel? You brewing up something for Nell's bruises? Good." Daddy's dark eyes met mine. "Tell me what happened, Nell."

I didn't know where to start, but the words that came from my mouth were, "Did you know? About the watchers in the deer stand?"

Daddy dropped his chin in an abbreviated nod. "I always had one man in the crew, Everett Lisby, who reported back to me. He kept the others from trying anything. But . . . earlier this week, things changed. Jackie sent the men home and by the time Everett found me and told me what happened, Jackie was back at the compound and Joshua was telling about a demon you called up.

"Just so we're clear, I don't believe you called up a demon. Priss said you threw a cat at him. He's got scratches and cuts that support that claim." Daddy's mouth turned up and he lifted a hand as if he might touch my face, but I flinched, just a hint, a micromovement of current pain and remembered whippings as a child. He halted and his fingers curled under. He dropped the hand. Being in this house, seeing my family, heated my blood with old anger, old fear, old pain, and new confusion; some of my anger was deserved, but just maybe, some wasn't.

Inside me, there was a new loneliness, an awareness of isolation because of what John and Leah had done . . . I believed it. I believed that John and Leah had lied to me, to keep me away from my family. And I didn't know how to move past all that. It was a barrier big as a mountain.

I looked into the eyes of my father and spoke without the

patois of my youth. "Yes. The day the regular spies were sent home by Jackie, three men came onto my property. Jackie, Joshua Purdy, and Brother Ephraim." Daddy's eyes tightened, little wrinkles radiating out from the corners as he listened, his expression intent and focused. "When they got close, they fired a few shots to draw me out. Blew out four of my windows. Damaged the house. I fired a few shotgun blasts back." I looked at Mama. "We all missed, but the gunfire messed up my garden something awful and killed some tomatoes, beans, and impatiens. Made me mad." Mama shook her head, knowing how I felt about my plants. I looked back at Daddy and held him with my eyes, "Then Joshua snuck up on me and coldcocked me." I touched the bruise on my jaw. "When I woke up, he had dragged me into the woods. He hit me some more. He cut my clothes."

Daddy's face went rigid, as unyielding as stone. So did Sam's. The two men looked at each other and Sam gave a tiny, stiff nod, his fists clenching. "Did he do you wrong?" Daddy asked me.

"He didn't rape me. A police officer heard the shots and came before he could. They'd been close by because of a heathen group called the Human Speakers of Truth. When the firing started, the police raced in and the churchmen ran off, all except Joshua, who got knocked around some and scraped up by a black cat. Not a demon. They had him, but they let Joshua go because I said I wasn't pressing charges."

Daddy was quiet for a moment, thinking it all through, watching me, studying my bruises. "Why not press charges?" Daddy seemed honestly curious at why I chose not to involve the law in my disputes. "You left the church and the protection it offered you. Why not call the law?"

I shrugged. "Fight the church? What good would it do me? Get Joshua locked up, have to go to court, see him get twenty days in jail and then be free to hurt me again? Maybe file a restraining order against him?" My voice got louder as I laid out my options. "A piece of paper between him and his guns? To then have him show up with his shotgun and more than two friends to help him? I am not interested in gang rape, *Deacon Nicholson*, or in having my house burned down, or in being burned at the stake." My daddy flinched when I called him by his honorific, and the sight of his discomfort made some heated, scorched, childhood part of me rise up in glee. "If the feds hadn't been there to help me, that might have been what happened. And *no one* in God's Cloud of Glory Church would have stood up for me when they brought me back for punishment. Just like *Mama*. Just like *Esther*."

A pained silence filled the big room and Mama looked down at her lap, at her white-knuckled, fisted hands. Mama, who had been to the punishment house with Brother Ephraim, whom I had killed. *Vengeance satisfied.* I kept that off my face only with effort, but had a feeling Daddy had seen something of it in my eyes.

Daddy looked down at his big hands too, his fingers interlaced in his lap, deceptively relaxed, but with a strange tension running beneath his skin like a creek at bankfull. "Sam?" he asked.

"Joshua said he had his way with Nell. Said she liked it." My head whipped around to meet my brother's eyes. He was staring at me with an intensity I had never seen before. "I beat his ass," Sam said fiercely.

"Sam!" Daddy said, at the language.

Sam ignored him, his eyes on me, and went on. "Me and the boys," he said, pointing to the outside door, referring to his—our—half brothers, the ones who had left the room. "We beat his ass and he admitted that he had lied about taking you. We beat his ass just like we did the time he laid hands on you, after you went to live with Ingram."

My mouth opened in surprise and confusion, and Sam nodded as if my reaction was something he'd expected. "According to Ingram, Jackie and Josh and some others tried to hurt you, tried to have their way with you when you went to the ladies' room one Sunday. Ingram said he got to you in time, that he laid on some fists in the right places, but we wanted them boys to know it was hands offa our sisters. We made it plain, and they stayed away, except for spying at the deer stand." Sam inclined his head to Daddy. "And like Daddy said, we made sure one of ours was always there.

"*This time*, me and my brothers made sure Joshua Purdy took a particular hurtin'." My brother's face softened with what might have been amusement at whatever expression was on my own. I closed my mouth and shook my head. Tears sparked hotly under my lids. More gently, Sam said, "What? John di'n' tell you we'uns beat Joshua and Jackie and them others up?"

I ducked my head and shook it no. I'd had no idea. John Ingram, the man who had saved me from the colonel's hands, had acted in cahoots *with* my family, and to keep me *from* my family, from the beginning and for years after. And he had never once told me about their efforts and actions on my behalf. He had taken credit not his own. He had implied that, except for him, I was alone in the world, that my family had disowned me for refusing the colonel. No matter the cause, it had been a deliberate cruelty on his part. John had helped me achieve independence, but he had also pushed me to become a hermit, and it hadn't been necessary. The silence stretched between us as I found a place inside me for the new truths, a dark and barren place that felt like broken rock and scorched stumps instead of my woods. But it was what I had and so I left it there, knowing that at some point, I would have to mourn for years and relationships lost. I raised my head and stared Daddy down again, blinking away the moisture in my eyes.

Sam added, "We jist come back from the Purdy place. Joshua ain't there. Don't know where he is. Esther ain't been there. The huntin' dogs didn't get a scent of her. But they got all squirrelly and we had to pen 'em."

Squirrelly. That word again.

"You got more to ask?" Daddy asked me, his tone kind and patient, things I hadn't known he could be. "More to say?"

"Anything going on at the Stubbins farm? Strangers visiting?"

"Not that I know. Sam?" My brother shook his head. So maybe I was wrong.

"Did you know, ahead of time, about John and Leah's proposal to me?" I asked. "To marry him and take care of her?"

Daddy nodded slowly. "After you caused that scene in the church, refusing the colonel." His expression lightened at the memory, but I was remembering the whipping Daddy had given me after that scene. The whipping had been a large part of why I'd left home with John and Leah. "The womenfolk and me talked it over," he said, "and we had to act fast. Seemed a wise decision to get you off compound property, and that left us with very few options. John was a good man, never beat his women. It was a painful choice, with him being unable to father little'uns, and the hardship that would pose to you, but it was the safest route. The women handle such things, and they dealt with the Ingrams."

Daddy cocked his head and the lantern light caught the gray in his hair, shining silver at his temples. His hair had been dark, with no gray, the last time I talked to him. But his eyes had been just as intense and shrewd. "Sister Erasmus tells me that John kept the truth from you. That he didn't inform you your family were partners in the decision."

I shook my head and blew out a slow breath, the sound suspiciously like tears. Bless Sister Erasmus for her gossiping ways.

"He always was a secretive old coot," Daddy said, his voice holding no judgment, but no forgiveness either.

Mama Carmel placed a cup of warm herbal tea in my hands. I could smell mint and burdock root, and the taste suggested bilberry and pineapple, the color turmeric. I drained half the cup of tea, which was sweet with honey and gave me an energy boost I needed.

"Esther?" I asked. "Did Jackie take her?"

"Jackie took her," Mud stated, sticking her head from behind a chair. "We'uns all know it."

"We *don't* know who took her," Daddy said. "We got no evidence. The boys have been searching all night. And that note you gave Sister Erasmus wasn't signed."

To Daddy, I said, "I came here for other reasons than just personal and family. If you heard the local and state news, you know that there have been kidnappings of four townie girls. The police who saved me from Joshua asked me if the church was responsible." Daddy reared back in affront. I ignored the insulted response. "They asked me if a homegrown terrorist group called the Human Speakers of Truth was using church land to regroup after the police raided them. He wondered if the church had fallen under even more evil since the colonel disappeared." Daddy started to interrupt, and I knew what he was going to say, so I talked louder, the way that Unit Eighteen did things, not the respectful way I was brought up. "I agree that the police hate the church and all it stands for because it doesn't fit with their religious and political belief systems, and are apt to accuse first and look for evidence later. I also agree that their feelings have some merit." Daddy opened his mouth to debate that too, and I shouted, "I won't argue that, Daddy!" He shut his mouth, surprised. "That's a discussion for another time. But the police are interested in the HST and the women they kidnapped.

"They have proof that two men, backsliders, were on church grounds just a few days ago, the same two who participated in a planned assassination attempt of PsyLED agents, them and Boaz Jenkins." I pulled out the laptop again and showed them the photographs. "These two and Boaz helped to shoot up a hotel room the police were using. I know all that because Sister Erasmus saw the men here, and I saw security video of them making a getaway from the shooting. And I was in the hotel room when they shot it up."

Daddy's eyes went wide with scandal. The mamas gasped.

"Working, Daddy. I was working. I have a job now. With the police. So I know that the police are seeing the church in a bad light. As people who are harboring criminals."

"This church was not involved with kidnapping," he said firmly. "No criminals stayed here."

I believed that he believed that, and looked from Sam to the womenfolk. "If the police find kidnapped women here, on church land, or even with a church family off the compound, at the Vaughns', or the Peays'," I added carefully, "or the *Stubbinses'*, the legal problems will be even worse than when child protective services came here. There will be police all over. For weeks. Maybe months. Some agency will find a legal way to deprive the church of its tax status. Some other agency will start an audit of all possible cash sales that didn't result in sales tax paid or income tax claimed. Another agency will accuse the church of breaking child labor laws. Things you'uns been expecting for decades. This time the church will be broken up and people will be jailed. It won't matter that the Nicholsons didn't have anything to do with the kidnappings. If there's *anything* going on, any hint of wrongdoing, the family may suffer anyway. If there's anything I should know, *tell me, Daddy*. I'll take it back to the police to protect you all."

Daddy was looking at his palms again, and without looking up, he said, "I know in my heart that no one has girls here, but I also know how far Jackie has strayed from the blood of his salvation . . ."

He sighed and turned his hands over, assessing the backs

as if they belonged to someone else. "This has been a long time coming." He looked up. "Sam. When the church bell rings and the compound is mostly empty, can you and the boys get a look inside Jackson's new punishment room, like we talked about, and rescue Esther, if she's there?"

Like we talked about, I thought, an ancient anger easing its way from my heart.

"You'll have to do it alone," Daddy added. "I'll be keeping everyone busy in the church."

"Yes, sir."

"Make it fast and clean. No bloodshed if you can help it."

Sam nodded, his jaw tight.

"When you finish with Jackie's, go inside the new guest quarters. Make sure Nell's kidnapped girls aren't there. Without getting hurt. Without being seen or causing a hullabaloo."

"Yes, sir. We'll go straight into the Jackson house first. Then we'll check the old punishment house through the trap-door." Sam said to me, "Daddy and me cut a trapdoor into the punishment house when Brother Ephraim took our mama."

My gaze jerked to Mama. She was looking at her hands still, a mimicry of Daddy. Her face was tight and pained and shamed. I kept my eyes on her as I asked, "Why did you let Mama go to the punishment house, Daddy?"

"That was my choice," Mama said, her voice so soft I might have missed her words if I hadn't been watching her so closely. "It was me or Phoebe. And I couldn't let her be hurt."

I shook my head in confusion. Phoebe was Mama's baby sister. "I don't understand."

Daddy said, "Phoebe was staying with us because she refused to marry Ephraim." He smiled, but his humor was thin. "Not quite as dramatically as you did, but she caused a ruckus. Dramatics run in your mama's family." Mama smiled at her lap, and Daddy continued his story. "Ephraim come to the house, demanding Phoebe for punishment. I was gone, buying wood to make some cabinets for a townie contractor. None of the boys was old enough or trained to defend the place. That's been rectified now," he said with a satisfaction that sounded like bones grinding. "All my boys know to defend against churchmen who come to take our women. But back then I wasn't prepared. The leadership of the church was changing, taking us into new and wicked directions, to mistreat our women, in direct contradiction of Scripture." He shook his head again and looked at Mama.

"Your mama is a brave woman," he said, his voice full of pride and pain both. "She hid Phoebe and sent Sam to find me. She told Ephraim it was her decision to refuse Phoebe to be his wife. Before I got back, he done dragged Cora off. The men with him wouldn't let me take her back. I appealed the punishment, but the colonel said she had acted with false pride and defiance and he upheld the ruling."

I felt as if the ground had opened up and swallowed me whole. "Where was I," I demanded, "when this happened?"

The look Sam gave me was surly. "You were with Mary, a girl who married Boaz Jenkins. You'd stolen my bubble gum and took off. Missed chores. Stayed gone all day. I spanked your bottom for that." I remembered the spanking. But I didn't remember anything of the rest of this tale.

"You were too young to be told," Mama said. "If things had been different we would a shared with you the family histories and stories when you became affianced. That didn't work out so good. You accepted John and Leah and took off. We never had the chance to share with you. Not a single thing."

Daddy said, "That night, a couple of the Campbell boys took the guards some drink and kept 'em busy while Sam and me cut a hole in the floor and rescued your mama. We was too late to save her from being hurt." He looked at his wife, love and tenderness in his eyes. "Your mama," he repeated with pride, "is a brave woman."

"Why do you stay here?" I asked. "I could give you land on my wood—"

The front door slammed open, banging on the wall, an icy draft blowing through, and I clamped down on my words. A man stood there, underdressed for the cold in a flannel shirt and jeans, a pump-action shotgun in his hands, held across his body. At his feet was a dog, a bluetick hound . . . acting *squirrelly*, his tail flashing, feet dancing, whining, a strange light in his eyes.

"Bascomb got a scent," the man said, gesturing to the dog with the stock of his shotgun. "He led me toward the new preacher's house." He stepped inside. "You gonna help me rescue my Esther or not?"

I figured the man was Jedidiah Whisnut, but the sound of the church bell ringing cut him off. A couple dozen pairs of feet banged down the stairs and a gaggle of young'uns and little'uns raced down and into the front room, which was suddenly filled with family.

Daddy said, "We're helping. Close the door, Jedidiah." To Sam he said, softly enough that Jedidiah couldn't have heard, "Change of plans, and you won't have much time. Keep Whisnut close. Tie him down if you have to. I don't want him doing something heroic and stupid and ruining things." Louder, he said, "Sam, Jackie'll be leaving his house in a few minutes. Skip what chores ain't done. Take charge of your brothers. Send Rethel and Narvin to the Campbells' and tell their boys we might need help. Send Rudolph to get the Vaughn boys to take security down just like we planned. Send Zeke and Harry to get the compound's dogs secured. You, Amos, Rufus, and Jedidiah follow Bascomb's nose. Find out if Esther is in Jackie's house or the old punishment house. Get her safe. And if there's signs of Jackie's own women being mistreated, take photos and bring 'em to me at the church. Looks like our plans are getting moved up a mite."

I didn't know what plans he was talking about, but it sounded like the Nicholsons, the Vaughns, and the Campbells had formed a faction and were going to cause a ruckus. In the compound and in the church itself. A small sinful part of me felt proud that I had shown them the way, but then maybe Mama's dramatic family had done that a long time ago. I reached into my pocket, took out the cell phone that had been given to me, and turned it on. I pulled up the last contact and dialed Rick.

"Damn it, Nell!" he answered.

I said, "My brothers and Esther's intended have been hunting for Esther. They're getting ready to check Jackson's house and the old punishment house. Then they're going to check on the Stubbins farm, to see what's going on there. I'll call back if I get intel." I thumbed the call off and made sure the ringtone was off, but I left the phone itself on. I placed it in Sam's hand. "If you find the girls and get in trouble, punch the word SEND. That'll redial that number. Tell the man who answers who you are and what's going on. Federal officers will come." Sam looked oddly amused as he pocketed the cell.

Daddy countermanded what I had said. "Don't call in *outsiders* unless you have to. Rescue Esther. If you see churchwomen that have been abused, but they ain't in immediate harm or bodily danger, get out and get back to me as per your training. Them rescues we'll handle as a family, us and our crowd. Iffen it's outsiders, leave 'em be but call your sister's police officer. Don't be messing with evidence." Sam raced off and Daddy handed me my coat, saying, "We'll make a fuss at the devotions ourselves." He looked at his wives, a severe set to his mouth. "I believe that an accusation against Joshua Purdy would be appropriate today. And it may come to an accusation against Preacher Jack."

Sam sent his younger brothers off to gather forces. Daddy sent others of his sons with messages to the Peays, Cohens, and Adens, warning that there would be "stringent verbal debate" at devotions. To his sons, he added, "And iffen there's trouble at the church, get back here and institute the safety measures. Understood?"

A dozen voices said, "Yes, sir!"

Having no idea what was about to happen, I picked up my basket and walked with my family to the chapel.

The chapel was on the far side of the compound from the Nicholson house, a cold walk in the gray light of dawn. The white clapboard building was centered in a ring of green grass and oak trees, and blooming, perennial fall flowers, many of which I had planted long ago and still flourished, testament to my gift with plants. The steeple was tall and narrow, mounted with a weathered wooden cross. Electric lights burned from within, through the clear panes of glass, some appearing irregular, and with air bubbles in them from when they had been hand-blown over a century ago. At one time, this building had been as much my home as anyplace on Earth. Now, after all the shattering revelations, I didn't know what to think about home or family or safety. *Why did my family stay here?*

Walking behind Daddy and Mama Carmel, one arm through Mama's and the other through Mama Grace's, surrounded by young'uns and effectively hidden by the family, I climbed the steps to the church and entered. The interior walls were still white-painted wallboard, the pews hand-shaped oak that had been treated recently, and was shiny, unlike my memories of them, seating as many as four hundred worshipers. The dais at the front placed the preacher three steps higher than the congregation, with a fancy carved wood podium. The floors were wood as well, and our feet were loud as we entered the church and Daddy led us to the Nicholson pews. My great-grandfather had shaped four of the pews, and his name was carved into the olive branch on the armrests. Every family had contributed at least one pew, and the family names were similarly carved. Daddy stood aside and we filed in.

I strained over Mama's shoulder to see the two pews that were carved with the words WELCOMED GUESTS, but they were empty. I sat and Mama pulled a scarf from a pocket and slid it over my head and around my shoulders, hiding who I was. I set my basket on the floor and stared at my hands, fisted in my lap, thinking about the family history. My own history. If I had known the truth, would I have built a life on my own when John died, or would I have gone back into the church and the safety of the Nicholsons, and been remarried at the behest of my daddy into some other home? Would I have young'uns by now, my own family? Would I have given up my land to the ownership of a man? I wasn't sure how to feel about any of it.

Mud pushed against Mama Grace and me, wriggled herself onto the bench beside me, and wrapped an arm around my waist. All by itself, my arm went around her and I pulled her tight.

"Welcome one and all to morning devotions. Welcome the day with thanksgiving." It was Jackie, his voice unable to boom as his daddy's had, unable to make the rafters shake with hellfire and damnation and politics couched in Biblical sayings, but strong just the same, thanks to the microphone, ringing in the vaulted space. I tuned Jackie out and kept my eyes downcast through the Bible reading and the hour-long service, wondering if Sam and my brothers had found and rescued Esther.

I was happier than a bluebird in spring that my family would have saved my sister even if I hadn't come. The Nicholsons were nothing like the people I had thought them to be. They were practically heroes. And yet I worried until Jackie's final prayer.

As he intoned, eyes closed and hands uplifted, from the corner of my eye, I saw Sam, Amos, and Rufus, walk down the aisle, all three carrying shotguns, all three silent. They took positions that looked carefully planned and choreographed, Sam standing beside Daddy, passing him a shotgun. That made four weapons in the house of God, five counting my revolver. The two half sibs went to the front of the church and took up places on opposite sides of the rows of pews.

Sam whispered into Daddy's ear, the words too low to hear. I glanced back and saw two other men. One was Caleb Campbell, Priss' husband. Fredi and Priss were in the Campbell pew behind me, faces pinched and white, holding hands. A tremor of fear racked through me at the number of unprotected men, women, and children, all in danger.

At the back of the church stood Elder Aden and Sister Erasmus, both faces uncompromising and austere. And Esther stood beside them, pale and drawn and bruised. There were bandages on her lower arms, with blood seeping through. Jedidiah Whisnut stood with her, holding her close beneath his arm, fury on his face so strong I thought he might explode, but his shotgun was nowhere in sight and I remembered Daddy saying to keep Jedidiah from causing more trouble. Sam might have taken the weapon.

But no one had taken mine. The heat of anger licked through me like wildfire, and I slipped my hand into my breadbasket, onto the gun, my hand on the grip, rage a low vibration in me. Jackie finished his prayer, saying, "Amen, brothers and sisters!"

At which point, my daddy stood and said, "Preacher, elders, deacons. I bring unto you a conundrum, a difficulty, and a sin that must be rooted out. An accusation to be judged by the elders and the deacons, as according to Scripture."

Jackie's eyes landed on the back of the church. Likely on Esther. He shouted, "Perhaps this evening's devotional might—"

"This will not be shelved!" my daddy shouted, his voice overpowering Jackie's.

A babble broke out among the families, and Old Man Campbell called, "I second Deacon Nicholson's right to speak to the congregation."

Elder Aden's distinctive, high voice piped up, "Where there be sin, it must be rooted out!"

A voice I didn't remember from my childhood said, "Has the scriptural methodology for settling of disputes been addressed?"

Keeping my head low, I darted my eyes around, taking in the congregation's expressions, trying to read body language. Trying to evaluate where the weapons were likely to be, besides those carried by my brothers and the Campbells. I knew next to nothing about paramilitary tactics, but from a hunter's point of view, if I had wanted to box in the exits and the podium both, I'd have put people just where my family had taken places, cornering them and cutting off anyone's retreat. And Elder Aden stood betwixt the congregation and the back door, boxing everyone in perfectly.

My daddy bellowed, "I call accusations against Joshua Purdy, who did lay hands upon my daughter the widder-woman Nell Nicholson Ingram, with intent to abuse her honor and her body, such actions bein' without consent of her family and approval of her church, and against her will."

The congregation went dead silent at the words and I dropped my head lower. This was not what I had expected.

Into the shocked silence Joshua shouted, "I call that lies. The woman did entice me into her bed! She is wicked and evil and has called upon demons to defend her!"

"You keep silent until you are allowed to speak, Joshua Purdy," Daddy said, his voice a growl I had never heard before. Daddy closed his shotgun with a *kerclunk-snap* and stepped out of the Nicholson pew. He lifted the shotgun and pointed it at the Purdy pew, where Joshua's voice had come from. "Iffen you open your mouth again, *boy*, I will personally and with great satisfaction knock out your'n teeth. And I contend that this church will allow such action as just and good punishment for your evil."

Sam's deep voice said, "I call accusations against Ernest Jackson Jr. for taking action meaning mischief upon my sister the widder-woman Nell Nicholson Ingram, to issue orders to bring harm upon her home, said action being taken with shotguns that did damage to her home, windows, outer walls, and that did require intermediation by the law enforcement Senior Special Agent Rick LaFleur with PsyLED in order to protect her.

"I call accusation against Jackson Jr. for laying hands upon my sister Esther Nicholson, stealing her away after dark last night, against her will and the will of her father who had given her into the keeping of her affianced as according to her will and to church law. And in so doing, causing bodily harm from stealth attack upon her affianced, Jedidiah Whisnut.

"And I call Jackie to account for the pain and suffering my sister Esther did suffer at his hands."

Following his words, there were whispers through the church that sounded like bees attacking. I had tilted my eyes to Sam in surprise as he spoke. He sounded like a lawyer. And for him to say all that, Sam had to have spoken to Rick. He had called the PsyLED agent on the cell I'd given him. Or he had answered the phone when Rick called.

Sam went on. "By all these actions did Joshua Purdy and Ernest Jackson Jr. bring shame upon this church, actions being in contradiction of the law of the land and against the law of the church and of Scripture. And then did Jackson Jr. and his cohorts lie about the situations and events, despite the earlier questions and the facts of clear evidence."

The babble became louder at the accusation against the preacher.

Jackson lowered a hand into the podium, into an open space where the big church Bible was kept, a nook that was big enough to hold a weapon too.

Sam pointed his shotgun at Jackie and said, simply, "Don't." Jackie didn't draw a gun or shoot anyone. Slowly he stood upright and placed both hands on the podium where they could be seen. His dark hair hung around his sweaty face, the curled tips sticking to his heated skin.

My chest hurt with fear and my lungs ached to draw breath, but something like pride welled up in me. My hands clenched painfully, as the congregational method of settling disputes continued. Mud clasped my elbow tightly.

"Last," my brother said, "I do bring accusations against the preacher, Jackson Jr., for abuse of his concubines, Havilah and Henrietta Sanders, who were just discovered shackled in the new punishment room in his home. I have evidence that they have been beaten and bitten and hurt, and are in dire condition, like unto death."

A woman's voice piped up, "I told you not to let that man have our girls!"

"Shut up, woman," a man said. I recognized Brother Sanders' tenor voice, raised in anger and embarrassment.

"I will *not* shut up."

I didn't turn around but heard a scuffle in the back of the church and a resounding smack. "I'll hit you again if you try to stop me, husband," the woman said. And I realized Mrs. Sanders had hit her husband, not the other way around. It was sinful, but I felt a flame of delight ignite in my heart. "I'm going to see my babies," she said.

Sam said, "Mrs. Sanders. I have called an ambulance. They'll meet you there. One of the Campbell brothers will see you safely to the preacher's house." Sam turned to me and even with my head down, I could feel him looking at me. He sounded like Daddy when he said, "And I've called the police." The church went silent at that, and I tilted my head so Sam could see my smile. He gave me one back and it lightened my heart.

"The church will address the second complaint first," Elder Aden said. "Where were Nell Ingram's family during said confrontation on the Ingram land?" he asked.

"We'uns was on church property," Daddy said. "We'uns was not properly informed about an action against Nell. Nor was we'uns allowed opportunity to attend such action with the church leaders as witnesses."

"Are there witnesses?" Elder Aden asked.

"None of the church that will speak truth," Daddy said. "But there were law enforcement officers there, police who saw those involved."

"Is there evidence?"

"There is evidence of damage to the house, such damage being repaired by widder-woman Ingram's insurance policy," Daddy said.

"Witnesses!" Jackie shouted. "I claim legal right to question witnesses."

"Is the policeman willing to testify to the damage and the culprits?" Elder Aden asked.

I nodded and Daddy said, "Yes."

"Good enough. I see Esther Nicholson in the back of the church. Can you speak to the charges laid, girl?" Esther must have nodded because Elder Aden continued. "Did Jackson Jr. abuse you unto dishonor? Let the record show she nodded yes. Did he abuse you with fists and teeth and threats? Let the record show she nodded yes. Did he bite you? Let the record show that she nodded yes. Anything you want to add Esther?"

I heard soft discussion in the back of the church and Jedidiah said, "My Esther said the preacher done drank her blood. Like he's some kinda blood-drinking vampire."

The entire church went silent as the members digested that revelation.

"Are there other complaints to be stated by the Nicholson family?" Elder Aden asked, his voice heavy. When Daddy said no, Elder Aden said, "Are there complaints and accusations from others in the congregation?"

The unknown voice said again, "Has the scriptural methodology for settling of disputes been addressed?"

"That will be addressed after the litany of complaints have been laid bare," Aden said. This time his voice came from a different location, and I saw that the old man had moved to the front of the church, to the side of the pulpit at an angle across from my armed brothers. He appeared to be unarmed, but his jacket hung far too large on his aged, bony shoulders; he could have been carrying a cannon and I wouldn't have noticed it.

From the back of the church a woman said, "Women are not chattel to be bought and sold or to be used as weapons. They are to be reverenced and given respect." It was Sister Erasmus, her distinctive, coarse voice taking up the accusations. "It is common knowledge among the womenfolk that Jackson Jr. has done evil to women. I can name half a dozen women who will provide spoken testimony against him. But their complaints have fallen on the deaf ears of the current deacons. I ask you, when did we fall so low? When did it become acceptable for menfolk to mistreat womenfolk? And when did Jackie start biting women? And why? Why is he drinking their blood like some kind of *vampire*? Has he become possessed by Satan? Have all our deacons become possessed?"

Elder Aden said, "Hang on there, wife. Are the complaints brought by the Nicholson clan all stated and have all been made public?"

"All Nicholson complaints have been stated before the church," Daddy said.

"We will first address the issues of violence against the widder-woman Mrs. Ingram. Miss Nicholson, Jedidiah, have yourselves a seat, unless there's need for immediate medical intervention? No? Good." In the silence of the church, I heard them sitting. Quoting the voice from the back of the church, Aden asked, "Has the scriptural methodology for settling of disputes been addressed?"

With not a hint of church accent in his voice, Daddy said, "The issue with my daughter has been addressed privately several times over the years. She is owed compensation for her prolonged abuse and compensation for her insurance deductible and compensation for any premiums that increase due to the destruction of property."

"I second the requirement for compensation," Caleb Campbell said. "I call for a voice vote."

Aden said, "All in favor?"

There was a firm, if scattered group of *ayes*.

"All against?"

The nays were much fewer and farther between. I'd be getting church money. I had never considered such a thing. And I had never heard such a fast and choreographed dispute. When I snuck a glance at Jackie, his face was flushed with turmoil, as if he might have a stroke on the spot.

"The ayes carry," Aden said. "Compensation and damages for Nell Ingram's house to be discussed at next meeting of the elders and the deacons, after devotionals tonight, said compensation to come from the Jackson and Purdy coffers and not the church coffers. As to the other accusation of the evil done to Esther Nicholson? Is there evidence?" Two seconds later Elder Aden said, "Did Jackie do all that? Let the record show that there are bruises and wounds upon the face and arms of Esther Nicholson. Are there other wounds?" he asked her. "Other wounds are present, such wounds to be addressed by medical professionals. Compensation?"

I frowned. They were going to give her money for her pain? *Money?* Jackie need to be in *jail*. Or his blood in my hands.

Daddy looked back and questioned, "Sufficient to provide for you for ten years?" He faced the front of the church again and said, "Ten years. And my daughters and my family shall make accusations to the police," Daddy said.

The church fell deeply silent. Jackie's face blanched and then bright red spots of wrath lit his cheekbones.

"We will not allow such conduct and evil to be hidden," Daddy said, his words ringing in the silence. "No longer. The old ways must change. These accusations and proof of evil are a harbinger of that change."

Unexpected pride welled up in me. Pride at my daddy. I never once in my whole life thought I'd be proud of a Nicholson.

"Agreed," Elder Aden said. "As to the accused abuse of Ernest Jackson Jr.'s concubines? What evidence is there?"

My brother said, "I got photographs."

"Let me see them pictures, Sam," Elder Aden said.

Sam pulled something from his pocket and stepped to Elder Aden. I couldn't see what it was without raising my head but I heard Elder Aden say, "By all that's holy. When did you take these?"

"Less than half an hour ago, at the new punishment room on the back of the preacher's house."

"Does it meet church methods of sanction?" Sister Erasmus asked.

Daddy said, "The issue of criminal abuse of women can no longer be considered a private church issue, but one that directly impacts the entire church. This is the first time of address, but meets church charter for direct and urgent threats against the people of the congregation by a member. Change is upon us and this church must not, will not, shrink from facing it."

"Agreed," Elder Aden said. He nodded to the congregation and then set a steely eye on Jackson Jr. "Set yourself down a spell, preacher. We'uns'll be here awhile."

Weapons were readied for firing, the *kerclunk* sound of a single-action bolt rifle, and something newer, with a sharper, higher-pitched *sh-shick* sound. A pump shotgun. Several semiautomatic handguns. I looked around and saw three armed men standing in one pew, what had to be a bunch of Jackie's cronies. Four weapons were aimed at them, held by Amos, Rufus, Jedidiah, and Elder Aden. Daddy had his old double-barreled shotgun squarely on Jackie at the front of the church.

Acid boiled under my breastbone and threatened to rise. My fingers and toes were tingling, my breath coming too fast. Beside me, a feeling of panic transmitted to me through Mud's fingertips on my arm.

"I said *set!*" Elder Aden thundered. The men sat, and he

placed his weapon in the hands of a middle-aged man in the pew behind him. "Disarm and guard them boys. Nicholson men'll remain standing and will be seeing that they behave until this is settled according to the laws of Scripture and the church charter. And the police."

Elder Aden accepted a second weapon, a huge six-shooter, from Sister Erasmus and assumed a two-hand stance, the gun aimed at the podium. "Jackie, iffen you pull that gun, I'll shoot you myself. *Set down in your chair.*"

Elder Aden was holding a handgun on Jackie. In church. I thought I might throw up. My flesh was buzzing with what felt like a storm of hornets stinging me. Confusion. Fear. Terrible fear. Worse than any I had ever felt, because this was my family in danger. And my family was standing up for me. For abused women. Mud squeezed my arm harder, and I squeezed the butt of the six-shooter harder.

The seconds stretched out, fraught with tension. Finally Jackie snarled and replaced whatever he had been holding behind the podium. He took his chair, a good four feet from the weapon.

From behind me, Joshua Purdy shouted, "I contest the compensation to the Ingram whore! I claim that the accusations against me are lies. I demand witnesses and evidence!" His voice quaked with anger and panic.

Gently, Daddy said, "Nell?"

I wanted nothing but to crawl under the pew, between the feet of the congregation, and out the door. But words and actions came to me, as if they had been growing like a vine in the back of my mind, all with purpose. Slowly, I peeled Mud's fingers off my arm and stood up, setting the basket on the pew seat, standing with the men of my family. Haltingly, I said, "I am Nell Nicholson Ingram, widow of John Ingram. Jackie and Joshua shot up my house." I left out mention of Brother Ephraim, preferring to leave him out altogether. "Joshua beat me." I dropped the shawl that had hidden me to my shoulders and held my face to the sunlight coming through the chapel windows. "And he cut away my clothes."

Sister Erasmus shouted, "Shame! Joshua Purdy is accused of bringing shame to a churchwoman, a widder-woman who was without dishonor."

Jackie started to reply and I shouted quickly, "Joshua and Jackie intended harm to me but were interrupted by the arrival of law enforcement officers. They wished for me to take this complaint to the court of the land and would be witnesses in that court of law. But first I brought this to my family and to the church as according to the Scriptures."

"Nell?" Daddy said again. I moved to the end of the pew and Daddy stepped to the side, making room for me in the aisle. I lifted my head and turned in a circle, making sure that my bruises were visible to all.

As I moved, someone finally spoke from the Purdy pew, sounding like Joshua's mother. "My son never beat your daughter. You got no proof! Your daughter is a wanton whore!"

"Nell Ingram called up a devil, a *demon*, to stop me from having my way with her!" Joshua said, his voice defiant, but his argument proving his guilt. "She's a witch! Look all you'uns! See what her demon did to me!" Joshua yanked down on his collar and showed us his neck and the scratches and piercings from Paka's claws. "She should be burned or stoned with stones as the Scripture commands."

My daddy said to Joshua, "To *stop you from having your way with her*? By thine own words thou art condemned."

Old Man Aden repeated, "By thine own words thou art condemned."

A too-long beat later, the congregation said, mostly together, but with clear sections of the church remaining silent and undecided, "By thine own words thou art condemned."

I said, "A black cat got you, Joshua. We can all see that. And if anyone summoned up a demon, it was you."

Joshua's eyes went wide. Clearly he had never been accused of witchcraft.

"Did you, Preacher Jackson, bite your concubines?" Sister Erasmus demanded, bringing the accusation back to Jackie. "Did you harm them in ways no decent man would, like some kinda vampire, biting them for their blood?"

At that, Jackie lunged for the podium. Elder Aden's gun tracked him, but the older man hesitated an instant too long and didn't fire. Jackie pulled a huge gun. He pointed it at me. And everything went to hell in a handbasket.

FIFTEEN

I remembered Rick's comment about a Mexican standoff, and for half a second, this looked like the same thing, except no one here would heal easily from gunshot wounds. We'd bleed and die like regular humans. That was the thought I had before Jackie's gun thundered, reverberating *blamblamblam* in the tall ceilings, the shots loud and too fast.

I had a moment's thought about the training Daddy had given his family, because all of them hit the floor as the first shot was fired, all but me. Daddy shoved me into the pew, to the floor, where I landed on top of Mama and a passel of Nicholson young'uns who were crawling for the exits. Daddy's shotgun blasted twice, then several others. Daddy fell on top of me, and his blood pulsed across my face. Without thinking, I pulled off the scarf Mama had wrapped me in, shoved it deep into Daddy's wound, and covered it with my hand, pressing. The pulsing stopped, but the gunfire went on. Deafening, breath-stealing, glass-shattering booms that went on forever. I could make out screaming, Some of it from the Nicholsons below and around me. Mama and Mud were still here, and my sister pulled off her jacket, applying it to another gunshot, this one a leaking hole in Daddy's leg, not the pulsing mess I was trying to stifle. Mud looked mad. Determined. Not afraid. Mama stretched out beside us, holding John's old revolver, which had tumbled in the carnage, as if she knew how to use it. The gunfight blasted away the dawn. Screams. Deafening concussions. Mama fired my gun at someone in the aisle.

Mama Carmel crawled across the empty space under the pew in front and slid up to Daddy, adding a pile of clean cloth diapers to my scarf. I had stopped breathing, and I remembered to inhale only when the blackness of oxygen deprivation closed in on my eyesight and I was near to passing out. With the breath came thoughts from my self-schooling, my mind bombarding me with trivia, searching for a way out of this. A quote by Patton came to me, one by Sun Tzu, both useless.

Then one by Harry Truman came to me, saying, *"Carry the battle to them."*

"Yeah," I whispered to myself. Now, *that* was helpful.

I rolled out from under Daddy so Mama Carmel could get to him better, and I took his shotgun with me. I felt around in his jacket pockets and found four more shotgun shells. In the cramped quarters, Daddy bleeding and maybe dying on one side, and the Nicholson women on my other side, I reloaded the shotgun.

Someone grabbed my arm and I jerked away, but it was only Priss, my sister, lying with her sister wife on the floor behind us, under the Campbell pew. *Cowering.* And that made me madder. We women didn't need to be cowering on the floor. We needed to be taking the battle to Jackie and whoever was helping him. We needed to be fighting back. Protecting *ourselves*, not waiting on a man to save us. But it would kill my sister to shoot another person. And I had ample proof that I wouldn't give a moment's thought about it.

At that thought, the awareness of blood, rich and thick and full of life, hit me. Blood everywhere. *So much blood.* But it wasn't on the ground and not on Soulwood, and the longing to take it for the land was muted. But the longing for vengeance beat in me, like a drum through my veins.

"Stay down," I shouted to Mud and Priss and the other Nicholson women. Mama shouted my name as I crawled to the front of the church, in the shadows beneath the pews, my knees and toes and elbows pushing and pulling me forward, my skirt dragging. Wishing I was in my overalls.

I reached the front of the church and spotted Jackie crouched behind the pulpit. He was reloading his revolver. I rolled to my knees and then to my feet, and pushed off the wood floor, into a sprint. Screaming, I took the three long steps to fall upon the dais. Half rolled to the side of the podium. Pointed the shotgun. Squeezed the trigger. The recoil slammed me back, bruising my shoulder. My heartbeat pounded in my ears. My breath heaved, hidden beneath the deafness from the concussion of shots.

Jackie was bleeding, but still on his knees, staring at me, his mouth a snarl of hatred. I resettled the shotgun and fired again. He staggered. I reloaded even as Jackie finished reloading his pistol. He lifted his gun to center it on me. I fired first. And again. By the last round, time had done something perplexing. It had slowed down. And it was as if I could see each shot leave the weapon, a puff of smoke, a shadow of shot pellets.

The shot was tightly centered at this distance. Right into the middle of Jackie Jr.'s torso and up his arms. Crimson blood gushed and pulsed into the room. The stink of gunfire and the smell of released bowels was foul on the air.

Blood spattered and pulsed. Jackie fell backward, and as I watched, his face went white. His hands loosed, and he dropped the big handgun. I watched it fall, and, without even thinking about it, I batted the gun away and back into Jackie's vacant chair, so it wouldn't land wrong and go off. In hindsight, that would be a move that I shouldn't have made, as hitting the gun could have caused the same firing problem I was trying to prevent, but at the time I was glad the gun was on the chair and out of his hands.

Jackie bounced on the floor and went still. His blood spread scarlet all across the dais, the pool widening fast. His legs bent backward beneath him. I peeked out from the podium and saw Joshua vault out the front door and off the small front porch, directly at Occam and Rick.

I rolled over and retched. And then Occam was there with me, taking away the shotgun and wiping it free of my fingerprints. He left the shotgun on the floor in the pool of Jackie's blood and lifted me like a baby. His skin was hot and feverish. Or I was going into shock and feeling too cold.

I looked down and saw the bloodstain on my good gray skirt. At first I thought, *Daddy's blood,* but it was spreading. *I'd been shot.* My mind scrambled for something to hold on to and it found Tecumseh's words. "'When your time comes to die . . .'" I whispered, "'sing your death song, and die like a hero going home.'" I wondered what kind of song I was supposed to sing when I was dying, and all I could think of was

"Onward Christian Soldiers" and, oddly, that made me laugh. Which hurt really bad.

"Nell? Nell! Medic! I need an ambulance!" Occam's voice was tinny with the damage to my ears, but even with the concussion damage, I could hear the growl in his throat. And his eyes were golden brown as he carried me out the back entrance of the church, the one behind the podium. "Gunfight at the damn O.K. Corral," he growled. "Fools with an arsenal in a church full of children. Medic!" He was right. Half the men and boys in the church must a had guns.

"Put me under that tree." I pointed to an oak I had hugged when I was child, hugged for the solace I needed after a whooping with Daddy's belt. I had come away soothed, and the tree had been soothed as well. Would it remember me? My own trees recognized me, but would this old friend? I took a breath and pain blossomed inside me, through me, like a bomb going off, like a cactus flower opening, though such things were opposites in every possible way. When Occam tried to take me around to the front of the church, I set my nails into his skin like a cat might and pushed on him with my mind. "Human medicine might hurt me more than help me. Take me to that tree." When he didn't turn around, I said, "Stop!"

Occam stopped, standing as still as the tree I wanted, uncertainty and confusion holding him in place, turmoil rushing through him so intense that I could feel his cat roil beneath the skin of his arms. "But we have SWAT and FBI and ambulances coming," he said.

"Please," I whispered, my fingers gripping his biceps.

He reversed course and carried me to the tree. "Put me down," I said. Moving stiffly, as if he was doing something he was already regretting, he set me on the ground, my back against the tree. His motions were jerky, and my body lurched, making pain pummel and twist through me. I couldn't hold back a moan. Occam growled, longer, louder.

I reached up and grabbed his chin with my bloody hand, and said, "Stop that. You cannot shift into your cat here. They will burn you."

Occam went as still as death for perhaps an entire second before he said, "Thank you, Nell, sugar."

"Now I need to be alone or I may die."

"And if I leave you alone, will you live?"

"I don't know. I ain't never— I *have* never . . . done a healing before, but it might work. It feels right to try." *It was possible that the tree could help. Or, no, I couldn't say that.*

"Then try. But I'm calling for an ambulance crew back here too, Nell, sugar. Every unit in the county is heading this way."

"Take care of my daddy first." My back was to the bark, and my legs were stretched out, spindly in the leggings beneath the bloody skirt. The tree's warmth hummed through the ground, content, as soothing as the last time I came to it for consolation. But would the tree recognize me? I laid back my head. Occam punched his cell phone, demanding an ambulance.

I put both of my hands into my rushing blood, and it was warmer and stickier than I expected. I placed both hands on the lower trunk, near the ground, propping myself. And I called to Soulwood through the tree. My trees didn't answer. Nothing but the soothing of this one tree, which wasn't mine. I called again. And again. My breath came fast and shallow. My heartbeat stumbling. And softly, distantly, a weak pulse of my land answered, Soulwood turning its attention to the feel/smell/taste of my blood trickling across the tree roots and soaking into the ground. Salty taste of death.

Within the tree behind me, something shivered, something loosened, some ineffable, warm *something*, shivered through the oak and out to me. *Recognition.* "Yes," I whispered. "Hey there." From far away, Soulwood beat through the ground, finding me. Enveloping the tree. Encircling me. The earth bubbled and roiled beneath my palms, the dirt vibrating up and over my fingers, covering my bloody hands, rootlets growing fast, trapping me.

Occam stepped back, swearing. Voice unsteady, he canceled the ambulance he had demanded for me.

Life throbbed from my wood and the earth answered, the trees recognizing me, even from here. Soulwood latched onto the oak, through the hill and the soil and the rocks. The tree behind me quivered, its leaves rustling in a wind that wasn't there. Its roots and the earth they were planted in drank down my blood, pulling it into the earth, sucking it greedily from my fingers.

They reached for my blood. Oak rootlets bent and distorted,

rotated and curled and rose from the ground, sending small plumes of dirt into the air. Roots wrapped around my hands and wrists, holding me tight.

I was too weak to fight, even had I wanted to. Other root-lets, thin, knobby things with even smaller fingers, spun and revolved and climbed across my skirt, sucking up the blood that flooded out of me. They drank it down. Empowered by my life force, by the blood that was pumping hot and fast, the roots grew in size and purpose, stealing breath and heat, and pressing into me. Into my wound where they pirouetted and looped and twined together and wove a knot, inside the wound. Another knot. They tightened. And they stilled.

My blood flow stopped. It just . . . stopped. I couldn't draw a breath. Couldn't move. My heart beat funny and fast, skipping like a toddler pounding on an overturned pot, no rhythm, no purpose. I wasn't sure I remembered *how* to breathe.

Occam leaned over me, shock and horror and bewilder-ment on his face. But no fear, no pulling away. I smiled at him and because I wanted to speak, I forced the breath I had for-gotten. Voice scratchy and rough as bark, I said, "It's okay. I'll live now. Don't cut me free until I ask you to."

Occam nodded, covered me with a shiny metallic sheet he had found somewhere, his voice directing people to do . . . things. I didn't pay attention. I was too tired to care. I closed my eyes and let the last of the breath flow from me, not need-ing it now. I needed my woods, and though I was not on them, there was enough of *me* here in this tree for my woods to reach across, enough of me here and enough of me there to bleed over from my woods. To connect *here*. To direct here.

I claimed this tree for my own, for Soulwood.

My heartbeat steadied and grew negligibly stronger. My breath, when I took one, much later, didn't hurt quite so bad. The sound of rushing water echoed in my ears, a distorted vibration, the sound of water below ground, the drumming of blood in my veins. I was healing. With roots inside of me.

Shadows shifted under the ground. I felt them through the earth, the dark things that hadn't been on my property until I gave Brother Ephraim to my wood. Once again, I trailed the dark shadows within the ground, the fractured and broken things, watching me, curious, intent, but also agitated and distressed—afraid. And that's when I realized, and knew I should have seen it instantly, but I'd been so busy with new people, new things, that I hadn't bothered to look at the earth, to see, to understand.

Unlike the man who had attacked me in the woods when I was fifteen, the man who had fed the woods and become one with them, Ephraim was still *whole*, still *sentient*, still *self-aware*. And he was trapped in my wood, not able to get free, even with the wood healing me from afar. I should have known it sooner, ever since I smelled his blood, metallic and pungent. Brother Ephraim hadn't been human. And he was not helping my wood. He was resisting it. He was trying to change Soulwood.

I didn't know what to do about him, buried there, beneath the soil, but his presence didn't mean my death in this moment, didn't affect my healing in this moment, and that was the only thing that mattered right now. Except . . . I remembered Daddy. Wondered if he was dead. If I could have saved him the same way I saved myself. And wondered if he would have shunned me as a witch if I had. I let sleep take me.

When I woke it was to feel Occam holding my forearm. I knew it was him by the sound of his purring breath. Without opening my eyes, I could tell that he was curled around me protectively. His body was heated as if with a fever, and shivers ran through his flesh, ripples of muscle spasms. He might have been about to shift into his leopard when I last remembered him. The spasms suggested that he was in a great deal of pain.

On my other side, curled firmly against me, but not quite so warm, was Tandy. His worry leached into me; I could feel his disquiet as if I were an empath myself. I had claimed Tandy just as I had claimed Paka. Both were probably huge mistakes.

My lips parted and I exhaled. Occam noticed the change in me and raised his head, the movement rustling the metallic sheet over me. "Nell?"

Tandy sat up as well, and I could feel him staring at my face.

"Yes," I breathed, the sibilant barely there. "I'll live." I managed another breath and felt just a hint stronger. "I think. How's Daddy?"

"Alive," Tandy said. "A woman named Carmel went with him to the hospital with a GSW—gunshot wound—to the middle of his torso and another to his thigh. There's some fear the round nicked what they called his descending aorta, which I understand is a big artery."

"Oh. That isn't good. Daddy hates hospitals. Why are you curled around me, Tandy?"

"You are the only stable place here. There is too much fear and anger and emotion except for right here, next to you."

"Ah," I said. "This tree is comforting. Always has been."

"It isn't the tree," Tandy said, his fingers wrapping over my bound ones. "It's you."

"Nell, sugar," Occam said gently. "You have . . . roots growing into your body."

He paused as if waiting for me to say something, but what could I say? I did have roots growing into me. I opened my eyes and looked down. Tandy lifted the sheet so I could see my exposed belly, roots climbing inside, just the way they climbed into cracks of rock when seeking water. They were over my arms and twined around my hands and fingers. And up my legs, sealing me to the ground. Claiming me.

"You told me to leave them alone," Occam said, his voice a Texan cat growl, "so I did, but them things are getting bigger and stronger. Soon it might be impossible to cut you free without carving out something important, like your liver or lungs or kidneys." I still didn't reply and he went on, his voice deepening as if this was the difficult part. "Rick wanted to cut you free. I made him go away."

"Thank you."

"He was kinda ornery about it all."

I smiled for real and said, "He's a mite prickly about being told how to run things, isn't he?"

"He's the senior agent. It's possible that I shouldn't have bitten him when he came at you with a knife."

I had a feeling that laughter would hurt rather badly, and so I just let my smile widen. "Probably not."

"Hindsight and all that," Occam said. When I didn't

respond, he asked, "When do you want to be cut free, Nell, sugar?"

I'd been evaluating my body while we talked and I said, "I think I'm as healed as I can get." Occam slid his hand from me and I heard him draw a knife from somewhere. I opened my eyes to see him take a root in his free hand and bend over me. "Be careful," I said. "The tree won't like it when you cut its roots. It's got opinions now and I think it wants to keep me here, so watch out. It might try to hurt you."

He paused. "A tree. With opinions." He sounded disconcerted.

"Trees are very opinionated," I said, "mostly about rain and sunlight and fire, as you might expect, but also about other things, like sharp blades cutting into them."

"A tree," he repeated, the Texan twang coming out strong. *"With opinions."*

Letting the smile into my voice, I said, "You turn into a jungle cat on the full moon, and other times too. Who are you to judge?"

After a moment he said, "True."

From one side, I heard Rick walk up, his feet so silent that only the vibrations through the rootlets told me he was close. From above us he asked, "You got a quote for this one?"

I settled on, "'All things must come to the soul through its roots, from where it's planted.' Teresa of Avila said that, or something like it. And right now I'm planted by this tree."

"What are you?" Rick asked in his cop voice.

I looked up to see him holding his psy-meter, measuring my psychometric energy. "I have no idea. But after today, I'm fairly certain I'm not human. I'm also not a tree. Beyond that I don't know. What do I read?" I asked, oddly curious.

"In the FBI office you read high in the human range, but still human. Right now, you aren't reading at all. I can't pick you up over Occam."

"Well. Right now I'm stuck inside a tree and it inside of me. Check it again when we get back to my woods." I thought I sounded very reasonable, but Occam frowned. "What?" I asked.

"Nothing. Cutting now. And watching out for roots that fight back."

Tandy said, "I'll grab them if the tree tries to trap you."

"Did SWAT or the FBI see the roots in me?" I asked.

"No," Rick said shortly. "Neither did your church people, though they can be demanding, especially your mother. We take care of our own."

My smile softened and I felt Occam cutting into the roots, a distant awareness that wasn't pain, but wasn't pleasure either. I said, "Thank you. But they aren't *my* church people. My family is still my family, yes, and maybe more so than I thought, but I don't have church people. They don't let the inhuman worship in their church."

"*Non*human," Occam said, slicing through a rootlet that roiled and snaked in his hand, fighting his blade. "Not *in*human. Different things entirely. I'm not human either, but I'm not *in*human in any way."

"Whatever," I said, borrowing a phrase from JoJo.

"Nell?" I made a *mmm* sound and Occam said, "This root? It's bleeding."

My eyes had closed and I forced them open again. Occam had cut open my shirts, revealing my midriff and abdomen, which was mostly healed over, with roots growing inside me, three of them, each nearly an inch in diameter. Occam's blade was poised over the cut root, which was moving, snakelike, severed about six inches from the ground and right at my skin. The woody root was bleeding. Interesting. Had my blood mutated the tree? I kept that thought to myself. "Better hurry," I said. "It's a mite antsy."

"Ouch," Occam said. "It bit me!"

Self-protecting trees? Carnivorous trees? Now, wouldn't that be something to see. I felt a tugging on my flesh as Occam cut, but no pain, which I figured meant good things, like the tree hadn't taken over my central nervous system or my brain. But I had a feeling that the tree had probably changed me as much as I had changed it. Mutations were likely mutual. I felt him sawing through the wood of a second root. "Ow!" I said, my eyes popping back open.

"Sorry," Occam said. The root had twisted my skin when it popped free, leaving a red abrasion. Dull red blood, thick as sap, gathered into a droplet on the root's cut end. Tandy reached out, grabbing the severed roots.

The empath hissed. "The tree is angry. It is thinking about growing thorns."

"Self-protective tree," I said speaking my earlier thought. "Thorns exist in the plant world, and the tree knows this." I wondered aloud if the tree would send out rootlets and roots and stems, reaching through soil and air, searching for something with thorns, to study or copy. And I wondered if the oak could steal the DNA pattern from thorns and incorporate them into its own DNA. Some plants could do that. But I kept all that silent until I had a chance to study DNA and RNA so I could sound, and be, intelligent and well-read on the subject. That is, if I talked about it at all.

Occam's blade severed the last root in my belly; this time the sting was much sharper, as if he had cut me, and I hissed with pain. I looked again and the blood from the tree root was thicker and darker. Inside me, deep in my belly, I felt something stirring, drawing tight. "I think . . ." I paused, paying attention to the movement inside me. "I think you better cut my body free fast."

"Yes," Tandy said, urgency in his tone. "Fast!"

Occam didn't question, but repositioned Tandy's hands on a root and applied his were-strength to the wood. Three rootlets severed fast but the blade nicked my skin. I hissed as my blood landed in a wide microsplatter. The ground beneath me sucked the blood down and a tiny vibration, a faint tremor, began in the soil. Occam's blade slicked through the smaller roots trapping my fingers and encircling my legs. I raised them, bending my knees, keeping my flesh off the ground. The blade sawed through the larger roots at my hips and shoulders, tree blood welling at each cut.

Occam attacked the final, midsized rootlets, which were wrapped around my wrists. They popped and the pain shocked through me, the root's red blood splattering my face, throat, and belly. "Move me," I said. "Move me now!"

Occam slid his arms around my back and under my knees and lifted me. Rootlets reached up from the earth, stretching and tearing, fresh rootlets ripping from my ankles and wrists and shredding my clothes as Occam jerked me two steps away from the oak.

"Move, move, move!" I said. "Out from the drip line." I

pointed and Occam started to take a step. Roots tore from the earth as he lifted his foot, where the oak had already wrapped around his feet. He whirled from the tree with cat grace, a slinking, supple, willowy step, almost dancing, or like a cat leaping for prey. Carrying me. I remembered being carried as a child, once or twice, until little'uns smaller than I was took my place.

His arms tightened around me as he landed. I was gasping, breath too fast, but I felt warm. Safe. Occam's body was warm, his arms muscled, keeping me . . . safe. Such an odd, rare feeling, safety. And not one I could let myself get used to. I twisted my head to see that Tandy was with us, safe as well. His skin was white, the Lichtenberg figures bright red on his skin, his face full of tension and fear. But he tucked the metallic sheet around me, hiding me, hiding my blood.

Occam carried me across the compound, which was full of police and ambulances and crime scene vehicles, to Unit Eighteen's van. He set me on the long middle bench seat, closed the door, and went around to the other side. He and Tandy climbed in. "We got two choices, sugar. I can take you home," he said, "Tandy and me. Or you can put on Paka's after-shift clothes and we can go back to work. Up to you. But you need to know there could be repercussions for you going into the compound against orders."

"I'll stay. I left my basket in the church, with my laptop inside."

"I'll notify Rick," Occam said as he tossed a gobag over the seat. "Get changed. I got me a ton of texts and e-mails while you were healing to go through." He climbed out of the van and shut the doors, giving me privacy, pulling his cell. While he talked, I zipped open the gobag. The catty scent of Paka met my nose. Occam didn't look my way, guarding the van. Like a cat, I thought, who sits in the window, knowing you are looking at him, and ignoring you, aware of your scrutiny, but not reacting to it. Which eased my embarrassment as I stripped off my shredded clothing.

Sunlight turned Occam's lightly tanned skin a pale gold, and made his amber-hazel eyes glow. He was wearing loose cotton pants and a stretchy T-shirt, the clothing dark blue with the words PsyLED stenciled on the shirt in white. And he was barefooted again, toes pawing the ground, the way a cat might milk the earth.

I realized he was wearing his gobag clothing. He had been in leopard form at some point this morning and had probably changed from his leopard form to his human one when he came to save me. That was why he eyes had glowed. I wondered, briefly, where he had been when the shooting started, how much ground he had covered, and how fast he had shifted and then dressed, to get to me so quickly. He was tall, all muscle and bone, long-limbed and lean, with long fingers and slender hands, like a guitar player or a pianist. His blondish hair was unevenly cut and ragged, hanging to his collarbones in places, longer now, perhaps a result of shifting several times in the last few days.

Tandy stood on the other side of the van, facing outward and he waved off a woman in an FBI jacket when she came too near. I felt terribly exposed to be changing in the van, so I slid to the floor, where I stripped off my skirt and pulled the elastic-waist sweatpants on over my blood-crusted undies. I couldn't make myself go without and there were no panties in the gobag, not that I felt I could wear another woman's undies anyway.

When I was dressed, the unfamiliar feeling of sweatpants on my legs, and my shoes back on my feet, I tapped on the door. Occam and Tandy opened them at the same moment and slid in. "Good timing," Occam said. "We're heading to the Stubbins farm through the old farm road. Rick says the FBI is there already, and he thinks one of churchmen ran off that way. Buckle up, Nell, sugar."

Occam drove across the compound, allowing for the ruts and the invisible bumps and holes hidden by weeds and grasses. He hit a particularly deep rut and we all bounced. When we settled, he looked back over his shoulder. "Sugar, you mighta walked into a firestorm of trouble back at the compound, but according to the texts that bombed my cell while you were healing, you just went from problem child to asset of the hour, the week, and the month. The FBI is drooling over what they've found since they responded to Rick's 'code ninety-nine and shots fired' alert. They got a gold mine at Jackson Jr.'s house and now a ton more at the Stubbins farm. And they didn't even have to get that subpoena."

I didn't know what a code ninety-nine was, but I understood the rest. "Are they happy enough that I won't get fired as a consultant for PsyLED?"

"I doubt anyone will even mention that possibility," Tandy said, a smile in his words.

Unexpected relief flooded through me. I nodded and pressed a hand to my middle, staring out at the little-used, narrow roadway, never paved, and with saplings grown in close. Beneath my hand, the rooty feeling of my belly seemed softer, as if things were settling.

Occam's cell rang, a quiet vibration with tinkling bells. He answered with, "Occam. What do you have, LaFleur?" Occam listened a long time before he said, "Understood. I'll tell her." He ended the call and looked my way. "Your daddy is out of surgery, Nell. He's expected to make it."

I closed my burning eyes. "That's good. Him and me—*he and I*—have a lot of things to catch up on. But Rick had a lot more to say, didn't he?"

"Yes. But that can wait until we get a gander at the Stubbins farm. Rick wants us on-site."

The van rolled out of the trees. The Stubbins house was set in a flat area about halfway down a slope, between two hills, with the gully where the hills met about a hundred fifty feet from the front door. A trickle of water ran through it, but the topography of the land suggested that the gully would carry a lot of runoff in big rains. The area around the house was hill mud, brown and grayish, with a goodly rock content. Not as good for farming as Soulwood, but okay for cattle. The extralong cattle trailer behind the house and the fences that cordoned off pastures to the south and west said it had been used for that purpose. The absent smell of cow manure said it had been a while. The place was a proverbial anthill of activity.

There were FBI vehicles, an ambulance, sheriff cars, two crime scene vans, and, in the distance, news vans behind a barricade. There were also ruts in the grass of the house's yard where eighteen-wheeler-sized trucks had been parked, and then had recently churned up the lawn, driving away.

There was a large group of men and women in white suits at the cattle trailer, mud to their ankles. And damp from a rain that hadn't fallen in the compound. Occam rolled down his window and tilted his head, as if listening to the wind. Tandy held still, watching the werecat, and I watched them both. When I couldn't stand it any longer, I asked, "What's over there?"

"Body," Occam said. "The feds are all over it like white on rice. According to what I'm overhearing, the body ties the Stubbinses to HST." He slanted a look at me and tapped the side of his head, sending his blondish hair swinging. "Cat ears. And they got a boy over there." He pointed to a small group of men near a car. A boy's familiar head was about chest high on them. The boy who had led the attack on my house. Occam tilted his head at a slightly different angle, listening. "He claims . . . he's Jael Stubbins, son of Nahum Stubbins. His daddy lost his job recently and they came back to stay on the family farm awhile."

Occam listened and I stayed so quiet I scarcely breathed. Nahum Stubbins had left the church, according to the Nicholson women. Had Nahum really lost his job or were these more backsliders staying at the Stubbins farm? Too much coincidence.

After a bit he said, "The boy was at the church when the shooting started and he hid under the floor of a house. When he got here, the place was deserted. His daddy and uncle and two of the mamas are gone. He's been abandoned. He's sniffling, crying."

He turned his head, picking up parts of conversations from different parts of the grounds. I made a note to never whisper secrets in his presence, and decided that my escape from my own house this morning had been sheer luck. A bit later, Occam said, "Jael's daddy and his uncle have been having company, what the older men call *townies*.

"The feds over there"—he pointed to a group standing on the front porch of the house—"found HST manifestos. We now have a clear link between the church, or at least a faction, and HST."

That meant that the FBI would be all over the church grounds. I didn't know whether be happy about that or miserable at the trouble it would eventually cause my daddy.

Another car pulled up and Rick got out, walking with a long-legged stride to the porch. The men there walked down the steps and away, not speaking. Ignoring Rick. Who was PsyLED and a were-leopard. It was a clear indication of the rampant prejudice in the state's law enforcement agencies, and it had to hurt. But Rick walked through them and inside as if he didn't notice.

Occam and Tandy got out of the van. I followed much more slowly. It had grown cold this morning, with a wind blowing, and low, wet clouds scudding across the hilltops. I had only a thin layer of clothing, no coat or sweater. Though the trees were still mostly green, colorful leaves swirled in the breeze and danced before me in loose spirals. I crossed my arms and followed the men across the rutted, muddy road and up the stairs.

Inside it was just as cold. The door closed behind us, cutting off the wind, which made me feel warmer, but inside, the smell of urine was horrible. Ammoniac, astringent, harsh, an eye-burning stench. I turned in a circle to see why. There were traces of urine running down the walls . . . everywhere. *Someone had peed on the walls.*

A white-clad crime scene tech looked up at me and laughed, not unkindly. She was wearing goggles and a face mask. "I know, right?" she said. *"Men."*

"Watch the sexism, Sharon," Rick said, semiteasing, his face as relaxed as if the ostracism on the front porch hadn't happened. But she was right. The smell was horrible. I covered my nose and breathed through the cracks between my fingers.

Rick said to Occam, "Same one?"

"I think so. What does Paka say?"

"Same one," Rick said. Neither one explained the exchange to me.

The house was a shambles. A hundred-year-old handmade wooden table lay on its side. Hand-turned spindle chairs were broken everywhere. Shattered pottery appeared to have been swept or kicked into the corners, spoiled food still on some surfaces. Pizza boxes and beer cans had been stacked and tossed. Chairs had been destroyed. The couch and a recliner looked like someone had slashed them with a knife, and stuffing erupted like a fluffy volcano.

Crime scene techs were working in every room. An older tech barked, "Stay between the markers. The walkway has been worked up already. The rest of this place is a disaster." I nodded in silent agreement and stepped into the walkway through the mess, the wood floor clean and marked with what looked like little pink plastic triangles. Yellow triangles, each of them numbered, were in other places. I figured the yellow ones were for evidence, the pink ones were for directions.

Holding my wrist against my nose, I took the pink-marked path. In the first-floor bedroom were more yellow markers. Books and papers were on the floor, files were strewn across the bare mattress. Rick stood in the room, alone, his face lined and drawn, staring at the file in his hands. From where I stood I could read the title stenciled on the front: PARANORMALS WITHIN OUR BORDERS. Beneath that, in larger print, were the words CIA: CLASSIFIED, and below that were the initials FYEO, which I didn't understand.

Tandy was standing close to me, and I was so cold that I could feel his body heat across the minuscule space. I met his reddish-brown gaze, looked to the file and back with a question on my face. Tandy leaned close and whispered, "A classified file from the Central Intelligence Agency marked 'For Your Eyes Only.'"

I thought about that and little pieces came together in my mind with almost audible clicks. This was the file with a list of all registered paranormals, which HST had been said to possess, but it hadn't been created by them. The data had been amassed by a government or law enforcement group—or better yet, by one or two researchers in such a group—and sent to one government person. That couldn't be good. That spoke of factions and maybe of one high-up individual using resources to a personal, paranormal-hating end. And then giving the list to the HST . . .

A second puzzle piece slid into place that suggested PsyLED had been provided with incomplete information into the FBI's abduction investigation of the human girls, for some purpose other than case jurisdiction, command structure, and decisions. Maybe because of this file, which proved the government had been tracking paranormals, and they didn't want the paranormal cops in PsyLED to know about it.

I remembered the ostracism on the porch and nodded my understanding.

"LaFleur," someone shouted from the front. "Where the hell are you?"

Rick looked up and handed me the file. "Under your shirt. Quick."

I tucked the file under my shirt, the icy papers cold on my skin. I wrapped my arms around myself and Tandy seemed to notice for the first time that I was underdressed. He pulled off his coat and hung it on my shoulders. I should have protested, but I had begun to shiver and the coat was marvelously warm.

To Tandy and Occam, Rick murmured, "See what else you can find that pertains to paranormals. Make it fast and get it out of here." To me he added, "You're our mule. Don't let anyone see."

I didn't know what was happening, but I didn't like this. Rick was hiding things from the FBI officers and the crime scene techs. Secrets always got me in trouble. But Rick walked away, leaving us in the bedroom surrounded by stacks of papers. Occam and Tandy moved fast, as if speed-reading everything and making decisions faster than light. Moments later, Occam handed me two more files and a paperback book titled, *How to Kill Paranormals*. I stuffed them up my shirt with the other file, and looked like I had gained twenty pounds, all in my belly.

Tandy used his cell phone to take photographs of dozens of other papers, but even I could tell that they were not near finished when Rick called them to head back to the van. We left behind important papers, four handguns, two assault rifles that Occam called Bushmaster Adaptive Combat Rifles, and the thousand rounds of nine- and ten-millimeter ammo he found under a floorboard in the closet, all boxed up. He had also found a large box of .223 Remington rounds and a box of 5.56 NATO rounds. Lots of weapons, lots of ammunition, and lots and lots of papers.

Holding the papers against my skin, and my arms crossed against the cold, I wandered back through the pink trail, looking lost and as innocent as I could manage. As we left the house, we passed several suited agents, all with muddy shoes and looks of disgust on their faces at the stench. It was a different and better-dressed group from the one that had shunned Rick, and I expected at any moment to be stopped and searched, but it didn't happen. We ended up outside in the icy air, which smelled wonderfully sweet and fresh, and then in the van, the van engine running and the heater on high. I stuck my booted feet into the heater blast and willed my toes warmer, but it seemed they weren't interested in obeying.

Rick took the top secret file and Tandy and Occam each took one of the others. I was left with the paperback book. What the title lacked in imagination, the book itself made up for in barbarity and cruelty. It was poorly spelled, improperly punctuated, and full of grisly descriptions of death, with accompanying illustrations drawn by an untrained hand. There were drawings of witches being burned at the stake, drowned, and skinned alive. There were pictures of werewolves being shot with silver, doused with caustic acid, and skinned alive. Skinning alive was the method of choice for many other forms of paranormal beings, most of which were mythical. The author was singularly unimaginative and with a bloody bent. I closed the book and when Rick stepped out of the van to talk to another federal agent, I asked, "Same one what?" Occam looked up, clearly confused, and I said, "When we went in the house, Rick, the werecat, asked you, the werecat, if *it* was the same one. And you said yes, you think so, and then asked Rick if Paka, also a werecat, thought so too. *Ergo dipso*, you smelled something humans can't. What did you smell?"

Occam gave me a half smile. "Do you mean '*Ergo, ipso facto*?'"

I gave him a hard look back. "Are you over being mad at me?"

"I don't know, sugar. You over getting shot and growing roots in your belly? Because that nearly did me in."

Which sounded like a Texan way of saying he had been scared for me. Which was nice. No one was ever scared for me. I offered a half smile back to him. "I'll do my best to not get shot. Since I don't know what I am, I can't promise I won't grow roots. And yes, I meant *ergo, ipso facto.*"

He said, "Yes. Smell. The dog that peed all over that house was the same one we smelled at the Claytons'. We smelled it on the compound today too. And our Nellie has a saying about coincidence and enemy action that seems to have become a rule in Unit Eighteen."

I ducked my head in pleasure at that one. Occam went on. "The feds' K-nine dog indicated that the first two kidnapped girls were at the Stubbins farm for a while. They found evidence that Girl One died there. Girl Two was kept there too. But not our girl. Not Girl Three, Mira Clayton. Yet the dog that was at Mira Clayton's house was here and kept inside long enough to mark the walls. A lot."

Which meant that somehow, Mira Clayton's kidnapping had been part of the same plan as the others, and had been carried out by the same people. Or a faction of the same people. I was mighty tired of thinking about factions and their possible convoluted plans.

"Could it be a werewolf?" Tandy asked.

"Not a were. Just a big, stinking dog that likes to mark its territory. The abductions are all related somehow, but we don't know how or why."

"So all the kidnappings are related to HST?" I asked.

"Related to, yes. And related to some members of the church, but we don't know the participants."

"Factions," I said. "It has to be factions of both."

Rick climbed back into the van and said, "We've been kicked out of this part of the investigation. We're picking up JoJo and T. Laine and going for lunch. We need a break and we're going to Sweet P's, where Girl Four was taken. We never checked out that location, and we need to see what it smells like."

SIXTEEN

The team was set up in a new hotel, not far from the old one, at Mainstay Suites. Seems they hadn't heard about the guns and the damage. Or didn't care.

It wasn't quite as fancy as the suite in the other hotel, but at least it wasn't all shot up either. Sweet Pea's was packed with a weekend lunch crowd, so we stopped at a mom-and-pop pizza place and picked up four large pies on the way to the hotel. Pies. Not pizzas. I was learning how the unit spoke, the jargon they shared. I was beginning to think that they were pizza addicts.

The team was on the fifth floor, and had taken three rooms, the one in the middle with a large seating area for group sessions. The overpowering scent of pizza filled the suite as JoJo opened the top box and dug in while Rick passed around colas. Everyone ate in the kind of silence that was dedicated to appeasing hunger. The moment he was finished with his part of the pie, Rick dried grease off his hands and said, "Update. I'll go first. As of three hours ago, the family of Girl Four received a ransom demand and proof of life. The money was transferred to the account in the Turks and the FBI is waiting to hear back on a recovery location. The family of Girl Two received a call that their daughter could be found in an abandoned storefront on Fletcher Luck Lane. Local LEOs and FBI went in and found the girl in the store, exactly where stated, alive and physically unharmed, if traumatized. There has been no demand for Mira Clayton.

"Crime scene techs are still at the Stubbins farm and the church compound, taking samples. Simon A. Dawson Jr., Nell's church outcast, has not been found. Boaz Jenkins is still missing. The Stubbins family is missing, except for the boy,

who's confused and uncooperative. The feds are still questioning members of the church, but so far, it looks like no one
knew any members of HST except the Dawsons, the Stubbinses, and Boaz Jenkins, and they didn't know that they
might be/were involved with HST. No one recognized any
members of HST in the photo lineup identification, and no one
assisted with the abductions. This leaves us with a tangled
mess that makes no sense. We clearly have kidnappings for
money, likely by the HST and few church members, for three
of the four girls taken. We just as clearly have one kidnapping
for other reasons by members of the same group."

Factions, I thought. *Maybe factions of both groups. Factions make us think one thing, and then another. Factions
make it tangled.*

"The farm was deserted except for a young boy, Jael Stubbins," Rick went on, "but there had been significant gunfire at
the church and plenty of time for anyone on-site to get away
before he got there. Tracks in the yard suggest that a few RVs
and one eighteen-wheeler were parked there for some time,
and hadn't been gone long."

"What about all those people by the cattle trailer?" I asked.

"The trailer was a different matter. There was blood spatter
there. The feds think the space had been used to keep a prisoner but the dogs went squirrelly—which seems to be a clue if
Nell's hypothesis about three times being more than coincidence. Crime scene did find a bloodied scarf that belonged to
Mira Clayton, so we have our proof that HST, or a splinter
group of HST and a splinter group of the church, had her at
one point. I'm trying to get the scarf and samples of the blood
spatter for scent comparisons, which will be much faster than
waiting on DNA. They also found a shoe that matches the one
Girl One was wearing when she was abducted."

I remembered the shiny blue shoe. A girl had died. A girl
had been stolen from her family. A girl had been killed. And
someone, or several someones, from God's Cloud of Glory
had been involved. I had survived. I touched my belly, the odd
rooty scars there hard and uneven.

Rick spread out the satellite and RVACs surveillance maps.
"The Stubbins farm wasn't part of the satellite photo recon-
naissance, but by piecing together edges of the shots, we now

have photos of the Stubbins farm." He tapped the papers he had printed and taped together. "Note the RVs and the eighteen-wheeler. All now gone."

JoJo said, "Rebel flags on this RV roof. Looks like that one has a missing AC cover. Should be easy to spot from above."

"The feds have eyes in the sky looking for the vehicles in the hope that they stayed together in a convoy that will allow us to pick them out of traffic. So far, we have nothing. The fear is that they went to ground and/or covered the RV tops.

"Inside the Stubbins house we found evidence of people living there for some time, with enough trace to keep the techies busy for months. We found a manifesto of sorts"—he nodded at me and I gave him the book—"a treatise on how to kill paranormals with extreme prejudice, published by HST. The forward demands all nonhumans be put in concentration camps and eventually destroyed, with the exception of the ones that are 'useful to humankind.'

"We also found a list of paranormals." His voice went toneless, though his words were still steady. "I've come to understand that the CIA created a formerly top secret list of paranormals. It seems that somehow HST stole or was provided a copy of the spreadsheet and added to it. The HST list is even more comprehensive than the original. Every paranormal member of this PsyLED unit, and every paranormal creature in the nation, is on the CIA list, with contact information and personal data, including every one of us, except for Nell." His mouth flashed me a smile that never touched his eyes. "Staying off the grid worked for the government. However, you *are* on the HST list, you and your sisters."

Sudden fear gripped my throat with skeletal fingers, and tears filled my eyes. HST knew about my family. But Rick didn't give me time to let the fear take hold.

"We at least know that HST spent a lot of time in that house, and it's the first *direct* link with HST that we've found. Credit for that goes to you, Nell, and your idiotic foray into the compound that allowed us access to the surrounding areas, looking for suspects. The Stubbins farm was not on the list of places the FBI had been trying to get warrants for." His tone suggested satisfaction that PsyLED had one-upped the feds. "However, if you go off again without orders, you are off this unit. Understood?" I nodded, my face flaming. Rick poured himself some cola and drank before continuing.

"One good thing came of the interviews on the church grounds. Your sister's family has been cleared of working with HST. Their passports were part of mission trip the church was planning, to Haiti, to dig wells and teach microfarming. And share the word of God according to God's Cloud." The last was said with a dose of sarcasm, and I didn't object. But a sense of relief feathered through me, alleviating my breathlessness, knowing that Caleb and Priss hadn't been part of HST.

"But we have a time crunch. According to Mrs. Clayton," Rick said, "Mira doesn't have long. We still don't know what species Mira is, and for all we know, she's a singularity, some-thing that made it through, or fell through, one of the liminal lines' weak spots, the places where there's a weakness in real-ity, but whatever the girl is, she'll be dead in just hours. That brings us back to looking at Nell's suspects, Simon A. Dawson Jr. and Boaz Jenkins."

Rick looked at me for a moment before continuing. "Accord-ing to statements made to police and FBI, and Sister Erasmus' statement, both Dawsons were on church property, visiting with family and friends, including Boaz Jenkins and the preacher, Ernest Jackson Jr., prior to the attack on us. Dawson Sr. was found dead, full of silver shot. No one's seen Dawson or Boaz Jenkins for forty-eight hours. We have the photos of them in the SUV at the shooting, Dawson's rehab, and his presence on church property. All that shows they are involved with HST, but not who, *exactly*, among our list of possible suspects, took Mira Clayton. The involvement of the Dawsons and Jenkins in the kidnapping of Mira Clayton is circumstantial at best, and what we have now would never hold up in court. Circumstantial also won't help us *find* Mira, if indeed they took her."

I didn't know what liminal lines were, or weak spots, though both sounded like the church's description of entrances to hell. Now wasn't the time for an education, however, and I didn't ask. I said, "So, there are four kidnappings, three by one group, Mira's by another group, probably a faction of the big-ger group?" Rick nodded his head, and, encouraged, I went on. "A few churchmen are part of group two, the smaller group.

And at the Stubbins farm, the two groups met, and maybe divided, leaving behind a boy who was away and a dead body?" Rick nodded again. "And we don't know where any of them, from either group, went?"

"Remind me to let you do summations from now on," Rick said with that tight smile.

"You said chasing suspects led you into the Stubbins farm."

"Joshua Purdy."

"What happened to Joshua?" I asked. "Last I saw, he was leaping through the air, right at you."

That tight nonsmile pulled Rick's face down into an emotion I didn't have a name for except it wasn't happy. "In the initial phases of the action, we had an . . . altercation. He shot a little boy, so I shot Joshua, cuffed him, and threw him in the back of a squad car. While I was applying pressure to the boy's wound, Joshua ripped apart the cuffs, tore the door off the squad, and got away, down toward the Stubbins farm."

My mouth hung open in front of a new slice of pizza. It stayed that way.

"The kid will be fine," Rick said gruffly. "But I lost the *one* person whose questioning could tie everything together."

I was now able to translate the expression on his face. It was loathing, for himself, for not being able to do everything right. "The boy's life is worth more than Joshua," I said. "We'll catch him."

"I don't need platitudes," he spat, fury crossing his face.

"I'm not offering platitudes," I said back, just as mean. "I was speaking fact. If you want to wallow in guilt and misery, by all means have at it. But wallow later. Right now you have a job to do. So do it."

The people in the room went still and silent, as if they'd never thought to tell Rick what he needed to hear. That was a shame. And it was something I seemed to have an unexpected talent for. That and summations.

A ghost of a smile crossed Rick's features and his shoulders relaxed. He shook his head and scrubbed his hands through his hair before dropping them to the chair arms. "Good advice. Okay. We have files on all the known HST members, and the info hasn't resulted in a single arrest. We have new squares, and those squares are Simon Dawson Jr., Joshua Purdy, Boaz Jenkins, and the dog scent at multiple sites. We need deep background on them all. They're connected to HST, and we need to find how they intersect with Mira Clayton. Mira is our single paranormal taken; she's the only abductee whose family hasn't received a ransom demand. It's possible that she was taken by an offshoot of HST for a reason different from the other girls. And based on the locations of the dog scent, it's also possible that the churchmen are that offshoot."

JoJo said, "Boaz was living on the church compound with his wives and children until two days ago, when he disappeared. He had zero intersection with society outside of the church. He had no property, no job, no friends, and no family outside of the church. His wives are clueless, but it's presumed he's with Joshua."

I thought about Mary, but there was nothing I could do to help my old childhood friend.

"I want JoJo and Tandy to visit the Master of the City, Ming, at the Glass Clan Home and talk to the vamps who used to feed Dawson. See if Ming's people showed him or told him anything about secure places where they kept blood-meals, a place he might keep an abductee. I want T. Laine and Occam in research, taking over all the intel from the feds, and paying attention to anything they're keeping from us."

Rick turned his full attention to me, "I want you on the church premises, talking and making nice-nice with the natives. Find out if we're on the right track with this. Get any locations Dawson or Jenkins might have gone to family property, hunting cabins, that sort of thing, and what weapons they have. They'll volunteer things to you, Nell, that they might not to us. You're our ace in the hole with the church."

I put down the pizza slice and pressed a hand to my stomach, feeling the gnarled scars. A pit opened in my middle at the thought of going back inside, but I understood the need. Until the young girls—human and not—were safe, my own lack of security was unimportant. I wondered if Mary would talk to me. If my family would. "Okay."

He said, "Check your e-mail on your laptop periodically."

I understood that the others would get dinged on their cells or tablets as needed, but my cell wasn't as smart as theirs. And I needed to get the stolen cell phone I had given to Sam back to the owner. "I will."

"Their answers might give you an idea who to talk to and what additional questions to ask. One thing," Rick added. "How many times did you shoot the preacher, Ernest Jackson Jr.?"

I felt the blood drain from my face. Tandy sat up straight, staring at Rick. Occam growled softly. My chin went up. "I shot him four times with one of Daddy's shotguns. Point-blank. Dead center. I reckon the FBI will want to question me. Am I gonna face charges?"

Rick leaned in, closer, into my personal space, his pretty black eyes staring into mine, his nostrils fluttering with scent. "No. Because Jackson Jr. got up from the crime scene and walked away."

I blinked, feeling as if I was on the brink of something, like a high cliff with nothing beneath me. Possibilities flitted and stung at the back of my mind like angry hornets, but nothing settled. When I didn't answer, Rick placed a series of crime scene photos in front of me. Three were photos of the place where I'd left Jackie lying, the blood pool looking as if a mop had been swished through it. A single set of bloody footprints raced away from the dais in the chapel. I studied the photos. No one had picked him up and carried him away. He had gotten up and run.

Jackie wasn't dead.

No one could have survived being shot four times with a shotgun at close range. It wasn't possible. I touched my shoulder. The recoil bruises told me it hadn't been a nightmare. I hadn't missed, and the gun hadn't been loaded with foam pellets or paintballs. I said, "I only got a glimpse of him after. His blood was pooling around him on the floor. His clothes were shredded, and pulped flesh showed through. His skin was going gray. He was *dead*. Deader than dead."

"Concur," Occam said. "Bowels had released. He smelled dead."

Rick said, "Yet he was seen running through the compound, bloodied and wild-eyed, according to some of the people questioned. Running toward the Stubbins farm. In the same direction as Joshua."

I remembered the woods' awareness that Jackie was running away, before Brother Ephraim died, moving faster than human. I remembered his note about the way my sisters smelled. I remembered the sense of awareness of something inhuman stalking on the far side of the new wall of thorns at the boundary of the Stubbinses' property and mine. The sense that the darkness that was Brother Ephraim had been trying to get to that inhuman entity. The sense of something not right about Jackie. I took a slow breath, tight and painful.

Were Jackie and Ephraim inhuman? Nonhuman? I sat back, hands open and empty in my lap. Was Joshua nonhuman? The same kind of nonhuman? Joshua had gotten away from police custody, and in pretty dramatic fashion. Jackie had come back from the dead. And . . . Brother Ephraim was a shadow in my land. Were they all—

"Nell?" Rick said, and there was a demand in his tone, his body leaning in toward mine in a fashion that reminded me of him prisoning me into my chair at the FBI headquarters.

I almost flinched, until I realized that was a churchwoman response. Rick was pushing my buttons, a phrase T. Laine had used during a card game when somebody had bluffed a hand. I leaned toward him, so close my nose was nearly touching his, and asked, "Did Paka get close to Jackie's blood? Close enough to smell if his blood smelled like Brother Ephraim's?"

"No," Paka said. "I am not officially PsyLED, but a consultant as you are. Pea and I were not at the crime scene."

I looked at Occam. "How about you? Did you smell his blood?"

Occam inclined his head as if processing memories. "There was too much GSR and too much human blood scent, but . . . yeah." His eyes were half closed, like a cat, thinking. "Something was off, now that I think about it."

"Metallic?" I asked.

His cat eyes found mine, glowing slightly in the hotel lights. "Yeah, Nell, sugar. Like metal and acid."

I nodded and thought of all the evidence, the odd things that didn't fit, and the one thing that stood out most was that Dawson Sr. had been killed with silver shot. "Can you get some of Jackie's blood to sniff?" I asked Rick. "'Cause I'm guessing he isn't human. Like Brother Ephraim wasn't human. And the Dawsons probably aren't, and weren't, human. Like maybe all of Jackie's closest cronies aren't human. I'm thinking this because Jackie had been biting his concubines and drinking their blood."

The senior agent had that strange expression on his face, the one where he was putting things together, connecting disparate elements into some kind of cohesive whole. One small part of what was going on in his brain had to be the legal aspects of everything that had happened, including the part where the FBI kept trying to keep us out of the investigation and the CIA had compiled a list of paranormal names.

I said as much and added, "Or factions of the CIA too. A few people here and there, with mutual prejudices, getting together to do a particular type of evil."

Rick flipped through the pages in the HST listing of nonhumans. "Jackie isn't listed. Neither are any of the other men from the church."

I said slowly something that had been percolating in the back of my mind. "If *Brother Ephraim* wasn't human, then human laws and grindylow laws didn't apply to him."

Rick's eyes crinkled and he tilted his head in acknowledgment, indicating that he had just come to the same conclusion as I had. If Brother Ephraim hadn't been human, then, because he was committing violence, his death would be considered self-defense. Paka would never have been guilty of breaking any law, not a were-taint law upheld by Pea, and not any law that Rick, as a PsyLED agent, had to uphold. Neither would I, at least about Brother Ephraim.

That did, however bring to mind the curiosity that Pea hadn't recognized the nonhuman blood of Brother Ephraim when he lay dying in the trees. Hadn't noted the odd smell of the man's blood. Or Joshua's blood in Paka's claws. Or . . . had she? She had allowed Joshua to be led away. She had given me a drop of Ephraim's blood. An offering. What did that mean?

Rick leaned back in his seat, now holding a travel mug of coffee, the smell strong and fresh. "Presuming Jackson's crew were a nonhuman faction, working with Dawson. Dawson Sr. was shot with silver, indicating that maybe the Dawsons aren't human. Also suggesting that there are problems in that faction or with the part of HST that they aligned with."

"HST would have killed Mira Clayton the moment they realized she wasn't human," JoJo said. "But if someone else took her—"

"Like a church faction that liked the way she smelled," T. Laine said. The girls bumped fists and, in a synchronized motion, they pointed all four index fingers at me.

"Factions joined with factions," JoJo said. "Just like Nell said."

"We talked about a copycat early on," Rick said. "But all the inconsistences make sense if a small nonhuman faction of God's Cloud was working with HST, and then broke away from that combined group and went out on their own. First that group tried to get Nell, then kidnapped Mira Clayton, then Nell's sister." Rick nodded, liking the conclusion. At one time I might have called it deductive reasoning, but it looked more like instinct.

"The colonel, Jackie's father, kidnapped vampires for blood in the past," I said, adding to my part of the debrief. "Word came out later that Jackie had cancer and was drinking the blood for healing."

"So taking Mira was deliberate, thinking she was a vamp?" T. Laine asked, sounding frustrated.

"No. Her social media was full of photos of her in daylight," Rick said. "They knew she wasn't a fanghead. But she's nonhuman, and her blood may be even better than vamp blood." Rick tapped a pencil on the table, little bounding taps, like a snare drum.

"Vampires can mind-bond with anyone who drinks their blood. Unless. . . . maybe if they aren't human," T. Laine said. "Why didn't we pick up on that before? Churchmen were drinking vampire blood and not getting mind-bound."

"Except Joshua," I said. "He got addicted."

"Which is not, technically, the same thing," Rick said, mulling things over.

"I'll go by the lab first thing in the morning," he said. "I'll sniff-test all the blood samples. And if they'll part with small samples, I'll bring them with me. I'll get them to run DNA on

Jackson's blood ASAP, for nonhuman markers." He looked at Occam. "I want you to take Nell to the compound and sniff the blood on the floor of the church building, now that other scents have cleared out."

Occam nodded.

"We have a lot of unanswered questions," Rick said. "Where is Jackie? Is he with Dawson? With HST or a splinter group? More important, *what* is Jackie?"

I might have added, *And how did Brother Ephraim maintain conscious awareness after I fed his soul to the earth?* I hadn't told them what had happened to Ephraim, hadn't shared the dark part of my magic. And because of Paka's involvement in his death, they hadn't asked. As if they were afraid of what might come out if they opened that particular can of worms. But . . . if Ephraim had been inhum—nonhuman, that might explain a lot.

More pieces fell into place and my mouth slowly opened. I said, "All the K-nines went squirrelly. Sam's hunting dogs went squirrelly. And the smell of strange dogs was everywhere. Scent-marking places. Could they be non-were, shapeshifting dogs?" Rick and the others looked at me and I realized that I was the last one to reach the potential conclusion. I pressed a hand harder to my middle and added one more mental question, perhaps the most important one. *What am I? What are my sisters? Because Mud, at least, is like me.*

Our meeting was over moments later, and I pondered the questions all the way back home to shower and change clothes, silent as Occam drove me, his thoughts closed to me and mine to him. He seemed content to be my personal driver. Or guardian. On my lap were my laptop and a new cell phone, provided by Rick because Sam had already returned his.

At Soulwood, as Occam waited in the unit's van, I cleaned up and dressed warmly, in layers: my last gray skirt over leggings. This time I brought a coat, gloves, and a muffler. On the way to the van, I picked up a potted plant, a batch of geraniums I had rooted, the pot protected from the weather, hidden in the walkway and still blooming. The temperatures had gone cool, and they were blooming, bright pink and white in the same pot. Mama might like it. Silent again, we made the drive back to the church grounds.

* * *

When we got a signal, I checked text messages. It felt strange to have access to such electronic things, expensive toys, just as strange as it did to be going back inside the church compound, for the second time in one day, after so long away. I was an outsider for real now. One working with the law enforcement of the United States of America, to uphold its laws, even ones I disagreed with. An outsider with electronic toys, and protected by a wereleopard.

As we reached the bottom of the mountain, the cell *ding*ed, and it was Rick. "I just heard from the local LEOs," he said without greeting. "Your father is out of recovery. He's awake and doing as well as can be expected."

Tears blurred my vision for a moment and my heart did some strange square-dancing beat before settling. I said, "Thank you. I gotta go." I ended the call, stuffed the cell into a pocket, and wiped my eyes. Occam, without taking his eyes from the road, patted my shoulder. It was oddly and unexpectedly comforting.

Instead of churchmen at the entrance to the church grounds, there was a double line of news vans and policemen guarding the road, two marked cars blocking access. One officer pulled his car out of the way so that Occam and I could motor through, cameras following us and reporters shouting questions that we ignored. Inside the fence, police squad cars and police were everywhere, from all different law enforcement branches, uniformed, men and women in business suits, along with crime scene vans and people in white jumpsuits, all so very busy.

Avoiding them all, Occam maneuvered toward my family's home and braked beside my truck. Occam said, "You'll be okay, Nell, sugar. You need me when you get inside, you call. I'll be here faster than you can blink. And I'll text you when I leave the compound."

I tried to think how to reply. *You are too kind* was too close to the formal phrase used by a churchwoman. I settled on, "Thank you. I'll be okay," and hoped I wasn't telling him a lie. I got out, placing my laptop and the potted geranium in my truck cab for now, and checking to see my keys were still where I left them, under the seat. Mama opened the door before I could knock and grabbed me into a hug so tight it hurt my recently healed belly. Unaccustomed to the contact—a contact I had seemingly missed, as my vision misted again—I hugged back briefly, and then took her hands into mine as I stepped away, trying to find something to say that wouldn't make my action a rejection. I blurted, "Daddy's out of recovery, Mama. He's doing okay so far."

Mama whirled away and burst into tears. She bent over, to place one fist over her heart, and the other hand on the arm of her rocking chair before she let herself fall into the seat. Tears coursed down her face, scalding her pale flesh. Mama Grace all but flew from the kitchen and I repeated the news. And then again several more times as my full and half sibs clattered in from the children's rooms and down the stairs, all talking and asking questions at once. I was hugged and patted and kissed on the cheek by children I didn't know, before four of them, led by Mud, dragged me to a chair with a padded seat and pushed me into it. The din was improbably reassuring.

Mud, seeming to notice that I was reacting oddly to it all, spread a crocheted afghan over my legs and pulled a low stool to my chair, to sit beside me, holding my hand in her small one. A little boy was standing by my chair, telling me about the gunfight in the church, his words mostly unintelligible. A little girl stood beside him, and she might have been telling me the same story from her viewpoint, but I could make out only one word in three. Seemed I'd lost my affinity for understanding the speech of little'uns.

Before I was allowed to conduct any kind of business, I was plied with food—a thick slice of bread carved from one of the loaves I had brought before dawn, smeared with homemade cashew butter spiced with peppers and honey, a cup of hot tea, a sliced apple. There hadn't been time for manners when I appeared at dawn, but there was time now, even if I didn't want to take the time.

I ate and said my thanks and listened to the remembered babble of my childhood as I was introduced to my extended family. The little boy was Ethan and the girl was Idabel. The other names flew from my head as quickly as they were spoken.

I was treated to a hymn sung by a bunch of young'uns who were no more than three feet tall, was shown embroidered samplers and newly made aprons by the girls, a newly seeded egg carton of basil by Mud, and hand-turned bowls and newel posts turned on a lathe by the boys.

As soon as seemed politely feasible, without that possible rejection I had worried about with Mama, I cleared my throat and handed my empty plate back to a middle'un. In my best church-speak, I said, "I need to talk to your mamas now. You'uns go upstairs and give us some privacy, you hear?"

When no one moved, Mama Grace said, "You heard your sister. Get on up. We'uns'll talk shortly about what she come to say."

The sound of retreating feet was much less enthusiastic than when they had arrived, but Nicholson young'uns were well trained and obedient. Daddy's belt had made certain of that. Except that Mud didn't move, a familiar mulish expression on her face, familiar because I'd felt it on my face before. Mama Grace narrowed her eyes at Mud and said, "Don't you start that."

Mud glowered and crossed her arms, but she stood. "It's not fair."

"No, it isn't. I don't aim to be fair. I aim to be one of the mamas. Now git."

Our own mother sat and watched the exchange with a faint smile on her face. I wondered how they had worked out such a partnership with so many mothers in one house, so many half-related siblings. At the thought, most of my good cheer fled and I stood, setting the afghan aside and smoothing my gray skirt into place. I took the poker and shuffled the wood coals in the fireplace, adding a log. Fireplace fires weren't as common as one might expect in the homes of the church folks. Most of the heat went out the chimney, which was a waste, and waste was a sin, but Daddy's fireplace had been fitted with a C-shaped, passive-action steel tube grate, one that used the thermodynamic action of heated air rising to pull in cool air below burning logs and release heated air into the room, above the flames and the rising smoke. While I worked the fire, Mud stomped upstairs and the two women took seats in the rockers by the fireplace.

When the mamas were settled, Mama Grace said, "Talk, baby girl." The words drew me further back into family, into the good memories I'd had as a child.

I sighed and pulled the soft yarn blanket back over me. "I don't know any more about Daddy," I said, "but I have a cell phone, and I'll be informed as soon as possible."

"Carmel called us hours ago on someone's cell phone," Mama said. "She told us that, because she isn't legally married to Micaiah, she can't be told his medical status," Mama said, her lips pinched. "They's only talking to his own *mama*."

"That's true," I said. "One of you needs to marry him legally, and he also needs to provide you with a medical power of attorney. It's the law."

"The government got no right—"

I held up my hand. "Stop. I'm not here to debate the law. We got talking to do and trouble to deal with."

That shut them both up.

"I've agreed to ask some questions of you and take the answers back to the federal officers. And before you can argue, you need to know that the police have connected Jackson Jr. to the Dawson backsliders to Boaz Jenkins, and through them to the organization that kidnapped the townie girls. One girl was delivered safely after the ransom was paid, two are still missing—a human and a nonhuman—and one is dead." The two women shared a long look as I spoke.

"Simon Dawson Jr.," Mama said with a faint huff. "That boy left the church years ago and took up with vampires, drinking vampire blood and sexing with them too. No surprise that he'd do something awful, him and them Stubbins boys. And that preacher boy has been heading for trouble for months."

"Wait," I said. "Simon Dawson Jr. and the Stubbins men were friends?"

"Couple of the younger men, that Nadab and Nahum Stubbins after old man Stubbins passed on. Them and Joshua Purdy and Jackson Jr. were all friends, up until the Dawson boy backslid again and left the church. Things fell apart a mite after that and Nahum left the church again, him and his son and three daughters. Broke my heart to see them all leave."

"Today's disgraceful troubles seem to be seated in the sin of the past. It appears that there might be a split in the church,"

Mama Grace said, her tone mourning, lifting her knitting
from a basket beside her chair. "A legal battle in the court of
the land, over the property of the church. Evil and *disgraceful*," she said. *Disgraceful* was Mama Grace's favorite word.

"Jackson Jr. ain't been right in the head in months, not
since the Avrils and the Bascoms took back their girls," Mama
said. "Jackson Jr. had claimed them as concubines and there
was whispers of mistreatment, though"—Mama took a breath
that sounded painful—"though nothing as vile as the biting
and bleeding Jackie done to Havilah and Henrietta Sanders
and my own Esther." Mama picked up a cup of coffee I hadn't
seen her pour and sipped the scalding black brew, her downcast gaze not quite hiding the tears in her eyes. I looked away
in proper church etiquette, respecting the privacy of another.

"How is Esther?" I asked.

"Back home from the hospital," Mama said. "Hurtin' in her
body and her heart. We talked about how a woman survives
such things. How to live with the memories. We'll talk some
more. Micaiah will talk to her man, see he knows how to help
her through. She'll . . ." Mama firmed her lips. "Esther will
survive and find joy again." Unsaid were the words, *but she'll
never be the same*. Mama knew that better than some.

After an appropriate amount of silence, as according to the
way churchwomen did things, Mama Grace cleared her throat.
"You was asking about Jackie. Two of his wives left him. They
said he was perverse and unnatural, just like his daddy done
growed to be in his later years. Wanting only young'uns. Wanting more than one in his bed at a time. *Disgraceful*. Unnatural.
Sinful."

"Wait," I said, catching up slowly after Mama's revelations.
"Someone took some of Jackie's concubines away? And his
wives left him too? How? Women can't—"

"We women ain't without power, baby girl," Mama Grace
interrupted. "Once upon a time we had as much power as the
men, in our own ways and in our own responsibilities, and we
women are taking back what we let slip away."

My mouth opened in shock and stayed that way. Mama
smiled slightly, and wiped her eyes with a handkerchief she
pulled from her sleeve. "Flies," she murmured and I closed my

mouth, remembering the saying about flies getting into a mouth that was open too much.

"No longer are we letting our girls and womenfolk be punished," Mama Grace continued, her needles clacking softly. "Enough was too much a that."

"But let's go back a bit and start at the beginning of the trouble," Mama said. "Back some few years, maybe eleven or twelve, word come that Jackson Jr. got cancer." I remembered my words to Rick earlier about the colonel's reason for drinking vampire blood. Mama sipped her coffee, holding the cup close, shaking her head, steam rising against her face. I had never known how Mama could drink nearly boiling coffee without being blistered. It looked painful. "Jackie got better. Then he got worse.

"About the same time, the colonel got to being all secretive. Going hunting with outsiders. Making changes here on the compound, working inside the storage caves, updating the security system in the compound with cameras and suchlike. The Jacksons and the Stubbins men, especially the young ones who come back and settled down and stayed, started spending time together. Then one night, the colonel went to every one of his wives' beds. All four of 'em. In *one night*. His wives said he hadn't visited the marriage bed for some time," Mama said.

"It continued every single night, him and *all four wives*." Mama Grace's tone said that was disgraceful too. Her voice hardened. "And sometime around then he asked for you as a fifth wife. That started a commotion, 'specially with you making such a scene in the church when he declared for you. Your mama and us, we got you to safety."

"And with you gone," Mama said, "and the women united against him taking a fifth wife, he went after young concubines. Took hisself four young ones by force. Too young. Sinful, evil, and disrespecting of the helpmeet."

"That's when we realized we churchwomen had let things go, hadn't taken proper care of our duties to the covenant of marriage and to the sanctity of the marriage bed." Mama Grace shook her head, her eyes on her knitting, and I could see her thinking, *Disgraceful*.

Mama cradled her mug. "We'd let ourselves down and now

we were suffering for it. Had been suffering for it for decades. But it looked like we was too late to effect changes. The men was considering deposing the colonel."

I felt like I was watching a Ping-Pong game, back and forth between them, letting them talk. I had to wonder how long they had kept it all dammed up inside, the way it was spewing forth. I kept my mouth shut and let them, nudging them only a little, with, "How did the colonel's taking new concubines create factions in the church?"

"Some of the older men wanted whatever the colonel had that gave him such . . . stamina," Mama said, "and that started dissension, as others of the men wanted him to leave their daughters alone. Groups was forming, gathering, and talking, not all together as the Scripture demands, but against church charter, one group here, another there. Church was close to splitting. Rancorous talking."

"Jackie was well by then, but he'd become a hellion, running all over church grounds, day and night. Then one night there was an uproar on the church grounds." The needles *click*ed and *clack*ed, adding an emotional commentary to her story, sounding agitated.

"Shots fired. No churchmen hurt, except that they had to bury a body the next day. Not a church member. And not buried on consecrated ground." Mama glanced at Mama Grace, who took up the narrative.

"We heard it was a vampire what got staked. That the colonel had been keeping him chained and drinking from him. Disgraceful," Mama Grace said with a fierce frown. "The men called themselves together for a meeting. We'uns wasn't there, but we heard. Some of the churchmen allowed as how they'd had a demon chained up more 'n once, and they begged forgiveness. The colonel once again stopped going to his wives and sent his concubines back home. And things settled down some, seemed better for a few years."

"Until the colonel started getting old again," Mama said. "And he began to remember what it had been like when he had vampire blood for the taking. That was when some a his cronies decided to steal them another demon and drink her blood." Mama punctuated that statement by drinking down a good portion of her coffee. Neither of them seemed to want to speak for a long time, and I heard the ticking of the big grand-father clock in the hallway, a counterpoint to the rhythm of the knitting needles.

Mama Grace spoke again but her voice was low. "The Cohens had a blood drinker in the family. Everyone knew it. So the colonel locked up two of the Cohen sisters in the punishment house and made sure the vampire knew. Then they took the blood drinker. Chained her up with silver chains and had their way with her. Cruel they was, according to what we'uns heard. And they drank her blood."

"Didn't give her none back to drink, neither. Starved her." Mama finished her coffee and shook her head. "But that weren't all." She nodded to Mama Grace to get her to take over the narrative while Mama went to the kitchen for another cup of strong brew for herself and poured one for Mama Grace, as well, adding cream to that mug, and a big spoonful of sugar. She didn't offer me one, just as she wouldn't have offered me cup when I was a child, and I didn't ask. I was gripping my hands tightly in my lap and had to force myself to relax and remember to breathe.

"No. 'Twasn't," Mama Grace said. "Jackie continued to change after that, in ways that seemed unnatural, growing more untamed and out of control, running the woods like a wild animal, half-naked, him and some of his friends. Disgraceful, they all was. And we'uns got to thinking that maybe Jackie was sick again and he was the *real* reason that the colonel done took the demon prisoner, trying to heal his son with the foul blood of the undead, as he had when Jackie was young. But then the vampires and that Cherokee woman come and took the vampire prisoner away."

They were talking about Jane Yellowrock. The vampire hunter who had started the changes in my life. I didn't know if I wanted to hug her or hit her, next time I saw her.

"And the social services people come and took our children," Mama Grace said. "And put some of us in jail, though we'd been doing our best to protect the little'uns. That's when Boaz joined Jackie's cronies, him and a few others."

My new cell phone made a little burbling sound, announcing a text. I picked it up to read a note from Occam. *Jackson's blood smells like the dog at the Claytons'. Hard to tell what he is, but not human. Finished here. Call if you need me.*

I realized that I didn't know how to send a text, so I set the phone on the table nearest and shrugged at Mama Grace. "Newfangled thing. Not sure how to use it yet."

Coming back from the kitchen, Mama said, "Then the colonel vanished without a trace. Some say them vampires come through your land. And they took the colonel."

I didn't respond, but it didn't seem to matter. The mamas had a lot to say, and continued with the story.

"With the colonel gone and the blood supply cut off, Jackie got worse," Mama Grace said, her wood needles clacking louder. "Pure scary. He come into our houses without knocking, frightening our little'uns, looking at our girls. We'uns had to *lock our doors*!"

"First time I remember that. Ever," Mama said, placing a mug on the small table beside Mama Grace. She sat, and pushed off with her toe, sending the hand-carved chair rocking, sipping on her second cup.

Unable to help myself, I asked, "Is Jackie human?"

"Can't say one way or another 'bout that." Mama Grace set her knitting in her lap, took her mug, and stirred it with soft tinkling sounds of the spoon, her eyes on her cup, staring, not looking at me. "But he was shot in the confrontation in the church at devotionals today, and some say that he walked away from it whole and healthy."

"Some say the same thing 'bout you," Mama said, "and I know for a solid fact you're human. First because you come from my womb, and second because we had you tested, and you are *not* a witch."

I almost pressed a hand against my belly, where I'd been shot and tree roots had grown into me, but I refrained. "What do you think he is?"

"We'uns got no idea. I saw him in the sawmill on the full moon a few months past and he was human, working, plain-sawing logs, so he ain't no were-demon."

"Can walk in the sunlight, so he ain't no vampire, even though he drank the demon's blood."

"But he's disgraceful. Evil. Dark of soul." Mama Grace's voice dropped to a whisper, "Demon possessed?"

"Churchmen done separated into factions again and our

own menfolk was getting ready to take him before the church and charge him with witchcraft. Such a charge would a ripped the church in two."

They went suddenly silent. Even the rockers went motionless on the wood floors. A charge of witchcraft, according to church law, meant a trial and if convicted, burning at the stake. A frisson of fear shot through me. That was the eventual, likely punishment that would have awaited me, had I stayed here. I said softly, "Thank you for saving me. Thank you for talking to Leah and John and getting me out of here." Things had taken a decidedly personal path, but I couldn't begrudge myself wanting my own truth and history, though I had been sent to discover a totally different kind of truth.

"Humph," Mama Grace said. "That's women's jobs."

"We'uns know our responsibilities, and we knew the colonel was evil."

Mama Grace tittered and picked up her knitting again. "That was the best thing to happen to that old coot in years, when you stood up and told him no and called him names."

"In front of the whole church." Mama laughed softly with her sister-wife and they exchanged knowing glances.

"Losing you to Ingram, him unable to give you babies," Mama Grace said, "was painful. But he promised to keep you safe. And he kept his word."

Staring into the flames, I shook my head. I had cleaved to John Ingram for saving me, when it had been my family all along. I had lived a lie. Knowing the truth was letting me see things inside me, emotions all snarled around, like the pot-bound roots of a captive plant, growing around and around, seeking an outlet when none was there. I took a breath that hurt, where the tree roots had entered, and imagined that I could feel them stirring inside me.

"We got a decade of catching up to do," Mama said.

"And we need to find you a man," Mama Grace said. "A good man in the church, one who can give you some young'uns."

My head came up fast, a denial on my lips, but Mama beat me to it. "Nell's a big girl. Iffen she wants a man, she can get her own, I'm thinking."

I chuckled, the sound forced and stiff, but at least polite. I said, "Thank you, Mama Grace, but I'm not the marrying kind anymore. I've been on my own too long." Mama Grace frowned at her knitting, but she didn't argue.

"And now I have to talk about something else, if you have the time." Both women nodded, and I led the topic back to the PsyLED interests. "I need to know more about the Dawsons' recent visit, the elder one and the younger one. Did either man spend any time on the compound? With or without Jackie?"

"They wasn't here but a day, maybe two," Mama Grace said. "Him and his daddy and Jackson spent some time in the winter storage cave."

Mama said, "You know Simon was addicted to vampire blood?" I nodded. "Living off church grounds, consorting with evil. Then he done something to make them vampires mad. They cut him off."

"He come to the church for help." Needles clacking, Mama Grace nodded to herself. "But that was after the vampire was rescued by the Cherokee woman, and by then, wasn't no vampire blood to be had, not around the church."

Mama's voice dropping, she said, "As evil as drinking blood is, if he'd a come to the Nicholsons', I like to think we would have helped him with his addiction. Found him a rehab facility somewhere."

Mama Grace seemed to think about that for a moment before agreeing. "Yes. That would a been the Christian thing to do. You're right, Sister Cora. You have a dependable moral compass and a good head on your shoulders. You should marry Micaiah according to the laws of the land. You or Sister Carmel."

Mama's eyebrows went up so high her forehead turned into furrows. The two women chatted back and forth about marrying under the law of the land and who should do it and why. I sat and listened. At one point, I left them to their chat and made a fresh pot of coffee in the big percolator on the kitchen's woodstove. I served us all when it was ready, trying to figure out what I needed to do next, what questions I needed to ask, when my cell rang. I retook my rocker and fumbled, hearing the strange, modern chime in the Nicholson house, then answered it. "Yes?"

"Nell? Rick. I have news about your father."

My heart plummeted and gave a painful electric splutter when it hit bottom. I tried to keep my reaction off my face, but the mamas were too good at reading body language. Mama Grace set down her needles. Mama placed her mug on a side table and gripped the arms of the rocking chair. "Okay," I said. "How's Daddy?"

"I'm at the hospital now. He's awake. He's asking for you. Can you talk?"

"Me? Ummm. Sure?" I mouthed to them, *Daddy wants to talk to me.*

The wives dropped everything and were suddenly kneeling at my rocking chair. It felt wrong to have them at my feet. Worse, Mama Grace was crying big tears like a broken faucet. I covered the end of the cell and whispered, "He's better." And he had to be, didn't he, for him to be talking on a phone?

I heard a change in the background noise, and then Daddy said, "Nell? These PsyLED police. You trust 'em?" His voice sounded scratchy and rough and weak, but it was enough to produce a relieved smile. I nodded at the two women.

"Daddy. Yes, I trust 'em. You can trust Rick. You okay?"

"What about Occam? The were-de . . . the wereleopard. You trust him?"

"Yes. And he ain't no demon," I said firmly, in church-speak.

Daddy laughed, but the sound cut off sharply as if the laughter had startled pain through him. When he started again, he sounded weaker and shaky. "If the police ain't found it yet, tell Sam to take you to the room at the back of the winter supply cave. Tell him I said to show you and the PsyLED police everything about it. Tell him to go armed in case something is back there again. And tell him I said, 'Gog and Magog.' He'll do what you say."

"Okay, Daddy. Mama Cora and Mama Grace are here. Will you talk to them? Daddy? Daddy?" That odd background muffled noise came again and Rick said, "The nurse gave him morphine and it just hit him. He's out of it, Nell. But your father was remarkably talkative."

"Wait a minute," I said, anger blazing up like fire. "You questioned my daddy when he was drugged?"

"And without reading him his rights or offering him a

lawyer. Meaning that anything he said is inadmissible in any court in the nation." Rick sounded entirely too pleased with himself.

My anger was snuffed out as quickly as it flared up. "You did that to protect him and the Nicholsons and me. Didn't you?"

Rick didn't reply to my question, saying instead, "Occam and I are on our way back to the church again. Tell your brother to hold his fire, okay? Gog and Magog sound dangerous."

I laughed, the sound as shaky as Daddy's voice had been. "Okay. See you soon." I ended the call and said, "They gave Daddy morphine and he's out cold again. But he told me to tell Sam to tell me everything about a room in the back of the winter supply cave. And to tell him, 'Gog and Magog.'"

Mama and Mama Grace looked at each other and stood together. Mama took Grace's hands and they bowed their heads. "Lord," Mama prayed. "Give us strength for the coming battles. Help us remain true to You and to Your Word. Amen."

"I'll send Amos and Rufus for the other families," Mama Grace said. "You get Sam and I'll get the middle'uns started on the weapons. 'Gog and Magog.' *Dear Jesus*, I never thought it would come to this. *Disgraceful*."

"Wait here, baby girl," Mama said. "I'll get Sam." Then Mama did something I had never expected in a million years. She reached into the basket of darning beside her rocker and pulled out a cell phone. It was an old-fashioned model, a flip phone, and she punched in a number. Stunned, all my senses alert, I heard Sam answer. Mama pressed the cell to her ear, cutting off his part of the conversation, and said, "Micaiah said, 'Gog and Magog,' to your sister Nell, and he gave her orders. Mama Grace is sending Amos and Rufus to get the others. You get here fast." She paused and said, "Yes. He's letting Nell and the PsyLED police run things." Another pause followed, and Mama's voice took on steel. "*Gog and Magog*, boy. Get moving." And she closed the cell phone.

Meanwhile Mama Grace had made several quick calls on her own cell phone and then she shouted for the children to "Get down here, all a you'uns! It's Gog and Magog!" She turned to me. "We're taking back the church leadership. And the land. And if we have to fight to make it happen, we're ready."

SEVENTEEN

I spent the next half an hour on as part of a texting group, making plans with Unit Eighteen. We had just finished up when Sam came in the front door, tall and lean and tough looking, and he walked directly to me through the melee of family, his long legs lifting across the little'uns, his work-booted feet landing solid and steady. Dependable. All grown-up. Eyes steely, he said, "Tell me *exactly* what Daddy said."

I closed my eyes. It had been years since I'd memorized or recalled anything more important than seeds to order or supplies to buy, but memory games and Bible verses had been part of my youth. I still had the skill, though it was rusty and slow. I quoted, "If the police haven't found it yet, tell Sam to take you to the room at the back of the winter supply cave. Tell him I said to show you and the PsyLED police everything about it. Tell him to go armed. And tell him I said, 'Gog and Magog.' He'll do what you say."

"Exactly that?" Sam asked. "Nothing more? And he said to let the PsyLED police into it all?"

I crossed my arms over my chest. I gave him the look, the one I had given him when we were children and he got bossy and questioned something I was doing or something I planned.

Sam waved my irritation away and laughed, his face lighting up. "Fine." He walked to the wall where the hunting rifles and shotguns were stored and unlocked the cabinet, returning with two weapons. He handed me a .30-30, one similar to John's old lever-action gun, and set ammo on the side table. He started loading his weapon and looked at me with raised eyebrows. "You forget how to load a gun, Nellie?"

I gave him the look again and loaded mine. And then the

others he brought out, until the kitchen table was filled side to side with weapons. Like the rest of the church families, Daddy had an arsenal prepared for the last days, when the remnant of the church had to fight demons and the government all at once. I remembered the gunfight in the church. It was more than scary how many guns were on church grounds.

When we were done, my brother grinned grimly, his blue eyes bright and intense. He handed me John's six-shooter. "I got it from Mama. It's still got three rounds in it. Let's go, baby sister."

He pivoted and made for the door, weaving through the organized chaos. He opened it and cursed, a word I'd never heard spoken on church land, jerking his shotgun up to fire. I rammed my body against his, and shoved him against the doorjamb. "They're with me."

"Demons?" he said, horrified.

"Wereleopards in cat form," I said, my tone derisive. "Not demons, you dopehead. Get them some water; they look like they've been running hard."

Sam rested his shotgun on his shoulder, the barrel pointing up, and snapped his fingers at the mass of young'uns that had gathered in the doorway when I shoulder-shoved my brother. "Get back to work," he said. "Mud, stop hiding and sneaking around. Get a . . . a dog bowl and water for the dem . . . for the cats." To me he added, "But they ain't coming inside, where they might hurt a young'un."

"They're not animals, you dumb boy." I grinned at Sam and he scowled at me. Just like old times.

I set the guns aside and settled on the shadowed steps of the front porch near the big-cats, Paka black and sleek, smaller than Occam's rangy, spotted, golden length, both panting, tongues hanging out. "Anybody see you?" I asked.

Occam shook his head side to side, a gesture that looked bizarre on a cat.

"You keep to the shadows? In the trees?"

Occam dropped his head and raised it back up, his pelt scratching on his gobag.

"That's just . . . wrong," Sam said watching from the door.

"Get over it, big brother. The world is a lot stranger and more interesting than you've been led to understand."

"And you're too big for your britches, little sister. Always was." Which was more old-times talk, and made me smile, dropping my head forward, a trail of hair hiding the pleasure on my face.

Mud brought a slopping bowl of water to the front door and I placed it on the porch. Paka shouldered her way to it first and slurped up half of the water. Occam looked up at me with golden eyes, and I reached out a tentative hand and stroked his head. The hair there was glossy and spotted black and gold. He butted my thigh with his head and dragged his jaw along my shirt, scent-marking me. I let go a breath that sounded like a chuff, and Occam chuffed back at me before bending over the water bowl for his share. When it was empty I picked the bowl up and handed it to Sam. "Get it filled while we're gone."

He handed it to Mud, who was staring unabashedly at the big-cats. She took the bowl and asked, "Why're they here?"

"I don't know. Something must a—must have—happened."

Occam sniffed, his nostrils fluttering. He did it again. And this time I got the message. "They're here to sniff around. Right?"

Occam dropped his head and raised it back up in a nod.

"Faster than waiting for K-nine dogs," I guessed. Occam nodded once again.

Studying the cats, Sam asked, "What the heck are they wearing?"

"Gobags, camouflaged for each coat type, stuffed with clothes and supplies. If they have to change back to human they'll need to dress." The bags also contained cell phones to call for help or backup, and there were weapons there too, but I didn't tell Sam that.

My brother shook his head at the strangeness of it all.

To the cats, I said, "Stick to the shadows. We're heading to some caves the other police might not have found, so you can sniff around. And you need to know: the church sounds like it's going to war, faction against faction, so we need to get out of here fast when we're done."

Both big-cats dropped their heads down, then back up in the cat nod. "Jump in the back of my truck and keep low," I said. I tossed the keys to Sam. "You're driving."

"So bossy . . . ," he murmured.

* * *

Most of the police cars and vans were gone. Except for the crime scene tape at the church, the drive to the caves indicated no problems anywhere, just another peaceful day in the compound, with women and men working in the gardens, harvesting cabbages, fall greens, pumpkins, and gourds, turning over the soil in winter ground prep, and bringing in tarps and mulch. The greenhouses were full of women starting herbs for winter use, and I had a sudden, visceral memory of being in the warm, damp greenhouse on a cold autumn day, the scent of fresh soil and mulch like a blessing to my senses. It was the first time I had been allowed into the greenhouse to help the elder women, and I had been given the job of spreading basil seeds and covering them with a scant layer of sandy soil. I had told the nascent plants they could "Grow now; it's time," and given them a small nudge. I remembered seeing the women smile at one another at how cute I was. But I wasn't being cute. I was being me, and sharing my gift with the plants. I had known it even then, and I couldn't have been much more than five.

Basils grew fast, but my basils had sent the women marveling over the speed at which the different varieties grew. By midwinter, they had nicknamed me *Green Thumb*. There had been good mixed in with the bad in my life in the compound. Maybe all life is like that: good with bad, chaos with order, war with peace, in parallel tracks, like railway lines. Or maybe it was always chaos, war, and bad, and we only imagined the good stuff. I didn't know. But the greenhouse was a good memory.

Maybe I could borrow some space in the church's greenhouses for my herbs and spring plants. If the church survived the coming split. I shook my head. Sam said, "What?"

"It doesn't matter. Park under the trees and away from the other vehicles if you can, so the cats can get into the lower limbs."

"You trust the devils?"

"I do."

Sam shook his head this time, his face looking away in church etiquette, as I did, and made a three-point turn, backing in under the big hemlocks that guarded the entrance to the cave where the church's winter supplies were kept. I felt the truck shift and wobble as the cats leaped into the tree branches overhead. Leaving the truck facing out toward the compound, so we could make a fast getaway, maybe, Sam turned off the engine. "Tell me about the room?" I asked.

"The cave access was reshaped with reinforced poured concrete, rebar, a layer of shock-absorbent wood, and stone, all hidden behind D-cut logs. The door is steel, covered by distressed oak, scarred by the attention of a few axes to look weak, like something that a small battering ram could bring down. But in reality, it would take something more like a batch of C4 explosives for anyone to gain entry, which is now known by the state, federal, city, and county law enforcement officers."

"That had to make the church elders mad, all their carefully constructed, end-of-the-world fortifications laid bare."

"It did. After the raid, though, me and the boys went exploring. We found a set of steel shelves on rollers, something the police had missed. When we rolled back the shelving, we found a . . . a room." Sam tilted his head and shot me a look. "A bad room. Like something out of a porno film, all that bondage stuff."

My eyes went wide and my brother shrugged, visible from the corners of my eyes, his face flushing. "Yeah. I've seen a film or two. When I went to university." I glanced at him and his flush went deeper red, as if he knew what I was thinking. For a moment there was an overlay of him when he was younger, towheaded, tanned, his blue eyes laughing, the eldest of Mama's children, a mischievous boy full of himself and certain of his position and importance in the family, the church, and his society.

A call burbled on my cell phone, and I answered. "Hey, Rick. The cats are in place. So are we."

"I'm pulling up the road," he said.

I turned off the cell and said, "Let's go."

The wide entry door was Xed over with crime-scene tape, sealing it for the police. Sam made a grunting sound that was remarkably like the one Daddy made when he was conflicted or surprised, or sometimes even amused.

Sam's face, however, went sober, a dour expression, carrying worry and a sense of responsibility beneath the bleakness. Visibly, he shook off the worry. "Take your gun," he said.

"Keep it pointed at the ground, finger off the trigger." He flashed me a grin that had couple of pounds of childhood teasing behind it. "Don't shoot your toes off."

"I can handle it," I grouched, opening the door to slide off the seat. "I can take care of myself." I stood on the ground, the .30-30 held in a loose grip at my side, and softly closed the truck door. I left my six-shooter under the seat. Side by side, we went to the cave entrance and Sam used the butt of his gun to tear the crime tape away. It trailed on the ground like holiday streamers. With a key, Sam opened the door. Inside the lights were off and he disappeared into the blackness. When the lights came on, Sam leaned out the door and said, "Call your pets."

A one-hundred-plus-pound black wereleopard landed silently in front of him and growled. Sam squeaked an undignified *geep* and was suddenly standing a few yards inside the building. I laughed at the effect Paka had on my tough brother. When Occam landed beside me, he hacked and chuffed, big-cat laughter. Rick pulled up next to my truck and hopped out. When he saw our weapons, he drew his own. Silent, together, we five went into the cave and shut the door.

The place was a shambles. The sheriff's deputies had opened every storage box, dropped dozens from tall pallets, the supplies inside scattered everywhere, broken, busted, strewn as if kicked around. I had a mental image of men laughing as they destroyed our winter supplies. The food supplies and seeds had suffered the most, with gallon jars of tomatoes broken and left to rot on the floor. I said something under my breath that might have been considered a curse word by the churchmen, but I didn't care.

Bags of winter feed of corn for the chickens and livestock had been opened and mixed in with the tomatoes. It was a mess and was starting to go bad. I made a mental note to tell Mama, so she and the other women could get in and clean. The church's pigs and chickens would be well fed and happy tonight. Rick tapped Occam's head. The wereleopard looked up, his eyes golden and beautiful. "You know how the kidnappers and their victims smelled, how Mira smelled. And you know how Jackson smelled. Take a sniff around."

Thinking about Dawson and his need for vampire blood, I added, "And you know how vampires smell. See if any vampires were here too."

Occam cocked his head as if considering what I was saying, and then he and Paka met, nose to nose, as if the senses of touch and smell were some kind of untamed, natural communication. They vectored off in different directions.

I jabbed my brother's arm. "Can you take photos with your cell phone?"

Sam pulled out his fancy cell phone, almost a tablet. "Yep. My generation ain't gonna be held back from knowing what's what in the world. Amos is going to MIT to learn computer stuff next fall. Rufus is going to MIT to learn chemistry, aerodynamics, and get a good grounding in making electricity off the grid. I don't have their brains, but I'm taking classes for my masters over the Internet in the business side of agriculture and animal husbandry."

At my startled expression, he said wryly, "The Campbells are sending their young'uns to school, one in constitutional law, the other to learn history, with an emphasis in medieval and postcivilization warfare. Other families are learning mining and smelting and the womenfolk have added the making of stoneware and ceramics to the soap making and weaving and sewing." He tilted his head to me as if conceding a point. "Two of the Nicholson's female little'uns might be some kinda prodigy in math. They're getting special tutoring, so it ain't gonna be schooling just for the men. When the end comes, we'll not only be able to survive, we'll be able to prosper. And if He doesn't come soon, then we'll be better suited to whatever kind of future comes our way." Sam had dropped the church accent while he was talking about school.

I said, "Daddy . . . Daddy plans for you to be in charge of the church, doesn't he?"

"Yeah, little sister. Gog and Magog." He face was harsh and lined, my brother looking older than a man still in his twenties should.

"Take a couple hundred photos," I said, ignoring everything of a warlike nature that might have been included in his statements. "Then call the Nicholson women and tell them about this mess. They need to get the families together to clean up."

Sam laughed softly, his tone mocking. "What about the cops' crime scene?"

"The cops can kiss my skinny pale backside about any

ruined crime scene. They can see the church in court about reparations too."

Rick glanced my way and put his cell away. "Already reported via text to the VIPs."

I followed Sam to the back of the cave, where I heard claws clicking on stone. Paka and Occam were in a dim corner, waiting for us.

My brother led to the way to a shelving unit against the back wall. The base was difficult to see in the weak cave light, but Sam kicked the shelf in three places, maybe unseating brakes, and pulled. The unit moved, revealing a door in the back wall. Using the keys he had brought, he unlocked it to reveal an unlit room. A dank scent flooded out and Occam sneezed. Paka stood at his shoulder, her ears pricked forward, sniffing, snarling. "I smell it too," Rick said.

Sam turned on the lights. Inside was an area with a poured concrete floor, smooth and slick except for four iron rings set deep in the middle. The cats were sniffing the room from the doorway, ears back flat to their heads.

There was something on the far side of the concrete pad, metal, like an erector set, or one of those robots that can change shape into a car or a plane, but this one was all in pieces, looking as if it had been tossed off the concrete and into a jumble of rods and metal mesh. It was a metal bed frame. A metal yard chair was next to it. A metal table. Everything twisted and destroyed. Including the handcuffs at each of the four bedposts. They had been twisted, deformed, and ripped, much like what Occam had done with the handcuffs on me in FBI headquarters, but with a lot more torque and violence.

Rick stepped into the room, using a psy-meter, taking measurements of paranormal activity in each part of the room, quartering it, taking notes on a little spiral notebook with a pen. The cats stood with the rest of us at the door, sniffing.

"Is this where vampire prisoners were kept?" I asked. Occam blew out a breath, his nostrils spreading and relaxing, his gaze too bright. He dropped his head and raised it. "Are those bloodstains in the concrete?" Occam repeated the nod. "Do you smell Jackie here? Others like him?" Occam nodded.

Rick said, "Recently?" Occam shook his head. "Do you smell Mira? Was she held here before she went to the Stubbins farm?"

Occam nodded and shook his head, uncertain. "Too much blood smell to tell for certain?" Rick asked. Occam nodded, but padded to the far side of the cave. He sat and put a paw out, tapping the concrete. "Maybe Mira was there?" Rick asked. "K-nine should check it out?" Occam's head dropped once in agreement. "I'm done," Rick said. "Check the room and then shift."

Sam, who had been silent for the whole time, said, "I got a tracker dog. Chrystal. A springer spaniel. She can sniff out a bird at a hundred paces. She ain't a police dog, but I'm willing to get her in here and see if she can pick up the girl's scent over the rest of this stink. That might save you some time and get started sooner." He glanced at the werecats and adjusted the position of his shotgun in what might be considered a menacing gesture. "'Course, your cats'll have to leave my dog alone or I'll have ta shoot 'em."

Occam and Paka both looked away, bored, before padding silently into the room to search, quartering the space as Rick had, noses to the ground. Sam, taking their body language as agreement, went to the cave entrance and made some calls, I supposed to get someone to bring Chrys to the cave. Minutes later, the cats raced back into the storage area and disappeared, to reappear, now in human form, dressed in light cotton clothing insufficient for the unchanging cold of the cave, with flip-flops on their feet. Voices low, they filled Rick and Sam and me in on the details they had learned.

It wasn't what I had expected.

They smelled the dog they had first smelled at the Clayton home. And there were others that scented of whatever creature the dog was. Dawson? Brother Ephraim? For sure, Jackson and the others like him who had been on the Stubbins farm. They had marked territory. And maybe someone had kept Mira in the cave, though only for a very short time.

On a shelf, Paka found another copy of the CIA's list, the HST's paranormal list, and more papers, written and published by Human Speakers of Stupidity. They were full of hatred couched in protection of the humans, and looked exactly like the kind of evil that said anyone not lily white or completely human should be enslaved. How had the dogs of Jackie's cadre associated with the people who would have killed them on sight?

I thought about Dawson Sr., killed by silver shot. Had the HST figured out he was wasn't human and killed him? Had Jackie given them the old man? When I said that to Rick, he shook his head. "We'll figure it out."

"Can the cats track Jackie and his friends?" I asked.

"No," Rick said. "Big-cats aren't trackers. We don't have the noses for anything but short-term scents. I called for the canine units earlier, but we're not getting them until the Stubbins farm is done."

"Hate dogs," Paka said, her voice rough and coarse, as if still in cat form.

I turned on her. "Well, you either need to get over that hate and start respecting a good tracker dog, or put your nose to the ground and start sniffing, Paka, because Mira Clayton is almost out of time."

Paka hissed. Occam's eyebrows went up in surprise and a slow smile spread across his face. "You look like some sweet lil' ol' thang," he said his Texan twang suddenly strong, "but you got some spunk, don'tchu, Nell, sugar?"

"Nell, *sugar*?" Sam said, menace in his tone.

"Occam can call me anything he wants," I said, eyeing the Texan cat. "I gave him permission, and I don't need yours."

Sam slanted his eyes at me but said to Occam, "She always did have a mouth on her."

"Did you pick up anything else?" Rick asked the cats.

Occam's face softened. "The blood of that bastard Jackson Jr. The blood of several captive vampires, at least three, as many as six, some who died here. And dogs everywhere. I think"—he paused, the fingers of his left hand counting against the thumb—"maybe four dogs?"

Sam look confused.

Paka said, "I smell the one who attacked your home and then"—her hand made a waffling motion—"then disappeared." She was talking about Brother Ephraim.

Brother Ephraim had just been proved to be nonhuman. The thought made my mouth go dry.

"He drank vampire blood here," she said. "Several dogs drank blood here. This place is a cage."

Rick looked back at the reinforced entrance. "Made when the fortifications were made?"

"That was when I was eight, I think," I said.

Sam nodded. "When Jackson Jr. first got cancer. He was about twelve. Maybe fourteen. Dogs?" he questioned.

"This place has been used as a prison for supernats for a long time," Occam said, glancing at Sam, "years off and on, according to my nose. And your preacher isn't human. He's a shifter of some kind."

Sam's eyes cleared. "That's what you meant by smelling dogs. And . . . that actually makes a lot of sense. There've been tracks . . ." His voice trailed away. He looked back toward the entrance, thinking. "Big tracks. And the security dogs have been more squirrelly than usual."

Occam chuckled. "*Squirrelly*. That's the word. Paka. You think it's similar to a wolf?" She cocked her head and squinted her eyes. "No. Dog of some sort. But not weredog. Pea would have noticed when the bad man went missing. And the musky scent is richer and more tart."

Occam's nose wrinkled. "Okay. I get that too. Dog it is."

"We need to seal this back room off as a paranormal crime scene," Rick said. "Looks like you'll be getting a chance to practice all your Spook School techniques."

Occam's eyes lit up in completely human excitement. I said, "I'll be in my truck."

While Rick and the others sealed off the back room, I sat in the truck cab, studying the photos of the destruction and property damage in the storage room. The photos made the mess look even worse than it had seemed.

Sam came by once as I worked, telling me, "Chrystal got a hit on the girl your people call Girl Three. She was on church land. But Rick says he'll do what he can to protect us. You trust him?"

I almost said, *As much as I trust any man,* but I kept it in, offering a nod and a shrug at the same to time to indicate my ambivalence. "Mostly."

My brother looked out over the compound, his face giving little away. "Sunset devotionals are likely to be dangerous. Just so you know. We'll be taking a vote on ousting Jackie and taking the land back from his daddy's estate. Our lawyer found some irregularities in the paperwork that gave the compound to

Jackie." He smiled grimly. "We aren't ready for Gog and Magog, but it's upon us. Or maybe I'm not ready. I was planning on marrying and starting a family first. Seems like the good Lord has other plans."

"Don't he always," I muttered. Sam snorted and moved away again.

By happenstance I discovered that my tablet could go online through my cell phone, which was simply amazing. I spent more time searching the Internet and PsyLED intranet for any mention of creatures that smelled like dogs, and in mythology, there were a lot of possibilities. The church taught that all mythological creatures were evil, possibly left over from the mating of angels and humans, and according to my research, the church might have been right about the evil part in many circumstances. A lot of creatures were indeed monsters—cannibals, child stealers, hellhounds, black dogs— dozens of varieties of dog-wolf-shifter types.

I was deeply engrossed in reading about some Germanic shifters when a tap on the cab window startled me. Occam stood on the other side, a half smile lighting his face when our eyes met. I rolled down the window.

"Nell, sugar, I got a question."

"Okay."

"Your brother's dog found a single drop of Mira Clayton's blood spatter in the cave. Rick says you can track creatures on your land. If I offered you the blood, do you think you could track her, through your land? Like maybe through the tree you, uhhh . . ." He floundered for a word, any word, and stumbled to a stop. He blinked once, slow, like a cat in the midst of ignoring his human, and said, "Rick suggested that you knew where things were on the land of your farm. He suggested that you could track on the land. Maybe *any* land."

"On my land, yes . . ." I stopped as possibilities flitted through me. When I'd been at the private school, in the wood near it, I hadn't been able to merge with the woods farther away, but my wood was close to the church land, and . . . and the tree here on the compound had stuck roots inside of me, had healed me.

Or I had made it happen.

My magic might be able to do things I had never thought about before. It might also make me into a tree or a rosebush or cabbage if I kept playing around with it. There's always a price to pay with magic.

At the thought, a strange emotion flitted through me, like bats on the wing. Was Soulwood sentient? Was the tree that had healed me sentient? Sentient because I willed it to be so when I was a child? Or was I the one who caused it to heal me, and sentience came to it after it tasted my blood? Or was it just a tree and I was imagining its independent actions?

I put a hand over my scarred middle and thought about the dark thing that chased its tail around in the earth of my land, confined there. If I reached to my land, now that I had merged with the bloody-rooted oak, would I accidentally unite the trees here with the trees of Soulwood? And if I did, would I upset the balance of the walls of my land and set the thing that used to be Brother Ephraim free? If it got free, what would it do? How much of *it* was still sentient? Worse, what might it become while kept captive?

Fluttery bat-wing thoughts, dark and chittering. They made my palms sweat and I rubbed them on my skirt. I had lots of things to think about, as soon I had a day free. "I honestly don't think so. The world's too big. But I can try."

Occam held out a paper bag, which I opened. There was a bright pink scarf inside. The scent of the missing Mira wafted out at me. Flowers. She smelled like flowers.

"I should try at the tree . . ." The bat thoughts spiraled and twirled and my stomach did a matching pirouette. "I can't promise anything, Occam."

He shrugged and got in my truck. We made good time back to the chapel and behind it. I stopped at the oak tree, which looked bigger and stronger and . . . maybe meaner than it had before. If I squatted down on the ground at its roots, would it try to stick them inside of me again, to trap me here? Before I could change my mind, I got out and knelt on the ground beside an exposed, gnarled root, one with a suspiciously fresh-looking cut on its upper side. At the thought, an odd new sensation trembled in my belly, not a bat-wing-fear flutter, but something green and warm, stretching like a vine in the sunlight on an early spring day. Before I could chicken out, I opened the paper sack and pulled out the scarf, holding it in one hand and placing the other firmly on the root.

The smell of Mira was buds and flowers and blossoms, all in the midst of anthesis—the midst of opening. Her scent filled my head, and for a moment, I thought this must be what dogs experienced when they took a scent. That bit of fancy faded away and I let myself flow into the root and the tree and into the ground.

An instant later, a rootlet snapped around my wrist, holding me still. Another root, one shaped like a thorn, pierced my thumb, drawing blood. I yelped and Occam cut me free with a knife I hadn't seen on him. With a spurt of adrenaline, I backed away from the tree, Occam beside me. He had his knuckles in his mouth, sucking his blood off them. I stuck my finger in my mouth and did the same. "Your tree? It's got teeth, Nell, sugar."

"Maybe we need to be at my house to try this," I said.

"Maybe so," he agreed, leading me back to the vehicles.

"But honestly, even if this *would* work, I think I'd need blood to track anyone except on Soulwood land."

"What about . . ." Occam looked back the way we had come. "What about trying in the winter cave? Where Mira was kept. Where we found the blood droplet."

Mira had been kept in the church compound. Vampires had been kept there. The things I had learned about the church—or, rather, about some of the people in power—were worse than anything I had ever imagined. There were few things in life I wanted less than to go into the back room of the cave and touch the blood and gore accumulated there. I wrapped my arms around myself. "I can try."

I was sitting in the dark, on a blanket Occam had spread on the cement slab. The metallic scent of the dogs' blood was all around me. The rotten stink of vampire blood. And death. I wasn't surprised the cats hadn't been able to detect a single drop of blood over the stench here. It was horrible to my human nose, and I didn't know how the werecats stood it. I didn't want to be here. I wanted to be anywhere but here. But Occam and Rick, standing nearby, seemed to think I might help.

As if he knew I was dithering, Rick said, "If you can just give a direction to start looking. We have land deeds and bank records for Jackson Jr. We have local law and sheriff deputies out searching each of the properties, and the Stubbins farm is locked down for CSI. We don't have time for standard, mundane law enforcement and evidence-gathering methods. We need to narrow and accelerate our search."

I placed my palm flat on to the slab, beside the speck of blood at Occam's fingertip. An icy chill flashed up, into my palm. I pushed beyond the cold, into the earth, through the concrete. The cave floor was limestone, like the walls, but pitted and dry, no longer a place for water to flow from glacier melt, or for water to drip through and slick everything with minerals, but a place where the earth breathed in fresh air. The earth beneath the stone floor was primeval soil and ancient broken stone and rounded boulders made from the creation time of the Earth. Streams flowed through the ground and across its surface, pooled below and above, the heart's blood of the earth. There were copper-bearing rocks in the stone and soil, and a huge fractured section of energy-sparking quartz carrying traces of gold. The heart of the mountain range and the soul of the valley arched up, then out and around, and it was . . . almost aware. Centered on Soulwood. Seen from here, the earth on and around my land was different from the land elsewhere. It had become responsive, interested, *discerning*.

But even the land away from Soulwood was different from what I expected. It was . . . awakening. As if sensing the new energies of man—nuclear, hydro, and electric. It was stirring, the energies changing the way the land thought and felt and communicated with its various different parts. The earth was awakened to the new energies as they buzzed through the ground, alien and annoying and itchy. And the earth was intrigued. I pressed through that awareness and searched for the life force of the dogs, the metallic scent of the foul blood. The awareness in the ground turned toward me, the way a blind slug turns toward its food source. Searching and seeking, slow and ponderous as lava pressing through cooler rock. The tree out front, near the church, was a dark thing, full of venom and anger and need. It turned to me too. The mutated tree . . . The tree I had changed and had no idea how to fix it. But I had other responsibilities just now.

"Okay," I breathed, so soft I was certain that nothing but the earth heard me. I returned through the rock and sand and clay and water to the limestone floor, rocketing from the ground into the concrete.

I hunted through the slab, with its myriad proteins and decaying effluvia. And I found the single drop of Mira's blood.

Light. Song. Blooming things. Bells ringing. That was Mira Clayton. I had her essence now, but it was fragile, delicate, hard to comprehend and harder to chase.

But . . . I smelled the dogs in the cage room, as well, dark and fetid, so easy to follow.

Without effort, my thoughts traced their scents, wet and dank and hungry, flowing through the cave floor and out the open door. Into the compound, a scent the earth knew. Beneath my hand, the land began to gather itself.

Time had passed, but time is nothing to the earth. I trailed the chemical traces of the dogs on the ground and scenting the air, all through the compound. And out. Up the hill, straight to the deer stand on my land. Then to the house. This was the last time they were all together. I backed away quickly, before Brother Ephraim noticed me, tracking the scents of Jackie and Joshua back to the compound. After that, it was even simpler to follow them away. I chose to shadow Jackie, his life force spiky and dark as lampblack, across the earth, along a path. To the Stubbins farm, where he had run after I killed him and he came back alive. Leaking blood. Then away, along a road. Harder to follow.

The asphalt where his trail led was a poisoned vein across the face of the land, tar in the wrong places, exhaust and refined gasoline and oil, all poisons, washed by rain into the grasses and herbs beside the road. The land opened and merged with me, Nell and earth, earth and Nell, and we tracked the trail of dog stink along the road. Jackie had left the Stubbins farm in a vehicle. Bleeding. Alive again. Along a road he had taken before, his traces stronger.

Here he and another dog had shot Old Man Dawson. A dog himself.

Farther along, *there* he had thrown the body. And close by, he had washed the blood from his truck bed.

The dog stink moved down the hills and through a town, through Oliver Springs, across Indian Creek, the waterway silted and sluggish. Jackie had slowed and stopped and parked. And then he moved across the surface of the land and into a building. He was there still. Carefully I reached out and searched all around him for the flowery traces of Mira, but all I found were potted plants, rosebushes, mums, narrow patches of greenery. If Mira was here, I couldn't sense her. Instead I was pulled to the scent and taste of *blood*. Human blood, soaked everywhere, in one building. Humans were inside. Dead. Dying slowly on a blood-soaked floor. My magic reached out for the blood, warm, alive, and pulsing. Dogs and human forms paced slowly among the bleeding humans, lapping at the blood, growling softly, the vibration of their snarls felt through the earth. I reined back on my magic, pulling the need for blood, the desire to feed the earth, away, back to me, gratified with the discovery that I could control it.

I noted where the building was and withdrew.

I concentrated on the doglike traces back at the compound, beneath my hand. I went after Joshua's . . . *scent* wasn't the correct word. His blood's life force, maybe.

Joshua's force was less spiked than Jackson's was. Less intense. Less dark, but more poisonous in other ways, ways the earth knew but I had no frame of reference for. A comprehensive timeline wasn't open to me, but he had left the compound before Jackson, for the Stubbins farm. They hadn't left the farm together. Joshua hadn't been found at the farm, and he hadn't come back. All I got was a direction and a sense of even that fading. Except . . . he wasn't alone. Another dog was with him. How many were there?

The vehicle he was in had turned onto Old Harriman Highway. The road was full of curves that followed the contours of the earth, and I liked the road, as it had become part of the earth. I had a general location and a direction. But of Mira I had nothing.

I pulled away, back into myself, and I would have fallen face-first onto the concrete slab if Occam hadn't caught me, his heated hands holding me steady. He put some juice to my mouth. Slimy, sugary, salty. Electrolyte water. I was leaning back against his chest, his body hotter than I expected. I leaned away fast and swallowed all at once, coughing on the liquid.

"Nell, sugar? You okay?"

"Yes." I coughed and swallowed. "I can't find Mira, but I found Jackie. I'm not sure where exactly, but a building in

Oliver Springs. And then I followed Joshua but lost him down
a road." I started shivering, even inside my coat, and Occam
picked me up bodily, carrying me to my truck, where he deposited me in the passenger seat, yelling for Rick. He turned on the
engine and heater full force and joined me in the cab. I had
been in the hidden room too long, and my teeth were still chattering when Rick climbed in and pushed Occam across the seat
against me, his warmth, like an oven stoked with winter wood,
burning bright. Occam told him what I had said, and Rick
placed a tablet in my lap, a map of Oliver Springs on screen.

"Can you narrow down the location of either man any?"
Rick asked.

With my fingertip on the screen, I followed the road into
Oliver Springs, across the town, remembering the creek and
the split-second feel of the road falling away to the water.
"Jackie was near here, somewhere. An abandoned building
maybe?" I asked, pointing to an area off East Spring Street.
"Joshua was out this way, somewhere before I lost him." I
pointed farther down Old Harriman Highway.

"The van is warm now," Rick said to Occam. "Bring her to
it." And he was gone.

"You're welcome, asshole," Occam said. "Beggin' your
pardon Nell, sugar."

I laughed, but it sounded weak and breathless. "You tell
him, Cat Man," I said. Occam shook his head and I bent to the
floor and picked up the pot filled with geraniums, the pot I had
meant to give to Mama. Instead I stuck my icy hand into the
soil from home and thought about Soulwood. Instantly I felt
warmer. Not a lot warmer, but my teeth stopped chattering, so
that was good.

Occam opened the door at my side and I realized I had lost
some time with my hand in the soil. The truck was off, though
still warm. The werecat slid his arms under me and lifted me
and the pot from the truck. "Come on, Nell, sugar. Boss' orders."

The van was full of the members of Unit Eighteen. Rick
swiveled in his seat and shoved the laptop at me again, his
finger on the screen. "Here? A churchman named Ingles
owned a warehouse near here."

"I don't know. But wherever it was, there were humans in
the warehouse dying and a lot of blood." And my magic was

attracted to blood, *wanted* blood, to give it to the land, which was a horrible thing to know, but I kept that new knowledge off my face. "Sister Erasmus said three entire families had moved out of the church compound in the last year. It didn't seem important at the time, but I think I might a found what's left of them. Mira wasn't there," I added. "I didn't sense her blood."

"So where is she?" Rick asked, his voice a snarl.

"I followed Joshua's trail. He was in an old vehicle. It felt like a truck, low and growly and powerful," I traced my fingers over the map in the general direction. "It may have turned onto a gravel drive out here somewhere. Not anyplace I've ever been. Sorry."

Rick said, "Drive." The van lurched into motion, the sound of keys clacking on multiple laptops, taking the road toward Oliver Springs. I closed my eyes, exhausted. In the dark, I heard voices, Rick talking on his cell, giving directions to someone, someone important, from the tone of his words.

Sleep flowed over me like water.

"Nell. Wake up." The voice was strident, harsh. My body jostled, my head lolling.

"If you shake her again, I'll have to hit you, boss." Occam. Defending me.

I almost found the energy for a smile. "It's okay, Occam. I'm awake. What do you need, Rick?"

"We have ten different properties to check, but Mira Clayton's mother is adamant that her daughter has to be found before dawn. We could get warrants and search each of the properties, but that would take a good week. We're out of time for the legal and the mundane. We need a direction. The cats can search in the dark."

Without warrants. I understood that Rick was willing to bend the law as it applied to paranormals, as Paka had suggested he might. I opened my eyes. It was nearly dark out, sunset hidden beneath lowering clouds. We were parked on a small flat place beside a two-lane road. There was no traffic at this time of day, on a weekend. I blinked and realized that my hand was still in the pot of flowers. I pulled out my fingers and flicked off the soil. "Where are we?"

Rick slid the laptop onto my lap again, knocking it against the potted plant. He pointed to the screen. "We followed your directions and we're on Old Harriman Highway." His voice dropped low. "Nell, can you put your hand in the earth and find her?"

I didn't want to say it aloud, but he deserved an answer. "I doubt it. But if I can it'll be only if she's been bleeding. And easier if she's still bleeding. And only if I have some of her blood."

"We've got her blood. Try," he said, and slid the van door open. A frozen wind swept in, smelling of cattle manure, pigs, maybe a chicken farm, rich and pungent and earthy. "Put her on the ground, Occam."

I felt the werecat's body tense, but I gripped his arm. "I want to try."

Occam growled again, but he lifted me from the van and set me on the ground. I was still holding my potted geraniums, and I spilled a little of the rich soil of Soulwood onto the gravel-filled ground. I pushed my fingers through the familiar soil and touched the earth beneath. "Give me some of her blood," I whispered.

Rick placed a bit of gauze into my free hand and I transferred it to the fingers on the ground. My magic recognized the presence of blood on the gauze. I had never used my magic this way, but I thought about the blood in my hand and about blood similar to it. Blood called to blood, and I felt the pull of the earth, faint and delicate. No more than a hint of scent on a fractious wind. I pointed. "That way." And I fell flat.

"According to Nell, Mira Clayton is somewhere outside of Oliver Springs." It was Rick's voice, guttural with exhaustion. My eyes fluttered open. "We have three potential properties, belonging to different former churchmen out this way. You cats need to shift and check them out. Stay together. Keep away from cameras and scopes." The van was stopped again but was angled so the cold wind whipped past instead of inside the open door. I felt Occam slide away from me, taking his extraheated body warmth. I hadn't realized he had been holding me on his lap. Totally improper but so very warm. I couldn't complain. And I missed that warmth. Using my magic in new ways had left me drained.

Outside the van, I heard the *snap* and *crack* of bones

breaking just before the van door closed. Paka and Occam were shifting into the their cat forms.

I was still clutching the tiny piece of gauze with Mira's blood on it, and had been . . . not simply aware of it, and not exactly talking to it, but . . . something. And I knew things now that I hadn't moments ago. I whispered to Rick, "I felt something you need to know. Mira's magic is similar enough to mine that I can feel her . . . calling to the earth and the sun, I guess is how to say it. She's been bled. Her blood supply is depleted." I licked my lips, which were dry and cracked, and Rick held a bottle of the slimy electrolyte water to my mouth. I drained it and asked for more. He opened a second bottle and I drank it down too. "Thanks," I said, taking the bottle from him. "She's weak." I stopped for a moment to catch my breath and to rest, so exhausted by speaking that I felt as if I'd sprinted miles at a dead run. "She's in a shed or a hut. That way." I pointed.

Rick jumped from the van and shared my information with the werecats. They padded away.

"You did good, Nell," Rick said when I woke again. "The abandoned building in the woods near Oliver Springs? There was an old auto repair shop near where you felt their blood. The sheriff's department and a SWAT team raided it an hour past. They found some of Jackie's paranormal dogs and two dozen humans, HST and church families, most of the survivors female. You did good work."

"But the women are in a bad way, aren't they? Jackie and his men raped them, didn't they? And bit them?"

Rick didn't answer, so I said, "Maybe killed and ate the males?" Again, Rick didn't answer, and I got the feeling he was trying to spare me something. "Jackie and his vile dogs were using the women to breed with and to drink from, weren't they?"

Rick hesitated a moment and then asked, "How did you know that?"

A smiled ghosted over my face and was gone. "Deductive reasoning. Jackie's note said my sisters 'smelled good.' Joshua wanted to claim me as a mate. So did the colonel before he disappeared. Jackson senior and junior had lots of wives and concubines, trying to breed babies like they were on an assembly line. Brother Ephraim raped my mama. Had himself a son on her. Jackie took my sister Esther and raped her. All this interest in one bloodline, what you might call one DNA type." Rick inhaled slowly, his eyes shifting back and forth as he took in what I was saying. "Jackie raped and bit his concubines. And you said the females survived, which means the men mostly didn't. And all the dogs we know about so far are male."

Rick stopped breathing entirely.

"I think they were drinking from and eating men and drinking from and breeding with women, looking for useful bloodlines." I thought about my half sib Zebulun, from Brother Ephraim, but I didn't say his name. "Maybe that's how they make more dogs."

"Yes," he said, the word slow and hissing with shock. "That makes sense. But they're safe now."

"Safe?" I asked, thinking about Esther. "How can you ever be safe again after something like that?"

From the front seat, T. Laine said softly, "Your mama survived. And so has Esther. I met them both at the hospital when they went to see your daddy today."

I hadn't realized that T. Laine was even in the van. JoJo as well.

T. Laine said, "The women in your family are strong, Nell. And we'll—*we all* will—see to it that the women are offered comprehensive treatment, physical and mental."

I shook my head. "Wounds don't always heal." Exhausted, I curled in my coat on the van seat, my potted plant in my arms. Before sleep took me under again, I saw car lights pull in behind us, and heard voices talking. But I was too tired to care what they were saying.

I woke to the feel of movement beneath me and heard Rick ask, "How many vehicles?"

"I see five cars, most sedans," JoJo said, her fingers tapping fast, "and three RVs in various states of disrepair on the vid. And one older eighteen-wheeler. The videos the cats got for you are all fuzzy and won't make it through the court system, having been downloaded from a leopard cam, but some appear to be the same make and model as the vehicles the feds were looking for from the Stubbins farm. I'm running the tag numbers the cats got for you now."

T. Laine said, "I can throw a pre-prepared sleepy time spell over the grounds. It's not big enough or strong enough to put the occupants unconscious, but I can make them drowsy enough to ignore most anything, up to a house fire."

The van slowed and bumped over rough ground before coming to a halt. The door opened, T. Laine slipped out into the darkness, leaving the sliding door open. The van rocked as two big cats—Paka and Occam—leaped inside. I sat up, pulled my fingers out of the soil, where they had migrated in my sleep. I stretched and checked my cell phone, to see that three hours had passed. Occam sat at my feet and stared at me, and I said, "You're a pretty cat, Occam." He yawned to show me his teeth in agreement.

Paka vocalized, a demanding sound, and butted Rick's leg.

"No, Paka," Rick said. "We don't have enough people. We have to wait for the hostage negotiator and SWAT backup." She butted him again, harder, and when he swatted her head, she sank her claws into his thigh. Rick cursed and jumped from the van, cursing again, steamy breath caught in the gleam of headlights. I covered my mouth. It shouldn't have been funny, but it was.

"Why is the cat harming him?" a woman's voice asked, the syllables stilted and old-fashioned sounding. I knew, without looking, that it was a vampire, and pulled my feet back onto the seat in case one of them came inside the van. Standing outside were the blond and redheaded vampires from Mrs. Clayton's house. Surprise laced through me like the roots in the pot I was holding.

"She says we should hurry," Rick said, his tone exasperated. "But we need Joshua in the room with her in order to have evidence worthy of charges. And we need armed law enforcement backup."

"We have waited over an hour for your law officers," she said. "We offered to be your *backup*." I peeked over the seat to see the blond-haired vampire, long and lanky and dangerous looking, with her fangs out and her eyes black. When she spoke, her breath didn't steam in the night air, which was unnerving. "We know where Mira is," she said. "We are done waiting." She turned to the dark and said, "We go. Now."

"Just in time." T. Laine appeared out of the night, startling even the vampire, who leaped back a dozen feet into the dark. T. Laine chuckled at the sight. She had been under a don't-see-me spell and even the vampires hadn't sensed her. "Sleepy time spell is in place, boss. Everyone went to bed and the music was muted. There's one man on the back porch of the house, smoking weed. He might be one of the Stubbinses, if the man in the social media photos grew a beard and started going gray." She stepped in front of the blond vampire and turned her back, which the vampire didn't like. The vamp snarled silently. I had a feeling that T. Laine was annoying her on purpose.

"And the best part?" T. Laine said. "Joshua just headed for the shed. According to what I overheard Joshua tell the man on the porch, Jackie doesn't know Joshua and his group took the girl. But they're expecting Jackie to find them eventually, at which point they plan to kill him and take over the church. Nell's factions are getting smaller and more murderous."

"I have all the cams integrated," JoJo said from the front passenger seat. "I can send the feds and the local law notice that we're ready to move."

"Do it," Rick said. "Paka, Occam, get into place. On a three click." He demonstrated by clicking something over his mike three times. The sound came from Occam's neck, where a head-set was wired next to his gobag. Occam and Paka chuffed and vanished into the night, leaving the van rocking again. "You two." He pointed to the vampires. "There will be no draining of anyone. He will be arrested and taken into custody."

The female vampire bowed from the waist, but it looked mocking. "The Mithran vampires of Blood Master Ming of Clan Glass do not drink down humans." I didn't know why, but it sounded like a lie.

The vampires raced into the shadows, Rick beside them. T. Laine ran in their wake, holding something round and shiny in her hand, like a Christmas tree ornament. JoJo, left in the van with me, tapped keys and muttered to herself.

"Where's Tandy?" I asked her.

"Back at the hotel. The sheriff's deputies used him on approach to the warehouse they took down, and it . . . it was hard on him." She glanced up from the screen, her eyes glowing in the LED light. Her fingers never stopped tapping.

"Did they get Jackson Jr.?"

"No."

I frowned. Something seemed wrong about that, but I put it away for now. I was too tired to make sense of it all. I was alone, but for JoJo, and the footsteps of the vampires and the other members of Unit Eighteen were quickly out of range. To find them I would have to put my hands into the earth, and I didn't think I could. But JoJo could see what they were doing, each little camera on her screen in its own little block. I leaned closer, watching. I followed them all, through the dark. Saw it when Occam and Paka leaped to the roof of a shed, four-legged. When T. Laine pulled back her arm, ready to release her ornament, I realized it was a spell to batter down the door. In the same instant, caught on T. Laine's camera, the two vampires gripped a vine-made crack in the wall, shoving their strong fingers along the vines and into the old, dry wood. Three *clicks* sounded over the computer.

"Takedown," JoJo muttered.

The takedown was fast and violent. The ornament ram hit the door with a splintering *bang*, and Rick slammed the door with his shoulder, just as the vampires ripped one wall off the shed. The two cats leaped inside from a shuttered side window, wood and glass smashing down together. It was a fast-moving montage of action and sound. I saw Occam's front legs, stretched into a leap, as his claws hooked into a man and bowled him down. He had Joshua Purdy on the ground.

Joshua, I thought. I had been chasing Joshua, but . . . where was Dawson? And Jackie? They should have been at the warehouse. *Something is wrong with this.*

The blond vampire twisted the metal shackles off the prisoner. The other one ripped his own arm with his fangs and held it to Mira's mouth. Nearly bloodless, she didn't respond at first. And then her eyes opened wide and she gripped his arm, sinking her own teeth—long and pointed all around like a shark's—in and sucking. The vampire said something in a foreign tongue, and I knew it was a pained curse, even without knowing or hearing the language.

I breathed out with a smile. Mira was a blood drinker of some sort. They hadn't told us that. But she was safe. The other vampire, the blond one, bit into Joshua's neck and sucked. JoJo said, "Blood to blood. Now the fangheads will know everything Joshua knows."

"That's not a myth?" I asked. "Drinking blood gives vampires control of their victims' minds?"

"Absolutely." JoJo frowned and looked over the seat back to me. "Well, maybe not the dogs. They did keep fangheads prisoner, which is pretty much unheard-of in the vamp world. So maybe vamps can't—"

The front doors of the car ripped open. A dark arm grabbed JoJo and her computer and threw her from the van. She landed ten feet away with a *thump* and a crack of broken plastic. JoJo didn't make a sound. As if I moved in taffy, too, too slow, I swiveled on my seat and reached for the van's side door.

The front doors closed with *bang*s. The engine started. The dark form in the passenger seat shoved me back and belted me in place as the van spun rocks and careened in a tight circle. With a roar of exhaust that blew inside, choking, it tore toward the road, knocking me back and forth, into the door and, without the seat belt, I'd have landed in the floor, rolling awkwardly.

I heard a *schnick* and the words, "I was after the girl that Joshua took from me, but you'll do. Move and I'll shoot your kneecap. Your blood and body will be just as good either way, wounded and gimpy forever or not."

In the dim greenish lights of the dash, I saw a hand adjust the rearview mirror, followed by a semiautomatic handgun pointed at me. On the other end of the gun was Jackie.

But he was different. Leaner. Joints more bulky. Short, midnight black hair covered his body like a thin coat, all except his face, which was pale as the moon rising over the treetops. He laughed, the sound coughing, and I saw a mouth full of pointed teeth, dog teeth, canines white and impossibly sharp. Shock struck through me like lightning, painful and heated. In the passenger seat was Simon Dawson Jr. But Dawson was mostly dog now, black fur and pointed muzzle, black nose. Glittering eyes. Pointed, tall ears. Lots of teeth, long and razor sharp.

The van's tires hit the highway and I knew I was lost to Occam, T. Laine, Rick, and Paka, who might have saved me. And JoJo was hurt.

EIGHTEEN

Jackie drove with one hand on the wheel and one hand holding a gun on me. Dawson stared at me like I was a steak, a red glow in his eyes. I felt in the seat crack for my cell phone, but it must have slid when the van skidded and fishtailed. My laptop was on the floor on the other side of the van, too far away to reach in a single lunge before I was shot dead. If I were closer I could bean the driver on the head with my geraniums, but I'd never get a backhanded hit to the front seat before Dawson simply took the clay pot away. Which left me with my wits and my crafty tongue. I figured that meant I was gonna die.

I heard a cell ring and Jackie's eyes focused on me in the rearview. He must have liked what he saw, because he put the gun down, glanced at the screen and answered. "Roxy. We didn't get her. But we did get the little church girl. Nell. Right." Jackie listened and said, "That might work. Since it was PsyLED, they might agree to an exchange." Jackie laughed, ended the call with a push of his thumb. The van sliding, rocking, he pulled over.

Moving faster than anything human ever could, he braked and was over the seat, both hands gripping my elbows, clamping them to the seat. Beside him, Dawson used a roll of duct tape to adhere me to the seat, panting as he pulled long lengths around me with that particular stripping sound of heavy tape, his hands more paws than human. When Dawson was done, Jackie patted me on the cheek, and I realized that his hands were clawed too, like a dog's paws—nonretractile claws, rigid and pointed. Like Dawson, his ears were pointed and situated high on his head. His nose was black and coarse, though unlike his friend's, still mostly human shaped. I remembered the smell of dog pee on the plants at Mira's house and all over the Stubbins farm. I had indeed found the dogs.

Dawson, back in the passenger seat, whuffed. He appeared to have changed completely to dog now, and he clawed the remains of clothes and shoes away from him, to the floor.

Jackie leaned in and sniffed me. "You smell like a werecat."

"What's it to you, *dog*?" I asked, thinking it might not be the smartest thing I ever did, picking on a black dog in some kind of partial shift.

Jackie's shoulders rose high, his nose wrinkling and his eyes going red. "Not just a *dog*. Not a *pet*. Nothing so *common*," he growled, the last word dripping in malice. "We are Welsh *gwyllgi*." The word sounded a bit like *gwee-shee*, and it was one in the long list of shifter dogs I had studied. One of the worst ones.

His nose moved along under my hair and up near my ear, sniffing, his breath heated and fast. "We like the stink of fear." Which I figured meant he really liked the way I smelled because I was flat-out terrified. He chuckled again, and pulled back, so I was reflected in his red-eyed stare, my own eyes wide. "Think of us as the faerie dog's scarier, darker cousin, but with a much better title—the dog of darrrknesssss." The last word came out as a growl, and spittle flew from his lips, hot and stinking of old meat.

I said nothing, and wished I could turn my gaze away, but that wasn't happening.

"You get to be a carrot, woman. And when we get the girl back, and the PsyLED team buried six feet under, I'll turn you over to Joshua and we'll get your land for our own, a safe place to hunt and kill. And you will bear our young, *gwyllgi* to build our pack." With that, he eased away from me, returned to his seat, pulling the van back onto the road and into the night, misshapen hands on the wheel, his claws tapping on it. If fear sweat hadn't been soaking my skin, I might have patted myself on the back for my deductions, but all I wanted was to throw up.

I tried to analyze what he had said. *The girl* had to be Mira. I had a feeling that he didn't know about the vampires who had come along to rescue Mira, and I had to wonder why he hadn't smelled them, despite his dog nose, unless the vampires had been downwind from him. They had never been inside the van.

But there was no way Mira was going to be exchanged for

me. It sounded as if T. Laine had been right. Jackie didn't know that Joshua was the one who had taken Mira from him. I had to assume he didn't know that the LEOs had raided the auto repair shop. Things I knew, that they didn't know, could give me leverage. But claws and fangs meant they would always have the upper hand.

I wondered if the vampires had drunk enough of Joshua's blood to get information out of him. If so, it was my fondest hope that the vampire drinking him down got so excited that Joshua got drained by accident. Of course, I also guessed that Joshua didn't taste too good, so that wasn't likely to happen. I had better use good ol' Josh now. I turned on my strongest churchwoman accent.

"Vampires was part of the raiding party, Jackie. And they done got Joshua Purdy."

The van swerved slightly before Jackie righted it. I'd hit a bull's-eye. "What?" he said, his voice a register lower.

"Joshua is the one who took Mira Clayton away from you, with help, of course. Him and . . ." I thought fast and found a twisted lie that might work. ". . . and probably the Dawsons. Simon here"—I kicked the front seat—"him and his daddy were both drinking on Mira with Joshua."

Simon made a doggy squeak of denial.

"Don't lie, dog," I said. "The PsyLED agents and vampires busted in. They got Mira. They got Joshua. They put all a your dogs to sleep so they can't fight and they're in custody right now. More important, no way will Joshua hold out against vampires. Everyone knows they can use compulsion to learn anything they want, and these vampires ain't chained. Even *gwyllgi* can't hold out against vampires who ain't prisoners." I didn't care that I might be lying. I needed to sow dissension. Divide and conquer.

Jackie growled, the note so low and deep it rattled the metal of the van. "Not against a *gwyllgi*," he said. "Vampires are nothing in the face of one of us."

Softer, speaking slowly, the way a good churchwoman should, I said, "They got two *master vampires* to drink him down," which might not be a lie, because I had no idea how powerful the vamps were, "and that means they'll quick-like know everything he knows. *Everything*, Jackie. Joshua is the same kind of creature you are? It won't help him. Not against two master vamps and him a prisoner. Table's turned, Jackie. The vamps is in charge." I remembered what he had said on the phone. "He knows who and what Roxy is? And where Roxy is?" I let my voice drop softer, almost into a whisper. "They'll know. Does Joshua know about your hideouts and your money?" I asked, sowing division in the ranks. And then I remembered one important thing. "And your friend here, the outcast Dawson." I tilted my jaw at the dog in the front seat. "Does he know you shot his daddy?" I pressed, remembering what reading the land had shown me, "Dawson Sr.?" I was risking everything on words, but they felt right, and Jackie flinched, just the smallest bit. "Shot him dead with silver shot?" Beside him, Simon the dog growled long and low and looked at Jackie with his hellfire eyes.

"Silver is the only thing that kills your kind, ain't it? I got me a feeling that you been working against your old friends, *and* against HST." I lowered my voice. "Was Joshua close enough to the Human Speakers to know who made the trips to the Turks and Caicos Islands to set up the bank accounts? Will Joshua give away all your hidey-holes? Will he tell them vampires *what you are*? Is *anything* safe, Jackie?" I had paraphrased the last line from a movie I had watched. Dawson panted. The smell of wet dog and dog breath filled the van, rank and sick.

"Somebody turned in the auto repair shop outside of Oliver Springs," I said. "The sheriff is still there. I wonder who turned that location in?" *Me. It was me.* "Your feeding places, your sanctuaries for your dog pack, have been raided today and tonight. You're on the run until you can find a safe place again. The church grounds, the Stubbins farm, the locked room behind the winter storage cave, and the repair shop near Oliver Springs," I said, almost musing, "all gone in one day. Who was it, I wonder?" *It was me. Me.* I wanted to say it so bad I could taste the words, but I kept them inside.

Dawson growled again, the vibrations stronger than the engine, shaking through my chest. Jackie moved, a blur in the dark. Gunshots stole all sound from me. The van braked and lurched and swerved to a stop.

The smell of metallic blood and gunfire burned the cold

night air. Simon Dawson Jr. whined. Jackie raised the gun and shot Dawson three more times. Dawson fell silent. Even his breathing died away. Tears I hadn't known I cried cooled and dried on my face. Not tears for Simon. Tears for . . . everything. This whole mess.

Jackie lifted the cell to his ear again and said, "Roxy. Three things. They got Joshua. The local cops raided the *gwyllgi* saloon. And Simon attacked me and I had to take him out. Yeah. Silver shot." He listened a long time. Then he said, "Yeah. They got the last of the HST members and the church families, not that we need the stupid males anymore, but they also got the pregnant females." He listened again. "Yeah. If we had to lose them, this was good timing." He added, "No. None of them know where you are." He ended the call.

Jackie looked back at me in the rearview and started making this choked, chuffing sound. I realized he was laughing. That couldn't be good. Maybe I had played into his hands— paws. I thought about my cell again, and tried to remember if it was turned on or off, and wondered if the team could track me through it. I didn't hear it vibrate or sing a tone, but it was a hope, no matter how faint. Or maybe they could track the van's GPS. Assuming it had one. All I had was a flowerpot. Against a paranormal, shape-shifting dog.

We drove through the night for a long time, first on 27, and later on the I-40 corridor, and the whole way, I tried to think of a way out of this. My brain felt like mush, which never happened to the women in the films I watched or books I read. I wasn't making any headway on an escape plan, beyond ripping off the tape, opening the door, and rolling out into the road. I tried the tape, but that stuff was strong. A sharp blade might cut it. The most I did was break a nail. Up front, dog blood dripped slowly onto the floor of the van, with little splats, metallic and foul.

I finally spotted my cell on the floor. If I could get the cell and call the PsyLED team . . . Yeah. Maybe I'd also grow wings and fly away. But it was the only chance I had, no matter how remote the possibility of success.

I stretched out my leg and pointed my foot, slid as far down in the seat as the duct tape allowed, but even when the tape was near to ripping my skin off, the cell was too far away. I pulled my flowerpot close to me. As a weapon, it wasn't much, but it was better than nothing.

I was out of ideas. The thought of being in Jackie's hands made my breath come fast, and sweat gathered, icy on my skin. That made Jackie turn his head, sniffing. He laughed that awful barking laughter. The blood dripped, slow and steady, metallic, almost caustic on the contained air.

We passed exits for towns I knew of but have never been to, until Jackie turned off I-40, onto a two-lane road and slowed the van. Farms passed on either side, and then thinned out into forest, the elevation began to rise, and I recognized mountains on the horizon. We were headed southeast on a road that hadn't been repaired in years, full of potholes and cracked pavement. It might be an old moonshiner's road, taking us to the Appalachian Mountains in North Carolina. Away from everything I knew.

Jackie turned onto an unpaved road that was little more than a rutted drive. My fear spiked and I heard hissing sounds close by, steady and sharp, like the unrelieved spitting of snakes or maybe dragons. Fanciful fears from reading too many books. From a childhood in the church.

The lane narrowed and trees leaned in close, as if looking into the van, branches scratching along the sides like the skinned and skeletal fingers of the dead. I loved trees, and they loved me, but there was something about this patch of land and these trees that was not lovely. They seemed menacing, though that had to be my own fear, as no tree was aware enough to menace anyone. Well, except for the vampire oak on church land.

The headlights picked out shapes in the night: outbuildings, trucks on blocks, a tractor, the remains of an old commercial chicken coop, yards long, with a rusting metal roof. A dilapidated barn listing to the side as if ready to collapse, doors missing. A ranch-style house appeared, windows curtained off, with only slits of light showing that it was inhabited. The door opened and a man appeared, a shotgun in hand. The van jolted and pitched and rolled on past.

The road curled again and went uphill, bumping and rough. And then we were back on a paved road, and I realized that we had taken some kind of shortcut. Minutes later, Jackie turned again, onto a well-kept tertiary road, and then onto a paved drive and up to a fancy house constructed of wood timbers, a log home that was a century and a half and a lot of high tech away from the log homes of the early settlers. This was a log mansion, with tall, vaulted ceilings, the windows in the peaks bright with light.

Jackie braked and turned off the engine, which ticked and hissed as it cooled; white steam curled up around the hood, swirling, caught in the headlights. At least I knew there weren't giant snakes or dragons nearby. The PsyLED van was about to blow a head gasket, if I was any kind of judge. Which meant it was not going to be a reliable way to get out of here, even if I got access to the keys.

Jackie opened his door, and the night air was damp and cold. I heard the hiss of the engine, but also the hiss of a low waterfall, splashing, dropping, landing wetly. Jackie opened my door and, with one claw, he ripped through the overlapped duct tape and yanked it off me in a fast tear. It took a patch of skin as he threw it aside, the pain instant, intense, and impossibly sharp; I cried out. He wrenched me out and tossed me. The pot landed first and shattered. I landed on top of it, on the ground beyond the drive, the torn skin of my arm on the manicured lawn . . . and the soil. Bleeding atop the potted dirt of Soulwood.

Face on the ground, my legs tangled in my skirts, I opened my hand on the ground, pressing the earth of home, to mix with the land beneath me and with my trickling blood. I dug my fingers into the mixed soils and curled them around a small fistful of dirt.

The grass, the land its roots grew in, and I woke up fast, as if I'd ingested a pot of Rick's coffee directly into my bloodstream. I *reached* into the ground. And I connected with . . . something. Not my land, not my woods, but something deep, something that rested in the dark, somnolent and content. I scratched my broken nails into the soil, mixing the dirt of here with Soulwood dirt, together with my blood. Jackie gripped my elbows behind me with his claws, piercing my skin, and I hissed, like the engine. Jackie laughed.

He lifted me to my feet and shook me. "Be good." With one hand, he pulled me after him toward the mansion, past upscale landscaping and an artificial pond with a waterfall. The door of the house opened. Roxy stood silhouetted in the light. A man. A man with clawed hands and hellfire eyes. Another *gwyllgi*. And I knew him. As a dozen children gathered around the dog in mostly human form, I put it all together. It had been there all along if I had just made the connections.

Roxbury T. Benton had been his ancestor and an early member of the church, the name misspelled in the newspaper as Roxbury T. *Bantin*. Four generations later, R. Thomas Benton the fourth ran the Knoxville FBI. And he had somehow made friends with Jackie. Maybe through Dawson, who had come through the legal system. Dogs recognizing dogs . . . Dawson led Roxy to Jackie. And now Dawson was dead.

More things fell into place, nearly clicking together as I comprehended each one.

Dogs might have bred true in some of the churchmen. Maybe recessive genes in some who had come from the old country among the first church settlers, like Mama's people. Out of multiple wives and so many children in each generation, there was a much greater chance of more dogs being bred.

Vampire blood maybe made the trait stronger.

Roxy might even have generated the relationship with HST. So he could know that the *gwyllgi* were safe from detection. That would explain why the HST had been trapped in the warehouse and drained dry. They hated paranormals. They would have hunted *gwyllgi* down and killed them, so Benton took the war to them first. That assumption in my sea of assumptions felt solid.

Whatever his motives, Roxy was the lynchpin who tied it all together. My fear spiked, sweaty and cold.

Benton smiled at me and I knew he was remembering my sassy talk in the FBI meeting when I had attempted to school him. Now I was at his feet. He said softly, "So much for your vaunted reasoning."

My lips wanted to quiver, but I clutched the dirt and blood in my fingers as more of my blood ran from my ripped flesh and pooled into my fist. I said, "I would have had to know that you and Jackie had two or more things in common in order to make an assumption that you would also have others in common. Had I known that *Roxy* was your nickname earlier, I might have made part of the connection. Had I checked to see who in the legal system Dawson had met, I might have made another part."

When the leader of the Knoxville FBI tilted his head, I continued. "I had no idea that your first ancestor to this area was a churchman, and therefore I could make no deductions or assumptions. Though now that I do know that, I can assume that the Dawsons, the Jacksons, and the Bentons are—or were—all in cahoots together. *Gwyllgi*. Dogs of darkness."

Benton stepped down the steps to the ground, his posture negligent, a big dog on his own hunting grounds, walking closer, studying me with unwavering eyes. He leaned in and sniffed. Like a dog. Coiled a hand in my hair and yanked me closer.

He and Jackie half carried me around the house, through a basement door and a bright room filled with lawn equipment, through a door that was well hidden. It opened into an area under the house—bare rock floor, concrete block walls, no windows. The lights glared, bright and intense after the dark of the night. They landed on a vampire, chained to the wall. It was skin and bones, with ratty long reddish hair wearing the remains of denim pants and a once-white shirt. It looked like a scarecrow until the scent of my blood hit it, and its eyes opened wide. It inhaled fast, its fangs snapping down with a sharp *click*. But the sclera of its eyes weren't red with blood-flush, rather they were a pale pink lined with darker veins, its pupils blacker than a moonless night. The *gwyllgi* had starved it and chained it to the wall with silver, hanging off the ground. Benton had done with the vampire what Jackie and his father had done.

Humans who drank of vampires became blood-drunk, open to compulsion, addicted. Not *gwyllgi*. They were free of the compulsion, and the blood made them stronger.

That would be the source of their power—to be able to drink vampire blood, to grow stronger and more powerful without becoming addicted, without becoming captive to the fanged ones. And they could also farm out the blood to the desperate, people who were hoping to drink vampire blood to remain young, to regain health, to survive when their own bodies turned against them. And if someone they sold or

traded blood to became addicted, that just gave them more
control.

That was the final, real reason why the *gwyllgi* had joined
with the HST. The CIA knew that the group had acquired the
list. And added to it. Benton found that out. To get the names and
personal information of the paranormals, he and his dogs had
found a way into the organization. To get the information on
which vampires might be easiest to take. Which women might
be easy to breed with. I understood it all. And it was too late.

They shackled me to a chair with handcuffs, which was
plumb stupid, as it was nothing more than an old captain's
chair, the wood dry and long-dead. I *know* wood. They thought
a chair and handcuffs would be enough to keep me cowed. But
my shoes rested on the stone floor. They turned off the lights
and left me there, in the dark, with a starving vampire, closing
the door behind them.

As my eyes futilely tried to adjust to total darkness, I
kicked off my boots—which took some time because I'd tied
them on tightly—and toed off my wool socks to place my bare
feet on the cold rock. The vampire hadn't been on this spot of
rock, so there was no sensation of maggots and death. I sighed
with relief. Behind me, my blood dripped off my fingers to
pool into the seat and trail down the turned wooden legs to the
rock.

"I thirst," the vampire whispered, the *sss*ing sibilants
bouncing through the underground room. "Feed me."

"No," I said, pushing my consciousness into the stone
beneath my feet, searching for contact with the dirt beneath it,
or to the side of it. But instead of soil I found rock, rock, and
more rock, a single massive, rounded boulder that extended far
beneath the ground, probably the result of some geologic event
so far in the past that even the earth itself had forgotten it. My
consciousness spread out and around and down, searching for
soil and moisture and life, looking for the strong sense of life
that I had found in the front yard. Roxy had chosen his housing
site well, and according to Biblical principles about building
one's house on rock, but . . . there was a small, hairline crack
and the first grains of soil filled with moisture, just . . . *there*.

I gasped with relief, following the moisture as it gathered
in the narrow crack of boulder and moved slowly, my mind

following it down through the stone and then up into dirt and rocks and decayed matter and . . . the roots of plants and grass. I knew where my awareness was—the backyard, just on the other side of the concrete block wall where the vamp hung.

I recognized the sense of life I had felt in the front yard, old and sleeping and *powerful*.

"What are you?" the vampire asked, its voice rasping like leather on bone. "You are not human."

I didn't have time, breath, or energy to respond, too busy trying to think of a way to contact my woods from so far away. I didn't know if the paltry bit of soil clenched in my fist and on the stone beneath me—Soulwood soil, from my busted pot— was enough. I dropped the bit of bloody Soulwood dirt onto the floor I *reached* . . .

My belly heaved, not with nausea, but as if the rooty muscles were straining, as if I were trying to do sit-ups. Or as if the roots inside me were stretching through solid ground, seeking water. Seeking life. Seeking home. My hands itched. I felt as if I were falling, the world twirling around me. I *reached*. And *reached*.

But it was too far. And I was too small. Too weak.

Bright lights flashed before my eyes, like stars falling. Pain beat through my bloodstream.

When I came to myself, I was gasping, pouring with sweat, muscles trembling. The world of blackness around me tilted and spun, a sickening whirl. I breathed deeply, trying to find some sort of stability in the blackness.

On the wall the vampire clanked its shackles. "Hungry . . . ," it rasped.

"Yes. I get that," I whispered, the words a faint echo from the concrete walls. Maybe, instead of reaching Soulwood, there was a way to stimulate the ancient power beneath the ground. Maybe I could get it to . . . do what? I wasn't sure, but I had few other options.

Breathing deeply, slowly, I reached into the soil toward the slumbering sentience. I touched the consciousness beneath the ground, the way I might stick a toe into a great pool. It slept on, unmoved by the slight pressure of my mental tap, though something passed between us: a flare of energy, or perhaps of life force. I was suddenly able to take a breath without pain or exhaustion; the strength of the consciousness flowed into me, filling me, the way water flows into a pool: effortlessly.

From far away, I felt something shift. Brighten. It was a feeling akin to the visual act of seeing a candle lighted on a distant mountain peak on a moonless night. A vague, remote spark in the far darkness, seen best when looking away, to the side, and not directly on.

"I smell your blood. I thirst." The vampire sounded stronger, more alert, and it clanged its shackles, the metal loud.

I *reached* toward the spark of light, the flicker of contact, a life force that was waking and stretching. The glow brightened on the distant mountain, suddenly familiar, oddly, unexpectedly aware of me. I realized that I was visualizing my actual home, not a virtual location in my own mind, but a place in time and reality; bouncing off contact with the sleeping sentience below me, I *reached* again through that life force. I touched the power of my woods. It latched onto me, wrapping itself around me, as if I was tied to it even more securely than I was tied to this old chair.

I had known that Soulwood was *my* land, *my* wood. I belonged to it as surely as it belonged to me. Perhaps more than I imagined.

My intestines twisted and writhed, rigid as wood within me. It hurt, the way a tree hurt after lightning hit, or when vines sent root tendrils into its bark. *Attack.* I felt as though I was responding to attack.

Across the room, I heard metal squeal. "I thirssst."

I reached out to my land. And, through my land, to Paka. *Here,* I thought at her. *I'm here.*

I felt her response. She was still in cat form, and her ears perked high, her whiskers shivered; she was aware of me. Paka nudged a warm, sleek body next to her and made a cat noise that was half scream, half challenge. She leaped out of a moving car's window. Occam followed, landing and jumping from the ground into a tree all in one move, claws sinking deep, to race along a branch. They were close. Very close.

How had they followed me?

Ah. Right. The cell phone.

Maggots followed the werecats, leaping, racing maggots. A vampire, *two* of them, on their trail, as fast as they were, perhaps faster.

Maggots crawled across the stone floor onto my feet.

Something clanked. Closer.

The vampire was getting free.

My eyes flew open in the darkness, like a cave, far underground. But I knew without being able to see that the vampire was no longer hanging on the wall. It had worked its shackles loose, had probably been working them loose for ages, as it was bled to feed the things in the house. And then I showed up, bleeding, the reek of lifeblood giving it the final impetus to wrench free. The maggoty feeling crossed the rock to me the moment it touched the floor. By the clanking and jangling sounds, I knew it was coming toward me. Dragging itself.

I reached out to Paka. *Hurry.*

But Paka was just now passing the abandoned chicken coop. They would be too late.

I rolled my weight forward and then back, the chair rising up on its back legs. I rocked forward and rocked back again, then forward, until the chair went far enough for my feet to take my weight. My ankles hadn't been chained to the chair legs, and so, bent over, I raced, if the shuffle of feet can be called such, for the wall I had seen in the moments of light, the wall farthest from the vampire. I *felt* the wall growing closer, a solid force. At the last moment, I twisted my body and *threw* myself back, the chair legs taking the brunt of the leap and my body's weight. They hit the wall with a splintering *crack*. I half bounced and rolled, bruising my knees and banging my head on the stone. Shards of dry wood pierced my side and back. It hurt, a stabbing, puncturing agony. There might be time for pain later, if I lived.

I rocked and rolled until I reached my feet again. And I threw myself at the wall, twisting to take the hit on the chair. But my aim was off, and one arm of the chair and my forearm took the hit instead. My head whiplashed and cracked. I saw more stars, white bursts of light that seemed to fall like snow. Dazed, I lay on the floor, blinking into the dark. My hair was caught under me, pulling my head back at an odd angle.

Something touched me.

The vampire laid her slimy, maggoty hand on my bare foot. Something scraped the stone beside the chair, a sound like shoe leather on rock, and I realized that the vampire was licking my blood from the stone floor, its tongue like jerky. An instant later, it bit down, fangs into the top of my foot, into the artery there. I couldn't help the gurgle of shock and pain. Nor the thought that the churchmen had been wrong. A vampire's bite was not pleasurable at all.

Maggots writhed over my bare foot, thrashing. Icy fire climbed up my leg, through my veins, leading to my heart and lungs. The vampire slid her fangs from me. *Yes,* I thought. *It's female.*

Stronger already, she pulled herself up my lower leg, claws sinking into shin and calf in spiked bursts of pain, and she lifted my leg. Her fangs sliced into the back of my knee. Flame and sleet blazed through me, hot and cold, burning as brands, intense as frozen knives. I screamed. And *reached.* Into the earth around the house, into the stone beneath my face. Instinct. Reaching for life, for control. A charged sensation zapped through me like lightning through soil.

The vampire whipped her head back. Squealed. Rolled away. But I had her now. My blood within her undead flesh. The earth beneath us. It was all I needed. I could feed her to the earth, body and soul, if she had a soul. But she rolled away, to lie against the far, cold, concrete wall. And she sobbed.

I had heard sobs like hers before, the night my mother was brought back from the punishment house. Shattered. Beaten. Wounded in ways I hadn't been able to imagine when I was a child. Broken, but alive. Mama had survived. So might the vampire prisoner. If I let her. If I *helped* her.

"I'm sorry," the vampire whispered. "I'm so sorry."

I lessened my hold on her. Slid the grip of my control away from her body and her blood. "Help's coming," I said. "Hang on."

"Too late," she whispered. "Can't you hear them? Their footsteps on the stairs? They come to bleed me once again. And this time they all come. Together."

I couldn't hear anything, but I imagined that a vampire's ears were far better than mine. I swallowed, trying to sense where Paka and Occam and the vampires were. Still down the road. And even after they got here, they would have to find a way into the basement and into the underground chamber. A pale light brightened around the cracks in the door. The muted sounds of male laughter followed.

"If you drink my blood, can you fight them off?"

"If I drink you dry unto death, I could take one or two. But the blood of one is not enough for me. And even if it were, there isn't time enough to heal, to find the strength to destroy so large a group. And they bring silver to torture me. To bind me. I can feel the poison upon them."

"With the blood you already took from me, can't you'un— *you*—can't *you* hurt them? It needs to be all of them. They need to bleed. It doesn't have to be a big injury, just blood on the floor. Can you spin like a dervish? Like one of those old-fashioned weapons—a mace, I think they called them, not to take them down, but just to bleed them. Scattering them, cutting each one. Can you do that, even if it means they get you after?"

"And you would help me after? To escape? To find food?"

"Yes." I nodded into the dark. *The vampires and the were-cats are coming. I just need a bit of time.* "Yes."

"I am not strong enough to be a mace, little nonhuman female. A small flail, perhaps," she said. "Yes, I can be a flail in the hand of my rescuer."

I wasn't certain what a flail was, or how I could be her rescuer, but our little chat was nearly over. Another light came on, brighter through the cracks. A man on the far side said, "Nothing in the world like it, my friend." A jangle of keys sounded on the far wall.

Fear and maggots still slimed my skin. "Can you break my handcuffs?"

"I'm not strong enough to break the steel, not with the silver shackles I still wear."

"Then break the chair," I grated out. "Just get me flat on the rock. And you attack them when they come through the door. I need their blood on this rock beneath me, or on the concrete out there." I jutted my chin to the light. "And then you can drink them dry for all I care. But . . . but stay off the floor, stay off the rock, or I might take you too." Her death, invisible to another, but real to me, bounced and wriggled, cascading over me as she shuffled near, fear in the sounds of her movements. "Hurry!" I demanded. *"Hurry!"*

The stretcher between the chair's legs broke and I tumbled back. The vampire caught me, one hand tangled in my hair, catching the back of my head. She broke the arms of the chair and I tumbled to the rock. I could feel her icy breath, fetid with rot against my face, and I thought for a moment that she would lose control and drain me. But as the door opened, she slid her hand away. With a soft *pop* of sound, she was gone.

Someone screamed. Several men screamed. Blood flew. The bloodlust of my magic lunged out and took me in its fist.

I stretched deep into the earth again, *reached* with whatever my gift was, whatever my magic might be. *Reached* out to the blood that flew and splattered. Eyes closed, I caught an essence of blood and darkness and dog, and essence of human male, and I took all the life forces into my grimy hand.

I fed a dog to the earth, spreading my fingers onto the rock, his body and soul into the stone. And then I took a human, screaming as he fell. That one I held still, compliant, draining him slowly, to weakness, not unto death. And let him go. He lay on the rock, gasping, drained.

Two more dogs. I gripped them both and felt them break and tear into a bloody slime. The heat and moisture of their bodies coalesced and trickled across the surface of the boulder, sucked into the earth. *Dead and gone.* I held their combined life force within me for a moment, making sure. *Knowing.* Accepting that I was doing this by choice. Not just instinct, not in fear of my life. But by choice. I gave them to the rock beneath me. Pushed their life force within the granite and the soil and the roots of the vine beyond the far wall. The vine stretched and put out blooms as the ground around it was saturated with the life of *gwyllgi*, the darkness of the dog. Other roots stretched for that life, and the somnolent thing beneath the ground woke and saw the death of the dog. It wanted more. It saw me as well. I eased away from it but gave it the body and soul of another *gwyllgi*. Its attention faltered, returning its focus to the life force as if recognizing a sacrifice long denied. But I was certain that it would know me again.

I held the lives of three more, not all dead, but all bleeding, all dying, pressing them into the stone of the floor, taking their blood and feeding it into the ground, more slowly this time, a steady trickle instead of a gushing flood. All but two of the males on the stone floor were *gwyllgi*. As was the man the vampire held trapped in the outer room. She was crouched on a table, the *gwyllgi* gripped in her hands. He was trying to shapeshift as she tore through his neck and sucked the life out of him.

Just as I was sucking the life out of the men in my grasp. I let the humans go, knowing they were too drained to be a danger. They were broken now. Diminished, but alive. And I fed the *gwyllgi* to the earth. Jackie. Fighting, Screaming. Howling. *Dead*. At last.

If they hadn't been planning on torturing a starving vampire and likely hurting me in other ways, I might have felt guilt and shame, but I felt nothing. Nothing at all.

I understood that the humans whom I had not totally drained had once been important people, considered so by themselves and by others. Now they crawled away, panting, hearts racing, aged and ruined and near empty of life. The dog with the vampire was conscious, fighting, yowling. Still alive somehow, but not for long.

Through the open door, I saw Occam leap into the outer storage room, Paka on his heels a little to the side, hunting formation. Occam saw the feeding vampire and screamed, altering course for her and her prey.

"No!" I shouted. "Occam! Paka! *No!*"

They skidded on tough paw pads, sliding on the concrete floor, claws extended, scratching, bodies bunching tight to change direction. Almost as one, they stretched into leaps and practically flew through the opening into the dark to land on the stone. One of the vampires was right behind them, her maggoty death-slime energies powerful. I might have gagged at the sensation, and I know I thrashed in horror when she picked me up bodily, the chair remains dangling from my handcuffs. It was like being carried by death herself, black shroud and sickle and rotting flesh, though my eyes told me she was flesh and blood and blond and beautiful, and familiar. Every footstep was an agony and I heard my own moan as she sped outside.

Rick said, "There," pointing into dark shadows cast by security lights.

She set me on the grass out back. Broke the cuffs with a simple twist of her powerful hands. She threw the wood away and pulled the shards out of my back and side and the skin of my arm, tossing splinters and stakes deep into the woods beyond the landscaped lawn. The earth felt the wood fall and the blood splatter, and the roots reached up, taking my blood into the ground, hungry, much like the starving vampire who still fed on the dog.

When I was free of wood and shackles, the blond vampire stepped away, staring down at me. "I don't know what manner of creature you are, but if my blood would help I am happy to off—"

A sick, oily, foul taste coated the back of my mouth and I gagged at the thought of rotten meat.

The vampire laughed, as if she knew what I was feeling and thought it was funny. It was a nice laugh, completely at odds with the blood-sucking, dead thing she was. But she seemed to understand and stepped away. The distance helped ease the sensation-thought-taste of rotten meat that glazed the back of my throat.

From the ground, I felt movement. Something pushed up through the soil, pliant and supple and full of life. Around it, other things pushed through. They were rootlets, seeking my blood. In the warmth beneath me, they burst into leaf and slithered around my body, into the tiny cuts. For a moment it hurt as if I was being pierced again, sharp and cutting. But they were healing me with the life I had sent into them. Dog of darkness life. Potent *gwyllgi* life, something out of mythology found to be real. I had taken, and now I was being given to. Healed. I relaxed into the roots and vines and they coiled into me, sharing.

Symbiotic. The word was there, and I understood it fully. The land and I were symbiotic, needing one another. Though I still didn't know how it worked, or what I truly was. Beneath the ground, the life there pulled in the souls it had captured and . . . swallowed them. Swallowed them whole. I heard Jackie beneath the earth, his soul screaming and thrashing. And Roxy, weeping like a child as the darkness sucked him under. Unlike Brother Ephraim, they were subsumed, as if eaten.

Occam was suddenly there, human shaped and steaming in the cold air, naked and beautiful in the stark light and shadows. "Nell. Nell, sugar?" His hands feathered along my body. "I smell your blood. Where are you hurt? Nell? Sugar?" When

I didn't answer fast enough, he growled, the vibration quivering through me.

I breathed out softly. "I'm gonna be fine, Occam. I just need to rest here awhile. But not too long. Okay? I'll tell you when."

"I take it we'll need to cut you free again?" Rick asked, something curious and amused and slightly mocking in his tone.

"Soon." I wasn't injured as badly as I had been when I was shot. This was more flesh wounds than organ damage. But I did wonder how many times I could be healed this way before growing leaves instead of hair, and the thought made me laugh softly. "Put some clothes on, Occam. It's cold out."

"Okay. Nell, sugar. If you're sure." A drop of his sweat landed on my cheek and steamed in the night air.

Rick squatted down beside me and asked softly, "Whose house are we at, Nell?"

I chuckled just as softly. "The *gwyllgi* home of Roxbury Thomas Benton, the fourth."

Rick cursed softly and stood. And then they were all gone, except the lanky blond vampire, who now crouched on a low brick garden wall, her weight on her toes and her fingertips, her knees bent into what, on a human, would have been an awkward crouch.

She was one of the vampires who had crossed my land to help Jane Yellowrock attack the church and rescue a captive vampire. She had been at Mira Clayton's home too, and she had carried me out of the basement, her fangs extended and her eyes all black. Her head was tilted oddly on her neck as she studied me. "Jane called you *Yummy*," I said, finally remembering.

"Jane said you were a fairy, one of the little people. Maybe a wood nymph, woodsy magic."

"Mixed with human," I said. "At the time, mostly human." I brought up the one of the words she had used to describe me. "*Yinehi*. Evil, soul-sucking *yinehi*."

"Fairies aren't evil, and you aren't exactly a fairy," Yummy said. "Fairies are private, though, yes. Elusive, preferring the woods to all other things." Her head cocked the other way. "They sacrificed to the mother earth. Fed her. Fed her powers that slept deep within. And they taught the Celts to do the same, to continue the tradition."

Well, that sounded like me for sure. I smiled without humor, feeling the anguish her words brought. "A tradition of murder." That felt right, deep within me. I was a creature of blood and death. I had to accept that, after all the lives I had taken tonight. And learn how to live with it. Despite it, maybe. "Tell them it's time to cut me free. And then I want to go home. I'm . . . tired. So very tired."

"You may have anything you want. Tonight the Human Speakers of Truth have taken a blow," Yummy said. "And you gave us back one of our own. We are in your debt. Ming of Glass has announced, 'Clan Glass owes you a boon.'"

"Is that a good thing?"

"It is the very best thing. Your life will never be the same."

But I had a feeling that was the case no matter what a maggoty blood-sucker might have to offer me.

NINETEEN

We left the estate on the North Carolina side of the line and drove sedately back into Tennessee. It was a long drive, and I slept the whole way, my body cuddled in my bloody coat on the van seat, safe with these people, who knew what I was and still seemed to accept me. They talked, their words a background hum that promised more safe, safe, so forever safe. The vampire Yummy was behind us, driving a lovely gold-flake 2015 convertible she called a Ferrari LaFerrari, a car she said was worth a million dollars, which surely was a joke, the vehicle having been liberated from Roxy's garage. My awareness of her was strong, nauseatingly strong, in North Carolina, but as we rode, that perception faded to nothing. In the car at the rear were the other two vampires, one of them the freed prisoner.

We drove into Oliver Springs long after midnight, and into a crime scene ringed by media vans and reporters and county and state and federal vehicles. Rick rolled down his window and a sheriff's deputy met us at the edge of the crime scene tape, saying, "Thanks for the tip. We got them all and we got Anne Rindfliesch, safe and sound." Anne Rindfliesch was Girl Four, I remembered.

When the deputy went back to work, Yummy sauntered up. She stopped at the van, where she leaned her head inside, without touching the body of the vehicle, which I appreciated. "They found seven women inside, some from families who 'left the church'"—she made little quotation marks in the air—"some from Knoxville, all of them in bad shape, three of them pregnant." She focused on me. "They have been there a long time, and have suffered horribly. I offer my blood and my gifts of healing should they deign to accept them."

To Rick, she continued, "The police also found forty-two

Human Speakers of Truth in the warehouse. They had been imprisoned there by Jackie and his splinter faction, some for as much as a week. There were also five mature human-dogs and a number of juveniles, all of which seem to be male. Either they kill and eat their own female offspring or they breed true along the male line only."

To me she said, "Next time you go hunting dogs of darkness or other things that go bump in the night, invite me. This was fun. And I simply adore my new car." With that, Yummy turned and walked away.

The metallic *clank* of the stove's wood box closing woke me. The smell of fresh wood and fresh fire, old ash, and coffee beans spoke of home. I was in my cot, which someone had placed in the downstairs bedroom. I vaguely remembered being bathed, my hair washed free of blood. Remembered JoJo and T. Laine arguing about how best to get me clean and clip off the last of the rootlets sticking out of me. Remembered hands drying me with towels and smoothing my skin with cream before laying me down in my narrow bed and pulling the covers over me as I shivered with cold.

I remembered a voice complaining that I had no electric blankets to heat me. ". . . dangerously hypothermic. She needs a hospital," T. Laine had said.

"Or a gardener," JoJo had said.

I had laughed. And JoJo had tucked a heated cast-iron frying pan wrapped in towels into the covers at my feet like an old-timey bed warmer. It was still there, still radiating a bit of warmth.

I rolled out of bed and to my feet. I felt . . . marvelous. Thirsty, but really, *really* good. Someone had placed three bottles of water at my side. I opened and drained all three and raced to the bathroom. Like someone had said recently, I needed to pee like a racehorse, though why a *race*horse I didn't know. All horses had to pee.

But, once I was awake enough to dress, I discovered that I had a problem. I was out of clothes. I had torn or ripped or bloodied every decent garment I owned. That left . . . I looked around the bedroom. That left Leah's clothes. In Leah's closet.

Leah had been one of the church's best seamstresses. She had given me her clothes when she died, but I had never been able to make myself wear them. I turned on the electric lights and opened the closet. The scent of her lemon verbena sachet flowed into the room. I replaced the sachets every fall. It was time again.

I had never touched Leah's clothes. Wonderful clothing. Something that might have been envy coiled through me as the lights fell on the clothes in the closet. Anxiety growing along with the envy, I pulled out a pale mint green skirt made of a silky material that caught the light.

My heart beat a funny rhythm as delight rose in me and I pulled out some shirts, pretty blouses, and a shawl I had always loved. Not Leah's anymore. Mine. Did I dare? I held the skirt up to me, studying my reflection in the long cheval mirror in the corner.

None of my underclothing was good enough to wear with such beautiful clothes. Unless . . . I stepped to my trousseau chest. Long ago I had placed it at the foot of John's bed, as a good wife should, though I had never used the things within it. I had never even opened it. The chest was handmade of cedar-heart wood, the colors rosy and cream, with my initials carved in the top, *NN*, with lots of swirls and curlicues. Daddy had carved the initials in the cap piece the day I was named, and had built the box before I was seven, as he did for all his daughters. I hadn't looked inside since I'd come to this house.

Girls in the church usually marry young, and when they leave their parents' home, they are still growing in height and girth. The things that a girl's mother, and sister-mothers, and elder sisters, and even aunts and friends, place in the chest for her wedding day have to be size adjustable, useful for many different occasions and activities. There are the practical things that are intended to help a girl set up housekeeping. There are other things intended for a girl's wedding night and that special first year of married life when everything is new and the falling-in-love part of marriage is still taking place. Hopefully. There would be useful things in it, like underwear. They might even be pretty.

Hesitantly, I lifted the lid and the old scent of red cedar rushed out onto the air and mixed with the lemon verbena. The scents should have clashed. They didn't. They mixed perfectly.

* * *

Excitement swept through me like a hot wind when I saw myself in the mirror, dressed in such wonderful clothes. I almost looked . . . pretty. And that vision of myself warmed my cheeks. I was no longer a churchwoman. I was just me.

I was wearing the silky mint green skirt and a soft floral blouse with pearl buttons that ran the collar high up my throat, with pretty, store-bought green slippers I had found in the trousseau chest. They were lined with something like sheep's wool, but didn't smell like sheep and they were warm. I was also wearing new underwear from a store, with lace on the bra, which itched, and on the top of the panties. They were pink and glossy and might have been a smidge too loose, but they both stayed up when I moved.

I was also wearing a tiny smear of lipstick, pale pink. It hadn't smelled real good and the taste suggested that lipstick could go bad, but the color had been so pretty with the green clothes and pink underwear that I had added a dab to my cheeks and smeared it in.

When I left the room, my heart was pounding and it was hard to breathe, as I stopped in the doorway observing the others. Listening.

Rick was standing, his back to me, debriefing, "There was nothing left of them but piles of ash. We know for a fact that Jackson Jr. is dead. Only one adult *gwyllgi* survived at Benton's mountain lodge, the one the captive vampire nearly drunk down. There were half a dozen in the house, all juveniles. We got three adults from the farm where Mira was kept, including Joshua, who survived the drinking down at the initial attack. This means that there are probably more *gwyllgi* around, people. Maybe lots more, as vampire blood makes the trait breed true."

"The scent is subtle," Occam said, "and so close to a dog's that it's difficult to differentiate, but we have it now. So does Sam Nicholson's tracker dog."

"Good. All of Benton's *gwyllgi* sons were secured by the state child services until they changed shape and attacked them. Paka and Occam had to change shape and teach them some manners." I could hear the amusement in his voice as he wrapped things up for his unit.

"After that," Rick continued, "they were turned over to a handler from PsyLED. They'll be taken to the werewolves of Montana to be trained in proper behavior. They aren't weres, but they're close, and sturdy enough to stand up to being taught proper manners, and the right way to hunt by werewolves. What happens after that will be up to the wolves."

"I get why the *gwyllgi* were tied in with the HST, but how did Benton manage to hide his condition from the entire FBI?" T. Laine asked. Beside her, Pea jumped from the couch to the window, to peer into the pale dawn light. I had slept clear through to morning.

"They aren't moon-called," Rick said, massaging one arm as if it pained him, "so they weren't conspicuously absent on full moons. They can work regular hours and regular jobs.

"Case summation," Rick said, changing the subject. "From what PsyLED Central in Virginia has put together, we were right when we postulated that Colonel Ernest Jackson Sr. had begun to breed for the *gwyllgi* trait, which proved easier when drinking vampire blood.

"Benton's family were formerly members of God's Cloud of Glory Church and, when Dawson ran into Benton during his trek through the juvenile system, that connection was reestablished. Dawson also brought HST, and information about their list of paranormals, to the church through an accomplice named Oliver Smithy, met in rehab. Smithy has been identified by dental records among the deceased at the warehouse.

"The Stubbinses were located and rejoined the group when Jael began exhibiting some dog traits.

"From the HST, the factional churchmen learned how to structure their finances and how to add to cash flow through kidnapping humans and blackmail of paranormals who weren't yet out of the closet. HST had no idea they were in bed with their worst nightmare, and had no idea the dogs were drinking vampire blood. At about this point, we became involved.

"We think the schismatic churchmen planned to kidnap a new vampire from Mira Clayton's home, one to drink from, but they got a whiff of Mira. They took her instead, and the abduction was attributed to HST. By acting on their own, they caused a rift among the members of HST, who were camping at the Stubbins farm, and when HST resisted, the dogs took over HST and made the men their dinners and the women their prisoners."

I must had made a sound, or my scent reached the were-cats, because Occam turned to me. His eyes lit from within, a glowing gold, holding my own as if he had taken me in his claws. My breath went tight. "Well, Nell, sugar," he said, standing and walking toward me. "You look right nice." He pulled one of my own chairs out for me and took my teakettle off the stove. Poured me a mug of my own spice tea. And held it out to me. "Come on, sugar." He smiled and that dimple I had almost seen a time or two went deep into his cheek. Something strange in my middle tumbled over. "Join us." There was distinctly odd tone in his words, as if I was being offered something more than a place at my own table. I was pretty sure I blushed.

"I've decided to cut my hair," I said to JoJo, hours later. "Twice now it's gotten caught under me and it hurts."

"You never cut it before?"

"No. Churchwomen don't cut their hair except for a trim or so every year. Mine's never been shorter than my waist." With a toe, I pushed off and the swing moved. We were alone on the porch, JoJo working on reports that would be filed later, me just thinking, and feeling the way the skirt brushed my bare legs. Nice. The day had grown warm, almost Indian summer, and the others were inside, or out back.

"But you do?"

"Now I do. Soon as I get paid by PsyLED. I'm gonna get a pedicure too, so my toenails are pretty. Maybe pink, like bubblegum pink. I used to like bubblegum. My sister Priss and Mary and me? We used to steal us each a piece from Sam's stash and chew it in the woods. It was a pretty color. I might even buy me a pink dress."

JoJo finished her report and pushed her laptop to the side. "Rick and I've been talking,"

I didn't think I liked the sound of that, and when I scowled at her she laughed, her black eyes sparkling.

"He has a few contacts with cell companies. What with Secret City and the TVA owning so many of the hills around

Knoxville, you could rent space to a cell tower company on the crest of the hill"—she pointed toward the church lands—"so you can enter the twenty-first century and get cell signals and TV, despite the magic that keeps this place so isolated."

"I beg your bless-ed pardon," I said, sounding entirely too much like a Nicholson, entertained and yet a tad affronted at the high-handedness.

JoJo shrugged. "You might have to run a cable or put an antenna or something, to get past the magic of the land, but T. Laine's been testing, and she thinks it extends only a few feet over the tops of the trees, like a bowl. She thinks you can get some signals in here, one way or another."

"Why would I want to do all that?"

Rick stepped into the doorway. Clearly he had been listening at the open window. "More paranormal species are being discovered every day, and PsyLED needs some of each on the payroll."

"So? I may be a backcountry hillbilly, but I read the newspapers," I said. "And if it's one thing all people brought up in the church know, it's how the government wants to control its citizens."

Rick lifted his fingers in a little wave, telling me he wasn't finished. At a glance from him, JoJo gathered up her laptop and went inside. He walked the rest of the way out the door and sat in a rocker. "How do you apply a sentence to a paranormal creature? A life sentence for a human is generally expected to be twenty to thirty years. That's nothing for a vampire or a were. A jail cell would have to be constructed out of sterling silver to hold a vamp. And how would you feed them? Turn them loose on the prison population?" Rick gave me a wry smile, maybe the one he had before he was bitten by a wereleopard, and all the joy was bled out of him. "How would you deal with the were-creatures during the full moon? And if you got a death penalty against one, would beheading be considered cruel and unusual punishment, if that was the only way to carry out the death sentence? Law enforcement is in a bad place. So PsyLED was created with special powers under the law. We police paranormals."

I crossed my arms over me, tipped my weight to one buttock in the swing, and gave him a look that came right off

Mama's face, all irritation and feigned patience. "I know all that. What's that got to do with cell towers on my land?"

"PsyLED's made an official offer for you to go to Spook School."

A strange heat raced through me at the words, that elusive excitement I had been ignoring, pushing away as impossible. I said, "I killed some *gwyllgi* in North Carolina. Hurt two humans. You're saying PsyLED would still want me?"

"Yes. The offer is on your desk in the great room. But you have to be reachable, Nell. Hence the cell tower."

My crossed arms fell to my sides, and I sat back in the swing, its motion going stationary as I thought through what he had just said. "But I like living off the grid."

From the yard, Occam called, "Nell, sugar, you can still live *partly* off the grid. You've got solar and wind and a septic system and a deep well, so you don't need city or county services, except the dump, and it ain't that far away. Just a cell system and maybe a little tie to the Knoxville electric grid."

I looked down at my green skirt as excitement zinged through me like a ricochet shot. I said, "I'll think about it." But I already knew my answer. I wasn't a churchwoman anymore. I might as well go all the way to hell.

"In other news," Rick said, "the head of Knoxville FBI is missing." He told me what the media, and most of the FBI itself, had been told. The real story was need-to-know and classified under PsyLED's mandate. As was everything about last night. Partly so the werecats had time to sniff out—literally—any other dark dogs in law enforcement and government positions. It wasn't illegal for paranormals to be in positions of authority, but it was a requirement to declare such. Which meant I'd have to tell them, tell the world, that I was . . . nonhuman.

"Benton's legal wife reported him and their sons missing when she came home from out of town. The investigators and special agents who responded to the call discovered a torture room under the house when they got there, and they found signs that a vampire had been kept chained to a wall. They also found a dead dog in the basement, big as a boar, drained of blood, and two old men that claimed they were a Tennessee senator and a preacher who led a megachurch in Nashville, though both were too old to be who they claimed to be. They're both in isolation for possible contagion while their DNA is compared to known samples.

"The investigators found piles of ash and two greasy smears in the basement that are being tested for genetic origins, because the two old men said they had been people until they crumbled to nothing after the captive vampire attacked. The vampire has not been located and is not expected to be found." Rick didn't look at me, but I understood that the ashy, squishy human remains were going to be blamed on a random vampire attack. I didn't know how to respond to that, but gestured that I understood. He said, "IDs nearby suggest that if the sludge and piles were indeed people, then we know the whereabouts of Boaz Jenkins and two other former churchmen.

"They also discovered that Benton had three other wives, all living in that house in the woods, across the state line into North Carolina."

Occam's tone bordered on sarcasm when he said, "Seems he was a polygamist. Shock is spreadin' everywhere."

Rick said, "I don't know what you remember about the old building, but the dogs decimated HST. They infiltrated the organization, took it over, and then used the women as . . ." He shook his head and settled on, "as breeding material. And the men for dinner."

Occam walked to the porch with the long, slinky gait of a cat in the sun. "You gonna join Unit Eighteen, Nell, sugar?"

I made a *mmm* sound, and said again, "I'll think about it."

"Let me know," Rick said. "There's forms to fill out."

"Of course there are," I said, trying on sarcasm. It seemed to fit just fine, proving that I was no longer a churchwoman— who would know better than use such a tone. I let what the unit called snark thread deeper into my tone and added, "There's always forms."

EPILOGUE

I wasn't terrified. I wasn't. I baked fresh bread, coffee, and tea every day. This was nothing new. I had all the proper serving dishes, and I knew how to use them. I had Leah's—my, it was mine now—good silverware. The good cloth napkins. Everything was in place, hot, warm, or cold as the foodstuffs demanded. The house was clean. The beds—including the new king-sized bed in my room—all were made and had fresh sheets. Clean towels were freshly folded in the bath. Extra rolls of toilet paper.

The cell tower going up on the hill was finally finished. Thank goodness. The woods had hated the noise and the vehicles rolling all over it.

A fresh dusting of snow was on the ground, and I had burned a lot of wood to heat the lower floor. The overhead fans were turning to redistribute the warm air that rose toward the ceiling.

My hands were sweating, palms itching.

I was having *company*. For the first time. And Not Mr. Thad and Deus and his big, noisy family, who brought Bojangles' takeout for dinner last Sunday. And not the PsyLED team. But *real* company. *Family*. My mama, maw-maw, Mama Grace, and Mama Carmel. My sisters, Priss, Mud, Esther, and Judith. And four half sisters. Coming to visit. Coming here.

I whirled and caught a view of myself in the mirror on the back of the bedroom door. I should change. I should definitely change. Pink was *not* a church color. A pale ice pink, to be sure, but pink. Pale pink layered shirts, slightly darker pink skirt. Rose leggings, mostly hidden beneath the skirt hem and the tall boots. My fingernails were painted. Clear, not pink or red, but still. *Painted*. I curled my fingers under as if to hide them.

And my hair was cut. I had stared at myself for long min-

utes in the mirror at the hair-cutting place. I was so different I
didn't recognize myself. My hair stopped at my shoulders and
curled forward just a bit. They had called it a long bob at the
salon. Not saloon. They had laughed when I mispronounced
it. But the moment the salon ladies discovered that I was from
the cult up the hill, the women had gathered together and chosen a cut that would be easy to style, easy to keep, and would
still fit back in a tail for working. They had taught me to wear
makeup too, stylishly and to "enhance my looks rather than
shout *pole dancer.*" Their words, not mine. I was wearing the
blush, lipstick, and a slight tint of mascara today.

I felt them coming up the mountain. Three cars and two
trucks, filled with females. My hot sweat went cold and shivery.

I walked back through the house, checking to make sure
the guns were safely stored away, except John's prize four-
barrel shotgun hanging on the stairwell wall. Rick had
informed me that the gun was a collector's item and might be
worth up to seventy thousand dollars. That kinda money
would go a long way to securing my financial future. I wiped
away a bit of ash dust at the base of the cookstove. Turned a
cup to its proper position.

My booted feet loud in the empty house, I walked to the
front door and leaned against the jamb, watching through the
windows as the first of the vehicles motored up the steep road.
I didn't move as they all pulled into the drive and up to the
parking area. They parked and got out, and adjusted their dull
gray-brown–sage green clothes. They were all carrying baskets. Guest gifts. I'd have plenty to eat when they left, and
childish embroidery and cross-stitch samplers to hang on my
nearly bare walls. Or maybe they would bring crocheted
scarves or hats. Each of them would take home a small jar of
my homemade, all-natural, organic caramel. It had taken me
eight hours to make it all. And it was delicious, according to
Occam and Paka, who had eaten an entire small jar all by
themselves last night. Darn cats.

The first car was full of women and girls, some I knew, others I didn't. Not yet. But Priss was driving and seemed to be in
charge, pointing and directing as the others got out, almost as
if she had been here before. I still needed to talk to Priss about
getting a passport, about going away to a foreign country to

witness, but that would be a private conversation, one between sisters about life and choices and opportunity, not something to be shared with this group. And, amazingly, I might have the chance to actually do that as the women seemed willing— eager, even—to get to know me. Which brought a smile to my face.

When the last truck pulled to a stop, a small form burst from the cab and raced across the front yard and leaped up onto the raised bed. She dropped to her knees and pushed her hands into the soil. And laughed. Her head to the sky, her mouth open. Laughing in delight and relief and something else I wasn't sure how to name but understood perfectly. Mud. Communing with my Soulwood. Just as I do. She scampered from one part of the raised beds to another, and even stopped at the dogwood tree in the large white pot, the one I would be planting in town at the ballet studio.

Mud looked from the tree to the house and met my eyes where I stood at the door. She was crying in happiness. And so was I. Because my life was full and getting ready to be even more full when I went to Spook School to become a real PsyLED agent.

Not that it was all perfect. I still had that rooty feeling in my middle. And I still had a shadow in my land, watching and willful, if impotent. There might be ways of dealing with that, when I was stronger.

But I cried mostly because I wasn't alone at all now. I had PsyLED Unit Eighteen. I had family. And I had Mud.

My baby sister, who was *yinehi*. Just like me.

Read on for an excerpt of the first book
in Faith Hunter's *New York Times* bestselling
Jane Yellowrock series,

SKINWALKER

Available wherever books are sold!

I wheeled my bike down Decatur Street and eased deeper into the French Quarter, the bike's engine purring. My shotgun, a Benelli M4 Super 90, was slung over my back and loaded for vamp with hand-packed silver fléchette rounds. I carried a selection of silver crosses in my belt, hidden under my leather jacket, and stakes, secured in loops on my jeans-clad thighs. The saddlebags on my bike were filled with my meager travel belongings—clothes in one side, tools of the trade in the other. As a vamp killer for hire, I travel light.

I'd need to put the vamp-hunting tools out of sight for my interview. My hostess might be offended. Not a good thing when said hostess held my next paycheck in her hands and possessed a set of fangs of her own.

A guy, a good-looking Joe standing in a doorway, turned his head to follow my progress as I motored past. He wore leather boots, a jacket, and jeans, like me, though his dark hair was short and mine was down to my hips when not braided out of the way, tight to my head, for fighting. A Kawasaki motorbike leaned on a stand nearby. I didn't like his interest, but he didn't prick my predatory or territorial instincts.

I maneuvered the bike down St. Louis and then onto Dauphine, weaving between nervous-looking shop workers heading home for the evening and a few early revelers out for fun. I spotted the address in the fading light. Katie's Ladies was the oldest continually operating whorehouse in the Quarter, in business since 1845, though at various locations, depending on hurricane, flood, the price of rent, and the agreeable nature of local law and its enforcement officers. I parked, set the kickstand, and unwound my long legs from the hog.

I had found two bikes in a junkyard in Charlotte, North Carolina, bodies rusted, rubber rotted. They were in bad shape. But Jacob, a semiretired Harley restoration mechanic/ Zen Harley priest living along the Catawba River, took my money, fixing one up, using the other for parts, ordering what else he needed over the Net. It took six months.

During that time I'd hunted for him, keeping his wife and four kids supplied with venison, rabbit, turkey—whatever I could catch, as maimed as I was—restocked supplies from the city with my hoarded money, and rehabbed my damaged body back into shape. It was the best I could do for the months it took me to heal. Even someone with my rapid healing and variable metabolism takes a long while to totally mend from a near beheading.

Now that I was a hundred percent, I needed work. My best bet was a job killing off a rogue vampire that was terrorizing the city of New Orleans. It had taken down three tourists and left a squad of cops, drained and smiling, dead where it dropped them. Scuttlebutt said it hadn't been satisfied with just blood—it had eaten their internal organs. All that suggested the rogue was old, powerful, and deadly—a whacked-out vamp. The nutty ones were always the worst.

Just last week, Katherine "Katie" Fonteneau, the proprietress and namesake of Katie's Ladies, had e-mailed me. According to my Web site, I had successfully taken down an entire blood-family in the mountains near Asheville. And I had. No lies on the Web site or in the media reports, not bald-faced ones anyway. Truth is, I'd nearly died, but I'd done the job, made a rep for myself, and then taken off a few months to invest my legitimately gotten gains. Or to heal, but spin is everything. A lengthy vacation sounded better than the complete truth.

I took off my helmet and the clip that held my hair, pulling my braids out of my jacket collar and letting them fall around me, beads clicking. I palmed a few tools of the trade—one stake, ash wood and silver tipped; a tiny gun; and a cross—and tucked them into the braids, rearranging them to hang smoothly with no lumps or bulges. I also breathed deeply, seeking to relax, to assure my safety through the upcoming interview. I was nervous, and being nervous around a vamp was just plain dumb.

The sun was setting, casting a red glow on the horizon, limning the ancient buildings, shuttered windows, and wrought-iron balconies in fuchsia. It was pretty in a purely human way. I opened my senses and let my Beast taste the world. She liked the smells and wanted to prowl. *Later*, I promised her. Predators usually growl when irritated. *Soon*—she sent mental claws into my soul, kneading. It was uncomfortable, but the claw pricks kept me alert, which I'd need for the interview. I had never met a civilized vamp, certainly never done business with one. So far as I knew, vamps and skinwalkers had never met. I was about to change that. This could get interesting.

I clipped my sunglasses onto my collar, lenses hanging out. I glanced at the witchy-locks on my saddlebags and, satisfied, I walked to the narrow red door and pushed the buzzer. The bald-headed man who answered was definitely human, but big enough to be something else: professional wrestler, steroid-augmented bodybuilder, or troll. All of the above, maybe. The thought made me smile. He blocked the door, standing with arms loose and ready. "Something funny?" he asked, voice like a horse-hoof rasp on stone.

"Not really. Tell Katie that Jane Yellowrock is here." Tough always works best on first acquaintance. That my knees were knocking wasn't a consideration.

"Card?" Troll asked. A man of few words. I liked him already. My new best pal. With two gloved fingers, I unzipped my leather jacket, fished a business card from an inside pocket, and extended it to him. It read JANE YELLOWROCK, HAVE STAKES WILL TRAVEL. Vamp killing is a bloody business. I had discovered that a little humor went a long way to making it all bearable.

Troll took the card and closed the door in my face. I might have to teach my new pal a few manners. But that was nearly axiomatic for all the men of my acquaintance.

I heard a bike two blocks away. It wasn't a Harley. Maybe a Kawasaki, like the bright red crotch rocket I had seen earlier. I wasn't surprised when it came into view and it was the Joe from Decatur Street. He pulled his bike up beside mine, powered down, and sat there, eyes hidden behind sunglasses. He had a toothpick in his mouth and it twitched once as he pulled his helmet and glasses off.

The Joe was a looker. A little taller than my six feet even, he had olive skin, black hair, black brows. Black jacket and jeans.

Black boots. Bit of overkill with all the black, but he made it work, with muscular legs wrapped around the red bike.

No silver in sight. No shotgun, but a suspicious bulge beneath his right arm. Made him a leftie. Something glinted in the back of his collar. A knife hilt, secured in a spine sheath. Maybe more than one blade. There were scuffs on his boots (Western, like mine, not Harley butt-stompers) but his were Fryes and mine were ostrich-skin Luccheses. I pulled in scents, my nostrils widening. His boots smelled of horse manure, fresh. Local boy, then, or one who had been in town long enough to find a mount. I smelled horse sweat and hay, a clean blend of scents. And cigar. It was the cigar that made me like him. The taint of steel, gun oil, and silver made me fall in love. Well, sorta. My Beast thought he was kinda cute, and maybe tough enough to be worthy of us. Yet there was a faint scent on the man, hidden beneath the surface smells, that made me wary.

The silence had lasted longer than expected. Since he had been the one to pull up, I just stared, and clearly our silence bothered the Joe, but it didn't bother me. I let a half grin curl my lip. He smiled back and eased off his bike. Behind me, inside Katie's, I heard footsteps. I maneuvered so that the Joe and the doorway were both visible. No way could I do it and be unobtrusive, but I raised a shoulder to show I had no hard feelings. Just playing it smart. Even for a pretty boy.

Troll opened the door and jerked his head to the side. I took it as the invitation it was and stepped inside. "You got interesting taste in friends," Troll said, as the door closed on the Joe.

"Never met him. Where you want the weapons?" Always better to offer than to have them removed. Power plays work all kinds of ways.

Troll opened an armoire. I unbuckled the shotgun holster and set it inside, pulling silver crosses from my belt and thighs and from beneath the coat until there was a nice pile. Thirteen crosses—excessive, but they distracted people from my backup weapons. Next came the wooden stakes and silver stakes. Thirteen of each. And the silver vial of holy water. One vial. If I carried thirteen, I'd slosh.

I hung the leather jacket on the hanger in the armoire and tucked the glasses in the inside pocket with the cell phone. I closed the armoire door and assumed the position so Troll could search me. He grunted as if surprised, but pleased, and did a thorough job. To give him credit, he didn't seem to enjoy it overmuch—used only the backs of his hands, no fingers, didn't linger or stroke where he shouldn't. Breathing didn't speed up, heart rate stayed regular; things I can sense if it's quiet enough. After a thorough feel inside the tops of my boots, he said, "This way."

I followed him down a narrow hallway that made two crooked turns toward the back of the house. We walked over old Persian carpets, past oils and watercolors done by famous and not-so-famous artists. The hallway was lit with stained-glass Lalique sconces, which looked real, not like reproductions, but maybe you can fake old; I didn't know. The walls were painted a soft butter color that worked with the sconces to illuminate the paintings. Classy joint for a whorehouse. The Christian children's home schoolgirl in me was both appalled and intrigued.

When Troll paused outside the red door at the end of the hallway, I stumbled, catching my foot on a rug. He caught me with one hand and I pushed off him with little body contact. I managed to look embarrassed; he shook his head. He knocked. I braced myself and palmed the cross he had missed. And the tiny two-shot derringer. Both hidden against my skull on the crown of my head, and covered by my braids, which men never, ever searched, as opposed to my boots, which men always had to stick their fingers in. He opened the door and stood aside. I stepped in.

The room was spartan but expensive, and each piece of furniture looked Spanish. Old Spanish. Like Queen-Isabella-and-Christopher-Columbus old. The woman, wearing a teal dress and soft slippers, standing beside the desk, could have passed for twenty until you looked in her eyes. Then she might have passed for said queen's older sister. Old, old, *old* eyes. Peaceful as she stepped toward me. Until she caught my scent.

In a single instant her eyes bled red, pupils went wide and black, and her fangs snapped down. She leaped. I dodged under her jump as I pulled the cross and derringer, quickly moving to the far wall, where I held out the weapons. The cross was for the vamp, the gun for the Troll. She hissed at me, fangs fully extended. Her claws were bone white and two inches long. Troll had pulled a gun. A big gun. Men and their pissing contests. *Crap*. Why couldn't they ever just let me be the only one with a gun?

"Predator," she hissed. "In my territory." Vamp anger pheromones filled the air, bitter as wormwood.

"I'm not human," I said, my voice steady. "That's what you smell." I couldn't do anything about the tripping heart rate, which I knew would drive her further over the edge; I'm an animal. Biological factors always kick in. So much for trying not to be nervous. The cross in my hand glowed with a cold white light, and Katie, if that was her original name, tucked her head, shielding her eyes. Not attacking, which meant that she was thinking. Good.

"Katie?" Troll asked.

"I'm not human," I repeated. "I'll really hate shooting your Troll here, to bleed all over your rugs, but I will."

"Troll?" Katie asked. Her body froze with that inhuman stillness vamps possess when thinking, resting, or whatever else it is they do when they aren't hunting, eating, or killing. Her shoulders dropped and her fangs clicked back into the roof of her mouth with a sudden spurt of humor. Vampires can't laugh and go vampy at the same time. They're two distinct parts of them, one part still human, one part rabid hunter. Well, that's likely insulting, but then this was the first so-called civilized vamp I'd ever met. All the others I'd had personal contact with were sick, twisted killers. And then dead. Really dead.

Troll's eyes narrowed behind the .45 aimed my way. I figured he didn't like being compared to the bad guy in a children's fairy tale. I was better at fighting, but negotiation seemed wise. "Tell him to back off. Let me talk." I nudged it a bit. "Or I'll take you and he'll never get a shot off." Unless he noticed that I had set the safety on his gun when I tripped. Then I'd *have* to shoot him. I wasn't betting on my .22 stopping him unless I got an eye shot. Chest hits wouldn't even slow him down. In fact they'd likely just make him mad.

When neither attacked, I said, "I'm not here to stake you. I'm Jane Yellowrock, here to interview for a job, to take out a rogue vamp that your own council declared an outlaw. But I don't smell human, so I take precautions. One cross, one stake, one two-shot derringer." The word "stake" didn't elude her. Or him. He'd missed three weapons. No Christmas bonus for Troll.

"What are you?" she asked.

"You tell me where you sleep during the day and I'll tell you what I am. Otherwise, we can agree to do business. Or I can leave."

Telling the location of a lair—where a vamp sleeps—is information for lovers, dearest friends, or family. Katie chuckled. It was one of the silky laughs that her kind can give, low and erotic, like vocal sex. My Beast purred. She liked the sound.

"Are you offering to be my toy for a while, intriguing nonhuman female?" When I didn't answer, she slid closer, despite the glowing cross, and said, "You are interesting. Tall, slender, young." She leaned in and breathed in my scent. "Or not so young. What are you?" she pressed, her voice heavy with fascination. Her eyes had gone back to their natural color, a sort of grayish hazel, but blood blush still marred her cheeks so I knew she was still primed for violence. That violence being my death.

"Secretive," she murmured, her voice taking on that tone they use to enthrall, a deep vibration that seems to stroke every gland. "Enticing scent. Likely tasty. Perhaps your blood would be worth the trade. Would you come to my bed if I offered?"

"No," I said. No inflection in my voice. No interest, no revulsion, no irritation, nothing. Nothing to tick off the vamp or her servant.

"Pity. Put down the gun, Tom. Get our guest something to drink."

I didn't wait for Tommy Troll to lower his weapon; I dropped mine. Beast wasn't happy, but she understood. I was the intruder in Katie's territory. While I couldn't show submission, I could show manners. Tom lowered his gun and his attitude at the same time and holstered the weapon as he moved into the room toward a well-stocked bar.

"Tom?" I said. "Uncheck your safety." He stopped midstride. "I set it when I fell against you in the hallway."

"Couldn't happen," he said.

"I'm fast. It's why your employer invited me for a job interview."

He inspected his .45 and nodded at his boss. Why anyone would want to go around with a holstered .45 with the safety off is beyond me. It smacks of either stupidity or quiet desperation, and Katie had lived too long to be stupid. I was guessing the rogue had made her truly apprehensive. I tucked the cross inside a little lead-foil-lined pocket in the leather belt holding up my Levi's, and eased the small gun in beside it, strapping it down. There was a safety, but on such a small gun, it was easy to knock the safety off with an accidental brush of my arm.

"Is that where you hid the weapons?" Katie asked. When I just looked at her, she shrugged as if my answer were unimportant and said, "Impressive. You are impressive."

Katie was one of those dark ash blondes with long straight hair so thick it whispered when she moved, falling across the teal silk that fit her like a second skin. She stood five feet and a smidge, but height was no measure of power in her kind. She could move as fast as I could and kill in an eyeblink. She had buffed nails that were short when she wasn't in killing mode, pale skin, and she wore exotic, Egyptian-style makeup around the eyes. Black liner overlaid with some kind of glitter. Not the kind of look I'd ever had the guts to try. I'd rather face down a grizzly than try to achieve "a look."

"What'll it be, Miz Yellowrock?" Tom asked.

"Cola's fine. No diet."

He popped the top on a Coke and poured it over ice that crackled and split when the liquid hit, placed a wedge of lime on the rim, and handed it to me. His employer got a tall fluted glass of something milky that smelled sharp and alcoholic. Well, at least it wasn't blood on ice. Ick.

"Thank you for coming such a distance," Katie said, taking one of two chairs and indicating the other for me. Both chairs were situated with backs to the door, which I didn't like, but I sat as she continued. "We never made proper introductions, and the In-ter-net," she said, separating the syllables as if the term was strange, "is no substitute for formal, proper introductions. I am Katherine Fonteneau." She offered the tips of her fingers, and I took them for a moment in my own before dropping them.

"Jane Yellowrock," I said, feeling as though it was all a little redundant. She sipped; I sipped. I figured that was enough etiquette. "Do I get the job?" I asked.

Katie waved away my impertinence. "I like to know the people with whom I do business. Tell me about yourself."

Cripes. The sun was down. I needed to be tooling around

town, getting the smell and the feel of the place. I had errands to run, an apartment to rent, rocks to find, meat to buy. "You've been to my Web site, no doubt read my bio. It's all there in black and white." Well, in full color graphics, but still.

Katie's brows rose politely. "Your bio is dull and uninformative. For instance, there is no mention that you appeared out of the forest at age twelve, a feral child raised by wolves, without even the rudiments of human behavior. That you were placed in a children's home, where you spent the next six years. And that you again vanished until you reappeared two years ago and started killing my kind."

My hackles started to rise, but I forced them down. I'd been baited by a roomful of teenaged girls before I even learned to speak English. After that, nothing was too painful. I grinned and threw a leg over the chair arm. Which took Katie, of the elegant attack, aback. "I wasn't raised by wolves. At least I don't think so. I don't feel an urge to howl at the moon, anyway. I have no memories of my first twelve years of life, so I can't answer you about them, but I think I'm probably Cherokee." I touched my black hair, then my face with its golden brown skin and sharp American Indian nose in explanation. "After that, I was raised in a Christian children's home in the mountains of South Carolina. I left when I was eighteen, traveled around a while, and took up an apprenticeship with a security firm for two years. Then I hung out my shingle, and eventually drifted into the vamp-hunting business.

"What about you? You going to share all your own deep dark secrets, Katie of Katie's Ladies? Who is known to the world as Katherine Fonteneau, aka Katherine Louisa Dupre, Katherine Pearl Duplantis, and Katherine Vuillemont, among others I uncovered. Who renewed her liquor license in February, is a registered Republican, votes religiously, pardon the term, sits on the local full vampiric council, has numerous offshore accounts in various names, a half interest in two local hotels, at least three restaurants, and several bars, and has enough money to buy and sell this entire city if she wanted to."

"We have both done our research, I see."

I had a feeling Katie found me amusing. Must be hard to live a few centuries and find yourself in a modern world where everyone knows what you are and is either infatuated with you or scared silly by you. I was neither, which she liked, if the small smile was any indication. "So. Do I have the job?" I asked again.

Katie considered me for a moment, as if weighing my responses and attitude. "Yes," she said. "I've arranged a small house for you, per the requirements on your In-ter-net web place."

My brows went up despite myself. She must have been pretty sure she was gonna hire me, then.

"It backs up to this property." She waved vaguely at the back of the room. "The small L-shaped garden at the side and back is walled in brick, and I had the stones you require delivered two days ago."

Okay. Now I was impressed. My Web site says I require close proximity to boulders or a rock garden, and that I won't take a job if such a place can't be found. And the woman—the vamp—had made sure that nothing would keep me from accepting the job. I wondered what she would have done if I'd said no.

At her glance, Tr— Tom took up the narrative. "The gardener had a conniption, but he figured out a way to get boulders into the garden with a crane, and then blended them into his landscaping. Grumbled about it, but it's done."

"Would you tell me why you need piles of stone?" Katie asked.

"Meditation." When she looked blank I said, "I use stone for meditation. It helps prepare me for a hunt." I knew she had no idea what I was talking about. It sounded pretty lame even to me, and I had made up the lie. I'd have to work on that one.

Katie stood and so did I, setting aside my Coke. Katie had drained her foul-smelling libation. On her breath it smelled vaguely like licorice. "Tom will give you the contract and a packet of information, the compiled evidence gathered about the rogue by the police and our own investigators. Tonight you may rest or indulge in whatever pursuits appeal to you.

"Tomorrow, once you deliver the signed contract, you are invited to join my girls for dinner before business commences. They will be attending a private party, and dinner will be served at seven of the evening. I will not be present, that they may speak freely. Through them you may learn something of import." It was a strange way to say seven p.m., and an even stranger request for me to interrogate her employees right off the bat, but I didn't react. Maybe one of them knew something about the rogue. And maybe Katie knew it. "After dinner, you may initiate your inquiries.

"The council's offer of a bonus stands. An extra twenty percent if you dispatch the rogue inside of ten days, without the media taking a stronger note of *us*." The last word had an inflection that let me know the "us" wasn't Katie and me. She meant the vamps. "Human media attention has been . . . difficult. And the rogue's feeding has strained relations in the vampiric council. It is *important*," she said.

I nodded. *Sure. Whatever. I want to get paid, so I aim to please.* But I didn't say it.

Katie extended a folder to me and I tucked it under my arm. "The police photos of the crime scenes you requested. Three samples of bloodied cloth from the necks of the most recent victims, carefully wiped to gather saliva," she said.

Vamp saliva, I thought. *Full of vamp scent. Good for tracking.*

"On a card is my contact at the NOPD. She is expecting a call from you. Let Tom know if you need anything else." Katie settled cold eyes on me in obvious dismissal. She had already turned her mind to other things. Like dinner? Yep. Her cheeks had paled again and she suddenly looked drawn with hunger. Her eyes slipped to my neck. Time to leave.

ABOUT THE AUTHOR

Faith Hunter is the *New York Times* bestselling author of the Jane Yellowrock series, including *Shadow Rites*, *Dark Heir*, and *Broken Soul*; the Soulwood series, set in the world of Jane Yellowrock, including *Blood of the Earth*; and the Rogue Mage series, including *Host*, *Seraphs*, and *Bloodring*. Visit her online at faithhunter.net, facebook.com/official.faith.hunter, and twitter.com/hunterfaith.

THE *NEW YORK TIMES* BESTSELLING
JANE YELLOWROCK SERIES
FROM

Faith Hunter

Skinwalker
Blood Cross
Mercy Blade
Raven Cursed
Death's Rival
Blood Trade
Black Arts
Broken Soul
Dark Heir
Shadow Rites
Blood in Her Veins: Nineteen Stories
From the World of Jane Yellowrock

Praise for the Jane Yellowrock novels:
"There is nothing as satisfying as the first time
reading a Jane Yellowrock novel."
—Fresh Fiction

"Jane is the best urban fantasy heroine around."
—Night Owl Reviews

Available wherever books are sold or at
penguin.com

R0223